W9-ANO-936

SILENT KILLER

An avid reader since childhood, Beverly Barton wrote her first book at the age of nine. Since then, she has gone on to write well over sixty novels and is a *New York Times* bestselling author. Beverly lives in Alabama.

For further information about Beverly Barton go to her website at www.beverlybarton.com.

By the same author:

Close Enough to Kill
Amnesia
The Dying Game
The Murder Game
Coldhearted
The Fifth Victim

BEVERLY BARTON

SILENT KILLER

AVON

AVON

A division of HarperCollins*Publishers*
77–85 Fulham Palace Road,
London W6 8JB

www.harpercollins.co.uk

This paperback edition 2012
1

First published in the U.S.A. by Kensington Publishing Corp.
New York, NY, 2009

A catalogue record for this book is
available from the British Library

ISBN: 978-0-00792-607-7

Printed and bound in Great Britain by
Clays Ltd, St Ives plc

MIX
Paper from
responsible sources

FSC
www.fsc.org
FSC® C007454

Prologue

Catherine Cantrell loved her husband. She hadn't always loved Mark, not in the beginning. But day by day, month by month, year by year, she had grown to care for him deeply. He had become her best friend as well as her husband. She only hoped that she was a worthy helpmate. God knew she tried her best to be everything he wanted in a wife.

The oven timer chimed, reminding her that the apple pie she had prepared from scratch was done. As she donned a pair of oven mitts, Mark breezed into the kitchen. When she smiled warmly at him, he returned her smile. She opened the oven door, reached inside and removed the hot pie, then set it on a cooling rack atop the granite counter.

"Something smells good," he told her as he placed his empty coffee mug in the dishwasher.

"Apple pie for dinner," she said.

When he nodded approval, something inherently feminine within her longed for him to touch her. She needed a kiss on the cheek or a pat on the butt or a little hug around her shoulders. Any basic act of affection would do. But Mark was not the affectionate type. She should have accepted that fact long ago. After all, it wasn't as if they were newlyweds or a couple who had been and always would be madly in love. But they did have a solid marriage, one based on mutual respect and admiration. That was far more than most couples had.

"How's next Sunday's sermon going?" Catherine asked.

"Not well. For some reason I can't seem to keep my mind on my work this afternoon."

On Mondays, Mark worked at home instead of his office at the church. And she was home on Mondays, too, since she and her business partner, Lorie Hammonds, closed their antique store on Sundays and Mondays.

"You were up late last night with the Jeffries family. I heard you come in after midnight." Catherine removed the oven mitts, stuffed them into the drawer with the pot holders and turned off the oven. "And you were so restless that I doubt you got more than a few hours' sleep. Maybe you need an afternoon nap."

"I couldn't get that family off my mind," Mark admitted. "It's been difficult for Debbie and Vern coping with the loss of their only child. It has truly tested their faith."

"Losing a child has to be the worst thing that could happen to a person. If anything ever happened to Seth, I don't know what I'd do."

"If, God forbid, that ever happened, and we lost our only child, we would do what I'm trying to get Debbie and Vern to do—put our trust in the Lord."

Catherine sighed quietly. A good minister's wife would never question God's plan for each of His children. But in her heart of hearts, she knew that if she ever lost Seth, she would die. Her son was her heart and soul.

When Mark looked at her, apparently wanting a reply to assure him that they were in agreement, she avoided making direct eye contact with him. She didn't doubt Mark's love for Seth, but she also knew that her husband would never love their child as much as she did.

"Catherine—"

The distinct doorbell chime saved her from having to either lie to her husband or disagree with him and be lovingly chastised for her lack of faith.

"I'll get it," she said. "Why don't you go in the den and take a nap?"

"Maybe later. I'll get the door. It could be FedEx delivering my birthday present."

Catherine smiled indulgently. "We just ordered that new set of golf clubs two days ago. They probably won't arrive until next week."

"A man can hope, can't he?"

Laughing softly, she shook her head as Mark, whistling to himself, hurried out of the kitchen. Her husband had four great loves: God, his family, his parishioners and golf.

She doubted that his much-anticipated fortieth birthday present had arrived so soon. More than likely their visitor was not FedEx but instead her mother, who had phoned shortly after lunch to ask if she could drop by on her way home from her weekly trip to the grocery store.

Catherine wiped her hands on a dish towel, laid it aside and removed her apron. She was a messy cook and had learned early on the necessity of wearing protective covering when she baked.

As she opened the kitchen door and made her way toward the foyer, she thought she heard the murmur of voices. Mark was talking to someone, but she couldn't tell if the visitor was male or female.

Just as she turned the corner in the hallway that led her by the staircase, an agonized scream echoed through the house. Shock waves shivered along her nerve endings. Dear God! Who was screaming in such pitiful torment?

She rushed into the foyer, planning to help Mark comfort the poor soul in misery. The front door stood wide open. Outside, on the front porch, Mark's six-foot body writhed in agony as lapping flames consumed his clothes and seared his flesh. Momentarily transfixed by the inconceivable sight,

Catherine screamed as she realized her husband was on fire.
Forcing her shock-frozen legs to move, she ran out onto the
porch, yelling at him, telling him to drop and roll, which he
did. While he lay on the concrete porch floor, hollering with
excruciating pain, she grabbed the doormat and beat at the
dying flames eating away his clothing.

She dropped to her knees beside him, inspecting his
charred body.

Oh God, God!

He was no longer screaming. He lay silent and unmoving.
But he was still breathing. Just barely.

"Hang on, Mark. Hang on."

She jumped up, ran into the house, grabbed the extension
phone in the living room and dialed 911. Barely recognizing
her own weak, quivering voice, Catherine managed to hold
herself together long enough to give their address and tell
the dispatcher that her husband was severely burned over his
entire body.

She carried the phone back onto the porch and sat down
beside Mark. He was still breathing. Still alive. But she didn't
dare touch him. There wasn't a spot on him that wasn't badly
burned. His face was charred beyond recognition, his flesh
melted as if it had been made of wax.

*Merciful Lord, please help Mark. He's such a good man.
Ask anything of me and I'll give it—just take care of him.*

Chapter One

Jackson Perdue stopped his car in front of the old home place. The last time he'd been here, five years ago, had been for his mother's funeral. He had stayed in Dunmore three days, and that had been three days too long. Both he and Maleah had booked rooms at the Hometown Inn. Their step-father had invited them to stay at the house, but Jack knew that Nolan had been relieved when they both declined his reluctant offer. When he left town, he had felt certain he would never return.

Never say never.

Things change. Life doesn't stay the same. Nolan Reaves was dead. The old bastard had keeled over in his workshop behind the house eight months ago. Heart attack.

Funny thing was, Jack had thought the son of a bitch didn't have a heart.

Neither he nor Maleah had come back to Dunmore for the funeral. He didn't know who had hated their stepfather more, he or his sister.

Maleah had come down from Knoxville six months ago, hired a realtor and put their mother's home up for sale. With the economy heading into a recession and real estate moving at a snail's pace, there hadn't been any offers on the three-story Victorian that had been in his family for four generations.

Jack turned off the engine, snatched the keys from the ignition and opened the driver's side door. When his feet hit the pavement, he stretched to get the kinks out of his back and neck and pocketed the keys. Rounding the hood, he stepped up on the sidewalk and stared at his childhood home. His thoughts went back to a time when this place had housed a happy family, when his world had been filled with love and laughter. Before his father had been killed. Before his mother had married Nolan Reaves.

Jack left the city sidewalk and moved onto the brick walkway that led to the front porch. He stopped halfway to the porch and looked up at the windows on the left side of the second story, where his old room was located. He doubted anything of his remained. When they'd been here briefly for Mama's funeral, he had gone no farther than the downstairs parlor. For the first twelve years of his life, this old house had been home. And for the next six years, it had been hell.

Could he actually live here again? Even if he got rid of everything that reminded him of his stepfather, he couldn't erase the memories.

He hated the cold, austere gray color Nolan had insisted the house be painted. Mama had wept quietly when the drab gray and white covered the beautiful green, cream and rose that the house had been for generations, colors true to the time period. If he actually moved into the house, the first thing he would do was hire painters to take the Victorian back to her colorful roots. He would have the house repainted—for his mother.

"God knows I'll never move back to Dunmore, but if I did, I wouldn't live in that house," Maleah had told him. "As far as I'm concerned, the house is yours if you want it."

But that was the million-dollar question: Did he want it?

Maybe. He didn't have to decide right away. He could stay here a few weeks and see how it went. It was either that or rent a motel room by the week. Not a pleasant prospect. Besides, if his new job didn't work out, it would be easier to move on if he hadn't leased an apartment or a house.

He had been at loose ends when Mike Birkett phoned and offered him the job. Otherwise, he probably wouldn't have considered coming back to Alabama. He had been honorably discharged from the army last year, after four months in the hospital recuperating from a bomb explosion that had nearly killed him. The surgeons had reconstructed the left side of his face, neck and shoulder and had done a damn good job. Only those who had known him before the reconstruction would suspect that he'd been put back together piece by piece.

"Hey, the job is yours if you want it," Mike had told him. "The pay isn't much, but it's in line with the low cost of living in Dunmore."

"Let me think about it."

"Come home. Take the job. Let's get reacquainted. If after a few months you hate it, you can always quit."

In the end, Mike had convinced him to give it a try. He'd known his old buddy had pulled a few strings to get him okayed for the position. Even though he was in really good physical shape now, he'd never be 100 percent ever again. Jack wasn't sure he'd make a good deputy just because he'd been a top-notch soldier, but God knew he needed something to do, something to keep him sane.

He stepped up on the porch, faced the front door and paused. After taking a deep breath, he removed the house key from his pocket. He unlocked and opened the door, then walked inside. A whiff of muskiness hit him the moment he entered the foyer. The house needed airing out after being closed up for so many months. First thing in the morning, he'd open every window in the place. Since it was spring and the temps were in the seventies, it was the perfect time.

As if his feet were planted in cement, he found it impossible to move beyond where he stood just over the threshold. Glancing in every direction—left, right, up and down—he clenched his teeth together tightly. He could feel Nolan's presence, could even smell a hint of the pipe tobacco his stepfather had used. Maybe this was a huge mistake. Maybe he'd been wrong to think that he could live here. It wasn't too late to turn around, walk away from the house and rent a room for tonight.

God damn it, no! He wouldn't let Nolan run him off, not the way he had when Jack was eighteen. Nolan was dead. Jack was thirty-seven, a decorated war hero, and this house was his now, his and Maleah's, as it had once been their mother's. If it was the last thing he ever did, he intended to erase Nolan Reaves from their ancestral home, starting with the old carriage house where their stepfather had doled out his own unique brand of punishment.

Catherine Cantrell had asked her best friend, Lorie Hammonds, to drive her by her old home, just outside the city limits. She and Mark had lived there for nearly six years before his death eighteen months ago.

"Are you sure you want to do this?" Lorie asked.

"I'm sure. I have to face the past sooner or later."

"But does it have to be today?"

Cathy sighed. Yes, it had to be today. One of the many things her therapist at Haven Home had taught her was that putting off unpleasant things didn't make them go away. The sooner she faced it, whatever "it" was, and dealt with it, the sooner it ceased to be a monster hidden in a dark closet ready to pounce on her when she least expected it.

Lorie got out of her Ford Edge, went around the hood and met Cathy as she stood at the border of the street, her gaze scanning the porch. This was where Mark had been doused with gasoline and set on fire. This was where she had waited with him, praying with every breath, until the ambulance arrived. This was where her safe, contented life had ended. Eighteen months, three weeks and five days ago.

Every nerve in her body shivered; every muscle tensed. With her eyes wide open, she could see Mark as he had been that horrible day, his flesh charred, melted, his life draining from his body. She could hear his agonized screams and then the deadly silence that had followed.

She closed her eyes and took a deep, fortifying breath.

Lorie put her arm around Cathy's quivering shoulders and gave her a reassuring squeeze. "Come on. Let's go."

Cathy opened her eyes and shook her head. "Not yet."

"Don't do this to yourself. Enough's enough."

"I imagine the new minister's wife redecorated," Cathy said. "No woman wants to live in a house decorated by a former owner."

"The new minister is a widower with a teenage daughter. No wife."

"All the same, this isn't my house any longer. My things aren't here. The home I created with Mark is gone."

"Your furniture and other things are in storage," Lorie reminded her. "When you buy a new place, you can—"

She turned quickly and faced her oldest and dearest friend. "Thank you for letting me stay with you until I find a place." Lorie and she were BFF—best friends forever—their friendship going back to when they wore diapers. Their parents had been good friends, and they had lived only blocks apart when they were growing up.

"Your mother wants you to stay with her, you know."

"What my mother wants isn't as important to me as what I want."

Lorie let out a loud, low whistle. "I don't know what they did to you at Haven Home, but I like it. The old Cathy would never have said something like that and meant it."

"The old Cathy no longer exists. I think she began dying the day Mark died." She looked directly at Lorie. "I couldn't say this to just anyone, because they wouldn't understand, they'd take it the wrong way . . . but it took something as traumatic as Mark's gruesome murder to finally give me the courage to become my own person."

Mark's death and a year of therapy.

Cathy took one final look at the porch and then ran her gaze over the neatly manicured lawn. "I'm ready to go now."

She followed Lorie back to the SUV. She had faced one of many demons that she had left behind a year ago when she had checked herself in at Haven Home, a mental-rehabilitation center outside of Birmingham. After the first six months, she had become an outpatient but had stayed on as a part-time employee in the cafeteria. Her mother and Mark's parents had visited her several times and had brought Seth with them. She had missed her son unbearably, but she had known living with his grandparents had been the best thing for him until she was able to provide him with a mentally stable mother.

Mark's death had almost destroyed her, and only with Dr. Milton's help had she been able to fully recover. She had gone into the intensive therapy blaming herself for Mark's death and believing that his parents and Seth blamed her for not being able to save him. But Dr. Milton had worked with her until she had been able to admit to herself that the guilt she felt wasn't because she blamed herself for not being able to save Mark. Realistically, logically, she knew that would have been impossible. She had done everything within her power. No, what Cathy felt guilty about, what she had had great difficulty admitting to Dr. Milton and to herself, was that she had never loved her husband. She had married him not loving him, and although she had tried to convince herself that she loved him, she hadn't. She had cared deeply for him, had respected and admired him, but she had never been able to feel for Mark that deep, passionate love a woman should feel for her husband.

"Do you want to stop by J.B. and Mona's to see Seth?" Lorie asked.

"No, not yet. I'm supposed to have dinner with them and Mother tomorrow, after church. I'll wait until then."

"J.B. and Mona may not give Seth up without a fight." Lorie inserted the key into the ignition. "I took the liberty of hiring Elliott Floyd to represent you, just in case Mark's parents aren't willing to turn your son over to you now that you're well."

Gasping softly, Cathy snapped her head around and stared at her friend. "I don't think a lawyer will be necessary. But thank you all the same. Seth is my child. I appreciate all that J.B. and Mona have done for him since Mark's death, but you can't possibly believe that they would try to take him away from me."

Lorie shrugged. "You never know what people will do. If for any reason the Cantrells think you're unfit to—"

"I'm fit," Cathy said. "I believe that I'm better prepared to be a good mother to my son now than ever before, and I was a damn good mother in the past."

Lorie eyed Cathy with speculative curiosity. "You are aware of the fact that you just said *damn* and didn't blink an eye, aren't you?"

Cathy smiled. "Surprised?"

"Shocked." Lorie laughed. "Know any other forbidden words?"

"A whole slew of them. And sooner or later, you'll probably hear me say all of them."

"I want to meet your Dr. Milton one of these days," Lorie said. "I want to shake his hand and thank him for releasing the real Catherine Nelson Cantrell from that holier-than-thou prison she stuck herself in trying to please her husband and her mother and her in-laws."

"The days of my trying to please everyone else are over. I've come home to start a new life, not to rebuild my old one. I owe it to myself and to Seth to be strong and independent and live the rest of my life to the fullest, and that's just what I intend to do."

                          *   *   *

Nicole Powell dreaded going home to Griffin's Rest. She and her friend, Maleah Perdue, had been gone a week, just the two of them alone in a Gatlinburg cabin in the Smoky Mountains. They had eaten out a few times and done a little shopping, but mostly they had kicked back at the cabin and done little or nothing. They had watched chick-flick DVDs, soaked in the hot tub, taken long walks on the nearby hiking trails and pigged out on the array of bad-for-you food they had purchased at a local grocery store.

The past year had been difficult for Maleah. Her older brother, Jack, had been critically wounded on his last assignment in the Middle East. She had spent weeks at his bedside, hoping and praying that he would survive. He had, but at a great cost. He had undergone several surgeries to his face and neck to rebuild what the explosion had ripped away.

During their stay at the cabin, Nic and Maleah had confided in each other, sharing things that they wouldn't or couldn't share with anyone else. In the two years that Nic had been married to Griffin Powell and had been co-owner of the Powell Private Security and Investigation Agency, she had become acquainted with all of their agents. Only a handful of their employees were women, and of those few, Nic had bonded with only two, Maleah and Barbara Jean Hughes.

"Have you decided what you're going to do? Are you going to talk to Griff and tell him how you feel?" Maleah asked as Nic pulled her Escalade up in front of the huge iron gates at Griffin's Rest. Two massive stone arches, with bronze griffins implanted in the stone, flanked the entrance.

Nic rolled down the window and said her name. The identification security system instantly recognized her voice and activated the Open function on the gates. This voice-ID system was new here at the Powell compound.

Once they were inside the estate and the gates closed behind them, Nic glanced at Maleah. "I can talk to him and try to explain, but he won't understand."

"He might. You won't know until you—"

"I know. Believe me. He will not understand. I can't ask him to choose between Yvette and me." She could, but she was afraid to ask her husband to make that choice, because deep down inside she wasn't completely certain that he would choose her.

"It's not a matter of choosing between the two of you," Maleah said. "Not really. It's a matter of making him understand how you feel."

"I feel jealous, and Griff doesn't understand why because Yvette is his friend, because she's like a sister to him, because he owes her his life. He's not in love with her. He's in love with me, but . . ."

"But recently you feel that he is putting her first. You're his wife. You have every right to expect him to always put you first."

Nic heaved a heavy sigh. "Griff has become so involved in whatever it is that Yvette is doing with that project of hers, that school or laboratory or sanctuary or whatever the hell it is, that he has all but turned over the running of the Powell Agency to me."

"I still don't see why you won't take my suggestion and get involved in Yvette's project yourself, if for no other reason than to find out what's going on. And it would give you more time with Griff."

"I suppose if I insisted, he'd ask Yvette to include me, but she's been so secretive about the whole thing, and whenever she comes for dinner and I mention the project, she clams up."

"Look, none of this is my business, except that you and I are friends and you've shared your concerns with me," Maleah said. "But you're Griff's wife and co-owner of the Powell Agency and of Griffin's Rest. You have every right to know what kind of operation Yvette Meng has going on in those buildings that Griff had built for her less than a mile from your home."

"I just don't want to come off sounding like a jealous wife, even if that's what I am. But if I don't get some of this off my chest pretty soon, I'm going to explode, and that won't be good for me or my marriage."

"So talk to Griff. Talk to him tonight."

Nic nodded. Maleah was right, of course. These feelings had been growing gradually, beginning with the day Griff told her that he would be constructing a housing complex for Dr. Yvette Meng at Griffin's Rest, a place where some of her gifted "psychic" students would be safe and protected from the outside world.

But when Yvette had arrived six months ago to oversee the project, Nic's concerns had escalated, and not without foundation. Even though she didn't doubt Griff's love for her, she couldn't shake the suspicion that neither he nor Yvette had been totally honest with her about their past relationship.

She trusted Griff as she had never trusted another person in her entire life. She loved him so much that sometimes it frightened her. That combination of love and trust was now being tested.

He did not deserve to live. He was like the others, pretending to be good when, in his heart, he was evil.

I have to punish him.

That's what You want me to do, isn't it, God?

Yes, yes, I hear You. I accept that it is my purpose in life to rain hellfire and brimstone down on the false prophets.

I will do Your bidding, Lord. I will seek out those who profess to do Your work and instead are in league with the devil. The liars. The blasphemers. The adulterers. The most vile of all sinners, those who transgress against Your holy word.

I didn't understand completely, not at first, but I do now. I cannot wait for them to reveal themselves to me. I must search for them and do so with all diligence.

Give me the strength to do what I must do. Show me the way. I am, now and always, Your obedient servant.

What?

Yes, Lord, I see him. And I know him for what he truly is. The priest has harmed dozens of little boys, and he's gotten away with his crimes over and over again. He must be stopped. He must be punished.

Chapter Two

Jack had gotten, at most, a total of two hours' sleep. He was still occasionally having nightmares about his last Rangers' assignment, and since his return to Dunmore, old boyhood nightmares had resurfaced and gotten all mixed up with the ones about the war. These days if he got four hours of sleep and didn't wake in a cold sweat, he called it a good night.

He had slept in his old room, on the same antique double bed and lumpy mattress that were almost as old as he was. If he stayed, he'd have to buy a new mattress. He hadn't ventured into any of the other upstairs rooms yesterday, but if he intended to air out the place, he would have to go into every room, including his mother's bedroom, a room she had shared with Nolan.

Tossing back the musty blanket and sheet, he got out of bed, stretched, scratched his chest and tromped toward the bathroom down the hall. After taking a leak, he peered into the dusty mirror over the pedestal sink and barely recognized the man looking back at him. He was no longer the teenage boy who had run away from Dunmore to escape his tyrannical stepfather, nor was he the angry man who had returned five years ago for his mother's funeral. Although the surgeons had done an excellent job, the left side of his face would never be the same. *He* would never be the same. He was still reasonably young—just turned thirty-seven. And despite his extensive injuries, the doctors had put Humpty Dumpty back together again so that he was strong and healthy. And although his career in the army was over, he now had a new job that offered him a chance to start over, to build a new life.

Out with the old and in with the new. Starting today.

Jack dressed hurriedly in faded jeans and a gray T-shirt, then headed up the stairs to the third story. He opened all the windows that hadn't been painted shut and descended the stairs, back to the second floor, and went from room to room, tying back curtains and lifting windows to let in the fresh springtime air. When he reached his mother's bedroom, he paused, steeled his nerves and opened the door. Except for the massive pieces of burl walnut furniture that had been in this room for generations, Jack didn't recognize anything. The room was as cold and dreary as his stepfather had been, the walls an off-white, now faded, the wooden floor unpolished for only God knew how many years. Heavy, brown brocade drapes closed out all light from the row of windows, and a matching bedspread covered the antique bed, the bed in which his maternal grandmother had been born.

As he closed his eyes just for a second, memories of his childhood flashed through his mind. He and Maleah running into their parents' bedroom and jumping into bed with them. His beautiful blond mother's arms opening wide to embrace them. His big, rugged father smiling as he ruffled Jack's hair and planted a kiss on Maleah's forehead.

Jack marched across the room, reached up and yanked the drapes, rods and all, from the windows and left them lying in dusty heaps on the floor. Morning sunlight flooded the room. He managed to open two of the four windows. As he stood and looked at his handiwork, he knew then that this would be the first room he would clear out, clean and restore.

With the windows open and the house airing out, Jack went down the back stairs and into the kitchen, which hadn't been remodeled in a good twenty years. He'd made a stop at a mini-mart on his way into Dunmore yesterday and picked up a few supplies, enough to tide him over for a few days. All the nonperishable items remained on the kitchen counter, where he'd left them last night.

After searching through the cabinets, he found the coffee-maker, washed it thoroughly and then put on a pot of coffee. Once the strong brew was ready, he poured himself a cupful and headed out the back door.

He had faced one demon—his mother's bedroom. How many times had he walked by her closed door and heard her crying?

He might as well face another demon, the one that made repeat performances in his nightmares. Standing in the middle of the backyard, he stared at the old carriage house, now little more than a dilapidated, unpainted hulk. He was surprised a high wind hadn't already toppled the rickety structure. His father had kept his fishing boat there, nothing fancy, just a sturdy utility boat with a 5-HP 4-cycle motor that they had taken out on a regular basis for their excursions on the nearby Tennessee River. Nolan had sold Bill Perdue's boat less than six months after his marriage to Bill's widow. Jack and Maleah had watched from the kitchen window as the new owner hitched the boat trailer to his truck and drove away. While holding his arm comfortingly around Maleah's trembling shoulders as she cried, it had been all the thirteen-year-old Jack could do not to cry himself. Selling their father's boat had been the least of Nolan Reaves's crimes, but it had been a forerunner of things to come.

Jack inhaled deeply, taking in the sweet smell of honey-suckles covering the back fence. His stepfather had kept the wayward vine cut to the ground, calling it an insect magnet and otherwise worthless. Jack allowed his gaze to travel over the overgrown shrubbery and the ankle-deep grass. Nolan had been a stickler for keeping the yard neat. Flowers were not allowed, despite the fact that Jack's mother had loved them. He would never forget the expression on her face when Nolan had cut down every bush in her beloved rose garden and then dug up the roots and burned them.

Jack finished his coffee, set the mug on the ground and marched toward the carriage house. He swung open the wooden gate that led from the backyard to the gravel drive. The closer each step took him to the side door of the carriage house, the louder and faster his heart beat. The last time his stepfather had beaten him, he had been a sophomore in high school and had just turned sixteen. He had stood there and taken the punishment Nolan Reaves administered with such deliberate pleasure. A strap across Jack's back, butt and legs. That time, the beating was not to atone for a mistake Nolan believed Jack had made, but one he thought Maleah had made. Three years earlier, after the first time Jack saw the bloody stripes across his eight-year-old sister's legs, he had made a bargain with the devil—from that day forward, he would take his own punishment and Maleah's, too. The deal had seemed to please Nolan, who took a sick delight in beating the daylights out of Jack on a regular basis.

Jack's hand trembled—actually shook like he had palsy—when he grasped the doorknob. Son of a bitch! Old demons died hard. He was a trained soldier, an Army Ranger, one of the best of the best, and yet here he was acting like a scared kid.

The boogeyman is dead. Remember? And even if he were still alive, there would be no reason to fear him.

He tightened his grip on the doorknob, turned it and opened the door. Nolan had always kept the door locked. Jack had no idea where the key was or even if there was a key. Neither he nor Maleah had mentioned the carriage house when they had discussed the possibility of him living here.

Leaving the door wide open, Jack entered the dark, dank interior of his teenage hell. In the shadowy darkness, he could make out the workbench, the rows of waist-high tool-boxes, the table saw, the push mower, the Weed Eater and various other yard-work devices. His gaze crawled over the dirt floor, around the filthy windows and cobweb-infested walls, to the triangular wooden ceiling. He stopped and stared at the row of menacing leather straps that hung across the back wall. He counted them. Six. At one time or another, Jack had felt the painful sting of each strap.

"You don't have to do this, you know." Lorie Hammonds poured herself a second cup of coffee, laced it liberally with sugar and cream and set the purple mug on the bar that separated the kitchen from the den.

Cathy glanced at a silk-nightgown–clad Lorie as she hoisted herself up on the bronze metal barstool, picked up her cup and took a sip. Lorie was thirty-five, a year older than Cathy, and sophisticated and worldly-wise. She was also beautiful in a voluptuous, sultry way that drew men to her like bears to honey. Her long, auburn hair hung freely over her bare shoulders, streaks of strawberry-blond highlights framing her oval face. She stared pensively at Cathy, a concerned look in her chocolate-brown eyes.

"Call your mother and tell her to bring Seth over here this afternoon," Lorie said. "Just because J.B. and Mona demanded a command performance doesn't mean you have to oblige them."

Cathy sighed. "They expected me to show up for services this morning, with Mother. I'm surprised she hasn't called me by now." Cathy glanced at the kitchen wall-clock. "Church probably let out about fifteen minutes ago."

"If you weren't ready to make an appearance at church today, what makes you think you're ready for a family dinner?"

"I have to be ready. I want to see Seth. I need to talk to him. And by agreeing to dinner with my in-laws and my mother, I'm showing all of them that I am more than willing to meet them halfway. The last thing I want is to alienate Mona and J.B."

Her mother was another matter entirely. There had been a time when she had jumped through hoops to please her mother. But after a year of therapy, Cathy had come to realize that pleasing Elaine Nelson was impossible. Pleasing her in-laws might be just as impossible, but she felt she at least had to try because they were her son's legal guardians, something she intended to change as soon as possible. And for Seth's sake and in honor of Mark's memory, she intended to remain on good terms with the Cantrells.

"Want some advice?" Lorie asked.

"Something tells me that you're giving it to me whether I want it or not."

"Just come right out and tell Mark's parents that you plan to find a house soon, and, when you do, you expect Seth to live with you."

"What if Seth doesn't want to leave his grandparents? After all, he's been living with them for a year now and—"

"You're his mother. He loves you. He'll want to live with you."

"I'm a mother who had a nervous breakdown and fell apart in front of him. Every time he came to see me at Haven Home, I could tell how nervous he was just being around me, as if he was afraid I'd go loco at any minute."

"The more time you spend with Seth, the more he's going to see that you're the wonderful mother who raised him." Lorie took another sip of coffee.

"But that's just it," Cathy said. "I'm not that same person. I'm different."

"Yeah, I know, but you're still Seth's mother. You still love him. He's still the most important person in your life. None of that has changed." Grinning, Lorie cupped the purple mug in her hands. "Besides that, you're different in a good way."

Cathy nodded agreement. The changes in her *were* good changes. She had no doubts about that fact. She was stronger, more confident, more independent and absolutely determined to never, under any circumstances, allow anyone or anything to undermine her new, hard-won self-confidence. Gone forever was the meek, subordinate pleaser who had deliberately buried the real Cathy Nelson Cantrell deep inside her.

"You're right." Cathy straightened the Peter Pan collar on her simple, navy blue shirtwaist dress, touched the single strand of pearls resting on her chest and smoothed the pleated shirt. "How do I look?"

Lorie inspected her from head to toe. "We need to go shopping and buy you a new wardrobe. God, honey, that dress is awful. It screams dowdy housewife."

Cathy smiled. "Mark liked this dress. It's suitable attire for a minister's wife. J.B. and Mona will approve."

Lorie shook her head. "I thought trying to please other people is no longer on your agenda."

"It's not, but just for today I don't want to do anything to antagonize my in-laws. I want them to turn Seth over to me without a fight, and if that means placating them, at least temporarily, I'm willing to make that compromise."

"And if they're not willing to meet you halfway, just remind them that your wicked friend, Lorie, has Elliott Floyd's phone number on speed dial. Everyone in North Alabama knows Elliott is a top-notch attorney who hasn't lost a case in the past fifteen years."

Mona and J.B. Cantrell had lived in the same house since they were newlyweds. The house had belonged to J.B.'s parents, with whom the couple had lived their entire married life, until his father died eighteen years ago and his mother had moved to an assisted-living facility. The elder Mrs. Cantrell had died four years ago at the age of eighty-nine. Mark's paternal grandmother had disliked Cathy on sight and had made her disapproval abundantly clear to everyone. J.B. had always been cordial to Cathy, but she suspected he shared his mother's opinion of her as an unsuitable mate for "our Mark." On the other hand, Mona had been friendly and had accepted her from the moment Mark announced their engagement.

"I've always wanted a daughter," Mona had said as she'd placed a kiss on Cathy's cheek.

From that day forward, Cathy had used her mother-in-law as a role model, hoping to please Mark, his father and his grandmother in the same way Mona did. And over the years, that was exactly what she had done—proven herself to be a supportive, agreeable, above-reproach helpmate. In retrospect, she now realized that what she had become was an almost robotic doormat.

She parked Lorie's Edge in the driveway, but after killing the motor, she sat there for a few minutes, garnering her courage.

She could do this. She had to do this!

While giving herself a pep talk, she ran her gaze over the 1940s bungalow. The original wood-shingled exterior had been covered with red brick sometime in the sixties. Black shutters and a black architectural roof added to the traditional appearance of the house, as did the six-foot-high white picket fence surrounding the backyard. Mona's green thumb was evident in the beauty of her late-blooming azaleas and various springtime flowers dotting the flower beds.

Cathy got out of the SUV, squared her shoulders and marched confidently to the front porch. When she reached out to ring the doorbell, the front door swung open and her

mother shoved her backward as she came out onto the porch
and closed the storm door behind her.

"Why weren't you at church this morning?" Elaine demanded, her hazel-blue eyes filled with condemnation.

"Hello, Mother. Nice to see you, too."

Elaine Nelson was a petite brunette who had allowed her
hair to go salt-and-pepper in her late forties. Neat and attractive, she always looked her best.

"Do not be sarcastic with me, Catherine Amelia. I have
your best interests at heart, as I always have." Elaine
frowned, deepening the soft age lines around her eyes and
mouth. "People asked about you. You were expected. If you
have any hopes of returning to your old life, you have to
prove to everyone that you aren't a raving lunatic just because you spent a year in that awful place." The last half of
her sentence came out in a soft, embarrassed whisper.

Cathy knew her mother was ashamed of the fact that she
had checked herself into Haven Home, horribly ashamed
that the good people of Dunmore knew Mark Cantrell's
widow had suffered a nervous breakdown. Nothing was
more important to Elaine Nelson than keeping up appear-
ances. The motto by which she lived was *What will people
think?*

"I will probably be at church next Sunday." Cathy looked
directly at her mother, a sympathetic smile on her lips but
solid-steel determination in her heart. Her mother had bul-
lied her for the last time. "But if or when I go to church, it
will be my decision, not yours." She slipped her hand around
and behind her mother and reached for the storm-door handle.

Elaine clutched Cathy's shoulder, but before she could
utter another chastising word, the door opened and Seth
looked outside at the two of them.

"Is everything all right?" he asked, his azure-blue eyes
searching her face for a truthful answer.

"Everything is fine," Cathy lied. "Grandmother was just welcoming me home."

The tension in her son's handsome face relaxed, and he smiled as he held open the door. Cathy paused when she entered the house and hesitantly lifted her hand to caress Seth's face. He leaned over and kissed her cheek.

"I'm glad you're okay now," he said. She heard the unasked question: *You are all right now, aren't you, Mom?* "Nana and Granddad thought you'd be at church this morning. I looked for you."

More than anything, Cathy wanted to wrap her arms around Seth and hug him. He might be six feet tall and have to shave every day, but he was still her baby. Her heart ached with love for him.

"I wasn't quite ready to see everyone at church. Maybe next Sunday."

"Or you could try Wednesday night services," Seth suggested. "Fewer people."

How very wise her almost sixteen-year-old son was. "You're right. I think Wednesday night would be a better time."

Only after Seth reached down and took her hand did she realize how truly nervous she was. Undoubtedly her astute son had realized she was trembling ever so slightly and wanted to give her his support. He led her into the living room, where J.B. and Mona stood side by side in front of the fireplace, and by the expressions on their faces she could tell that they were as uncertain about this first meeting as she was. Her plump, blond mother-in-law could be extremely attractive if she wore a little makeup, dressed in something other than polyester and didn't wear her hair in a neat little bun at the nape of her neck. On the other hand, J.B. was a good-looking silver-haired man who dressed fit to kill; he was a strutting peacock, the exact opposite of his brown-hen wife.

Cathy caught a glimpse of her mother as Elaine eased up alongside her.

"Cathy overslept this morning," Elaine said. "The trip from Birmingham—"

"I didn't oversleep," Cathy corrected. "I'm sorry if I disappointed all of you by not showing up for church this morning, but the truth is that I simply wasn't ready to see anyone other than Lorie and the four of you."

Mona looked pleadingly at her husband.

J.B. cleared his throat and then said, "There's always next Sunday."

"Of course there is." Mona rushed toward Cathy, opened her arms and hugged her. When she released Cathy, she wiped the tears from her eyes. "It is so good to have you home where you belong. We've missed you, each of us, but Seth most of all."

Cathy breathed a tentative sigh of relief. Maybe Lorie was wrong. Maybe everything was going to be all right. Maybe her in-laws understood that Seth belonged with her.

I hate him. He is such a fake, pretending to be a man of God, acting the part of a priest. Father Brian is young and handsome and charming—and a pedophile. At these interfaith Sunday afternoon socials, I've noticed how friendly he is with all the children, but especially the boys. Those poor babies being molested by that monster. It is up to me to put a stop to his evil.

He thinks no one suspects, that because none of the children have told anyone about what he's doing, he is safe. He's not safe. Not from me. I am God's instrument of punishment. I have been appointed to be judge, jury and executioner. It is my duty to seek out and destroy evil, the kind of evil that hides behind a priest's robes, a minister's white collar and a preacher's holier-than-thou façade.

No one understands why Mark Cantrell and Charles Randolph had to be punished. Mark Cantrell. Good Saint Mark. No one knew about his secret sin. But I knew. I saw him with that woman—a woman who was not his wife—stroking her, caressing her. He knew I saw him, and he even tried to explain, but I didn't believe his lies. He claimed he was merely comforting her when she fell apart in his arms because she had miscarried for the third time in less than two years. And Charles Randolph had stolen money from his church, but instead of being sent to prison, he was going to be allowed to resign from the ministry and simply repay what he had taken. Couldn't they see that he deserved God's wrath?

Mark Cantrell had been a liar. A fornicator. A sinner. Charles Randolph had been a liar and a thief. A sinner. And Father Brian is pure evil, a monster disguised as a kind and caring priest.

You're next. I'm coming for you. Soon.

"And I will punish the world for their evil, and the wicked for their iniquity." Isaiah 13:11.

God's wrath will rain down on you, Father Brian, and you will burn in Hell's fire.

Chapter Three

Meaningful conversation at the dinner table had been nonexistent. Idle chitchat was minimal, even though Mona had done her best to keep the mood light and cheerful. Despite her best efforts to defuse the tension in the room, Mona had received little coöperation from J.B. and Elaine. Seth had commented a couple of times in response to questions Cathy had asked him, but he was a bright boy and quickly realized the less said the better. In this household, everyone had learned to take their cues from J.B. And Cathy's father-in-law was not in a talkative mood this Sunday.

When Cathy offered to help clear away the table and clean up in the kitchen, Mona smiled and said, "Don't bother, dear. Elaine will help me. I know you want to spend some time with Seth." Mona glanced at J.B., silently pleading with him.

A tiny frisson of foreboding jangled along Cathy's nerve endings. Reading between the lines of her mother-in-law's statement, she wondered if this had been Mona's subtle way of saying *You can visit him here, but J.B. will not allow you to take him away from us.*

"Thank you," Cathy replied, her voice strong and even,

not indicating the unease she felt. "Seth, why don't you and I take a walk? It's a lovely afternoon."

Seth stopped midstride on his way out of the dining room and glanced back at his grandfather, obviously seeking permission. *Damn it, I'm your mother,* she wanted to scream. *You don't have to ask him if you can take a walk with me.*

J.B. nodded. "Don't be long. Remember you need to go over your song a few times before tonight's services."

"I remember, Granddad," Seth said. "We'll just walk a few blocks."

Cathy felt the immediate release of tension that permeated the room, as if everyone had been holding their breaths, waiting for J.B.'s decision. Her father-in-law was not a bad man, not evil or cruel, but he adhered to the old biblical teachings that a man ruled his household, his wife and his children. His word was law.

Mark had been reared in a home where his mother had been subservient to his father, and although he had tended to be more modern in his thinking, on occasion Cathy had seen glimpses of J.B. in Mark. For the most part, he had inherited his mother's gentle, sweet nature, but Cathy had learned early on in their marriage that when they did things Mark's way, it made life easier for all of them.

As soon as Cathy and Seth left the house, she asked, "What was that about your going over a song for tonight's services?"

"Don't you remember, Mom? Once a month, on Sunday night, the teenage guys take turns acting as the song leader."

"Oh. Yes, of course. If I'd known you were going to be doing that this evening, I'd have made plans to be there."

He shrugged as they left the porch. "It's no big deal. Besides, we'll do it again next month."

"I'll be there then."

"Yeah, sure."

They walked side by side, heading west toward the center of town, which was only four blocks away. A couple of times, neighbors sitting on their front porches or out in their front yards gawked as they passed, as if they were shocked to see the crazy widow walking the streets with her son. A couple of neighbors threw up a hand, waved and spoke. Seth returned their greetings.

One block passed and then another, neither she nor her son speaking to each other again. Cathy hated the awkward silence. It was as if she and her own child were strangers. *Just make conversation,* she told herself. *Nothing heavy.*

"School's out in a couple of weeks, huh?"

"Ten days," he said. "Exams are next Thursday and Friday."

"I can hardly believe that my baby boy will be a junior in high school this fall. It seems like only a few years ago that you were in kindergarten."

"Yeah, that's what Nana says all the time."

"Your nana is a wonderful lady," Cathy told him, completely sincere. She loved Mona, who had in many ways been more of a mother to her in the past sixteen years than her own mother had ever been. "I'm grateful that she's been here for you while I've been gone."

Seth didn't respond. He just kept walking at a slow, steady pace, keeping his gaze fixed straight ahead.

They crossed the intersection at Mulberry and Fifth without encountering even one vehicle. Dunmore was quiet and peaceful on Sunday midafternoons. After church, people either went home or out to eat. By now everyone had reached their destination.

"What are your plans for the summer?" she asked. "Are you doing anything special? Playing ball or—"

Seth stopped abruptly. "Mom, I play baseball and football. Have you forgotten that, too?" He stared at her, studying her with his intense, narrowed gaze.

"No, of course I didn't forget. I just . . . The question came out before I thought. I've been trying so hard to think

of something to say, to come up with casual conversation."
She looked him square in the eye. "I'm fine, honey. Don't
worry. I'm not sick anymore. I'm completely well."

His gaze hardened. His brow wrinkled.

She could tell that he desperately wanted to believe her.
But Seth had been there that day, when she had run down the
hall, alternately laughing and crying hysterically before
locking herself in her bedroom and refusing to come out. He
had stood outside the door, beating on it, begging her to
open up and let him come in. He had listened to the sounds
of her emotional meltdown, the laughing and crying that she
could not control. She had known she was losing it, but she
had been unable to stop.

She vaguely remembered that sometime later, her mother
had knocked on the door, called her name and demanded she
stop all the nonsense and come out immediately.

"Catherine, you're frightening your son." When she hadn't
responded, her mother had continued calling her name over
and over. "Cathy? Cathy, can you hear me? Cathy!"

They would never forget what she had said to her mother
that day before she fell across the bed in a fit of uncontrol-
lable, manic laughter.

"Cathy's not here. Cathy's dead."

That had been a year ago. A year of therapy. A year of
healing. A year of learning to accept herself as she was, to
acknowledge her true feelings and to come into her own as a
grown woman. And most importantly, to forgive herself for
not being perfect. Her words that day had been prophetic.
The old Cathy was dead.

She reached out and grasped Seth's arm. "I'll be there for
every game from now on. I promise."

"Okay. Sure."

She saw a glimmer of hope in his beautiful blue eyes.

She had disappointed him, had let him down. She would
never allow that to happen again. But he didn't know that. It

was up to her to prove to him that she was completely well, that she was whole and that for the rest of his life he could count on her.

She released her tight grip on his arm. "You know I'm staying with Lorie, but just for a little while. I plan to find a house for us soon. I'm going to start looking next week."

"Mom, I . . . I can't come and live with you." He stared down at the sidewalk, avoiding direct eye contact.

"Of course you can, and you will. I'm your mother. You belong with me."

Don't push so hard. Don't demand. Ask. "I want you to live with me. Don't you want that, too?"

"Granddad says you're not ready for the responsibility, that you might not ever be. He thinks I should stay with him and Nana until I leave for college in a few years." With his head still bowed, he lifted his gaze just enough to glance at her quickly. "You can visit me anytime you want, and . . . and once you're settled in and all, I could come visit you."

I don't want you to visit me. I want you to live with me. "That's what J.B. wants. What do you want, Seth?"

That's it, Cathy. Put your son on the spot. Make him choose between you and his grandfather.

"Mom, I don't want to hurt your feelings. . ."

"If you want to stay with J.B. and Mona for a little while longer, then that's what you'll do." Agreeing to give up her son even for a few more weeks was one of the most difficult things she'd ever done. "I'll find a house for us . . . for me. And I'll go back to work at the antique shop with Lorie. I'll visit you, and you'll visit me. We'll take this one day at a time. Does that work for you?"

"Yes, ma'am." His lips curved into a hesitant smile. "Thanks, Mom, for . . . Well, for . . ."

"It's only another block into town," she said. "Want to stop at the Ice Palace and get Cherry Cokes?"

"Yeah, that sounds great."

Baby steps. One day at a time. That was how she had recovered. And it was the way she would regain her son's trust.

On her drive home from the interfaith Sunday afternoon
social she had attended at St. Mary's in Huntsville this afternoon, Lorie questioned her motives for taking part in any
event even vaguely associated with religion. Her strict Baptist upbringing, her parents both fanatics of the first order,
had turned her against religion as a teenager. It had seemed
to her that everything that was fun was also a sin. And if
there was one thing Lorie had learned about the hard way, it
was sin. She had paid a heavy price for her teenage rebellion. She had lost her parents. They had never been able to
forgive her for what her father had called her unforgivable
sins. She had lost her innocence, her self-respect and almost
her life. And she had lost the only man she had ever truly
loved.

Religion was just a word to her, and up until the past few
years, it had been an ugly word. She had blamed her youthful rebellion and her gradual descent into degradation and
shame on religion. But her friendship with Reverend Patsy
Floyd had shown her that it was not religion but religious fanaticism that should be feared and avoided at all costs. Patsy
was one of a handful of female Methodist ministers in Alabama. She taught love, understanding and forgiveness. The
interfaith socials that brought young people of different religions together so that they could better understand one another had been Patsy's brainchild. And although Lorie was
still unable to bring herself to attend church services, she
had agreed to help Patsy with the monthly socials held at
various churches in North Alabama every month.

If she could help just one kid not to make the kind of mistakes she had made . . .

Originally, her motives for taking part in these socials

had been completely selfless, but she had to admit that for the past six months she'd had a selfish motive. It gave her a chance to get to know Mike Birkett's two kids, his eight-year-old daughter, Hannah, and his ten-year-old son, M.J. Being with Mike's children was always a bittersweet experience. She knew that if she had never left Dunmore for the bright lights of Hollywood, California, seventeen years ago, Hannah and M.J. would probably be her children, hers and Mike's.

Of all her many mistakes, leaving Mike was her biggest regret.

Jack tossed the last toolbox on the stack of garbage that he had thrown into a heap in the alley and then returned to the carriage house, which he had stripped to the bare walls. After removing a switchblade from his pants pocket, he cut down the corded leather straps from the ceiling. The whips were the last items to go. Clutching the straps in his hands as he fought the bad memories, Jack made his way across the backyard and flung them into the fire. They needed to be destroyed so that no one could ever use them again. Every damn thing that had belonged to Nolan Reaves was now either awaiting the garbage truck or smoldering in the large metal barrel that his stepfather had used to burn leaves and trash. He had thought about tearing the carriage house down to the ground, but if he did that he would erase the good memories along with the bad. Next week he'd get a carpenter in here to give him an estimate on what it would cost to restore the building.

It would take time and money to bring the old painted lady, the carriage house and the grounds back to the way they'd once been, but Jack had plenty of time and enough money so that he wouldn't have to cut corners on the restoration. Odd how one night in the old homestead had convinced him to stay here in Dunmore, in his ancestral home, and somehow, someway, build a new life for himself.

He'd been so immersed in his thoughts that although he'd heard the car, he hadn't noticed that it had stopped in his driveway. But he heard the crunch of gravel beneath the man's feet as he approached. Just as Jack turned to face the intruder, the man spoke.

"Have you got a burn permit for that?" Mike Birkett asked, a wide grin on his deeply tanned face.

"Nope. Do I need one?" Jack swiped his palms down the front of his dirty jeans.

"I'll let it pass this time," Mike said. "But next time, get one. It won't look right if my new deputy keeps breaking the law."

Jack nodded. "Yeah, okay." He ran his gaze over his old friend, who wore gray dress slacks and a white dress shirt with a charcoal gray collar. "Been to church?"

"Yeah, earlier today. Then the kids and I had lunch over at City Restaurant before I saw them off with Reverend Floyd for their monthly interfaith social."

Jack chuckled. "You've done all right for yourself, haven't you? A solid citizen. A real family man. The sheriff of the county, church every Sunday, a couple of kids."

"I can't complain. I've been damn lucky, and I know it, except . . ." Mike's voice trailed off into thoughtful silence as he stared into the flames inside the barrel. Mike was one of the few people on earth who knew about the times when Nolan had beaten Jack with those leather straps. "I'm surprised you didn't burn the place down." He glanced at the carriage house.

"I thought about it." Jack reached over and placed a hand on Mike's shoulder. "I'm sorry about your wife. I should have come back for her funeral."

Mike shrugged. "You called."

"Yeah, five months later."

"Don't sweat it."

"I haven't been much of a friend, have I?"

"Good enough."

Jack took a deep breath. Mike cleared his throat.

"I thought I'd run an idea by you," Mike said. "That's the reason I came over uninvited."

"You never need an invitation."

"Don't happen to have a couple of beers in the house, do you?"

"As a matter of fact, I do." Jack hitched his thumb toward the back porch. "Want to come inside, or would you rather sit out here?" He glanced at the rusty metal lawn chairs on the porch.

"Let's sit out here and enjoy this weather while it lasts. You know what it'll be like in another month. Hot as hell and humid as a steam bath."

"Take a seat. I'll be right back."

Jack returned with the last two beers he had in the refrigerator. *Note to self: buy more beer.* He handed his old buddy one of the cans, then sat down beside him in the faded green metal chair and popped the tab on his can. They stayed there, sipping the cold brews as they stared out at the large backyard, the pile of junk awaiting the garbage truck and the smoke spiraling up and away from the old trash barrel.

"So what's this idea you want to run by me?"

Mike took another swig from his beer, then held the can between his spread knees. "I sheriff a small, mostly rural county, and our funds are limited."

"Is this where you tell me you've realized you can't afford another deputy?"

"I can afford you, but just barely," Mike admitted. "I'm aware of the fact that you have some physical limitations, but I can't see where that would keep you from becoming a good deputy." Mike paused, obviously weighing his next words carefully. "I thought it might be best if we broke you into the job gradually."

"Meaning?" Jack wasn't sure he liked the sound of this.

"The sheriff's department doesn't actually have anyone working our cold cases, but we've got several unsolved murders that family members have asked us to look into again. I thought it could be a good place for you to start."

"Working the county's cold cases?"

"Yeah. What do you think?"

"I think you've created a job for me, one that sounds a lot like charity."

Mike finished off his beer, then crushed the can between his huge hands. "Damn it, man, that's exactly what I didn't want you to think. And it isn't true. I need another deputy. Ernie Poole is retiring in a few months, and I need a man to fill his shoes. In the meantime, I want you to work these unsolved murder cases and get the county commissioners and the good citizens off my back."

Okay, there was enough truth to Mike's words for Jack to accept that he hadn't been hired as an act of charity by his old high school buddy.

"How many cold-case murders?" Jack asked.

"Several."

"Several as in three, six, ten . . ."

"Two," Mike said.

"Two?"

Mike nodded. "I'll have the files on both murders on your desk first thing in the morning. Look them over, study them, dig around to see if you can come up with anything that will shed a new light on either of them."

"How old are the cases?"

"One is five years old. George Clayton, an old geezer, nearly eighty. Somebody robbed him and beat him to death. There were several suspects, but no real proof. We figured his nephew did it, but the boy had an airtight alibi."

"Does the nephew still live around here?"

"He's still in Alabama," Mike said. "He was convicted of

assault and battery and is serving time. He's in the Limestone Correctional Facility."

"What about the other case?"

"That murder case is eighteen months cold. We investigated, but didn't come up with even one suspect." Mike said. "There was another, similar murder over in Athens a year ago. The police chief and I compared notes and agreed that it could have been the same killer, but neither of us had a legit suspect."

"Want to give me some details or . . ."

"Both our victim and the Athens victim were ministers. Ours a Church of Christ preacher and theirs a Lutheran priest. Both men were doused with gasoline and set on fire."

"Damn." Jack's breath hissed between his clenched teeth. "Just the two murders? Nothing since?"

"That's right. Just the two."

"Any connection between the two victims other than the fact they were both clergymen?"

"We couldn't find a link of any kind. As far as we know, Father Randolph and Brother Cantrell didn't know each other, had never met, had no friends or family in common."

"Brother Cantrell? Mark Cantrell?"

"Yeah, Mark Cantrell."

"The guy Cathy Nelson married?"

"One and the same."

"Cathy's a widow?"

"Yep."

Jack looked directly at Mike. "Once we get all the new deputy hoopla over with in the morning, I'll take a look at those files and figure out where to go from there."

"If you're thinking about contacting Cathy . . ."

"Is there any reason I should?"

"None that pertains to her husband's case," Mike said. "Her statement is on file. She was never a suspect. She heard the killer's voice from a distance, but couldn't tell if it was male or female. There's no reason to bother her unless we wind up reopening the case."

"Agreed."

Mike studied Jack. "Mind if I give you some advice?"

"About Cathy?"

"Yeah."

"Go ahead."

"Stay away from her. If you've got an itch that needs scratching, find another woman."

"Are you warning me to stay away from the widow because you've already staked your claim?" Jack asked.

"Nope. Cathy's just a friend. Nothing more. Never has been, never will be. But she's a good woman who's been to hell and back. I don't want to see her hurt any more than she's already been hurt."

"And naturally, a guy like me would hurt her." Jack grunted. "Don't worry. I'm not interested in a good woman. I prefer the other kind."

Chapter Four

"How'd you do on that Algebra exam?" Felicity Harper caught up with Seth just as he slammed his locker shut.

Although Felicity was a year older than he was, they were both sophomores because of when their birthdays fell during the calendar year.

He had caught a glimpse of her when they left Mr. Bange's classroom. Although he hadn't turned around to check, he had known she was following him. After being practically stalked by her for the past seven months, he'd become accustomed to her shadowing him and using any excuse she could find to get his attention. If only he'd moved a little faster, he might have gotten away before she cornered him. He had thought she might get caught up in the crowd of students milling around in the hallways long enough for him to get his backpack out of his locker and escape through the side entrance. No such luck.

It wasn't that he disliked her. She was okay, considering she was a bit of a weirdo, and he was sort of flattered that she obviously had a crush on him. But she just wasn't his type. Besides, since she was his mom's best friend's cousin, he had to try to be nice to her.

Seth shrugged. "I did okay on the exam, I think."

"I'll bet you aced it." She gazed up at him adoringly. "You're so smart."

The way she stared at him gave him the creeps. Heck, most of the time she gave him the creeps. Felicity wore violet-colored contacts, circled her eyes with black liner and painted the lids with purple eye shadow. She wore black clothes nearly all the time and had ever since eighth grade, when she had gotten on some Goth kick. And that dagger tattoo on her neck turned him off completely, as did the small fire-breathing dragon circling her left wrist. She sure didn't look like a preacher's kid. Judging by her appearance, you'd never expect that her parents and older sister seemed pretty much normal.

"You don't have any other exams today, do you?" Felicity asked.

Seth picked up his backpack off the floor and flung it over his shoulder. "Nope. I'm through for today."

"Want a ride home?"

"Is your mother picking you up?" he asked.

"Nooo . . ." She dragged the word out, exasperation in her voice. "Don't you remember? Charity got a new car for her eighteenth birthday last month. She won't mind giving you a lift."

His grandparents' house was a good eight-block walk, one he made almost every day. Nana dropped him off at Dunmore High each morning, having overruled Granddad's objections, something she seldom did. But his grandfather had expressly forbidden Nana to pick him up in the afternoons. He considered doing that would only coddle Seth.

He had overheard Granddad say to Nana, "You and Elaine spoil that boy way too much. He'll never be a real man with his two grandmothers hovering over him the way y'all do."

If today had been just another warm and sunny May day, he'd have opted to walk instead of considering catching a ride home with kooky Felicity and her sister, Charity. But it had been raining cats and dogs for the past hour, and he didn't look forward to getting drenched in the downpour.

"Sure, thanks," Seth said. "If you don't think Charity will mind."

Felicity lit up like a Christmas tree, as if his agreeing to accept a ride home had been an answer to her prayers. Yeah, okay, so he knew she liked him. She'd sort of had a thing for him for nearly a year now, even though he'd never done anything to encourage her. The last thing he'd ever want to do was hurt her feelings, but sooner or later he was going to have to tell her to back off.

"Come on." Felicity grabbed his arm. "We've got to hurry. Charity will be waiting out front, and she can't stay parked in the tow-away zone forever."

They barely made it out the front door before Felicity popped open a huge black umbrella to shield them from the rain. She led him to the late-model Chevy, a reliable, sturdy vehicle that most teenagers wouldn't be caught dead driving. She opened the back door and said, "Get in."

Once he and Felicity were inside, Charity pulled out of the tow-away area, not glancing back at them or saying a word. It was only after Felicity had closed the umbrella and Seth had fastened his seat belt and looked forward that he noticed the girl sitting in the front seat with Charity. He knew, without seeing her face, who she was. His heartbeat accelerated. His face flushed. And his penis came alive.

Damn! Get that thing under control.

While he concentrated on how his body was reacting to the beautiful Missy Hovater, she turned around and smiled at him.

"Hi, Seth."

God, she knew his name!

Don't be an idiot, of course she knows your name. Her father took your dad's job. He's the minister where you and your grandparents go to church. You're in Sunday school class with her.

"Hi, Missy." His words came out sounding like a frog's croak.

When Missy laughed, the dimples in her cheeks deepened and her eyes sparkled.

Felicity punched him in the ribs and giggled. "What's up with that voice? Were you trying to do an imitation of a bullfrog?"

Shit!

Oh, damn!

I shouldn't even think those words. It's wrong to curse, even in your mind. And I shouldn't be fighting a hard-on. Sins of the flesh. Stay chaste. Don't think evil thoughts. Oh, God, help me.

Seth didn't know which was worse—being concerned about his numerous sins or the red flush no doubt covering his face. It was hell being sixteen—well, almost sixteen—and no one except another teenager could possibly understand how he felt right this minute. His grandparents certainly wouldn't understand.

"Yeah," Seth managed to say in his normal voice. "I'm practicing for tryouts for the school play, *The Frog Prince.*"

When everyone laughed, even the quiet, shy Charity, Seth relaxed.

He could feel Felicity watching him, but he couldn't manage to take his eyes off Missy. She had to be the prettiest girl he'd ever seen, every feature on her face perfect, and her body was bad, really bad. He hated to admit it, but the first thing he had noticed about her, after her gorgeous face and mane of blond hair, was her big boobs. He might be a preacher's son and the grandson of a church elder, but he was human and couldn't help it if a girl's breasts fascinated him.

Felicity leaned against him, her long, straight black hair

brushing his arm, her actions demanding his attention. When he glanced at her, he realized she was practically in his face.

"Why don't you come home with us?" Felicity asked. "Mom will fix us all lunch, and then you and I can study for our American History test together."

"I don't know." *Think of some excuse other than your grandmother is expecting you to come home.* "I sort of promised Tyler that we'd hang out together later today."

"So call him and invite him over. Mom won't mind. She loves for us to have company, doesn't she, Charity?" When her sister didn't respond, Felicity punched the back of her sister's seat.

"Uh, no, Mother won't mind at all," Charity said.

"I'm going home with Charity and spending the afternoon," Missy told him. "I don't like to disturb my father when he's busy working on a sermon."

"I . . . uh . . . sure, thanks, I'd like to have lunch with y'all." *Liar. You don't want to have lunch with all of them, only with Missy.* "But I need to give Nana a quick call, so she won't worry. You know how grandmothers are."

Seth fumbled in his pocket and managed to retrieve his phone without dropping it. *Please, God, let Nana answer and not Granddad.* Nana wouldn't give him a hard time about not coming straight home. He understood that Granddad was strict with him for his own good, just as his own dad would have been. But sometimes he wished his grandfather could remember what it was like to be nearly sixteen.

Cathy looked at the address written on the notepad: 121 West Fourth Street. This had to be a mistake. That was the address for the old Perdue house. Hadn't Mona mentioned something about that house being empty, that it had been up for sale for nearly six months? Maybe someone had bought the place, and the new owner needed interior-decorating advice, an extra service they provided at Treasures of the Past Antiques and Interiors.

"Is something wrong?" Ruth Ann Harper asked. "You have the strangest expression on your face."

Cathy forced a smile. She liked Ruth Ann, who was married to Lorie's cousin, the local First Baptist Church's minister. Ruth Ann had been working part-time helping Lorie with the antique shop while Cathy had been at Haven Home.

"No, nothing's wrong. I was just puzzled by the address. I didn't realize anyone had bought the old Perdue house." Cathy looked right at Ruth Ann. "Are you sure you wrote down the correct address?"

"Yes, I'm sure."

"And Lorie told you to ask me to meet with the client at four-thirty this afternoon at this address?"

"Yes." Ruth Ann looked puzzled. "When she phoned from the auction in Fayetteville, I told her about the gentleman who had called and asked if y'all could help him with decorating his house. He said it was an old Victorian, that he was having some restoration work done on the place and he didn't know anything about decorating."

"Did he happen to tell you his name and if he and his wife would be meeting with me or . . . ?"

"He didn't mention a wife. And come to think of it, he didn't give me his name. I think he thought I knew who he was. How, I don't know. Local gossip, maybe."

"I see. And you told Lorie which house it was? You mentioned the address to her, right?"

"Well, actually, no, I don't think I mentioned the address. I just told her what the man had said, and she told me to ask you to meet with him since she wouldn't make it back from the auction by four-thirty."

"Oh."

"Is there a problem of some kind?"

Cathy shook her head. "No, no problem at all." She checked her wristwatch. "I'd better leave now since it's already four-twenty. Would you mind closing up today? It would save me from having to come back instead of going straight home. Seth is coming for dinner tonight."

"He's such a fine young man. So well mannered and friendly," Ruth Ann said. "He was at the house today for lunch. He came by with my girls and their friend Missy after exams. I think my youngest has a major crush on him. And God knows he'd be a wonderful influence on her. I'm afraid Felicity is going through a rebellious stage."

"Good for her."

Cathy didn't realize she had spoken out loud until she saw the surprised expression on Ruth Ann's face. Her dark eyes widened, and her mouth opened in a half-smile/half-frown, as if she was uncertain how to take Cathy's comment.

"I'm sure you don't have anything to worry about with either of your girls, not with the wonderful example you and John Earl have always set for them. I just think it's good to allow teenagers to think for themselves and for them not to always be expected to do everything their parents want them to do."

"Actually, I agree with you. Despite the slight embarrassment Felicity's tattoos, outlandish makeup and black attire cause us, John Earl and I believe that allowing her the freedom to express herself will help her grow up to be her own person, a young woman we'll be quite proud of."

"You're very wise. Your girls are so lucky to have a mother like you." Cathy took the car keys out of her purse, hung the strap over her shoulder and headed for the back door. "See you tomorrow."

Ruth Ann waved as Cathy left the shop.

She paused beneath the metal canopy over the door and looked up at the gray sky. The morning's heavy rain had left puddles of standing water. The light drizzle falling now wasn't discernible to the eye, but when she walked toward her parked SUV, she felt the light moisture misting her face.

With her consent, her in-laws had sold Mark's Lexus and

put the money in Seth's college fund, and they had given Cathy's ten-year-old Jeep Cherokee to Elaine, who had stored it in her garage.

"I had it serviced for you when I found out you were coming home," her mother had told her. "I wasn't sure if you'd be driving, but I assumed you would. After all, you wouldn't have left that place if you weren't completely well, would you?"

Ignoring the comment about her mental health, Cathy had simply said "Thank you, Mother," taken the keys and left. One of the many truths she had accepted while at Haven Home was the fact that Elaine Nelson would never change. She couldn't change her mother, but she could change the way she reacted to her.

Cathy slid behind the wheel, started the engine and sat there in the alley behind the antique shop. During the eight days she had been back in Dunmore, she had met and survived several challenges. Not allowing her mother to intimidate her had actually been easier than she'd thought it would be. But facing her in-laws had not been easy, nor had accepting the fact that she would have to regain her son's trust before she could fight the Cantrells for custody. One of the lesser challenges had been forcing herself to pretend she didn't hear the whispers or notice the curious stares when she attended Sunday morning services yesterday. And whenever a customer commented about her year away and how horrible it must have been in *that place*, she simply forced a smile and told them it was wonderful to be home and back at work.

Of all the challenges that she had known she would face and could deal with, helping the new owner decorate the old Perdue house had not been one of them.

You can do this. It's just a house. Mr. and Mrs. Reaves are both dead. Maleah lives somewhere in the Knoxville area. And Jack . . .

She gripped the steering wheel with white-knuckled strength.

"Jackson Perdue." There, she'd said his name aloud, and the earth hadn't opened up and swallowed her. God hadn't struck her dead. "Jack." She spoke his name softly.

Cathy wasn't surprised that Jack and Maleah had sold their mother's house, considering how much they had both hated their stepfather and how quickly they had both left home when each had turned eighteen. They had returned briefly for their mother's funeral five years ago. She had caught a glimpse of them, from the back of the church, when she had slipped in and sat in the very last pew. She hadn't spoken to either of them at the church and hadn't gone to the cemetery or to the house.

Cathy put the SUV in reverse, backed up and drove down the alley to the side street. On the short drive from Main Street, where their shop was located, to West Fourth, she wondered about the people who had bought the old house. Were they a young couple, middle-aged or elderly? Were they locals or people from another town or even another state?

When she parked in the gravel drive at 121 West Fourth, she noticed the door to the carriage house stood wide open. The interior of the in-need-of-repair structure was bare to the bones. Apparently the new owners had already started clearing out things in preparation for the renovations. She got out of the Jeep and searched for the owner's vehicle, but didn't see one. Was it possible the potential client had forgotten about their appointment? If no one was here, she could wait for them, but not for long. Seth was coming to Lorie's tonight for dinner. Nothing, not even a rich client, was more important.

As she made her way to the sidewalk, her leather high heels marring up in the wet ground, she inspected the three-story house, one of several Victorian painted ladies that still graced the downtown streets of Dunmore. How dark and dreary this place looked, the gray paint peeling, the faded white shutters in need of repair, the wide porch empty. She rang the doorbell.

Seconds ticked by and quickly turned into minutes.

She rang the doorbell again.

Silence.

Apparently no one was at home. Should she go or should she wait?

Before she could decide, a sheriff's car zipped into the drive and pulled up alongside her SUV. She turned and watched as the tall, muscular man in uniform emerged from the Crown Victoria.

As he approached the front porch, Cathy's chest tightened. Her heartbeat accelerated. With slow, easy strides, he came up the walkway. His hair was darker now, a rich sandy blond, and just a tad longer than a regulation military cut. When he stepped up on the porch, he removed his sunglasses, squinted and stared at her.

"Sorry I'm a few minutes late," he said, then stopped dead still when less than six feet separated them.

He was the same and yet different. Older, broader shouldered, harder. And battle scarred. The boyish smoothness of his handsome face was gone, replaced with an imperfect roughness.

"Hello, Jack."

He stood there speechless, staring at Cathy Nelson. No, not Cathy Nelson—Cathy Cantrell, Mark Cantrell's widow. He had figured that sooner or later he'd run into her, considering that Dunmore was a small town. But he sure as hell hadn't expected to react this way—as if he'd been hit between the eyes with a two-by-four.

As a teenager, Cathy had been a pretty girl in her own shy, sweet way. But the woman standing there, her blue-green eyes fixed on his face, her mouth open in shock as if she'd seen a ghost, was more than pretty. She was beautiful.

Her long brown hair, flowing freely around her shoulders, shimmered with damp highlights caused by the misty rain. Her body had matured. Her breasts were fuller than he remembered, and she was slimmer. Not skinny, just trim.

"Hello, Cathy."

She surveyed him from head to toe, taking in his deputy's uniform. "I—I wasn't expecting to see you. I thought you and Maleah had probably sold the house."

"I thought I left my name when I called. Maybe I didn't. I guess you hadn't heard that Mike Birkett hired me as a deputy. I've moved back to Dunmore."

"Permanently?"

He nodded. "Possibly. Depends."

"Depends on what?"

"If the deputy job works out."

"Yes, of course. You've left the army?"

"Yeah."

She glanced at the porch and front of the house. "And you're going to restore this place?"

"That's the plan." When he moved toward her, she backed up as if she were afraid of him. Odd. "Why don't you come on inside and take a look? I can put on some coffee, or, if you prefer, there's beer in the—No beer. As I recall, you don't drink. Unless your tastes have changed."

She stepped out of his way as he retrieved the key from his pocket and headed for the front door. "I wasn't sure who would show up," Jack said. "I sort of thought it would be Lorie."

"Lorie's at an auction in Fayetteville."

Jack held open the front door. "Come on in."

When he noted her hesitation, he forced a wide smile, hoping to put her at ease. Apparently at least a part of the shy young girl he had once known still existed inside the adult Cathy.

"How about some coffee?" Jack asked. "We can go in the

kitchen and talk. I can explain what I want to do to this old place, and you can tell me what you think."

"All right." After she entered the house, he came in behind her. Then she followed him to the kitchen. "If you'd prefer working with Lorie, we can reschedule. I've been away from the business for nearly a year, so I might be a little rusty."

She was nervous.

Was she nervous because she was alone with him or because she only recently had left a mental-rehab center and was having difficulty readjusting?

"You'll do just fine," he said. "If you'd like the job. I haven't even hired a contractor yet. What I need from you is someone who knows something about restoring and decorating historical houses, about fine antiques and things like that. I know little to nothing. I want this place to look the way it did when I was a kid, only better. Modern bathrooms, a modern kitchen . . ."

"The kitchen and bathrooms could be modern and yet reflect the Victorian style of the house. Claw-foot tubs in the bathrooms. A farmhouse sink in the kitchen. Cabinetry that has the look of antique furniture." Cathy's face lit up as she talked, her expression reflecting her enthusiasm about the proposed project. "This house could easily be a showplace." She glanced at him, her gaze almost timid. "Returning this house to her former glory will be expensive."

Jack grinned. "And you're wondering how I can afford it on a deputy's salary."

"I didn't mean to imply that you can't afford—"

"I've invested my money wisely," he told her. "Nearly twenty years in the army with no wife and kids, I was able to save a lot, and I made some lucrative investments over the years."

"I'm sorry. It's really none of my business."

"Let me put on the coffee. Then, if you'd like, I'll walk

you through the house. You've never been inside before, have you?"

"Uh . . . no. No, I haven't," she lied. She had been here one other time.

Jack hurriedly prepared the coffeemaker and then began the tour of his home, taking her from room to room.

When he had phoned Treasures of the Past and set up this appointment, he had hoped Cathy would show up. Mike had warned him to stay away from her. During this past week, as he had gone over the file on Mark Cantrell's murder, he had asked Mike a number of questions and had learned about the hell Cathy had been through these past eighteen months. The last thing he wanted to do was create more problems in her life. But he had been curious about Cathy. His Cathy. The only girl who had ever broken his heart.

Chapter Five

Father Brian hung up the telephone and immediately wondered if he had made a mistake by agreeing too quickly to his caller's request. But how could he have refused such a pitiful plea for help? Not only was it his duty to help others, but he felt a deep kinship with the oppressed, children and teens in particular, because of what he had been through as a young boy. Having been subjected to drug-addicted parents who, stoned out of their minds most of the time, had beaten him on a regular basis, he knew how truly helpless the young could feel and how hopeless their lives could be. He had run away at thirteen and lived on the streets, where he had come into contact with the vilest human beings imaginable. But a kind and caring priest in Louisville had saved his life, both literally and figuratively.

Father James had not only taught the goodness of our Lord and Savior to Brian but had shown him that goodness in action on a daily basis. Thanks to the gentle old priest, Brian had come to realize that ministering to others, especially the young, was his true calling.

"Please, you have to help me," the frightened, almost hysterical caller had said. "I can't come to you. You have to meet me. It's the only way. If you don't, I'll kill myself. I swear I will."

His better judgment warned him against meeting his caller at a public park in Dunmore this evening, but his heart insisted that he must do whatever was necessary to save a life. The wisest course of action would be to tell Father Francis, but he knew that the parish priest would advise him against going, perhaps even forbid him to go. It wasn't that Father Francis wasn't a good and caring man. He was. But he was a priest who followed the rules, who adhered to the letter of the law, so to speak.

During his brief conversation with the caller, he had done his best to persuade the woman—or was she actually a teenaged girl or boy?—to come here to the church. But no matter how sincerely he had promised protection and anonymity, she had refused. The voice over the phone had been oddly hoarse, as if the person was trying to disguise it, but he believed the caller had been female. If a male, then his voice was alto in tone.

"No one must ever know," she had said. "If he ever found out . . ." She had burst into tears.

"Everything will be all right. I promise that I will meet you this evening at eleven. And I will do what I can to help you."

Father Brian had no idea who the mysterious *he* the caller had referred to was, but it had been apparent that she was terrified of this person. Her father? A male relative? A boyfriend? Whoever he was, he frightened her and had tormented her to the point that she was seriously contemplating suicide.

He, too, had once known that abject feeling of utter hopelessness. The night Father James had found him huddled in a corner of the church in Louisville, his body bloody and bruised and his spirit broken, he had been thinking about killing himself. He had been fifteen years old.

Father Brian dropped to his knees on the floor of his sitting room, folded his hands together and prayed. A prayer of heartfelt thanks for Father James, gone now these past ten years. And he prayed for the life of the person who had called, pleading with him for help. He needed God's guidance. No matter what was going on in her life, no matter how horrible her situation, he must find a way to help her without betraying her trust. But he knew that if she was being beaten or molested, he would have to find a way to convince her to allow him to contact the authorities.

Erin McKinley reapplied her lip gloss and blush before leaving the restroom located across from Reverend Harper's office in the basement of the First Baptist Church. It was already after six, half an hour past time for her eight-hour day to end, but as she did every day, she would knock on John Earl's door and say good-bye before heading home. Each day she hoped that he would notice her, would see her as a woman and not just a fixture in his office. She had been his secretary for four years and had fallen in love with him almost immediately. She simply couldn't help herself. Who wouldn't love John Earl? Not only was he incredibly handsome, with thick, curly brown hair streaked with thin silver strands, stormy gray eyes and a tall, athletic body, but he was a truly good man. He lived his religion every day of his life. He was kind, considerate, patient and gentle. And Erin worshipped the ground he walked on. Yes, she knew it was a sin to lust after a married man, to dream of taking him to her bed and allowing him to ravish her. But she could no more stop herself from loving John Earl than she could stop the sun from rising in the east tomorrow morning.

She squared her shoulders, thrust her breasts forward, marched through the reception area and knocked before opening the door to John Earl's office. She gasped softly when she saw that the reverend was not alone. He held his wife in his arms.

Ruth Ann Harper tilted her head and smiled at Erin. "Please, come in. I just came by to pick up John Earl. He and I have a date for a movie and dinner out this evening."

He kissed his wife's cheek with great affection.

Erin stiffened, but managed to force a friendly smile. She didn't actually hate Ruth Ann. The woman was nice enough, and she did seem to truly love John Earl. *But not as much as I love him.*

Erin envied Ruth Ann, and in darker moments, when hopelessness and despair took over, she even thought about killing her. Not that she ever would, of course. But how could she ever compete with a woman such as Mrs. Harper, who seemed so perfect, always smiling and friendly, always perfectly groomed with nary a dark hair out of place? A fine wife, a good mother, a real lady. Tall, slender and elegant in that Jackie Kennedy/Grace Kelly kind of way, as if she had been born knowing all the correct things to say and do.

Not for the first time, Erin wondered what the oh-so-perfect Ruth Ann was like in bed. Was she as perfect at fucking as she seemed to be at everything else? Or was she, as Erin suspected, a frigid ice queen? After all, the woman had to have some faults, didn't she? And if her shortcomings were inadequacies in the bedroom, that meant that Erin had a shot at giving John Earl something his wife could not. Other than being a damn good secretary, Erin was a damn good lay.

"It's good to see you, Mrs. Harper," Erin said. "I just wanted to say good-bye to Reverend Harper." She looked directly at him, doing her best to hide the longing in her eyes.

"Good-bye, Erin. See you tomorrow," John Earl replied, but he never took his eyes off his wife. Having dismissed his secretary, he said to Ruth Ann, "Do the girls have plans tonight or are they staying in with your mother?"

Just as Erin started to close the door, she heard Ruth Ann say, "The girls have plans. Felicity is going to the mall with some of her girlfriends, and Charity is going to the library."

"Charity spends too much time in the library," John Earl said. "She needs to have a little fun."

"Are you saying our eighteen-year-old daughter needs a boyfriend?"

John Earl chuckled. "That's a father's worst nightmare—his baby girl dating. But yes, it's time Charity started dating. Some nice young man who attends church here, a boy whose parents we know."

Erin closed the door quietly and walked away, tears trickling down her cheeks. John Earl was a man devoted to his wife and daughters. If she hadn't been able to seduce him in four years, what made her think she ever could? And with no hope of John Earl ever returning her love, her life simply wasn't worth living.

"You knew that Jackson Perdue was back in Dunmore and you didn't bother to tell me!" Cathy stood in the middle of the kitchen, hands on hips, and glared at her best friend.

"I didn't mention it because I thought you needed time to adjust to being back home and settling into your new place next week and . . ." Lorie threw her hands in the air in a gesture that was half plea and half exasperation. "I thought I was protecting you. After all, you've got enough on your plate without having to deal with Jack Perdue showing up in Dunmore after all these years." Lorie reached out and grabbed both of Cathy's hands. "I swear to you that when Ruth Ann told me some man had called and wanted to hire Treasures as decorating consultants, I had no idea it was Jack."

"I believe you." Cathy squeezed Lorie's hands, then pulled free and turned back to the stove, where she had several pots and pans bubbling, boiling and simmering. She was making Seth's favorite meal: meatloaf, green peas, creamed potatoes, deviled eggs, biscuits and caramel pie for dessert. This morning, she had prepared the pie and placed it in the refrigerator and had made the meatloaf that was now warming in the oven. And only a few minutes ago, right before Lorie arrived home from Fayetteville, Cathy had topped the pie with whipped cream and Maraschino cherries.

Lorie came up behind Cathy and placed her hand on Cathy's shoulder. "How was it, seeing him again?"

Cathy lifted the lid off the green peas, stirred them, turned the stove down low and replaced the lid. "I'm not sure. At first, I was nervous. Seeing him was such a shock."

"Oh, honey, I'm sorry. If I'd had any idea this would happen, I'd have told you he was back in town."

Cathy checked on the bubbling pot of sliced potatoes, then faced her friend. "He's staying permanently. He's moved into his mother's house. He's going to restore the old place, and he offered me the job as his design consultant." Cathy giggled nervously. "Never in a million years would I have thought that someday Jack and I would . . ." Realizing she was on the verge of crying, she took several deep, calming breaths. "He's different. And not just because he's older and was injured in the war. He used to be so angry and tense all the time, but now he seems . . . I'm not sure—not so angry. Steadier somehow."

"Did he tell you that he's taken a job as one of Mike's deputies?" Lorie asked.

Cathy nodded. "He was wearing his uniform and drove up in a county sheriff's car."

"Is he still as handsome as sin?"

"Yes."

"Any old feelings resurface?"

"A few."

"Well, listen to you, being honest with yourself and with me."

"I don't lie to myself anymore." Cathy picked up two oven mitts from the counter, opened the oven door and checked on the warming meatloaf. "There's nothing wrong with admitting that I'm still attracted to Jack. Most women probably are. He always did attract the opposite sex. Besides, he's single and so am I."

"Amen, sister." Lorie patted her on the back.

"He told me that Mike has assigned him to work on two cold-case files for the sheriff's department, and one of those cases is Mark's murder."

"What?"

"He was entirely up front about it." Cathy looked directly at Lorie. "He told me he was sorry about what had happened to my husband, and then he explained that he was going over the county's cold-cases—the unsolved homicides—including Mark's murder."

"But why? What possible reason would Mike have to re-open Mark's case?"

"He's not reopening the case," Cathy said. "Jack is studying the files, and he's going to compare notes with the police in Athens, where Charles Randolph, the Lutheran minister, was killed last year in the same way Mark was."

Lorie put her arm around Cathy's shoulders. "Oh, honey, you shouldn't have to deal with any of this. You shouldn't have to go over all those bad memories about the day Mark died. And you certainly shouldn't have to work with Jack Perdue. I'll step in and handle the consulting job myself, and that way you won't have to—"

"No, that won't be necessary. I can work with Jack. I'm not running away from the past. I faced a great many hard truths while I was in therapy. I learned that I can't change the past. I can't bring Mark back any more than I could have saved him the day he died. And I can't deny that a part of me still loves Jack Perdue and probably always will."

"Oh, Cathy . . . Honey, no, no . . ."

"It's all right, really it is. I have no illusions about Jack. But he's not the same now, and neither am I. I'm not expecting happily ever after, not with Jack or any other man. Whatever does or doesn't happen between us, I can handle it."

"Can you?"

"Yes."

"What about Seth?"

Cathy swallowed hard. "What about Seth?"

"How do you think Seth would react if he found out the man you were in love with before you married Mark has come back into your life?"

"There's no reason for Seth to know about my past with Jack."

"Oh, honey, you're lying to yourself if you think the truth won't come out eventually. If you get involved with Jack again, all your secret little birds will come home to roost."

He moaned and groaned and trembled with his release. She lay beneath him silent and unmoving, hating him, wishing him dead. His heavy weight pinned her to the bed—her canopy bed with white, lace-trimmed linens—as he kissed her tenderly and whispered the same words he always said when he had finished with her.

"I love you, sweetheart."

When he lifted himself up and off her, she turned over, grabbed the sheet and pulled it over her naked body as she curled into a ball. She didn't watch him leave her room, but she heard the door close behind him. He would go to his bathroom, remove the condom he had worn and take a shower. Then he would go into his den and spend the rest of the evening in his disguise as a man of God.

Lying there, her tender young breasts bruised from his rough hands and her whole body throbbing with shame and anger, she wanted to cry. But she didn't cry anymore. Tears were useless. She was trapped in a nightmare without end. The only way to escape would be to end her life. But she wasn't that brave. Not yet.

She got out of bed, took a shower to wash off his smell, dressed hurriedly and sneaked out through her bedroom window, leaving it cracked open so she could come back in later. It was nearly eight-thirty and had gotten dark early this evening because of the rain clouds. Tonight, the sky had partially cleared, enough so that the three-quarter moon peeked through the threads of murky clouds. She could stay out as late as she wanted, go anywhere, do anything, as long as no one recognized her and reported back to her father. He wouldn't check on her again tonight. Once he raped her, he didn't bother her again. Not until the next time. During the day, their lives were hypocritically normal. They ate their meals together every morning and evening. He asked her about her homework, her teachers and her friends. He acted like any father might. He attended all her school functions, charmed her teachers and her friends, and had the whole world fooled. Everyone believed he was the ideal father. No one suspected what happened between them several nights each week in the privacy of her bedroom.

"This is our secret," he had told her the first time he had raped her, when she was thirteen. "No one else must ever know. No one would understand."

He was right. No one would understand.

She didn't understand.

"Mom, I think it's great that you've rented your own place." Seth finished off the last bite of caramel pie and scooted his chair away from the kitchen table.

"It's not as large as our old house," Cathy told him. "But it's only three blocks from Nana and Granddad, over on Madison Avenue, and there's plenty of room for the two of us. Your room is a really good size, and you'll have your own bathroom."

Seth's smile, which she had enjoyed all evening, faded quickly at the mention of him living with her. "Mom, I . . . I . . ."

"You don't have to move in with me next week when I take our furniture out of storage, but sooner or later, I want you to come home where you belong—with me."

"I know what you want, Mom. It's just that Granddad's not going to agree, and I don't think he'll change his mind. You know how stubborn he is."

"Yes, I know. And I would prefer to have your grandfather's approval. But with or without it, I want you to live with me. You're my son, not his. You belong with me."

When she saw the confused expression on Seth's face, she almost wished she could take back the adamant claim to her maternal rights. Almost. She would never make Seth do something he didn't want to do, but she suspected that his reluctance to live with her had more to do with him not wanting to displease J.B. than it did with any doubts he had about moving in with her.

"Granddad and Nana are my legal guardians," Seth reminded her. "When you went to Haven Home, you agreed that it was the best thing for me."

"At the time, it was. But that was then and this is now. I'm completely well. I'm strong and healthy and totally competent."

He stared at her, a look of uncertainty in his blue eyes.

Eyes identical to his father's.

"I had a nervous breakdown. I chose to get the help I needed. I did that as much for you as for me. We had just lost Mark, lost your dad, and I knew you needed me. The only way I could be the mother you needed was to get well, completely well."

"I know all that, but it doesn't change the fact that you . . . Well, you totally lost it and spent a year in that place, and some people think you're still . . . Gee, Mom, I don't think you're crazy or anything. It's just that Granddad—"

"I understand." Cathy steeled her nerves. Oh, she understood, all right. J.B. intended to retain legal custody of her son and would do whatever he thought necessary to keep a barrier between Seth and her. The old Cathy wouldn't have fought back; she would have convinced herself that J.B. knew what was best. Well, that was the old Cathy. The new and improved Cathy would give her father-in-law the fight of his life. "But I'd still like for you to come by this weekend and see the house. And please, invite your grandparents to come with you."

Seth's face brightened. "Yeah, sure. That would be great. I know Granddad will eventually let me come over and spend the night."

Cathy forced a smile and somehow managed to keep it in place for the next hour of Seth's visit.

J.B. picked Seth up promptly at nine-thirty, but didn't bother coming to the door. He honked the horn and waited outside. Seth kissed Cathy's cheek and gave her a hug.

"Tonight was great," he told her. "I'll see you this weekend."

She stood in the doorway and watched him get in the car with his grandfather. When J.B. glanced her way and nodded, she lifted her hand, waved and plastered an ear-to-ear grin across her face.

Just as the red taillights on J.B.'s Lincoln disappeared around the corner at the end of the block, Lorie came up beside Cathy.

"J.B.'s being a real bastard about Seth," Lorie said.

"Yes, he is."

"What are you going to do about it?"

"I'm going to call in the morning and make an appointment with Elliott Floyd. I believe it's time I hired a lawyer."

When Father Brian parked his Honda Civic, he noted that his was the only vehicle in the small paved lot adjacent to the park entrance. On several trips to Dunmore during the past couple of years, he had passed by Spring Creek Park, but he had never stopped and checked it out. The entrance was well lit, as the entire park seemed to be, with pole lights placed strategically throughout the acreage. After closing the car door, he took in a deep, steadying breath and instantly caught the scent of damp earth. He closed his eyes for a peaceful moment and inhaled that glorious smell left behind after a good, soaking rain.

He sighed, opened his eyes and checked his lighted digital wristwatch. Ten fifty-seven.

She should be here soon, if she showed up at all.

Please, God, let her come to me so that I can help her.

Although it was late May and the daytime temperatures ranged from the high seventies to the low eighties, the nights were still often quite chilly. Feeling the cool breeze whipping through the trees, he was glad he had worn his jacket.

The stone archway that led into the park appeared to be quite old. No doubt this park had been in existence for generations. Often parks were located near underground springs and other bodies of water, so he assumed Spring Creek Park was near Spring Creek. The sidewalk ended abruptly less than fifteen feet inside the park. Three dirt paths, leading in different directions, branched off from the sidewalk.

He paused, looked around, getting the lay of the land, so to speak, and felt an instant shiver of apprehension shoot through his body. Standing perfectly still, he listened to the quiet nighttime chorus of wind and nearby water and the gentle song of unseen creatures.

Suddenly the headlights of a passing car flashed across the park entrance and startled him. No reason to panic, he told himself. But what if the car had belonged to a policeman? What if he was questioned about what he was doing here, alone in the park, at this time of night? Why hadn't he considered the possibility that someone might mistake him for one of those men who performed deviant sex acts in public places?

A flutter of noise erupted from a nearby tree, and two

birds emerged from the thick foliage and sailed into the starless sky, their silhouettes spotlighted by the shadowed moonlight. The sound startled him, so much so that his heartbeat accelerated and his hands trembled. An anxious unease settled over him, accompanied by the thought that he shouldn't be here.

He checked his watch again. Five after eleven. He would wait another ten minutes. Even though his gut instinct told him to leave now, his heartfelt concern for the person who had called him, begging for his help, overruled his common sense. Some poor, lost soul might take her own life tonight if he didn't stay here and offer her hope for the future.

"Father Brian," the voice called to him.

"Yes, I'm here." His gaze circled the area around him, but he saw no one. "Where are you?"

Silence.

Had he imagined her calling his name? Had it simply been the wind?

"Please, show yourself. I'm Father Brian. I'm here to help you, my child."

"Father Brian." The eerily soft voice said his name again, and this time he noted from which direction it had come.

He followed the path that led past the small rose garden and two sets of concrete park benches. "Don't be afraid." He held out his hands in a gesture that he hoped indicated concern and caring. "Whatever is wrong in your life, God can help you. All things are possible through Jesus Christ, our Lord and Savior."

A dark figure bolted from the unlit area of trees and tall shrubs and came at him so quickly that he didn't have time to react before he felt a cool, foul-smelling liquid splatter over him from his face to his feet.

What had just happened?

Father Brian looked into the face of death, realizing too late that he had walked into a skillfully planned trap. He saw the tiny, yellow-orange flame at the tip of the Pocket Torch lighter half a second before she tossed it on him, setting him on fire.

She moved back, away from the flames, and stood there listening to the priest's screams. She watched in utter silence, smiling. He would never again harm another child.

Vengeance is mine, thus sayeth the Lord. She was the Lord's instrument of punishment. He had chosen her to rid the world of men such as Father Brian. Slowly, quietly, as silent as the grave, she turned and walked away.

Burn in hell for your sins, Father Brian! Burn in everlasting torment.

Chapter Six

Tasha Phillips parked one of the two Spring Creek Missionary Baptist Church vans carrying the church's preschoolers, and her husband, Dewan, pulled the second van up beside the first. Three SUVs followed, each carrying the same precious cargo. Every year on the final Tuesday prior to the Wednesday evening church services where the little ones participated in a graduation ceremony, the minister and his wife hosted a picnic at Spring Creek Park. As the director of the church's preschool and day-care programs, Tasha took great pride in her accomplishments—not that they equaled Dewan's, of course. Since they had come to Dunmore nearly ten years ago, the local church had flourished under her husband's charismatic leadership. The once small, floundering congregation now boasted over two hundred members, a large number in a town of less than eight thousand residents, with only 10 percent of those African-American.

Mothers and fathers carrying picnic baskets and coolers emerged from their vehicles, and the teachers lined the preschoolers up and counted heads.

Once the group had congregated at the arched entrance to the park, Dewan raised his hands and called for a moment of silence. To a person, every man, woman and child quieted instantly. The murmur of the warm spring breeze and the trickle of springwater flowing over the nearby streambed provided background music for the prayer.

"Almighty God, creator of all things, benevolent and understanding, we come before You this morning asking for Your blessings for these our beloved children and thanking You for this fine day."

Tasha bowed her head and closed her eyes as she listened to Dewan's booming, authoritative voice speaking directly to the Lord. She was as mesmerized by him today as she had been twelve years ago when they had been introduced by mutual friends. For her, it had been love at first sight. She had never met anyone like Dewan Phillips, a man so sure of his calling to preach, a man who could have been anything he wanted and yet chose service to God and his fellow man. And when given the opportunity to be an assistant minister at a large church in Birmingham, he had chosen instead to accept the job as pastor of a needy church in the small North Alabama town of Dunmore.

At the end of Dewan's prayer, a resounding shout of "Amen" signaled the children that they could laugh and talk, which they immediately did.

As the teachers and parents entered the park, Tasha slipped her arm through her husband's and smiled up at him. At six-three, Dewan towered over her by a good ten inches. He leaned down, kissed her forehead and then laid his big hand tenderly over her slightly protruding belly. After ten years of marriage, ten years of praying for a child, they were, at long last, expecting a little boy in three months. They had already decided to name him after their fathers, Sidney Demetrius Phillips, but they couldn't agree on what they would call him. She preferred Sid, after her dad, and he preferred Demetrius, after his dad. She suspected that, in the end, Dewan would win her over. He always did.

"You go on in," he told her. "I need to get those folding chairs out of the back of the van."

Tasha joined the others in the park, following the mothers as they walked directly toward the tables near the rose garden. There was more shade in that area because of the enormous old oak trees growing nearby. The teachers herded the children toward the play equipment suitable for their age groups while the parents busied themselves with picnic preparations. When Mariah Johnson pulled a red-checkered tablecloth from her basket and unfolded it, Tasha grabbed one end and helped her spread it across the nearest table.

"The day couldn't be more perfect, could it?" Mariah said. "It's as if the Lord is smiling down on us."

While chitchatting happily, they retrieved another tablecloth from Mariah's basket. Then, just as they lifted the cloth over the next table, a loud, terrified scream shattered the adults' cheerful conversation and the children's beautiful laughter. Tasha stopped dead still, the ends of the tablecloth clutched in her hands. Two of the fathers, Eli Richardson and Galvin Johnson, ran toward the screaming Monetia Simmons, who stood stiff as a granite statue, her wide eyes fixed on something lying on the ground behind the concrete tables at the far side of the rose garden. As the men neared Monetia, they paused when they saw what had made her scream.

Dewan came racing toward Tasha. "What's wrong? I heard someone screaming."

Eli went over to Monetia and put his arm protectively around her trembling shoulders while Galvin hurried toward Dewan. He said in a low, calm voice, "Call the police, Reverend Phillips. There's a dead man over there. It looks like he burned to death."

"Merciful Lord," Tasha gasped.

Dewan gripped her arm. "You and the other ladies gather up the children and take them back to the church. I'll contact the police, and the men and I will stay here until they arrive."

* * *

Jack stared at the photographs of Mark Cantrell's charred body. Autopsy photos. What kind of person could douse another human being with gasoline and set him on fire? Someone completely devoid of any type of normal emotions—someone incapable of empathy or sympathy?

His own body retained the scars left from an explosion, scars no surgeon's scalpel could ever completely erase. But he had been in the middle of a war zone when he'd been severely injured. And he had survived. Casualties were expected during a war. Mark Cantrell had been living in a small, quiet Alabama town. He had been a minister, a man of God, someone who taught love and compassion and forgiveness. His death had been unexpected and horrific in nature.

What must it have been like for Cathy to have watched her husband burn to death, knowing there was absolutely nothing she could do to save him?

Jack set aside the Cantrell file and picked up the file containing the copies of the Athens police department's report on the death of Charles Randolph. Six months after Mark Cantrell's vicious murder, the forty-nine-year-old Randolph, a Lutheran pastor, had been covered with gasoline and set on fire. His wife had heard his screams and rushed into the backyard. She had found him burning to death in the alley, where he had gone to place their garbage for the next day's trash pickup. Randolph had lived less than twelve hours after being rushed to the hospital. In his condition, he had been unable to tell the police anything. And neither his wife nor any of the neighbors had seen or heard anything suspicious.

Jack shoved aside the files, leaned back in the swivel chair at his desk, lifted his arms behind him and cupped the back of his head with his entwined fingers.

Other than the fact they were both clergymen, the two victims had nothing in common, nothing that would link them to each other or to the same killer.

These files told only part of the story, the official part, and that's all that should concern him.

"Less than a week after Pastor Randolph's murder, Cathy Cantrell had a nervous breakdown," Mike had told him. "She spent several days in the hospital here in Dunmore, and then her mother drove her down to Birmingham, where Cathy checked herself into Haven Home, a mental-rehab center."

Jack knew a little something about post-traumatic stress. During his recuperation from the bomb explosion, he'd gone through his own psychiatric treatment. And even now, there were times when he got the shakes and occasionally had nightmares. He hated to think about Cathy going through the torment of the damned.

Since seeing her yesterday afternoon, he had thought of little else. He was a damn fool. Whatever had been between Cathy and him had been over and done with long ago. When he'd been a kid of twenty, he had thought he was in love and had believed she felt the same. But shortly after his leave ended, his Rangers unit had been sent to the Middle East and he had wound up spending six months as a POW in Iraq before escaping.

And Cathy had married someone else.

A sharp knock on the door snapped Jack out of his musings about the past. Mike opened the door, stuck his head in and said, "I just got a call from Wade Ballard, Dunmore chief of police. A group from a local Baptist church went to Spring Creek Park this morning for a picnic and found a dead body. Looks like the victim burned to death."

Jack shot up out of the chair. "Any idea who the victim is?"

"They found a car at the park they believe belonged to the victim. The church folks said the car was there when they arrived. Wade ran a check on the license plate. The car is registered to Brian Myers, a Catholic priest from Huntsville."

"Son of a bitch," Jack grumbled under his breath. "Victim number three."

"Yeah, it could be. We'll know more when the crime-scene guys finish up and after we get a look at the autopsy results."

Jack kept up with Mike's hurried pace as they exited the sheriff's office complex and headed toward Mike's heavy-duty Ford pickup.

"There were six months between murders one and two. Why wait a whole year before striking again?" Jack might be jumping to conclusions, but his gut told him that whoever killed the priest was the same person who had murdered Charles Randolph and Mark Cantrell.

Someone was killing clergymen. What was their motive? And why had they chosen such a gruesome way to execute their victims?

Lorie gift wrapped the set of coasters and the matching placemats that Mrs. Webber had purchased for her grand-niece's bridal shower. She took extra care with this gift, choosing the most expensive paper and ribbon she kept on hand at Treasures. Margaret Webber was one of their best customers and one of the grand old dames of Dunmore society. If someone such as she could accept Lorie, even as a lowly peon, there was hope that someday a lot of other people in her hometown would also accept her. Maybe even Michael Birkett.

After placing a Treasures of the Past gold sticker on the gift, she inserted the beautifully wrapped box into one of their largest bags with handles and offered it to Mrs. Webber.

"Here you are," Lorie said. "And please give my best wishes to your niece."

"Thank you, my dear."

"Have a nice day."

"And you, too."

Just as Mrs. Webber headed out the door, Lorie's cell phone, which lay on the glass checkout counter, jingled. Before answering, she checked caller ID. She did a double take when she saw the name. What an odd coincidence. Michael Birkett. Her heart stopped. Why on earth would Mike be calling her?

With an unsteady hand, she picked up the phone. "Hello."

"Lorie?"

She cleared her throat. "Yes, this is Lorie Hammonds."

"Mike Birkett here. Is Cathy there with you?"

"She's here, but she's in the stockroom doing some end-of-the-month inventory. Would you like to speak to her?" Why the hell hadn't he called the store phone? Why her cell phone? And just how did he get her private number? *He's the sheriff,* she reminded herself. *He can get anybody's number.*

"No, I don't want to speak to her. I called you directly because I didn't want to risk Cathy answering the store phone. There's no easy way to say this. . . ." His voice trailed off as if he was having a difficult time with whatever news he had to share.

"You're scaring me. Has something happened to Seth?"

"No, nothing like that," Mike assured her.

"My God, whatever it is, just tell me."

"There's been another murder. The pastor, his wife and some members of the local black Baptist church found a body at Spring Creek Park this morning when they went there for a picnic." Mike paused. "The victim burned to death. Andy Gamble says that it looks like he was drenched in gasoline. And one more thing—we're pretty sure the guy was a Catholic priest from over in Huntsville."

Sour bile rose up Lorie's esophagus and burned her throat. "Damn! How can I tell Cathy about this? You know what happened when that Lutheran pastor over in Athens was killed last year."

"You don't have to tell her. I'll do it. But word's got out already, and I thought I should warn you before somebody comes into the shop and blurts it out."

"Oh God, oh God."

"Pull yourself together," Mike told her. "Jack and I will be there in twenty minutes or less."

"Jack? Why bring him?"

"Jack's one of my deputies, and since I put him in charge of the department's old cases, including Mark Cantrell's murder, he's been exchanging info with the detectives in Athens who headed up the Randolph murder. With this third murder, we'll probably be calling in the Alabama Bureau of Investigation and forming a task force. I'll be assigning Jack to work with the other law-enforcement agencies involved with this new murder investigation."

"Cathy is going to have a hard enough time today hearing the news about another murder similar to Mark's. She doesn't need to have to deal with Jackson Perdue at the same time."

"You're overreacting, aren't you? Jack and Cathy's little romance lasted what? Two weeks? And that was nearly twenty years ago."

"No, Cathy and Jack's little romance wasn't quite that long ago," she said. "It ended about the same time ours did, right after I left Dunmore and went to LA."

Silence. Mike didn't make a sound.

Why on earth had she brought up their past history? Now was not the right time. Actually there probably never would be a right time.

"Sorry," Lorie said. "We weren't talking about us, were we? But then there is no us and there'll never be an us, not ever again."

"Do what you can to keep Cathy from finding out about the murder before I can talk to her." Mike ignored her comment about the two of them. "And . . . uh, I won't bring Jack with me."

"Thanks. I'll lock the front door and put up the CLOSED sign. When you get here, come to the back door."

"All right." He ended their conversation abruptly with those two words.

Mike had been right to ignore her outburst. It wasn't as if she had any hope whatsoever that he would ever forgive her for what she'd done. Even if she would settle for the two of them being nothing more than friends, he wasn't interested. He didn't want to have anything to do with her, and he'd made that abundantly clear more than once in the years since she had returned to Dunmore, tail tucked between her legs and her reputation in tatters.

Stop feeling sorry for yourself.

You have to take care of Cathy and help her not to fall apart when she hears the news about the priest's ghastly murder.

Lorie removed the keychain from the drawer beneath the counter, walked across the shop and locked the front door. After flipping the OPEN sign to where it read CLOSED, she went to the back storeroom, where Cathy stood at the top of a stepladder.

"Need some help?" Lorie asked.

Cathy glanced down at her. "Who's looking after our customers?"

"Mrs. Webber just left, and the place is empty. You know that Tuesdays are never very busy. Besides, it's nearly noon, and I thought we could go ahead and take our lunch break."

Cathy stepped down off the ladder. "Since Tuesdays are slow days as a general rule, maybe we should think about doing something special to draw in customers every Tuesday. We could have a sale day on certain items or serve refreshments on Tuesdays or—"

"It all sounds great. We can discuss your ideas over lunch." She draped her arm through Cathy's. "Come on. You take those tuna-salad sandwiches you made this morning out of the refrigerator, put on a pot of fresh coffee and I'll run back out front and get us a box of those sinfully rich McTavish shortbread cookies."

Cathy eyed Lorie suspiciously. "Are you all right? You're acting kind of funny."

"I'm okay. Just hungry." She gave Cathy a gentle shove toward the hallway that led from the stockroom to the kitchenette. "Feed me and I'll be fine."

Lorie hated being less than honest with Cathy, but she couldn't bring herself to tell her about this new murder, another death so similar to Mark's. Maybe Cathy was emotionally strong enough to hear the news and deal with it, but what if she wasn't? What if she fell apart again?

It was best for Mike to tell her, just in case.

Mike parked his truck in the alley behind Treasures of the Past, but instead of getting out immediately, he killed the engine and sat there collecting his thoughts. He hadn't dreaded anything this much in a long time. He had known Cathy since she was a kid. He'd grown up with her, gone to church where she went, lived on the same block. And he had been crazy in love with her best friend for as far back as he could remember. There hadn't been anyone else for him except Lorie Hammonds, from elementary school through high school and his first two years at the junior college. He and Lorie had often double-dated with Cathy and whatever friend of his he could talk into taking Cathy out. It wasn't that Cathy hadn't been cute, but she'd been shy and bookish, and all the guys knew they wouldn't get past first base with her.

And then Jack Perdue had noticed Cathy. He'd been home on leave from the army and visiting Mike and his family. From the minute Jack had asked Cathy for a date, the two had been inseparable for the remaining two weeks of Jack's stay in Dunmore.

If he'd ever seen two people in love . . .

Mike didn't know what had happened between them, why things hadn't worked out. All he knew was that less than three months later, Cathy married Mark Cantrell, and shortly after that he'd accepted a preaching position at a church in another state. And that same year, Lorie had won a talent contest and flown off to Los Angeles to become a Hollywood star.

Mike slammed his fist down on the steering wheel.

It had taken him a long time to stop loving Lorie, but eventually he'd met someone else, a sweet girl named Molly. They'd had six great years and two fabulous kids together before he'd lost her. When Lorie had finally come back to Dunmore, he'd been too busy caring for his dying wife and his two small children to take much notice.

The sound of a car horn coming from the nearby street jerked Mike out of his memories and reminded him of where he was and why he was here.

Stop putting things off. Go do what you have to do.

He got out of the truck, walked over to the back door of Treasures and knocked. Ordering Jack to stay at the scene of the crime had been the only way to keep him from coming along.

"I need you here at the park," Mike had told him. "I'm making you the liaison between the sheriff's department and the police department on this murder case. If you want to help Cathy, then do your job and help us find the killer."

Jack hadn't put up an argument. Instead he had said, "Yeah, sure. There's no reason for me to go with you. There's nothing I can do for her."

Mike hated to admit that Lorie had been right—Cathy didn't need to deal with Jack, not right now. He hadn't wanted to believe that there might still be some unresolved feelings between Cathy and Jack, because if he did, he'd have to face the fact that he still had some unresolved feelings for Lorie.

When no one came to the back door, he knocked again, louder and harder.

"Coming," Lorie called.

He took a deep breath.

Lorie opened the door and looked up at him with those big brown eyes that had haunted his dreams for years. "She's in the kitchenette. I got her to eat a bite, because I figured once she hears the news, she'll lose her appetite."

When Lorie moved aside, allowing him to enter, he asked, "Have you said anything to her?"

Lorie shook her head. "No, but I've been so jittery that I think she knows something's up. She's asked me a couple of times if I'm all right."

"How is she? I mean really, how is she? Can she take this news without cracking up?"

"She's been doing better than fine since she came home. She smiles and laughs, and she's been holding her own against Elaine and the Cantrells. She's the same wonderful Cathy she always was, only better. She's stronger and more self-confident."

"So you think she'll handle this okay, then?"

"God, I hope so."

"I thought you said—"

"This news will force her to relive the day Mark died. I don't know how she'll cope with that. I think she'll do okay, but . . . Damn, bad things just shouldn't happen to good people like Cathy."

"Bad things happen to good people all the time." Molly had been one of the finest women he'd ever known, and yet she had suffered unbearably for the last year of her life.

Cathy came out of the kitchenette. "Hey, is that you, Mike?"

"Yeah, it's me." He moved past Lorie and went straight to Cathy.

Lorie came up beside him. Cathy looked from one to the other.

"What's wrong? What's happened? It's not Seth . . . ?"

"Seth is fine," Lorie and Mike said in unison.

"Then what is it?"

"Why don't we go sit down," Mike suggested.

Cathy shook her head. "No. Whatever it is, tell me now."

Mike sucked in air and blew out a frustrated breath. "We've had a homicide in Dunmore. Andy—you know Andy Gamble is the county coroner now—anyway, Andy thinks the man was killed sometime last night."

Cathy stared at him, her blue-green eyes wide and her lips slightly parted. Lorie grabbed Cathy's arm.

"How was this man killed?" Cathy asked.

Mike grimaced. "It looks like he was set on fire."

Cathy staggered. Lorie tightened her grip and held fast.

"I wanted to tell you before you heard it from somebody else," Mike said. "We don't have an official ID yet, but we believe the victim was Father Brian Myers, a Catholic priest from Huntsville."

"Another clergyman was set on fire." Cathy reached out and clasped Lorie's hand. "It's the same person who killed Mark and Reverend Randolph, isn't it?"

"We aren't sure, but yeah, we think maybe it is."

Chapter Seven

Jack stood off to the side talking to Chief Ballard while Andy Gamble's two-person crew carried the body bag out of the park. Jack had gone to school with the lanky, red-headed Andy, who'd been a senior when Jack was a freshman. Burly, bald Wade Ballard was ten years older than Jack, but everybody in Dunmore knew he'd been the local high school baseball star who had gone on to play for the Atlanta Braves for five years until a car wreck had messed up his pitching arm.

The crime scene had been effectively closed off by a ring of tape, but the entire park was temporarily off-limits to all except authorized personnel. A single entry and exit route had been marked off in order to manage the number of people who had access to the scene.

"The ABI guys are on their way," Wade said. "Mike and I agree that it looks like we just might have ourselves a serial killer, considering this was the third preacher set on fire in the past eighteen months."

"Technically, this is your case since the park is in the city limits," Jack said. "But with this crime possibly connected to the Mark Cantrell case, we would appreciate your allowing us to join forces with your team."

"I figure I need all the help I can get. I put in a call to Chief O'Dell over in Athens, where that other preacher was killed last year." Scowling, Wade threw up his hand and hollered, "Where the hell did that dog come from? Get him out of here. I want this crime scene as pristine as possible for the state boys."

While two uniformed policemen chased off the stray dog, Wade grumbled under his breath. Heaving a deep sigh that expanded his massive chest and beer belly, he turned back to Jack. "Reverend Phillips swore that no one in his party got anywhere near the body, but Lord only knows how they might have accidentally contaminated the site."

"I'd say other than finding an eyewitness to the crime, which is highly unlikely, the most important thing is to get the answers to a few questions. Did the victim die from his burns? Was he doused with gasoline? And can we, with some degree of certainty, connect this crime to the deaths of Mark Cantrell and Charles Randolph?"

"Yeah, you're right." Wade nodded, then settled his gaze directly on Jack's face. "Tell me something. What kind of person would do something like this?"

"I'm far from an expert, but my guess would be that it's someone who hates clergymen."

Wade grunted. "Yeah, but why burn them to death? Why not just shoot 'em?"

"Figuring that out is probably a job for a professional profiler," Jack said.

"Well, we sure don't have one of them on our payroll, and I don't know if the ABI boys have got one, either."

"I think I might know someone who can pull a few strings and get us a former FBI profiler."

Wade's beady brown eyes widened with interest. "Tell me more."

But before Jack could respond, he caught a glimpse of the coroner meandering toward them, seemingly in no hurry. Andy's long legs created a slow, easy stride. "Hell of a thing to see, a man burned like that," Andy said as he paused alongside Jack. "It's enough to give a person nightmares."

Jack understood only too well how the sight of something so atrocious could embed itself in a guy's mind and haunt him for years. Even the most seasoned soldier never became completely immune.

"Any preliminary findings you'd like to share?" Wade asked.

Andy shrugged. "I'd say our victim was doused with gasoline, but the lab folks will make a definite determination. I'll make sure any pieces of clothing that didn't burn up are stored in an oven bag."

"Oven bag?" Jack asked.

"Yeah. An oven bag is a polyinylidene bag used for the proper storage of volatile accelerants, especially those that evaporate easily," Andy explained.

Wade rubbed his meaty fingers across the back of his thick neck. "Can you say for certain that he wasn't killed first and then set on fire?"

"I can't say anything for certain officially, not yet, but from my routine exam here at the scene, I'd say he died from his burns. The burns covering the body had inflamed edges where the red blood cells worked to fix the damage."

"How soon will you be able to give us a positive ID?" Wade asked.

"Depends on how soon we can get hold of Father Brian's dental records," Andy said. "That will be the quickest way to ID him, assuming the car that y'all found belonged to our dead guy."

"We're ninety percent sure," Jack said. "Father Brian is missing. No one has seen him since late yesterday evening."

"Jack here thinks he can get us a professional profiler to compare the three murders." Grinning, Wade clamped his hand over Jack's shoulder. "Of course, the city can't afford any kind of big fee."

"How about for free?" Jack looked at Andy. "You remember my kid sister, Maleah? She works for the Powell Agency, and they keep a profiler on retainer."

"Yeah, I remember Maleah," Andy said. "Do you think she can pull a few strings with her boss and get this guy involved?"

"Maybe," Jack replied.

"It would sure help if we had some idea what kind of person is doing the killing, assuming all three murders were committed by the same perpetrator," Wade said.

"Whoever the hell he is, he's one sick puppy." Andy glanced at the area near the rose garden—the scene of the crime.

Maleah could barely keep up with Nic as they jogged along the dirt trail by the lake. The problems between Nic and Griff were still unresolved. She had suspected as much the minute Nic called her last night and asked her to come to Griffin's Rest, not on an assignment but as a friend.

"You'll be on the payroll," she had assured Maleah. "But without someone other than Barbara Jean to talk to, I'm going to wind up doing something stupid." Barbara Jean, the wheelchair-bound girlfriend of Griff's best friend and right-hand man, Sanders, worked full time at Griffin's Rest. Since Nic's marriage to Griff, the two women had become close friends.

"Barbara Jean advises me to be patient and understanding with Griff and accept the situation with Yvette," Nic had said last night. "She doesn't question Sanders's past or present friendship with Yvette. But that's the way she handles things. I can't do it her way. I'm on the verge of exploding."

"I'll be there first thing in the morning," Maleah had promised.

She had left her Knoxville apartment at five this morning and arrived in time for breakfast with Nic and Griff. It had taken her less than five minutes to ascertain the situation between her boss and his wife had gotten worse. They had each carried on a conversation with her, but hadn't said two words to each other. And when Griff left for a business trip, he'd kissed Nic on the cheek. That was a sure sign of trouble in paradise.

So here Nic and she were this afternoon, running like madwomen for the second time today. She hated to tell Nic that all this physical activity wasn't a cure-all for her troubles.

"Good grief, hold up, will you?" Maleah called to Nic, who was at least fifteen feet ahead of her.

Nic slowed her pace, then stopped and turned around to face Maleah. Perspiration dotted her face and soaked her white T-shirt and gray cotton shorts. "What's wrong?" She inhaled deeply and exhaled slowly. "Have you got a cramp?"

"No cramp." Maleah gasped the reply, then leaned over and sucked in large gulps of air. "Let's sit down and talk. I'm worn to a frazzle."

"We've been talking, but it hasn't helped much. I'm still pissed as hell."

Pulling herself up straight, Maleah walked over, lifted her arm and put it around Nic's shoulders.

"Let's sit down over there by the lake. If you don't want to talk, we won't, but I'm exhausted. I can't run another twenty feet, let alone another mile."

"Okay." Nic offered Maleah a halfhearted smile. "Sorry that I've been putting you through this marathon. It's either this or pack my bags and leave again."

"What's leaving going to solve?"

"I don't know. Nothing, I guess."

Nic followed Maleah to the edge of the lake, where they found a grassy spot to sit. Nic bent her knees, circled them with her arms and pulled her legs toward her body.

Maleah removed her running shoes and thick cotton socks, then immersed her feet in the cool lake water. "Are we talking or sitting quietly?"

"What is there left to say? I've talked your ear off today. I've ranted and raved and gone over the same crap time and again." Nic laughed, the sound hollow and unhappy. "I feel as if I'm spinning my wheels and going nowhere."

"Haven't you talked to Griff and told him what's going on with you?"

"I've tried several times this past week to have a conversation with him about how I feel, and his solution is to drag me off to bed and screw me."

Maleah grinned.

"Don't you dare laugh," Nic said. "It's not the least bit funny."

"Sorry. I was just thinking how many women would love to have Griffin Powell drag them off to bed and screw them."

Nic buried her face in her hands.

Maleah patted her back. "I really am sorry. I shouldn't make light of your problems. I understand. I wouldn't be happy if I felt as if I were sharing my man with another woman. If I had a man, which I don't have and do not want."

"I know Griff loves me, and sex has never been the problem. My insecurities and Griff's unwillingness to share the whole truth about his past are the problems. And that past includes Yvette and Sanders."

"If trying to talk to Griff doesn't work, talk to Yvette," Maleah suggested.

Nic snapped around and glared at Maleah. "And just what do I say to her? Do I ask her why there's so much secrecy surrounding this project Griff is helping her with? Or do I ask her why she and Griff haven't been totally honest with me about their past relationship?"

"Ask her about both. Be honest with her, and maybe she'll be honest with you. Tell her that Griff's involvement with her sanctuary for her psychic students is creating tension in your relationship with your husband. From what you've told me about Yvette, and from what I've learned firsthand, I get the feeling that the last thing she'd ever want to do is cause a rift between you and Griff."

"I know you're right about that, but at the same time, I'm not sure she'd tell me anything if I asked her," Nic said.

"You won't know until you ask."

"You're right. And there's no better time than now, since Griff will be gone to Switzerland for a few days, tending to some financial matters. Or at least that's what he told me."

Nic crossed her arms over her chest in a hugging motion. *It must be terrible to feel as if you can't completely trust the man you love,* Maleah thought. She knew Griff as her boss, and as her friend's husband. While working for him, she had come to realize that Griffin Powell was a very complicated man. But on that score, Nic and Griff were a good match. Nic was rather complex herself.

While Maleah considered what else to say about Nic confronting Dr. Yvette Meng with questions that Griff seemed reluctant to answer, her phone rang. Her ringtone was the theme song from the old *Peter Gunn* TV series.

She unhooked the phone from where she'd clipped it to the elastic waist of her running shorts and checked the caller ID "Jack, can I call you back later?"

"Sure. When?" he asked.

Nic clasped Maleah's arm. "No, go ahead and talk to your brother. I'll head back to the house. After I grab a shower and change clothes, I plan to go see Yvette."

"Okay." She gave her friend a reassuring smile. "Afterward, if you want to talk, just knock on my door."

"Sure thing." Nic surged to her feet and jogged back toward the house.

Maleah returned to her call. "Okay, I can talk now. What's up? Things going okay with your job? And how are your plans going for renovations to the old home place?"

"The job's fine," Jack told her. "As for the house—I've got a couple of contractors coming by later this week to give me estimates on what it'll cost to put the old beauty in tip-top shape."

"So, did you call for a specific reason or just to . . . ?"

"I need a favor."

"Sure. Just ask." She adored her big brother, always had and always would. In her eyes, he could do no wrong. For as long as she lived, she would owe him more than she could ever repay for protecting her as best he could from their stepfather, that sadistic son of a bitch.

"There's a chance we've got a serial killer on the loose here in northern Alabama. There have been three almost identical murders in the past eighteen months. It would help us if we could get a profile done of the possible killer. Any chance you could help us out?"

Maleah groaned inwardly. Yes, she could help them, and she would. But damn it all, she really hated the thought of asking Derek Lawrence for a favor. From the instant they met, he had rubbed her the wrong way. He was just a little too good-looking and a little too suave and sophisticated for her tastes. And the man was a damn know-it-all. Yes, he was brilliant, with an IQ bordering on genius. And from what Nic had told her, he had come from old money, thus explaining his attitude of superiority, although rumor was that the family had lost most of their vast fortune. Some bad investments and several hefty divorce settlements made by his father and uncle.

"I'll get in touch with Derek Lawrence tonight," Maleah said. "Derek doesn't come cheap, but the Powell Agency has him on retainer, and the agency often provides his services without charge. All I'll need to do is get Nic to sign off on it, and I know she will."

"Thanks, Sis. I appreciate it."

"I take it that this case is connected to one of your cold-case files?"

"Yeah."

"Which one?"

"The minister who was doused with gasoline and set on fire."

"Oh."

"Oh, what?"

"Nothing," Maleah said. "It's just that I know that minister was Cathy Nelson's husband and—"

"Cathy has nothing to do with this."

"Don't give me that. I remember the summer you came home on leave and stayed with Mike and his family. I might have been only fifteen, but I was old enough to know what was going on between you and Cathy." Maleah paused and considered what she was going to say next. "And I remember later on how you reacted when you found out that she'd married Mark Cantrell."

"Past history," Jack said.

"She's a widow now."

"Yeah, so she is." He paused briefly before changing the subject. "So, let me know if you can line up that profiler. If you can, I'll fax him all the info we have."

"I'll call you as soon as I know something for sure."

"Thanks. I appreciate your doing this."

"No problem."

" 'Bye."

"Take care of yourself, okay?"

"Sure thing."

" 'Bye."

Maleah clipped her phone back on to the waistband of her shorts but didn't get up immediately. She could postpone getting in touch with Derek. She could go back to the house, shower and eat dinner first. But delaying the inevitable wasn't her style. Just do it and get it over with was her motto.

She pulled on her socks, put on her shoes and tied them. After standing up and stretching, she looked out over the lake. She loved staying at Griffin's Rest, loved the acres and acres of woods, the dirt pathways that meandered here and there, the lake itself and the solitude she found here.

She retrieved her phone, hit the preprogrammed number and waited for Derek to answer. But instead of speaking to the arrogant man himself, she got his voice mail. Breathing a sigh of relief, she left a message, succinctly explaining what she needed from him and giving him Jack's phone number. If she were lucky, she wouldn't have to deal with Derek directly.

After Mike had delivered the news about the latest victim, Lorie had closed Treasures for the day. They had come home nearly an hour ago. Cathy's mother had arrived first, and she'd been in the middle of reassuring her mom that she was perfectly all right when J.B. and Mona arrived on Lorie's doorstep.

Sensing that everyone, with the possible exception of Lorie, expected her to come unglued at any moment, Cathy felt she needed to say something that would ease their fears. After all, it wasn't unreasonable for them to expect the worst. A year ago, she had proven just how emotionally unstable she'd been.

While Lorie excused herself and went into the kitchen to prepare iced tea for their guests, Cathy cleared her throat loudly. All eyes focused on her.

"I know y'all are worried about me and you've rushed over here because you're concerned." She took a deep, calming breath. "I appreciate that, but I promise you that I'm fine. I'm not going to have another breakdown. Not today or tomorrow or ever again."

"I know you believe that, but this was such a horrible shock," Elaine said. "Not just for you, but for all of us. To think that the person who killed our dear Mark has killed again. . ." With tears misting her eyes, she covered her mouth with her open hand and bowed her head.

Mona reached out and clasped Cathy's hands. "We're here because we love you. We care. If there's anything we can do . . . We should have been there for you the last time. If only we'd known how fragile you were."

Cathy hugged her mother-in-law, then pulled away and told her, "There's nothing you could have done. I think my breakdown was inevitable. But I'm completely well now. I'm much stronger, and I can deal with whatever happens."

"It's good that you feel you can handle this," J.B. said, his voice deceptively kind and soothing. "And naturally if there's anything we can do to help you, we will. But all things considered, I feel it's best that we cancel Seth's visits with you . . . for the time being. Just until we're sure you'll be all right."

Damn him! If he thought he was going to use this as an excuse to keep her son away from her, then he'd better think again. She, not J.B. or anyone else, would decide what was best for Seth.

Cathy all but shoved Mona aside as she marched up to J.B. and glowered at him.

"You must understand that J.B is doing what he thinks is best for you and for Seth," Mona said pleadingly, apparently afraid of a confrontation between her husband and daughter-in-law.

"Of course she understands." Elaine glanced back and forth between Cathy and J.B. "Don't you, dear? J.B. is doing what he knows is best for Seth. That's what you want, what we all want." When Cathy didn't respond, her mother added, "Please tell J.B. and Mona that you agree with their decision, that Seth's welfare is what's most important."

Cathy's gaze never wavered. She kept it focused directly on her father-in-law. "Of course Seth's welfare is what's most important." Both Elaine and Mona sighed with relief. "But as Seth's mother, I believe I should be the one to make the decisions concerning Seth, not you, J.B."

Pulsating with a nervous silence, the room became deadly quiet.

"You're not in any condition to make decisions for my grandson." J.B.'s tone had changed to an icy control. "You haven't been out of that mental institution for two full weeks yet."

Cathy squared her shoulders and stiffened her spine. There had been a time when she never would have stood up to her father-in-law, but those days were over. He was wrong about her. And she would prove it to him and to anyone else who had doubts about her mental stability.

"I'm not going to argue with you," she told him. "Not now. But I think you should know—"

"Tea, anyone?" Lorie came into the room carrying a tray of tall, chilled glasses.

And then the doorbell rang.

Lorie handed Cathy the tray, leaned in and whispered, "Keep your cool. Now is not the time or place to do battle with the old buzzard." Then she went straight into the foyer and opened the front door.

The tension that had been vibrating like a live wire dissipated somewhat as they all turned to see who Lorie had invited into her home. As Lorie escorted the man into the living room, J.B. came forward immediately and held out his hand.

"It's good of you to come, Brother Hovater." J.B. shook hands with him, and Mona rushed over and gave him a hug.

While Elaine joined the others in welcoming the newcomer, Lorie subtly eased toward Cathy until she was close enough to say in a soft, low voice, "Looks like your father-in-law called in reinforcements."

Cathy had met Brother Donnie Hovater, the minister who had been hired as Mark's permanent replacement, this past Sunday morning when she had attended church services. Her mother had informed her that he'd been in Dunmore for nearly ten months now, he was a widower and his teenage daughter went to school with Seth. Her mother had also informed her that all the single ladies in town considered him quite a catch.

Cathy studied the young and attractive minister. He was no older than Mark had been, perhaps even a few years younger, and he actually reminded her of her late husband. Broad-shouldered and slender, he looked neat as a pin in his tan slacks and navy, short-sleeved shirt.

When Brother Hovater approached her, his hand out, ready to take hers, she hesitated. *Don't be paranoid. Don't assume they're all ganging up on you. They're not. Everyone here, including J.B., is concerned about you.*

"I hope you don't mind my barging in this way," he said. "But your father-in-law thought perhaps I could help."

She shook hands with the minister. "In what way did J.B. think you could help?"

He seemed surprised by her question, but after a moment's uncertainty, he smiled. "The unfortunate murder that occurred last night in the park has stirred up unpleasant memories for J.B. and Mona, and for you, too, I'm sure. I'm here as your minister and a friend of the family to offer whatever support and advice you might need."

Cathy stared into his eyes, trying to decide just how sincere he was. She had no reason to doubt him, of course. He was probably a good man who had the best intentions, but the fact that he seemed so chummy with J.B. bothered her. It shouldn't. After all, J.B. was an elder in the church, and it was only natural that he and the new minister would be on friendly terms.

"That's very kind of you," Cathy said. "I appreciate everyone's concern. I'm sure my father-in-law filled you in on the details of how I reacted the last time a clergyman was brutally murdered in the same fashion my husband was." She paused to take a breath, and then continued before the preacher could respond. "I can assure you that I'm not on the verge of another nervous breakdown."

"I apologize if I gave you the impression that I came here because I or your in-laws question your mental health," Brother Hovater told her, sympathy evident in his hazel eyes. "I'm here for no other reason than to be of service to you, if you need me."

"Thank you. But what I need right now is to be left alone to deal with my memories and my feelings. I am not an emotional cripple. And what would help me tremendously is if my mother and my in-laws could get it through their heads that I'm not crazy." Cathy turned and ran out of the living room, knowing her actions would be misconstrued as evidence she was indeed crazy.

She hurried into the kitchen, taking the quickest and easiest escape route out the back door and onto the side yard that separated Lorie's house from her nearest neighbor's. Seeking sanctuary under the sheltering weeping willow, Cathy braced her open palms against the tree trunk, tilted her chin down and closed her eyes.

You overreacted, and you know it. You did just what Lorie told you not to do. You lost your cool. You lashed out from sheer frustration.

What would Dr. Milton say?

Cathy smiled.

Give yourself permission to be human, to make mistakes. Having a hissy fit occasionally can be good for you. Don't bottle up all your emotions.

"Catherine!" Elaine stomped off the back porch and marched toward Cathy, a stern, disapproving expression on her face.

Oh God, just what she didn't need—her mother reading her the riot act.

She lifted her head, tilted her chin up and squared her shoulders, preparing for battle. It seemed to her that most of the conversations she'd had with her mother from the time she was a little girl had been a battle of wills, battles her mother always won.

Coming up to Cathy there beneath the willow tree, Elaine glared at her. "If you wanted to convince everyone that you're still emotionally unstable, that little scene back there proved it. Your rudeness to Brother Hovater was uncalled for. And how dare you treat J.B. in such a disrespectful manner. I raised you better than that, or at least I thought I did. I can't tell you how disappointed I am in you, young lady. You should go back inside right this minute and apologize to everyone."

"No," Cathy said.

"What do you mean no?" Elaine stared at her in disbelief.

"I regret that I was rude to Brother Hovater, and I will probably apologize to him, but not this evening. Later. Perhaps at tomorrow evening's prayer meeting. But as for J.B.— it will be a cold day in hell before I apologize to that man ever again."

Elaine gasped.

"And another thing, Mother, I don't give a rat's ass how disappointed you are in me. Your opinion of me no longer matters."

Cathy walked off, leaving her stunned mother standing alone in the side yard.

God, she felt good!

Chapter Eight

Cathy couldn't ever remember feeling so damn good about doing something so bad. She had talked back to her mother, no doubt a sin that would condemn her to eternal hellfire. And she didn't care. She had done what she had once believed would be impossible—she had stood up to her mother and survived. Not only had she survived, but she had been set free from a lifetime of knowing she would never live up to Elaine Nelson's expectations.

As she strolled down the sidewalk at a leisurely pace, her mind savoring the preceding moments of personal glory, she didn't pay any attention to the passing vehicles on the street.

"Running away from home?" a voice called out to her.

As she stopped and turned toward the sound of the voice, her breath caught in her throat when she saw that Jack Perdue had pulled his car over to the curb and had rolled down the passenger window.

"I might be," she told him. "Got any suggestions where I should go?"

He slid across the seat, opened the door and said, "Yeah. Run away with me."

"Okay." Without hesitation, she got in the car with Jack.

He was right in her face; her shoulder pressed against his chest. They stared at each other for a full minute, one of the longest minutes of Cathy's life. And then he slid back across the seat to the driver's side, and she slammed the door shut.

"Where are we going?" she asked.

He grinned. "How about an early dinner somewhere?"

"Where?"

"Is the Catfish Shack still in business?"

"As far as I know. I haven't been there in years." Not since the last time he had taken her there.

The Catfish Shack was a seen-better-days restaurant and bar down by the river. The proprietor had a reputation for serving the best catfish and hush puppies in six counties. The music was loud, the beer flowed like water and all the food was to die for. And better yet, Cathy was relatively sure none of her churchgoing friends would be there. The place was a little too lively for their tastes. And much too sinful.

She had been there only once, years ago, on a date with Jack. She had been seventeen and madly in love.

Jack glanced over his shoulder, back at Lorie's house. "Do you need to tell anyone where you're going?"

She shook her head.

"You really are running away, aren't you?"

"Temporarily."

"Want to talk about it?" he asked.

"No, not really. I'd rather not think about what happened today or a year ago or eighteen months ago. I'd like to forget about all of it, just for a little while."

"I'll see what I can do to give you what you want."

John Earl took his wife's hands and held them in his. He wasn't looking forward to telling her the news that was spreading around town like a deadly wildfire. But she had to be told. The local authorities believed there was a serial killer targeting clergymen. If the man found dead in the park today was indeed Father Brian Myers, he would be the killer's third victim.

"What is it?" Ruth Ann asked. "I can tell by your expression that this isn't going to be good news."

He loved Ruth Ann for so many reasons, not the least of which was her strength and resilience. As a team, they had weathered many of life's storms together. His wife was indeed his helpmate. He could not imagine his life without her, and he knew she felt the same about him. They were friends, life partners and lovers.

"There was a man's body found this morning in Spring Creek Park," John Earl said. "The police believe it was murder."

"Oh, how terrible. It wasn't someone we know, was it?"

He shook his head. "No."

She studied him intently. "There's more to it than just a body being found, isn't there?"

Tightening his hold on her hands, he nodded. "The victim has not been identified yet, but they believe he was a Catholic priest from Huntsville."

Ruth Ann drew in a startled breath.

"The man burned to death. They think he was set on fire."

Emotion swelled in her chest and rose to lodge in her throat.

"There is a good chance that someone out there is targeting clergymen," John Earl said.

She swallowed hard. "First Mark Cantrell and then that minister from Athens and now . . ."

"I don't want you to worry about me. I know that after Mark was killed, you were concerned, and when the second clergyman was killed, your fears only increased. I know how both deaths brought back some painful memories for you and your mother."

"I think maybe we should consider moving out of state." Ruth Ann pulled away from him. "Perhaps it's time for you to do some mission work. We could leave the girls here with Mother, and you and I could spend six months or a year—"

"We can't just pull up stakes and leave," he reminded her. "I would have to apply for any type of transfer, and it could take months or longer for me to be reassigned. Besides that, both Charity and Felicity are at an age when they need our guidance more than ever before. And your mother isn't in good health. She could never cope with two teenagers."

Ruth Ann wrung her hands together. "I know. I know. It's just . . ." She slipped into John Earl's open arms. "I couldn't bear to lose you."

He clasped her chin and lifted her face to his. Then he kissed her forehead. "You're not going to lose me."

When she looked into his eyes so pleadingly, he lowered his head and took her mouth with a hunger that bound him to her as surely as their marriage vows did. She clung to him with a desperation that he felt all the way to his bones. He understood. Not only was she battling her fears for him, but the memories of a long-ago night when her parents' house had burned to the ground. The night her father had died, consumed by the blaze that the fire marshal had later ruled arson.

"You need to tell your mother," John Earl said as he eased out of her tenacious hold. "While you're doing that, I'll speak to the girls and do my best to allay any fears they might have."

Their gazes locked, each aware of what the other was thinking. In a marriage such as theirs, when the love and commitment were both strong, words were often unnecessary.

John Earl watched his wife as she walked out of his study, a room she had personally decorated for him. He was a very lucky man to have such a devoted wife. Years ago, in the early days of their marriage, he had been uncertain of her love, but never of her devotion. As the years went by, he had come to trust the love she professed for him and now knew beyond any doubt that she was as much in love with him as he was with her.

"Help me, dear Lord, to say whatever my daughters need

to hear. I've done all within my power to protect them from the ugliness of this world. I need Your continued guidance to lead them along the path of righteousness."

"Daddy?" Charity called from the open doorway.

He forced a confident, all-is-well smile and motioned to her, inviting her to enter. She came toward him, her younger sister directly behind her. His daughters were quite different in appearance and personality. Although Charity was as pretty as her mother, with her dark hair and eyes, she shied away from makeup and fashionable clothes. She possessed Ruth Ann's gentle nature and was their studious, conscientious child, the one who strived so hard to please. On the other hand, Felicity had his fairer coloring, his gray eyes and wide mouth, and although not quite as pretty as her older sister, she was far more flamboyant. She kept her hair dyed that hideous black, wore violet contacts and bore the most vulgar tattoos that he had reluctantly agreed for her to get, as proudly as if they were badges of honor. She was his little rebel.

John Earl indicated the overstuffed settee. "Sit down, please. I need to talk to both of you."

"Whatever it is, I didn't do it," Felicity said.

His lips curved in a genuine smile. How many times had his parents heard him, as a teenager, say those very same words of denial? Considering what a hellion he had been in his youth, he had every reason to believe there was hope for Felicity.

Ruth Ann knocked on her mother's closed bedroom door. "Yes?"

"May I come in?" Ruth Ann asked.

"Yes, of course."

When she opened the door, she found her mother sitting on the window seat gazing down at the backyard below. Faye Long was two years shy of her sixtieth birthday, yet she looked much older, as if life had worn her out prematurely. As a child, Ruth Ann had thought her mother was the most beautiful woman in the world, with her willowy figure, her long, lustrous dark hair and her large, expressive brown eyes. Her hair had turned salt and pepper, and her brown eyes were now void of emotion. Dead eyes.

Faye turned halfway around on the window seat and looked up at Ruth Ann. "Are we having dinner early this evening?"

"No, Mother, dinner will be at six-thirty, as usual."

She wished she could go to her mother, sit at her feet and be wrapped in her arms. But Faye was not capable of giving her the maternal comfort she craved. The last time her mother had touched her had been the night she had dragged her from their burning home. The night her father, Reverend Charles Long, had burned to death.

"John Earl is talking to the girls. We thought it best that he speak to them while I told you about what has happened."

"My goodness. What on earth is wrong?" Faye rose to her feet.

"Another clergyman was found dead this morning. The authorities believe he was a Catholic priest from Huntsville and that he was deliberately set on fire."

"Merciful Lord!"

"If there is someone out there killing clergymen in North Alabama, then not one man of God is safe. John Earl could be in danger." She took several tentative steps toward Faye. "I can't endure the thought that my husband might become a victim."

"Don't you trust the Lord to take care of John Earl?"

"It's not a matter of trusting the Lord." Ruth Ann paused in front of her mother and hovered over her, needing an answer to a question she was too afraid to ask. "Mother . . . please . . ."

Her mother lifted her head and met Ruth Ann's questioning gaze head-on, without flinching or even blinking. "I am very fond of John Earl. He's a good man, a good husband and a good father. I can't imagine why anyone would want to harm such a man."

Ruth Ann sighed. "I agree. Thank you."

Faye folded her hands in her lap, turned back around and looked out the window again.

"I'll call you when dinner is ready."

When Ruth Ann stepped over the threshold into the hall-way, her mother called her name and then said, "Do you really think I'm that much of a monster?"

Ruth Ann did not reply. She closed the door to her mother's room. As she walked down the hall and into the kitchen, her eyes misted with tears.

Yvette Meng was one of the most exotically beautiful women that Nic had ever seen. She moved with a fluid grace that made her seem to float instead of merely walk. Every small, perfect feature, from her almond-shaped eyes to her full, sensuous lips, proclaimed her Eurasian heritage. Her re-markable beauty and intelligence was a unique combination of her Chinese father and French mother.

"Please come in." Yvette gestured a warm welcome with the sweep of her slender arm.

"I appreciate your meeting with me this evening."

The moment Yvette smiled, Nic realized that she sus-pected why Nic was here. Maybe it had been a mistake to come here with the intention of confronting her husband's old and dear friend. But it was too late to back out now. In for a penny, in for a pound.

"My private quarters are not completed yet, but my office is," Yvette said, her voice like a soft, soothing melody. "We will go there so that we will not be disturbed. I sensed from your phone call that we have much to discuss."

As Yvette led her out of the large, marble foyer and down the hallway to the right, Nic noted the pale green walls and dark wooden floors. And she was acutely aware of how quiet it was, so quiet you could almost hear a pin drop. Where were all of Dr. Meng's psychic students?

"Where is everyone?" Nic asked.

Yvette paused by a set of closed French doors, glanced over her shoulder and smiled. "This is my private wing of the retreat. My students have rooms on the other side of the building."

Yvette swung the double doors open to reveal an eighteen-by-eighteen square foot room with a fireplace and sitting area in one corner and an enormous bay window spanning half the back wall. Her private office reflected her Asian heritage, with a black lacquer desk and chair, no doubt both priceless antiques, facing the windows. Two massive, hand-painted black lacquer chests flanked the fireplace.

Yvette glided toward the windows, paused and gazed out at the lake behind the retreat that Griffin had built for her. Hesitantly, Nic walked over and stood beside her.

"I should have invited you here sooner," Yvette said. "I have been very busy with the contractor and with making sure my students are settled."

"You refer to this place as a retreat—is that how you see it?"

Yvette faced Nic. "It is my retreat, yes, but it is more a sanctuary for my students than anything else. And I refer to them as students for lack of a more appropriate term. They are people with unusual gifts that have alienated them from their families, talents that have turned them into outcasts. I, too, have always been an outcast."

"So everyone living here has psychic abilities of some kind?"

"Yes, and their abilities vary in degree. Most are marginally talented, while two are far more gifted than I am."

"How many students do you have living here?"

"Seven. Three men and four women." Yvette focused on Nic's face. "I see that Griffin has kept his word and not shared any information about my students, not even with you."

"Then you asked him to keep me in the dark about—"

"Oh, Nicole, I am so very sorry." Yvette stared at Nic, realization in her dark eyes. "I should have given him permission to tell you. I can see that you are upset because—"

"My husband shouldn't have needed your permission to tell me what is going on here at Griffin's Rest. Griff and I are married, and to me that means we don't keep secrets from each other. We share everything. But for the past year, since you sent your first student, Meredith Sinclair here to live and Griff began construction on your retreat or sanctuary or whatever you want to call it, he has been secretive and so involved with you and your pet project that he's neglected me and our marriage."

When Yvette reached out to touch her, Nic jumped back, avoiding skin-to-skin contact. She didn't want Yvette probing into her mind, sensing her innermost thoughts and feelings.

"I truly had no idea," Yvette said. "But I should have. My only excuse is that constructing this sanctuary has been a dream fulfilled for me. I apologize most sincerely for allowing my needs and the needs of my students to create problems between you and Griffin."

Nic stood ramrod straight, every muscle in her body tight, every nerve pulsating. "I won't apologize to you or to Griff for the way I feel. You had no right to swear him to secrecy. And he had no right to agree."

"Does Griffin know how you feel?"

"I've tried to talk to him more than once, but he acts as if he thinks I'm being silly."

"You have felt this way for all these months and did not come to me. Why?"

Good question. She's got you there. Why didn't you come here sooner and demand to know what was going on and why Griff was so secretive?

"I think I was afraid of what I might learn."

"If you had objections to Griffin building this retreat for me, why did you not tell him when he first mentioned it to you?"

"And sound like a jealous wife?" Nic chuckled sarcastically. "I know that everything Griff has, he has because of you. You and Sanders. Even his life. I know that all his billions were rightfully yours. So if you want or need something from Griff, he's in no position to refuse you, is he?"

"Griffin should have told me that you were unhappy with my living here. But I assumed that since Sanders lives in the house with you, you would have no objections to my living a mile away."

"Sanders may know my husband better than I do, just as you do, but he isn't a beautiful woman. Griff isn't in love with Sanders."

"And Griffin is not now nor ever has been in love with me," Yvette said with absolute certainty. "He is very much in love with you."

Damn it, don't you dare cry.

"I want to believe you. I've tried to believe what you're telling me is the truth, but . . . When a man's allegiance to one woman supersedes his allegiance to another—to his wife—then a person has to question the reason why."

"This is my fault entirely. Please, Nicole, forgive me. Do not blame Griffin. Because of what happened in the past, because of the horrors Griffin and Sanders and I shared, we have a bond that I realize no one else truly understands. But that bond in no way is a threat to your marriage."

"You're wrong. Whatever secrets Griff has not shared with me do pose a threat to our marriage."

"When Griffin returns home, you must speak to him and make him understand how you feel. But you must be prepared for whatever he chooses to share with you."

"Will he admit that the two of you were once lovers?"

"No. We were never lovers. I swear this to you."

God, how she wanted to believe that was true. But if the

dark secret that Griff wouldn't share with her was not that he and Yvette had been lovers, then what was it?

"Would you like a tour of the retreat?" Yvette asked as she led Nic out of her office and back into the hall. "If you will come back in the morning, I will give you the grand tour, and I will introduce you to my students."

"Yes, I'd like that. What time should I come back in the morning?"

"Is ten o'clock suitable for you?"

"That's fine."

"And from this moment on, there will be no more secrets about the retreat. You and I must learn to trust each other more completely. I should have shared everything about my plans with you. As Griffin's wife, you had every right to be included."

"I'm glad you understand."

"I believed we were friends, but I see now that I have not earned your trust and friendship. I will work harder to be a better friend."

"Good night. I'll see you in the morning.

Yvette nodded.

Nic hurried ahead, not waiting for Yvette to escort her to the door. She had gotten what she came for, at least partially. And in a few days, when Griff came home, she would demand the complete truth from him. She needed to know more about his past. She needed to know his deepest, darkest secret.

As soon as they placed their order—fried catfish, hush puppies, steak fries, slaw and a pitcher of beer—Cathy relaxed for the first time since Mike Birkett had shown up at Treasures this afternoon. She looked across the table at the man who had whisked her off the sidewalk and run away with her. For half a minute she felt seventeen again, seventeen and doing something frighteningly sinful.

"You're smiling," Jack said.

"Am I?"

"You should run away more often. It seems to agree with you."

"Mother would say that I acted irresponsibly, and I suppose, in this case, she might be right. No one knows where I am, and I'm sure they're all worried sick wondering if I jumped off the Spring Creek Bridge."

Jack removed his phone from the belt clip and handed it to her. "Call somebody and tell them you're okay."

She stared at the iPhone in the palm of his big hand. After hesitating for a moment, she took the phone and punched in Lorie's number. Lorie answered on the second ring.

Apparently Jack's name had appeared on her home phone caller ID, because the first thing she said was, "Is Cathy with you? Please, tell me she is."

"Lorie, it's me, Cathy. And yes, I'm with Jack."

"Thank God. I've been worried sick. After I got rid of your mother, your in-laws and their preacher by lying to them and telling them that a wrong-number phone call was from you and you were fine, I started looking for you. One of my neighbors said they saw you get in a car with a good looking guy and I put two and two together and . . . Damn it, Cathy! I don't blame you for escaping from the zoo, but did you have to run off with Jackson Perdue?"

"I didn't have to, but I wanted to."

"Oh, I see. Just where are you? I hear a lot of background noise."

"We're at the Catfish Shack. We just ordered dinner."

"I hope you know what you're doing," Lorie said. "Please don't do anything stupid just because you're upset."

"Don't worry about me. And don't wait up."

"You didn't take your purse," Lorie reminded her. "That means you don't have a key, but it doesn't matter, because I'd have waited up for you regardless."

"See you later." Cathy ended the conversation and handed Jack his phone. "Thanks."

"I guess Lorie was worried about you," Jack said.

"She's a good friend."

"I always liked Lorie back when she and Mike were together." Jack shook his head. "Damn shame about those two. I'd have laid odds back then that by now they'd be married and have a houseful of kids."

"Life seldom works out the way we think it will. Fate can play some cruel tricks on us."

"You've had it awfully rough, haven't you, honey?"

She looked into his eyes, and their gazes locked. He reached across the table, clasped her hand and held it tenderly.

"Discussing the past or anything unpleasant is off-limits tonight, okay?" She couldn't bear to think about Mark and how he had died—how, for the entire length of their marriage, she had cheated him. And she certainly didn't want to talk to Jack about how she had spent this past year at Haven Home.

"Sure thing. Tonight we'll pretend that God's in His heaven and all's right with the world." He tugged on her hand. "Come on, Kit-Cat, let's dance."

Kit-Cat.

Cathy's heartbeat accelerated. No one else had ever called her Kit-Cat. It had been Jack's pet name for her that long-ago autumn when they had been lovers.

She rose to her feet and allowed him to lead her onto the dance floor. Without a moment's hesitation, she went into his arms. He held her close, but not too close, their bodies almost touching. And then she closed the narrow gap between them as she laid her head on his shoulder.

Chapter Nine

Where man's laws fail, God's laws do not. No one is above the wrath of the Lord Almighty. Sinners must be punished. God's law demands retribution.

What I have done, I have done in the name of Jesus Christ, my Lord and Savior. He has given me this holy duty to stop the evildoers from defiling His name. These wolves have hidden themselves in sheep's clothing and have preyed on the weak.

"And I will punish the world for their evil, and the wicked for their iniquity." Isaiah 13:11. I hear You, Lord. I know there are others who must be punished. I will find them and destroy them.

Sitting here alone in my room, I gaze out the window at the stars and wonder if heaven is out there, far away, beyond the moon and stars. Or is heaven another dimension, not a part of the universe as we humans know it?

I long to be in heaven, to walk the streets paved with gold, to hear the angels sing, to sit at God's feet and know His goodness. Who I am here on earth will not matter in heaven. All my burdens will be eased, all my heartaches soothed, all my sins forgiven.

I must not cry. Tears serve no purpose. I must be a strong soldier for the Lord. I must fight the good fight if I want to receive my eternal reward.

I have sent three wicked men to the fires of hell. I know that Satan has marked their names in his book of eternal damnation.

Mark Cantrell—adulterer; Charles Randolph—thief; and Brian Myers—pedophile.

I will not stop until I have done all within my power to rid the world of such perverted evil. And God will be pleased with all that I do. He will transform me from a child conceived in sin, born in shame and degradation, the living proof of man's evil, to a place of honor at His side. I will be purified by His power.

Show me the way, Lord. Take my hand and lead me to the others who must be punished.

Jack figured he was a fool, because only a fool would play with fire. And that's just what Cathy Cantrell was—hot and dangerous. She had no more idea now than she'd had all those years ago just what kind of effect she had on him. Yeah, him and the male sex in general. She possessed a kind of womanly sweetness that made it damn near impossible for a man to resist her.

He'd had his share of women over the years, but there had been only one he'd never forgotten. Maybe it was because he had been her first. Or maybe it was because he'd honest to God been in love with her. When he'd first found out that she'd married someone else, he'd been as mad as hell. But he hadn't held on to his anger and bitterness. He had learned that it didn't pay to judge others unless you walked a mile in their shoes. He figured Cathy had had her reasons for marrying someone else, for giving up hope, for not waiting for him to come back. And he knew that that reason could have been as simple as her falling out of love with him and in love with Mark Cantrell.

He'd spent the past hour watching Cathy as she devoured their greasy meal. She'd eaten with gusto, as if she were starved to death. And she'd downed several glasses of beer, which probably was the reason she was smiling now. A couple of times, when she'd licked her fingertips, his racy thoughts had given him a hard-on.

"Want dessert?" he asked, forced to talk loud to be heard over the din of conversation, laughter and music pounding from the old jukebox.

Laughing, she leaned back in her chair and rubbed her stomach. "I don't know where I'd put it. I'm stuffed."

He glanced at the nearly empty pitcher on the table. "I could order some more beer."

She groaned. "I've had my limit. Actually, I drank more beer with dinner tonight than I've drunk in years."

"What about some coffee?" He was trying to find a way to keep her here for a while longer. Food, drinks, conversation, whatever would persuade her not to go.

"Maybe some decaf later." She scooted back her chair and stood. "What I want right now is to dance." She held out her hand.

Dance with Cathy again? Cheek to cheek. Bodies pressed together.

"Are you sure?" he asked.

Grinning, she shook her head and clicked her tongue. "You aren't afraid to dance with me again, are you?"

He rounded the table, took her hand and led her onto the crowded dance floor. She slipped into his arms as naturally as if she'd done it a thousand times. He pulled her close. She was soft and warm. When she laid her head against his shoulder, he pressed his cheek against her silky hair.

If she were some other woman, a woman he'd just picked up here at the Catfish Shack, he would maneuver her out of the door and to the nearest bed as quickly as possible. But this was Cathy, and unless he missed his guess, she still wasn't the type of woman who had casual sex. And if he were a different kind of man, he would take advantage of her vulnerability. She was working hard at trying to have a good time. He understood why. He'd been there. More than once. She was holding on for dear life, the control over her emotions hanging by a mere thread, that modicum of control not easily achieved or maintained.

"If you need to talk, I've been told I'm a pretty good listener," he said, his lips brushing the tip of her ear.

When she shuddered involuntarily, he clenched his teeth. Her reaction probably wasn't anything personal. He figured she hadn't had sex since she lost her husband.

"Who told you that you were a good listener?" She lifted her head and gazed into his eyes. "One of your many women?"

Jack chuckled. "Well, actually, the only woman who told me I was a good listener was my sister, Maleah."

Cathy smiled. "How is your sister? I heard she lives in Knoxville now. Is she married? Does she have children?"

"Maleah's still single. I guess after witnessing the horror of our mother's second marriage, we're both gun-shy when it comes to wedded bliss."

"All marriages aren't like that. Your parents' marriage wasn't."

"What about your marriage? Were you happy with Mark Cantrell?"

Cathy's smile faded as she glanced away, her gaze focusing on something over his shoulder. "Mark was a good man, a good husband and a good father."

Yeah, he'd figured as much. After all, the man had been a preacher. Cathy's husband had been one of the good guys. But she hadn't said they'd had a good marriage, that she'd been happy.

"If it bothers you to talk about him . . ."

"It doesn't. Not anymore. But I'd just as soon not talk

about the past, not tonight. I spent nearly a year talking to my therapist at Haven Home in Birmingham. I'm pretty much all talked out."

One jukebox selection ended and another began, "Love in the First Degree" by Alabama. Even though the rhythm was upbeat, they continued dancing at a slow, clinging pace.

"Been there, done that and have a T-shirt that reads *Graduate of the Psych Ward*." He splayed his hand across the small of her back and pulled her closer.

They stared at each other, and he figured she saw her own pain and guilt and loneliness reflected in his eyes. And a similar steely determination to maintain sanity at any cost. He suspected she sensed that they were kindred spirits. He knew he damn well felt it.

"I guess you heard about what happened to me last year when Reverend Randolph was murdered," she said.

Jack nodded.

"This time, I didn't fall apart. I won't fall apart. Not ever again. I have to be strong for my son." She broke eye contact.

Jack reached down, cupped her chin and tilted her face upward. "Why don't you tell me about your son? What's his name?"

"Seth. We named him in honor of Mark's younger brother, who died when he was only a few days old."

"That was a nice thing to do."

"It pleased Mark and his parents. Mark was so good to me. I wanted to make him happy."

Did he make you happy, Cathy? "Seth's an only child?" Jack asked.

"Yes. And I love him more than anything in the world."

"It's good for a kid to know he's loved like that. Your son's a lucky boy to have you for his mother."

"I'm the lucky one. Seth is a wonderful boy. He's good and kind. He's smart, makes good grades in school and has never given us a moment's trouble. And he's a handsome boy, if I do say so myself."

He liked the way her face lit up when she talked about her son. The love she felt for the boy was there in her expression, in the glow of her cheeks and the sparkle in her eyes.

"I suppose he reminds you of his father."

Jack felt her tense and wondered why. Damn it, why had he gone and mentioned Mark Cantrell when Cathy had been so happy talking about her son?

"Actually, Seth is more like me," she said. "He even looks like me."

"Then I believe you when you say he's handsome."

That comment brought a smile to her lips.

Another oldie came on the jukebox: "Young Love" by Sonny James.

Jack wondered if she remembered that this song had been playing the first time he brought her here and they had danced together. Right before the song had ended, he had kissed her for the first time. That had been a lifetime ago. They had been two different people then.

Cathy pulled out of his arms. "I think it's time for me to go. I don't want to keep Lorie up too late."

He grabbed her hand. She stopped, turned around, looked at him and said, "Yes, I remember."

He reached out, circled her neck with his other hand and lowered his head. God, what he'd give to relive that first kiss, to feel the way he'd felt that night, to know she felt the same way.

"Please don't," she whispered.

"Cathy?"

"Not yet. Not tonight. I'm not ready for this. I'm not ready to handle the way you still make me feel."

He lifted his head and released her. "You're right. We're practically strangers. We need to get to know each other all over again, don't we?"

"We will. I'll be working with your contractor and you as you restore your house. We'll see a lot of each other."

"Yeah, I guess we will. But . . . what if I asked you for a date? What would you say?"

"I'd say that I'm not going to rush into anything, not with you or anyone else. I've only recently become my own woman, and I need time to get my bearings. My life is a brand-new unexplored territory."

"Sounds like we're in the same boat," Jack told her. "I just ended a long career in the Rangers, and I've moved back to Dunmore and started a new job. I'm taking things one day at a time, getting used to my new life."

"How about taking me home now?"

"Sure thing."

"Jack?"

"Huh?"

"Thanks for tonight. It was just what I needed."

"You're welcome, Kit-Cat. Glad to be of service."

She squeezed his hand and smiled. He felt ten feet tall and twenty years old again.

His hot breath fanned her neck, moved across her collarbone and swept across her breasts. She lay beneath him, her body rigid with fear and revulsion. His mouth pressed against her breast, surrounding her nipple through her cotton pajama top.

Please, God, make him stop. Don't let him hurt me again. I'd rather die than endure what he's going to do to me.

His hand slipped inside her pajama bottoms and cupped her intimately.

Tensing, she held her thighs tightly together, fighting his probing fingers.

"I don't want to hurt you," he told her, his voice a dark, evil whisper. "But if you force me to hurt you, it will be your own fault."

It's not my fault. It's not. I don't want this. I hate you. I hate what you do to me.

He forced his hand between her legs.

Tears lodged in her throat, tears she would not shed. No matter what he did to her, she would never cry, not ever again.

His fingers thrust into her. She bit down on her lip to keep from screaming. But in her mind, she screamed and screamed and screamed.

John Earl leaned over the bed and grasped his wife's trembling shoulders. "Wake up, Ruth Ann. Wake up, honey." He shook her gently.

Her eyelids flew open, and she stared up at him, her gaze filled with terror.

"It's all right," he told her as he sat on the edge of the bed. "You were having a nightmare. That's all."

Shivering uncontrollably, she nodded and reached out for him. He took both of her unsteady hands in his, brought her cupped hands to his mouth and kissed the tips of her fingers.

"You're safe." More than anything, John Earl wanted to erase that expression of fear from Ruth Ann's beautiful dark eyes. He never saw that look except after she had one of those horrific nightmares. She seldom had them now; as a matter of fact, it had been well over a year since the last one.

She pulled her hands from his and eased up in bed, then offered him a reassuring look. "Did I wake you? If I did, I'm sorry." Her gaze scanned over him, apparently noting that he was wearing his pajama bottoms.

"I wasn't asleep," he said. "I was sitting up over there reading"—he indicated the chair by the window—"when I heard you whimpering."

"I was screaming. Inside my head. Begging God for help."

"Hush now. Hush." John Earl pulled her into his arms and

stroked her back. "Don't relive it. Let it go, sweetheart. Let it go."

She gasped, then began to weep quietly. He soothed her with his touch and loving words, praying for God to help him comfort her.

In the first few months of their marriage, the nightmares had plagued her every night, but eventually they had become less frequent until he thought they had finally gone away forever. And then Mark Cantrell was killed. Burned alive as Ruth Ann's father had been burned alive on that long-ago night when someone had set fire to their home.

Ruth Ann lifted her tear-stained face and looked directly at him. "Sometimes I wish I knew for sure who set that fire, but then, when I think about the possibility that it might have been—"

"It wasn't. You know it wasn't."

"That's just it—I don't know. What if I've always known and just blotted it out?"

"Ruth Ann, I thought we agreed years ago that neither you nor your mother knows who set the fire that killed your father. It serves no purpose to do this to yourself."

"But what if . . . if . . ." She brushed the tears from her face, took a deep breath, grabbed John Earl's upper arms and held on tightly. "What if the person who set fire to our house and killed my father is the same person who killed Mark and the Lutheran minister and the Catholic priest?"

"Merciful Lord, do you honestly believe that's possible? Is that what has you so upset, why you had another one of those nightmares?"

"Tell me that I'm wrong." Her nails bit into his biceps. "Tell me I have no cause to worry."

He pulled loose of her tenacious grip, held her hands between them and said, "You're wrong. You have no reason to worry. I'm safe. You're safe. Your father's death nearly twenty years ago has nothing to do with what happened to Mark or the others."

I am right, aren't I, dear Lord? Please, let me be right.

"You don't have to walk me to the door," Cathy said when Jack offered to help her out of the car, but she took his hand all the same.

If two weeks ago someone had told her that she would have dinner with Jackson Perdue at the Catfish Shack, she wouldn't have believed it possible. But not only had she shared dinner with Jack, she had laughed with him and danced with him. And he had helped her hold back the memories that threatened her hard-won sanity, memories of the day Mark had died.

Jack had been true to his word. He had given her what she had told him she wanted—not to think about what had happened today or a year ago or eighteen months ago. She had desperately needed to forget about all of it, just for a little while.

They walked up the sidewalk, hand in hand, and then, halfway to Lorie's porch, Jack stopped, looked up at the night sky and said, "It's a beautiful night."

Cathy gazed up into the star-studded sky and remembered a long-ago time when they had lain on a blanket in the park and gazed up at a night sky equally as beautiful. Was he remembering that night, too?

He slipped his arm around her waist but didn't pull her against him. "I'd like to kiss you good-night, but you've already laid down the law about that. So how about a kiss on the cheek?"

"I think that after your playing my knight in shining armor and running away with me, you deserve a kiss on the cheek." She lifted her hand and caressed the side of his face.

He tensed instantly and grabbed her hand.

"What's wrong?" she asked.

He held her hand against his cheek, then eased it down his neck and beneath the collar of his shirt. Her fingertips encountered a rough patch of flesh at the base of his neck.

"Feel it? The doctors did a good job on my face, but my shoulder and arm and part of my chest aren't so pretty."

"Then you were badly wounded, weren't you? Is that why you left the army?"

"I'm not the man I used to be. I wanted you to know, up front, that I've got battle scars on my body and, according to the psychiatrist, on my soul, too."

"I've got my own battle scars," she told him. "They're invisible because they're on my heart and my soul, so I truly understand."

"We're just a couple of wounded warriors, aren't we, honey?" He lifted her hand away from his face and brought her open palm to his mouth.

When he kissed the center of her palm, she drew in a deep breath. "I—I'm not a warrior."

"Yes, you are." He released her hand. "You waged war in your own mind. You fought your demons and won."

"For the most part," she said. "Sometimes I still have to fight them. Like today. You helped me more than you can ever know. Thank you."

He shrugged. "I know quite a bit about fighting demons. I have a few of my own. So anytime I can help you . . ."

Cathy stood on tiptoe and, without touching him, kissed Jack on the mouth. She had acted purely on instinct. When he kissed her back, she withdrew quickly and said, "I think it's time for me to say good-night."

Neither of them said anything else. He walked alongside her up the stone pathway and onto the porch. Just as they neared the front door, a dark silhouette rose up out of the porch swing.

"Where have you been?" Seth demanded as he emerged from the shadows. "And who is he?"

Chapter Ten

"Seth?" Cathy gasped his name. "What are you doing here?"

"I was worried about you," he told her, but his gaze surveyed Jack from head to toe.

Jack held out his hand. "I'm Jackson Perdue. I'm the new deputy Sheriff Birkett hired."

So this was Cathy's son. She was right—he looked like her. Same glossy brown hair, same full mouth, same oval face. He was a handsome boy, tall and lanky.

Seth stared at Jack's hand, then grabbed it firmly. They exchanged a man-to-man handshake.

"I'm Seth Cantrell. I'm her son." He inclined his head in a quick nod toward his mother, then turned to Cathy. "Are you okay? Did something happen?" He looked at Jack. "Why is my mom with you? Is she in some sort of trouble or . . . ?"

"Seth!" Cathy's tone implied a mixture of censure and surprise.

Jack tried not to grin. He respected Seth's protective attitude toward his mother. It was obvious that the boy loved her.

"It's okay, son. Your mom's not in any trouble," Jack explained. "Your mother and I are old friends. We knew each other when she was a teenager. I took her out for dinner this evening."

"You took her out for dinner?" Seth turned to Cathy. "Granddad said you were all right, but I worried all the same. I called Lorie, and she said you were out with a friend, but I had no idea you'd go out on a date. Not after what happened today."

"It wasn't a date," Cathy said. "Not exactly."

"You kissed him," Seth said. "I saw you."

"We weren't on a date. Tonight was about a couple of old friends getting reacquainted," Jack told him. "Your mother was upset and needed a distraction. She kissed me to thank me. That's all there is to it."

Cathy placed her hand on her son's arm, which gained his full attention. "Do your grandparents know where you are?"

"No, ma'am. I slipped out after they went to bed." He lowered his head. "I didn't think Granddad would approve, but I had to make sure you were okay."

"Why don't you come inside, and we'll talk," Cathy said, then looked at Jack. "Thanks again for tonight."

"You're welcome. Any time."

He guessed that was his cue to leave. Cathy needed time alone with her son, and he needed some fresh air to clear his head

As soon as Jack said good-night and headed for his car, Cathy rang the doorbell. Lorie, in her satin pajamas, opened the door, glanced from mother to son, then stepped back and waited for them to come inside.

"Want to tell me what's going on?" Lorie looked outside to where Jack stood beside his car. He threw up his hand and waved before opening the door and sliding in behind the wheel.

After they entered the house, Cathy closed the front door behind her. "Jack was just dropping me off, and we found Seth sitting in the swing waiting for me."

"Oh, I see. So Jack and Seth met, huh?"

"I think I just said that, didn't I?"

"Who is that guy to you?" Seth asked. "I know he said you two were old friends, but I never heard of him. And why would you go out to dinner with him?"

Lorie's eyes widened in an uh-oh gesture. "I think I'll head for bed and give you two some privacy. Cathy, if you want to talk later, I probably won't be asleep."

Cathy nodded, and as soon as Lorie left her alone with Seth, she said, "Why don't we sit down?"

"Answer my questions, will you?" Seth paced around the living room. "I thought after you heard about their finding that priest's body today, you'd be all torn up because you'd be remembering the day Dad died and thinking about him and . . . But instead you went out on a date with a guy you knew when you were a teenager. I don't understand."

"Are you saying that you're disappointed I didn't fall apart?"

He glared directly at her face. "No, of course not. It's just I don't understand why you'd pick tonight of all times to go out on your first date since Dad died. It somehow seems disrespectful to Dad's memory."

Cathy heaved a heavy sigh. Her son's words mimicked J.B. Cantrell's sentiments. She didn't like that. All the more reason to regain custody as soon as possible.

She approached Seth, who stood in the middle of the room, his gaze never leaving her face.

"I told you that dinner with Jack wasn't exactly a date. Not the way you mean. It was just what he said. I needed a distraction, something—anything—to keep me from thinking about the day Mark died, from remembering how I'd nearly lost my mind in the weeks following his funeral and how I had a complete breakdown when Reverend Randolph was murdered.

"Jack and I were friends a long time ago. He moved away from Dunmore, and I haven't seen him in nearly seventeen years. He's renovating the house where he grew up, and he's hired Treasures to act as consultants on the renovating and decorating. I'll be seeing more of him in the future."

"Just as friends?" Seth asked.

Good question. Did she think she could really be only friends with Jack? "That's all we are right now, just two old friends becoming reacquainted."

"Are you going to date him again?"

"I don't know. Maybe. If he asks me."

"I don't have to like him, you know. And I don't have to like the idea of your dating him or anybody else for that matter."

"No, you don't have to like him." Cathy laid her hand on Seth's arm. "But you don't know Jack, so you have no idea if you'd like him or not. Once you get to know him—"

Seth yanked his arm away. "I may not want to get to know him. Doesn't it matter to you what I think, how I feel?"

"Yes, it matters to me a great deal. But I thought I taught you better than to judge a person before you actually know them. If I choose to date Jack or someone else, it will be my decision. Not yours or my mother's and certainly not your grandfather's."

"What if I told you that if you date that guy, I won't ever come and live with you?"

"Is that what you're saying? Do you think you have the right to make that kind of threat in order to force me to do what you want?" What would she do if she had to choose between her son's wishes and remaining in control of her own life?

"No, of course not. It's just . . ." Seth slumped down on the sofa and dropped his clasped hands between his spread thighs. "I want things back the way they were before Dad died. I want Dad."

Cathy sat down beside her son and put her arm around his shoulders. "I know you do. And if I could give you that, I would." She reached out and shoved back soft strands of hair from his forehead.

Seth turned around and went into her arms the way he had often done as a small boy. She held him close as he cried silently.

Bruce Kelley watched his wife of forty years as she prepared for bed. There was something comforting and reassuring in life's little daily routines. Morning coffee while glancing over the newspaper. Lunch at twelve-thirty every weekday. Sunday dinner with their children and grandchildren. And Sandie's nightly ritual. She always put on her gown and house slippers before smearing makeup remover from forehead to chin and then washing her face. After that, she sat at her small dressing table in the corner of their bedroom and brushed her hair. Her once strawberry-blond hair was now streaked with silver, but it was still long and silky, and he enjoyed the feel of it beneath his fingertips.

He walked over and stood behind her. She tilted her head back, glanced up at him and smiled. Her lovely smile had been the first thing that had attracted him to her when they'd first met forty-two years ago. They had both been students at the University of Alabama.

Today had been one of Sandie's good days. Thankfully, she had more good days than bad, but Bruce knew that it was only a matter of time before that changed. She had been diagnosed with Alzheimer's three years ago, and the insidious disease had finally begun to alter her personality. Only recently their children, Kim, Kira and Kevin, had spoken to him about hiring a companion for their mother.

"You don't want to wait until she wanders off one day and we have to call the police," Kevin had said. He was their youngest and had just graduated from law school.

"Kira and I will find someone for you," said Kim, their eldest, who taught mentally challenged children and adults and was the mother of three precious little girls.

"Even if you retire next year as you're planning to do, you can't look after Mama twenty-four hours a day, seven days a week," said Kira, the middle child, with her mother's beauty and tender heart, the artist who had chosen not to marry, as she had taken his hand in hers. "We're as concerned about you, Daddy, as we are about Mama."

He had resisted hiring a companion for Sandie, knowing that their comfortable, reassuring life would change forever when they brought another person into their home full time.

But their life had already changed. On the days when he had to be in his office at the church or when there were matters he couldn't turn over to his young assistant minister, Bruce had to rely on ladies from the church to come and sit with Sandie while he was gone. He hated to impose on others, but his congregation had rallied around him in his time of need.

Bruce leaned down and kissed Sandie's forehead. She sighed, then rose from the vanity bench and walked over to the bed. After she got in, he pulled the covers up above her waist and reached to turn off the bedside lamp. She grabbed his hand.

"I love you," she told him.

"I love you, too, my darling." Tears misted his eyes.

Their golden years were not supposed to be like this. They had planned to travel when he retired. Tour the country by train. Take an Alaskan cruise. Visit all the capitals of Europe.

"I'm going to stay up and read for a while," he told her. "I'll be in my study if you need me."

She smiled, then closed her eyes and turned over on her side. He switched off the light and left her to rest.

As soon as he entered his study, he walked over to his

desk and picked up the phone. He dialed Kim's number and waited.

"Daddy?"

He could hear the panic in her voice. "Everything is all right, sweetheart. I—I wanted to ask you to go ahead and look into finding a companion for your mother."

"Did she have a bad day today?"

"No. Today was a good day."

"Oh, Daddy . . ."

"Find someone kind and caring, someone your mother would like."

"I've already found somebody," Kim told him. "I've just been waiting for you to say the word."

"Who is she?"

"Mirabelle Rutledge. She's one of my students."

"You want to send me a young woman who is retarded to look after your mother?"

"Mirabelle is simply a little slow, Daddy. And you know how I hate the word *retarded*."

"I'm sorry I'm not being politically correct. In my day, calling someone who was retarded retarded wasn't an insult."

"I know, but times have changed. And words can and do hurt."

"Tell me something—how can she take care of your mother if she can't take care of herself?"

"She can take care of herself," Kim assured him. "She's perfectly capable of cooking and cleaning, and she can read and write. Besides that, she's young and strong and . . . and she needs a home. She needs you and Mother as badly as y'all need her."

Bruce sighed. "Then why don't you bring Mirabelle to dinner this coming Sunday, and we'll see how she and your mother interact."

"Thank you, Daddy. Thank you. This will be good for Mother and for Mirabelle. Just you wait and see."

* * *

Felicity hated sharing a room with her older sister. Charity was such a neat freak. She loved pastel colors and ribbons and lace and disliked everything Felicity liked, especially her music and her clothes. Charity was such a goody-goody, Mama and Daddy's perfect darling. If Grandma didn't live with them, she could have her own room. But her mom's mom had lived with them as long as she could remember. It wasn't that she didn't love Grandma. She did. Even if the old lady disapproved of everything about her, from her dyed hair to her violet contacts and dagger tattoos.

"Are you going to stay up all night?" Charity, who was curled up in her twin bed, looked over at Felicity, a frown wrinkling her forehead.

Felicity, still wearing her black jeans and dark purple T-shirt, eased the earphones connected to her iPod down to hang around her neck. "I can't sleep. I'm worried."

"What are you worried about? Afraid Seth Cantrell likes Missy better than he does you?"

"What a hateful thing to say. Besides, Seth can like whoever he wants to like. It's not as if I own him or anything." Felicity glowered at her sister. "And for your information, I'm worried about Daddy."

"Why would you be worried about Daddy?"

"Because of what happened today. You know, they found that priest's body in the park, and he was burned alive just like Seth's father was."

"What has that got to do with Daddy?"

"Somebody has murdered three preachers—well, two preachers and a priest. Daddy's a preacher. What if that person tries to kill Daddy?"

"Nobody is going to hurt Daddy. He's a good man. There's no reason why anyone would want to harm him."

"Everybody thought Seth's father was a good man." Felicity laid a pillow against the headboard and sat up straight.

"And I'm sure everybody believes that those other two men were good, too."

"Maybe they weren't as good as everyone thought they were," Charity said. "You never know about people."

"Do you think whoever murdered them did it because he thought they had done something wrong?"

Charity groaned. "How should I know? I just said that to get you to shut up and go to sleep. I have to get up at six in the morning. I start my summer job tomorrow."

"It would make more sense, wouldn't it, if they'd all done something terrible, something that made the killer think they deserved being punished."

"Oh, shut up, will you, and go to sleep. You're talking nonsense anyway."

Felicity stuck out her tongue at her sister.

Charity just rolled her eyes and shook her head, then reached out, turned off her bedside lamp and closed her eyes.

Sometimes Felicity wondered how she and Charity could be sisters. They were so different. But when she'd mentioned this to her father, he'd smiled indulgently and told her that Charity took after Mama and that she took after him.

"I was quite the rebel in my day," he'd told her, a statement she found difficult to believe. But his comparing her to him when he'd been a teenager had made her feel better about herself.

She wished she were prettier and smarter and a nicer person. And she wished Seth Cantrell liked her as more than just a friend. Charity had been right—she was jealous of Missy. If she possessed special powers like the heroines of the books she read and movies she watched, she'd make Missy vanish and put a spell on Seth to make him love her and only her.

Felicity laid her iPod and earphones on her nightstand, then turned off her lamp and scooted down in her bed. She closed her eyes and thought about how she could stop Missy from stealing Seth away from her.

Mike Birkett, barefoot and wearing only a pair of well-worn gray sweat pants, opened his front door, took one look at Jack and asked, "Do you know what time it is?"

"I know it's late, but I need to talk to you."

Mike stepped aside. "Come on in, but be quiet, will you? M.J. and Hannah are asleep."

"I'm sorry about stopping by at this time of night."

"Is it something to do with the new murder case?"

"Not really," Jack said as he followed Mike into the kitchen. "Maybe indirectly."

"Sit down." Mike pointed to a kitchen chair. "I was fixing to get myself a glass of milk, but if you'd like I can put on some coffee or get you a beer."

"Nothing for me, thanks." Jack pulled out a chair from the table and sat.

Mike turned a chair backward, straddled the seat and rested his crossed arms over the back. "I'm listening."

Jack fidgeted. "I took Cathy out to dinner tonight. We went to the Catfish Shack."

Mike didn't respond verbally. He just sat there staring at Jack.

"Say something, will you."

"What do you want me to say?" Mike asked.

"Chew my ass out. Tell me again to stay away from Cathy. Remind me that I'm not good for her. Just handling my own baggage is a full-time job without having to deal with hers."

"What did you do, go over to Lorie's and ask Cathy out?"

"Nope. We just happened to meet up."

"Is that right? How did you two just happen to meet up?"

"I was on my way home, and I took a detour by Lorie's," Jack said. "I don't know why. I didn't plan on stopping or anything. I had Cathy on my mind and wondered how she was taking the news about the burned body found in the park this morning. And lo and behold, there Cathy was walking down the sidewalk about half a block from Lorie's."

"Let me guess—you stopped, asked her for a date and she said yes." Mike shook his head. "She never could resist you, could she?"

"She needed to get away, to escape and not think about what happened to her husband and the possibility that he was the first victim of some lunatic running around killing clergymen."

Mike nodded. "I see. You were playing white knight, huh?"

Jack shoved back the chair and shot to his feet. "Damn it, Mike, I don't want to hurt her. I swear to God, I don't. But I'm not sure I can keep my distance. She'll be helping me with the house renovations, so we'll see each other quite a bit. If something develops between us . . . I know I'm a screwed-up mess and not fit company for any woman. But as crazy as it sounds, I think maybe Cathy and I might be good for each other."

"Kind of like the blind leading the blind."

"I trust you, Mike. I trust you to be honest with me, to tell it like it is."

Mike looked up at Jack. "You can't go back. You can't be the two people you once were. Believe me, I know. Usually you get one grab for the brass ring, and if you miss it, that's it. You've always been a pretty tough son of a bitch, but it still hurt like hell when you found out she'd married Mark Cantrell. And don't try to tell me it didn't."

"Okay, I won't."

"I think you'd be taking a big risk for yourself and for Cathy. Don't forget that she has a son to think about. It wouldn't be just her life you'd be messing with, but Seth's, too."

"Is that the reason you won't give Lorie a second chance—because of your kids?"

Mike frowned. "I'm not discussing Lorie with you. But as for you and Cathy . . . You're both consenting adults. I'd just hate to see either of you get hurt."

When Cathy came out of the bathroom, makeup removed, teeth brushed and pajamas on, she came face-to-face with Lorie.

"I thought you'd gone to bed," Cathy said.

"No. I thought you might need to talk."

"About Jack?"

Lorie's mouth curved into a strained smile.

"It just happened," Cathy told her. "Neither of us planned it. He happened to be driving by and saw me. He stopped. We talked. I told him I wanted to run away, and he invited me to run away with him."

"And you did."

"Uh-huh. And I'll be honest with you—it felt good to be with him. It felt good to go someplace with loud music and laughter all around us, to eat greasy, fattening food and to dance and forget about everything else."

"But with Jackson Perdue, of all people."

"Why not with Jack?"

"Good Lord, do I have to remind you of how your first love affair with him ended?"

"I'm not a naïve seventeen-year-old girl."

"Oh, honey, you're still halfway in love with him, aren't you?"

She started to staunchly deny it, but the words died on her lips. "I don't know. Maybe just a little bit. Don't they say that you never forget your first love?"

"I guess you know what a risk you'd be taking getting involved with him. J.B. and Mona aren't likely to approve. And heaven help you when your mother finds out."

"Mother isn't running my life anymore, and neither are

my in-laws. I plan to make all my own decisions for the rest of my life. If I want to date Jack, I'll date Jack."

"I'm the last person in this world to argue against rekindling an old romance," Lorie said. "God knows, I'd like nothing better than to get a second chance with Mike. But there's more to consider than what you want or how your mother and in-laws will react."

"You're talking about Seth."

"Yes, I am. If his reaction tonight is any indication, he's not going to be happy about your dating anybody. And if by some miracle he gets to know and like Jack, how are you going to deal with that?" Lorie gently grasped Cathy's shoulders. "Jack is no fool, you know. Sooner or later, he'll figure it out."

Chapter Eleven

Jack folded the morning newspapers—the *Dunmore Daily*, the *Huntsville Times* and the *Decatur Daily*—and dumped them into the wastebasket. Four days ago, after Father Brian's charred body had been found at the park, a hotshot *Huntsville Times* reporter named Grant Sharpe had given the killer a particularly appropriate label, dubbing him the Fire and Brimstone Killer. The local and regional press had picked up on the title, and now even the folks at the sheriff's department were using the phrase. So here they were, ninety-six hours after the priest's horrific murder, without even one suspect, a fact that the press pointed out in bold headlines. Sharpe's coverage of the case stated that the task force, comprised of members from both local and state law-enforcement agencies, had a serial killer on their hands and apparently weren't equipped to deal with that type of case. The reporter had all but referred to the task-force members as a bunch of redneck yokels who couldn't stick their finger up their ass with both hands.

The autopsy results weren't in yet, but no one expected the findings to reveal anything more than the initial report had told them. Brian Myers had been doused with gasoline and set on fire. Possibly, the severe third-degree burns over most of his body hadn't killed him. Not instantly. Shock had probably set in, and without immediate medical attention, the priest's body had shut down. But even if he had been discovered quickly and rushed to the hospital, his odds wouldn't have been good. After all, Mark Cantrell and Charles Randolph hadn't survived.

Jack gathered up the crime-scene photos spread out before him and opened the file folder to replace them, but when he heard someone say his name, he laid everything down on his gray, metal desk. Glancing around the open office area—his desk was located on the left, near the windows—he saw one of his fellow officers talking to a stranger and pointing his way. The tall, lanky guy, dressed in casual yet obviously expensive slacks, shirt and jacket, smiled at the officer, thanked him and walked straight toward Jack. As he approached, Jack sized him up: mid-to-late thirties; about six-two; wavy, black hair in need of cutting; intelligent dark eyes; and an easy smile that projected self-confidence.

"Jackson Perdue?" the man asked.

"Yeah, that's me."

"I'm Derek Lawrence." The former FBI profiler offered his hand.

Jack shook hands with the guy. "I didn't expect you to show up. I thought you'd just call or e-mail."

"That was the original plan when Maleah first asked me to come in on this case. But once I received the information and went over it, I realized that I'd never seen a situation quite like this before. Your killer fascinates me."

Jack looked Derek right in the eye. "Does he? Why is that?"

"He—or she—has chosen unlikely victims—clergymen. And his method is not only cruel and painfully violent, it sends a message, one that our killer wants the world to hear."

Beverly Barton

Jack nodded. "Have a seat. I want to hear your theory." Jack hitched his thumb in the general direction of the coffee-maker. "Would you like some coffee?"

"No, thanks. I'm fine."

Jack pulled up an empty chair and placed it in front of his desk. The two men settled into their seats, the desk separating them, and then Jack asked, "What message is our killer sending?"

"You've probably already figured it out. Our killer is saying—no, he or she is screaming, *'I hate you. I'm punishing you, and I want you to burn for your sins, for what you did to me.'*"

Jack grunted. "So we're dealing with a person who at some point in his or her life was somehow wronged by a clergyman, and now he's killing that minister or priest over and over again?"

"That's pretty much it in a nutshell."

"Like you said, we figured that our killer hates preachers, but I don't see how knowing this helps us catch the guy."

"It doesn't," Derek said. "I've gone through ViCAP—the FBI's Violent Criminal Apprehension Program data base—and come up with similar crimes, but none that are actual matches to your three Fire and Brimstone murders. Setting people on fire isn't something new. And clergymen have been killed before. What we have to concentrate on is what makes these three crimes different and what links them together."

"You're the expert. You tell me."

"Your killer doesn't fall completely into either the organized or disorganized offender category, but that's not unusual. An offender doesn't always reflect all the crime-scene characteristics or personal characteristics of one or the other."

"Look, you're going to have to speak plain English to me," Jack admitted. "I'm new at this. I'm an ex-soldier. My experience is limited. I've been with the sheriff's department for only a few weeks."

Derek eyed Jack speculatively. "I'm surprised the sheriff chose you to work on the task force."

"The sheriff assigned the department's cold cases to me, sort of a way to break me in, I guess. The Cantrell murder was one of those cases."

"Even so, I'd have thought he'd put a more seasoned deputy on the task force. Do you feel as if you're in over your head?"

"Maybe." Jack shrugged. "Guess I'll learn as I go. And I did bring in an expert to help us out, didn't I?"

Derek chuckled. "Yes, so you did. That probably earned you a few brownie points with your boss."

Jack grinned. "So tell me, Mr. Expert, all about how you can't pigeonhole our killer."

"Be glad to. It's simple. The killer planned these murders, chose his victims in advance and personalized the victims, all characteristics of an organized killer. But on the other hand, he probably knew his victims or at least knew who they were. He left his victims in plain view at the scene of the crime, and with the use of gasoline and the Pocket Torch lighters left at the scene, the weapon couldn't be hidden. Those are all characteristics of a disorganized killer."

"A killer with a split personality?"

"Our killer is what we refer to as a 'mixed personality,' which is actually fairly common."

"Are you saying that in trying to come up with a profile of our killer, you've struck out?"

"No, I wouldn't say that." Derek grinned. "How about that cup of coffee?"

"Cream? Sugar?" Jack asked.

"Black."

Jack got up, went to the coffeemaker and poured two Styrofoam cups three-fourths full of the strong, black brew. He returned to his desk, handed Derek one of the cups and sat back down.

After taking a couple of sips, Derek said, "We assume the same person killed the two ministers and the priest. Why?"

"All three victims were clergymen. All three lived within a fifty-mile radius of one another. All three were doused with gasoline and set on fire, using a torch lighter that enabled him to lock the flame before using it. And all three murders occurred within an eighteen-month time span."

"It's unlikely that the similarities of the murders were co-incidental. So think about it. What other similarities were there?"

"So far, all the victims have been white. All have been between thirty and fifty years old, and all have been Christians."

"Charles Randolph had been accused of stealing from his congregation. Had the other two committed any type of crime?" Derek asked.

"No. If they had, I'd have included that information in the files I sent you."

"Hmm . . . Stealing is a sin, right? So what if the other two ministers didn't commit crimes, but did commit sins?"

"And just how would we go about trying to discover what sins these men might have committed, if they actually did?"

"Talk to people who knew them."

Jack tapped the manila folder on his desk. "That's been done. Family and friends were interviewed extensively after each murder. Mark Cantrell was a saint according to everyone who knew him. His only weakness seems to have been his love for golf. And so far, Father Brian is coming across as damn near perfect."

"No one is perfect." Derek took another sip of coffee. "All humans have numerous weaknesses, and few are true saints. Perhaps our killer either knew something no one else knew or he projected someone else's sins onto these men. In his mind, our offender is probably killing the same person over and over again, perhaps punishing him for his sins."

"How does this help identify our killer?"

Derek picked up his cup and took a couple of swigs of the cooling coffee.

"Using the info we have at this point, it's likely that our killer is a young, white male with a 'mixed' personality who is punishing his victims for the sins of someone who possibly harmed him in some way. He's also mobile. His victims, though living within a fifty-mile radius, did not live in the same town, which means he probably either owns a car or has access to one."

"That certainly narrows it down," Jack said sarcastically. He finished off his coffee, crushed the cup and tossed it into the wastebasket atop the morning's newspapers.

"Profiling is not an exact science. It's mostly putting puzzle pieces together and coming up with an educated guess. I hate to say this, but the more murders the offender commits, the more clues we'll have, and that means a more thorough profile."

Jack huffed. "I suppose I expected too much from you."

"Sorry I can't pinpoint your guy and hand him to you on a silver platter. But if you don't mind, I'd like to go over all the files again and stick around, maybe talk to a few people."

"Who do you want to talk to?"

"People who knew the victims. Friends and family."

"Not going to happen."

"Why not?"

"Don't you think the families have been through enough without being questioned again?"

"Even if it might help catch the killer?"

Jack looked Derek square in the eyes. "Can you promise me that it will?"

"No, of course not, but—"

"Run your request by Sheriff Birkett," Jack said, reasonably certain that Mike would say no.

"Thanks, I'll do that." Derek dropped his empty coffee cup into Jack's wastebasket, paused, eyed the newspapers and then glanced at Jack. "I'll put my official report in writing and give it to you before I leave Dunmore."

Elliott Floyd met Cathy in the middle of his tastefully decorated office. He glanced over her shoulder, smiled at his secretary, who closed the door, and then he reached out to take Cathy's hand.

"Come in and sit down, Mrs. Cantrell."

After they shook hands, he led her to one of two leather armchairs facing his large, mahogany desk. Once she'd taken a seat, she subtly studied him from the top of his thinning dark hair to his expensive Italian leather loafers. Probably in his late forties, Elliott Floyd dressed the part of a successful lawyer, his suit no doubt tailor-made to fit his trim, five-nine body.

"My friend Lorie Hammonds recommended you, Mr. Floyd," Cathy said as she folded her hands together in her lap.

"Yes, Lorie's a friend of my wife."

"I had hoped not to have to do this—hire a lawyer—but I realize that I don't actually have a choice, and, according to Lorie, you're the best lawyer in Dunmore, possibly in the whole state."

Elliott smiled, creating dimples in his apple-round cheeks. "I see. So, tell me why you need my services."

"A year ago, I had an emotional breakdown. I checked myself into Haven Home in Birmingham and underwent extensive psychiatric care. I was released as an outpatient six months ago and then given a clean bill of health last month. I have a fifteen-year-old son who has been living with my in-laws for the past year. They have legal custody of him." She leaned forward, her hands entwined in a prayerlike gesture. "I want custody of my son."

"I take it that his grandparents are opposed to your having custody."

"Yes."

"What does your son want?"

"Seth is torn between wanting to please his grandfather and not wanting to hurt me."

"Is there any reason why your in-laws are not proper guardians for your son?"

"No. J.B. and Mona are good Christian people. They're well liked and well respected by the community. J.B. is an elder in the church."

"I take it that you've tried talking to your in-laws about this and making some type of arrangement that—"

"My father-in-law has made it perfectly clear that he believes I'm emotionally unfit and he has no intention of allowing Seth to live with me now or ever."

"Will your psychiatrist testify to your emotional stability?"

"Yes."

"Can you financially support your son?"

"Yes."

"Is there anything in your personal life that would make you an unfit mother?"

"Other than the entire town knowing I've been at Haven Home?"

Elliott nodded.

"I can't think of anything else."

"You're a widow. Is that correct? Your husband was a local minister, the one murdered by the person the press is now referring to as the Fire and Brimstone Killer."

Cathy inhaled and exhaled, then replied, "Yes, that's correct."

"Seth is your only child?"

"Yes."

"Do you think he'd talk to me? I'd like to get a sense of what he wants and how he feels about his grandparents retaining custody."

"And how he feels about me?"

"Yes, that, too."

"Does this mean you'll take my case?"

"If it comes to that, yes, I'll represent you, Mrs. Cantrell."

Cathy rose to her feet. "Thank you. I'll speak to Seth, and if he agrees to talk to you, I'll call your secretary and make an appointment."

Elliott stood, rounded his desk and escorted Cathy out of his office. When they reached the outer door that led to the sidewalk, he patted her shoulder.

"We'll do everything we can to settle this matter without going to court."

She forced a smile.

When he turned around and went back inside, she stood there and looked at the renovated antebellum cottage that had been converted into Elliott Floyd's office. In the past dozen years or so, many of Dunmore's older downtown homes had undergone facelifts, some as simple as fresh coats of paint and new roofs, others far more extensive.

Cathy checked her watch. She had a lunchtime appointment with Jack and his contractor, Clay Yarbrough, whom she'd never met.

Lorie had offered to take over as the consultant on this job, cautioning her about what it might cost her to renew her friendship with Jackson Perdue. But she had spent a lifetime playing it safe, doing what was expected of her, fulfilling other people's wishes. Never again.

"You can't turn back the clock," Lorie had told her. "Even if you and Jack reconnect, it won't be the same."

No, it wouldn't be the same. She didn't expect it to be. Actually, she didn't expect anything in particular. But whether she worked with Jack professionally or dated him or became his lover again, the decisions were hers to make.

Seth had jumped at the chance to do Brother Hovater's yard work. He had three very good reasons: it pleased Granddad that their minister had asked Seth; it gave him a chance to earn some money this summer to save toward buying himself a car; and, last but most important, it gave him the opportunity to be near Missy.

Being here at his old home, cutting the grass and trimming the hedges that he had once helped his dad cut, seemed odd. He halfway expected his mom to come out the back door and bring him a bottle of Gatorade. But this was no longer his home. He and his mom and dad didn't live here anymore. Sometimes his old life seemed like little more than a dream, as if it had been some other guy's life.

"Hey, you," Felicity called loudly as she came up behind him. "Why don't you take a break? Missy and I are fixing to eat lunch, and we made enough sandwiches for all of us."

Seth turned off the Weed Eater, propped it against the fence and yanked a rag from the back pocket of his old, tattered shorts. As he swiped the perspiration off his forehead, he turned around and faced Felicity.

"Her dad's not here, if that's what's worrying you. He's gone to Decatur to set up a gospel meeting with the church over there."

Seth glanced past Felicity. Missy, all summer-tan brown in khaki walking shorts and a sleeveless red blouse, set a tray of sandwiches and iced tea down on the patio table. His gaze met hers. She smiled, then waved and motioned him to come on over.

"You like her, don't you?" Felicity asked.

When he didn't reply, she socked him in the arm. "What'd you do that for?" he asked.

"She's nearly eighteen, you know, and you're only fifteen. She's not going to date a guy younger than she is."

"I'll be sixteen soon," Seth said. "In August."

"You don't even have a car," Felicity reminded him. "Besides that, your grandparents won't let you date."

"What makes you think—?"

"Just how many dates have you had, not counting being Shannon Moore's Homecoming Court escort?"

"I'll be dating when I turn sixteen, and I'm going to get a car, too. That's one of the reasons I'm doing yard work this summer."

The gate that led from the back yard to the front swung open, and Charity stood there for a couple of minutes staring at Seth and Felicity.

"What are you looking at?" Felicity snapped at her sister.

"Sorry, I—I wasn't expecting to see Seth here today," Charity said.

"Yoo-hoo!" Missy called out and waved. "Come on, y'all, let's eat."

Within minutes the four of them sat around the patio table munching on ham sandwiches, chips and pickles and sipping on ice-cold sweet tea.

"Thanks for inviting us to lunch today," Charity said. "Mom's working at Treasures all day, and I dreaded having lunch with Grandma. I guess I shouldn't say such a thing, but—"

"But she's a weird old lady who scolds us all the time and reminds us to be good girls and watch out for all the evil in the world, especially evil men." Felicity laughed.

With his gaze glued to Missy, Seth noted an odd expression cross her face. Just a flicker, there and gone in a second. Then he glanced at Felicity and couldn't help comparing the two girls. Missy was prettier in a wholesome sort of way. She wore very little makeup and dressed in what his granddad would call a demure, ladylike manner. Of course, with her being a Church of Christ preacher's daughter, she had been taught to walk the straight and narrow. On the other hand, Felicity, too, was a minister's daughter, but for some reason her parents let her get away with murder. If she'd take off some of that makeup, remove her violet contact lenses and quit dying her hair jet black, Felicity would be a cute girl.

"How was your first morning at Bright Side?" Missy

asked Charity. "Is it weird to be around all those people with mental handicaps?"

"I'm working in Mrs. Maxwell's office. She's a very nice person. I'm answering the phone and filing stuff and entering information in the computer. I won't actually be around the students all that much. My first morning there has been great, except—" She quieted abruptly.

"Except what?" Felicity asked as she finished off her second sandwich.

"Nothing. I shouldn't say anything about it." Charity lifted her glass to her lips and sipped her tea.

"You have to tell us now," Felicity said. "Whatever it is, we can keep a secret, can't we, guys?" She looked from Missy to Seth and then back to her sister. "Come on, spill it."

"I really shouldn't, but . . . well . . . Mrs. Maxwell," Charity cleared her throat. "She told me to call her Kim."

"Good God, stop hem-hawing around." Felicity rolled her eyes in aggravation.

"Kim's father came by to see her this morning, and I couldn't help overhearing part of their conversation. They were talking pretty loud," Charity said. "Her father is a Presbyterian minister over in Decatur, and his wife is sick. From what I could make out, he doesn't want to take care of her himself, so Kim recommended one of her students to come live with Reverend Kelley and take care of his wife."

Felicity groaned. "Is that it? That's boring news. I thought you knew some deep, dark secret. Maybe something scandalous."

"It is scandalous when a man doesn't want to take care of his sick wife, don't you think?" Missy said. "If he really loved her . . ."

"The way your dad loved and took care of your mom when she was sick," Charity said.

When Missy didn't respond to Charity's comment, Felicity grabbed the bag of potato chips and shook out a tall stack onto her plate. "So were they arguing, Mrs. Maxwell and her father?"

"Yes, I think so." Charity shook her head. "I only heard bits and pieces of their conversation, but I think they were arguing about the best way to take care of Kim's mother. My guess is that Reverend Kelley wants to put her away somewhere so he doesn't have to be bothered with her."

Felicity faked several yawns as she patted her hand over her mouth. "Boring stuff. Let's talk about something more interesting."

Frowning, Charity gave her sister a condemning glare.

To break the tension in the air, Missy asked, "Are y'all going to the youth rally Reverend Floyd is hosting tomorrow night? Just about everybody from school is going."

"A youth rally," Felicity whined. "Jesus, Missy, you're as boring as Charity. You two really need to get a life."

"I'm going," Seth said. "To the rally. Granddad isn't much into my visiting other churches, but since this is being held at the community center and it's not any kind of church service, he's okay with my going."

Missy smiled at Seth, and suddenly everyone else disappeared. They were the only two people in the world. "I'm going, too. Would you like to ride with me? Dad's letting me take my car."

"Hey, if you two are going, count me in," Felicity said. "Pick me up, too, okay?"

Seth wanted to tell Felicity that she hadn't been invited to go with them, but he'd been taught not to be rude. Besides, before he had a chance to do more than process the fact that Felicity had just blown his big chance to be alone with Missy, Missy said, "Of course. All of you can ride with me. We'll make a night of it. You know the youth rally lasts until eight o'clock Saturday morning."

"Oh, I like the sound of that." Felicity looked right at Seth. "We could slip off in the night and have some real fun."

Chapter Twelve

Jack's phone rang just as he unlocked the patrol car. He glanced at the caller ID and grinned.

"Yes, he showed up, in person. He's quite a know-it-all," Jack said. "A man with a great deal of information and some interesting theories, but unfortunately nothing that pinpoints our killer."

Maleah laughed. "You didn't like him."

"Do not project your feelings onto me. You don't like him. I found Derek Lawrence to be intelligent, articulate and intuitive."

"You didn't like him," she repeated.

"I'm withholding judgment until I know him better."

"What does that mean?"

"It means that Mr. Lawrence has decided to stay in Dunmore for a while. Our Fire and Brimstone Killer fascinates him."

Maleah groaned. "I'm sorry, but you did ask for his help. I had no idea he'd do anything more than send you his report. Just remember that if he steps on any toes and pisses off the wrong people, I was just the go-between, at your request."

"I promise I won't shoot the messenger," Jack assured her.

"Are you at work or . . . ?"

"Heading out for lunch. I'm meeting the contractor, a guy named Clay Yarbrough. Mike recommended him. He added on a sunroom and a deck at Mike's place."

"Clay Yarbrough. The name doesn't sound familiar. He must not be from Dunmore originally."

"He's originally from Athens," Jack said.

"I still can't believe you're actually going to restore the old place and live there. A year ago, I'd have bet good money that you'd never ever even spend a night there."

"A lot has changed in a year."

"Is Cathy Nelson . . . uh, Cathy Cantrell still . . . ?"

"Yes. She's going to work with us on this project. As a matter of fact, she's meeting us for lunch."

"Would I be nosy if I asked . . . ?"

"Yes, you would."

"Well, I'm going to ask anyway. After all, I am your sister, and that gives me certain rights."

"That works both ways, you know," Jack told her.

"Yes, I guess it does."

"I'll answer your questions about Cathy if you answer a couple of questions about why you dislike Derek Lawrence so much."

"I'd think that after your meeting him, that would be obvious. He's a smug, conceited, know-it-all jerk."

"Hmm . . ."

"What does that mean?"

"It means if he did something to hurt you, as your big brother, then I'll have to beat the crap out of him." Jack barely managed not to chuckle.

"Oh, good God, you think . . . That's ridiculous . . . We never . . . I never," she sputtered. "Believe me, I'm not his type, no more than he's mine."

"So, baby sister, just what is your type?"

"Nice, sweet, boy next door. Good job, but not rich. Intelligent, but not a genius. Someone who respects my opinions as much as I respect his."

"In other words, everything that Derek Lawrence is not."

Maleah groaned. "My turn to ask you about Cathy. Are you going to ask her out on a real date?"

"Maybe. Yeah, I think I probably am."

"Take it slow and easy, okay? One step at a time. She broke your heart once. I don't want to see that happen again."

"You were just a kid when I was involved with Cathy. How do you know she broke my heart?"

"After they shipped you back home and you were in the hospital, full of pain medication, you talked about her," Maleah said.

"Oh."

"I love you, you know."

Jack heaved a heavy sigh. "Yeah, me, too."

"Have a nice lunch. And remember to take some photos while the remodeling is going on and send them to me. If you change the place enough where it looks completely different inside and out, I might actually come for a visit."

"I'll hold you to that."

When they said good-bye and Jack slipped his phone onto the belt clip, he tried not to think about the reasons Maleah hated their childhood home so much. As far as he knew, after he'd left to join the army, Nolan had never laid a hand on her again. He had warned his stepfather that he'd kill him if he ever touched Maleah. But she had lived in that house of horrors for nearly five years after he left, until she'd gone away to college. Even if Nolan hadn't abused her physically, Jack suspected the psychological abuse had been bad enough. Sometimes, he still felt guilty about leaving her there, but if he hadn't gotten away when he did, he would have wound up killing his stepfather.

* * *

Bruce Kelley folded his hands together and pressed them against his forehead. "Dear God, help me."

He hadn't wanted to sedate Sandie, but he'd had little choice. This morning's episode had been the worst she'd ever had. Although she had known who he was, he had been unable to convince her that their three children were now adults and living on their own. She had searched the house in a frenzy of fear and uncertainty, looking for Kim, Kira and Kevin.

"Someone has kidnapped my babies," she had told him, genuine terror in her eyes. "We have to call the police. Do you hear me, Bruce? Do something. Do something now!"

When he had tried to comfort her, she had balled her hands into tight fists and pummeled his chest repeatedly. And when he had tried to restrain her, she had fought him like a madwoman. He had begged and pleaded, doing his best to calm her without physically hurting her. But she had broken away from him and run out the front door and into the yard, screaming at the top of her lungs. Neighbors had come out of their houses, and when two of the ladies, Glenda Pittman and Judy Calhoun, realized what was happening, they had rushed over to help. But Sandie hadn't recognized the women, even though both had lived on either side of them for a good many years.

"She needs to be sedated," Glenda, a pediatric nurse, had told him. "Do you have anything?"

He had nodded. "Some pills the doctor gave us, but—"

"Get them. Judy and I will stay here with her. If we can't get her to take the tablets, we'll have to call 911."

When he had returned with the medication, Sandie had appeared calmer and even agreed to take a couple of the pills. But the moment he'd placed the medication in her mouth, she'd bitten his fingers.

Bruce unfolded his clasped hands and looked at the ban-

dage Glenda had taped over his right index finger after she
had stopped the bleeding and cleaned it with an antiseptic.

"She's sleeping." Judy Calhoun stood in the doorway of
his study. "Glenda said to tell you that she'll sit with her for
a while longer." She gazed at him sympathetically. "Why
don't you come over to the house and eat lunch with Bob
and me?"

"Thank you, but I don't think I could eat a bite."

"You need help, someone who can live in and look after
Sandie."

"Yes, I know. Kim is bringing a young woman to Sunday
dinner. The girl is one of her students. She's a bit slow, but
she's strong and healthy, and Kim assures me that she's very
kind." Tears sprang into his eyes. He turned his head and
cleared his throat.

Judy walked into the room, came over to him and placed
her hand on his shoulder. "Why don't you call Kim and see
if this young woman can start work today?"

Bruce squeezed his eyes tightly as he accepted the
painful reality of their situation. He nodded, but didn't look
at Judy. He didn't want to face her with tears in his eyes.

She patted his shoulder. "If you need us, call us. Bob and
I will do anything we can. You know we think the world of
you and Sandie."

He swallowed hard, gulping down the tears tightening his
throat. Several minutes later, alone in his study, Bruce rose
to his feet and walked over to his desk. He picked up the
phone and dialed his elder daughter's work number.

It is my duty to search for and find the unworthy, those
who profess to be servants of the Lord, who pass themselves
off as good shepherds but are sinners of the worst kind. I
have heard rumors about certain people, but I cannot punish
someone unless I am certain of their evil ways.

People say that Reverend Dewan Phillips is a good man, but he is a proud, boastful man. He likes to talk to hear his own voice, and although he sings the Lord's praises, he often takes credit for himself instead of giving credit to God. I must keep an eye on him. *When You give me a sign that he is a sinner in need of chastisement, I will obey Your command.*

And most people believe Patsy Floyd is above reproach, that as the first female minister in Dunmore, she should be admired for achieving equality for women in her church. But there are a few people who don't like her. I've heard some say that she does not conduct herself in a humble and pious manner, that she wears expensive clothes and jewelry and flaunts her wealth. *Has she displeased You, God? If I find all the accusations against her to be true, I will mark her name in my book, and she will be punished.*

And the rumors about the minister at the Presbyterian Church in Decatur cannot be ignored. If Bruce Kelley has hardened his heart and is shirking his duties as a husband, he must be dealt with severely. There is no more grievous sin than one committed against a member of one's own family. A husband who abuses or abandons his wife, a father who abuses or abandons his child, a son who neglects or mistreats his parents.

Not my will, O Lord but Thine be done. I know that You have chosen me to carry out Your will, that my suffering proves my worthiness, that I am special in Thine eyes. I am the Angel of Vengeance, the Destroyer of Evil, the Executioner of the Unworthy.

Jack didn't like the way that Clay Yarbrough was flirting with Cathy. He wished she would stop smiling at Clay. And why did she have to laugh at all his silly comments? Jack didn't think he was all that amusing.

"I sure didn't mean any disrespect to your late husband when I told you about my old man," Clay said, grinning like an idiot as he stared into Cathy's eyes. "But my father, God rest his sorry soul, was a mean old son of a bitch, preacher or no preacher."

Jack cleared his throat. Cathy and Clay looked at him. He tapped his wristwatch.

"I have to return to work in less than fifteen minutes," Jack said. "We need to get back on track here."

"Sorry about that." Clay bestowed his wide smile first on Cathy and then on Jack. "I tend to talk too much instead of listening, but I wanted Mrs. Cantrell to know how sorry I am about what happened to her husband. And whenever preachers come up in the conversation, I naturally think about my dad."

"You mentioned before we ate lunch that you think it would be a good idea for me to hire an architect to draw up plans for the renovations I want." Jack glanced at Cathy. "Do you think you could draw up the plans? It would save me the added expense of hiring an architect."

"Well, yes, I suppose I could," Cathy replied, a touch of surprise in her voice. "The plans wouldn't be the same as a professional architect would do, but . . ." She paused and smiled at Jack. "I can't believe that you remembered I wanted to be an architect."

"I remembered the plans you showed me for your dream house," Jack said. "If I recall correctly, the house was a modern version of a Victorian, with gingerbread trim, a turret and a porch gazebo."

"I don't have a problem with Mrs. Cantrell drawing up the plans," Clay said. "They don't have to be professional quality. I've had clients who drew up their own plans, and somehow, someway, I managed to give them what they wanted."

"Actually, I took some night classes at the junior college right after Lorie and I opened up Treasures of the Past." Cathy didn't even glance at Clay; her gaze focused directly on Jack. "If you'll tell me exactly what you want, I'll do my best to transfer that into something resembling what an architect would produce for you."

"Sounds great," Clay said. "And I'd be more than happy to help you out. Sometimes I have to sketch out things for a client myself, and if you need any tools of the trade, I'm sure I can round 'em up for you. What say we have dinner tonight and—"

"The lady already has dinner plans." The words were out of Jack's mouth before he realized that Cathy might object to his high-handed manner. He looked at her pleadingly. "That is . . ."

"Jack's right," Cathy said as she turned to Clay. "I'm having dinner with my son tonight. I appreciate the offer to loan me your supplies, but I have my own, everything from trimmers and drafting templates to a sketch board and parallel rulers and gliders."

"Well, another night then," Clay said. "Maybe you and your son would like to go over to Huntsville for dinner and a movie. How old is your boy?"

"Seth's fifteen. But, you see, I haven't started dating." She cut a quick glance Jack's way. "Not officially."

"If we take your boy along with us, it won't exactly be a date, but I tell you what—consider it an open invitation. When you do start dating, just let me know."

Clay slid back his chair and stood. He grinned at Cathy, and then offered Jack his hand. Jack stood.

"I'm ready to start when you are," Clay said. "I'll get an inspector out there on Monday to see where we need to start on structural repairs. And as soon as I get Mrs. Cantrell's plans, I'll have the carpenters go right to work."

Jack shook Clay's hand and walked him halfway to the restaurant's front entrance. He wanted to tell the man to stay away from Cathy, to back off and leave her alone. But he thought better of the idea, sensing that she would resent him running interference for her. She'd made it clear that she was in charge of her own life.

When he got back to the table, Cathy didn't question him about his attitude toward Clay; instead, she smiled warmly, a look of excitement in her blue-green eyes.

"Thank you for allowing me to draw up the plans for re-modeling your house. I haven't been this excited about a project in I don't know when. Never, actually." She laughed.

He liked the sound of her laughter. "I'm glad you're excited about it."

"I'll need your input as soon as possible, but since both of us have to go back to work right away and I'm having dinner with Seth and his grandparents tonight, maybe you could drop by my house tomorrow evening and we can discuss everything then. Tomorrow morning the movers are bringing my furniture out of storage to the house I'm renting, but by tomorrow evening, I'll need a break. Of course, if you have other plans . . ."

"You mean unless I have a date?"

"Yes."

"I don't have a date," he told her. "And I'd like to stop by and discuss my plans with you. But I'll tell you right now that although I have some basic ideas about restoring the old place, I'd like for you to help me decide just what to do. Like, what do you think of adding a gazebo on the porch? And you can design the master bathroom for me. I thought I could convert one of the bedrooms. Then there's the kitchen—you've already mentioned some ideas on how to modernize it and yet at the same time retain its Victorian heritage."

"You—you want me to make all these decisions? Are you sure? I mean, this is your home. It should reflect your tastes."

"It's a home meant for a family," he said. "That's what I want it to reflect. I want it to have a similar feel to the way it was when Maleah and I were kids, and my father . . ." He paused and huffed quietly. "I want to erase Nolan Reaves from every inch of the house and grounds."

She reached across the table and clasped his tight fist. He

stared at her small, delicate hand lying on top of his tense knuckles, and then he looked up at her. "I understand. You told me some of the things that horrible man did, the way he treated you and Maleah and your mother." She squeezed his hand. "I promise you that I'll help you make your house a home again."

After a surprisingly pleasant dinner with her in-laws, her mother, Seth, Brother Donnie Hovater and his daughter Missy, Cathy pulled her son aside and told him she needed to speak to him alone.

"That would be kind of rude, wouldn't it?" he said.

"I need five minutes of your time. Surely that's not too much to ask."

Seth nodded, then walked across the living room and spoke quietly to his grandfather. J.B. glanced across the room at her, a questioning glint in his eyes.

"I told Granddad that I wanted to show you my room," Seth said.

"Thank you for thinking of an excuse so that we can have a few minutes alone."

As they headed for the hallway, Seth said loud enough for the others to hear, "It's my dad's old room. Nana got some of Dad's stuff out of the attic, stuff like his baseball glove and bat. We hung them on the wall over my bed. And we put together a photo album of pictures of Dad from the time he was a baby to when I was born."

Seth opened the door to his bedroom and flipped the wall switch. The overhead light, with its two sixty-watt bulbs, illuminated the twelve-by-twelve space. This room didn't resemble Seth's old room in the parsonage; instead it looked, in an almost eerie way, like a shrine to Mark Cantrell.

Cathy swallowed and held her thoughts at bay, determined not to say or do anything that would upset her son.

But seeing this room only reinforced her determination to regain custody of Seth. She didn't want him to forget Mark, but holding Mark up as some saintly figure that Seth had to live up to was wrong. Had filling this room with all of Mark's boyhood things been Mona's idea or had it been J.B.'s? Or perhaps it had been a joint endeavor. After all, Mark had been their only child. His younger brother, for whom Seth was named, had died as an infant. What was it like for J.B. and Mona to have lost both of their children? Her heart ached for them, but she was not willing to give them her son as a replacement for his father.

"Why didn't you and Dad ever tell me that he'd been married before?" Seth asked, the question coming from out of the blue.

"What?"

"When Nana and I were going through the old photograph albums, I saw Dad's wedding pictures from his first marriage," Seth told her. "Nana said that Dad's first wife died. Her name was Joy."

"Yes, I know." Cathy hadn't thought about Mark's first wife in a long time. "She died when she was quite young."

"Nana said she had cancer."

"An inoperable brain tumor."

"Why didn't y'all tell me about her?"

"There was no reason to," Cathy explained. "Mark's first wife died several years before we married. She had nothing to do with our life, nothing to do with you. And, well, it made Mark unhappy to talk about Joy."

"Did you mind that he'd been married before?" Seth asked. "Were you jealous of her? Did you think Dad might have still loved her?"

"My goodness, what strange questions for a fifteen-year-old boy to ask."

"I asked Granddad about her."

"Did you?" She could only imagine what J.B. had had to

say about Saint Joy. During the first few years of her marriage to Mark, she had been forced to listen to her father-in-law sing the woman's praises.

"He said Dad never got over losing her, that, well, that she was the love of his life."

Damn, J.B. Why on earth would he say such a thing to Seth? "I was never jealous of Joy. Your father loved me. He was happy in our marriage, and he adored you."

Apparently remembering the good life the three of them had shared, Seth smiled. "I sure do miss Dad."

"I miss him, too."

"Do you?"

"Of course I do. And I miss you, Seth." He had given her the opening she needed. "You know how much I want you to come and live with me. I'll be moving our furniture into the rental house tomorrow morning."

Seth stared down at the floor. "Granddad doesn't believe—"

"I don't care what J.B. believes. I need to know what you want. Do you want to come and live with me?"

"Granddad would never agree. You know what he thinks."

"Yes, I know what he thinks. What do you think?"

"I guess I'd like to be two people." He glanced at her quickly and then looked back down at the floor. "One of me could stay here with Granddad and Nana and the other me could go live with you."

God, she hated doing this, hated making her son choose between her and his grandparents. But it wasn't her fault that he was being put in this position. It was J.B.'s fault.

"But there's only one you—only one Seth Nelson Cantrell. As much as your grandparents love you and you love them, you're my son, not theirs."

"Maybe, if we give Granddad time, he'll come around."

"And if he doesn't?" Cathy knew that waiting for J.B. to change his mind would be like waiting for the sun to rise in the west and set in the east.

"I don't know. What do you want me to say?" Seth curved his right hand into a fist and punched it into the open palm of his left hand.

Cathy curled her hand over his shoulder. He looked right at her. "I've hired a lawyer, Elliott Floyd. I want you to talk to Mr. Floyd and tell him how you feel about living with your grandparents and about the possibility of coming to live with me."

Seth's eyes widened. "Why did you hire a lawyer?"

"That's a very good question." Elaine stood outside in the hallway, her hard gaze directed at Cathy.

"This is none of your business, Mother. This is between my son and me."

"If you're thinking of suing for custody, I think you should know that I will side with J.B. and Mona, and I'll testify that I do not believe you're stable enough to—"

"You do whatever the hell you have to do." Cathy barely managed to control the anger inside her. "And I'll do what I have to do."

"Don't argue, please," Seth said. "Grandmother, don't say anything to Granddad and Nana about this."

"I think they should know what your mother has planned," Elaine told him.

"Please don't tell them." When Elaine hesitated, Seth added, "If I promise not to go and talk to Mr. Floyd, will you promise not to tell Granddad?"

Elaine smiled triumphantly. "I promise. Now go on back to the living room and tell everyone that your mother and I will be along shortly." Seth hesitated; then, without a backward glance, he left the room.

Elaine turned to Cathy. "Think about what Seth needs, not about what you need. You've become quite a selfish person, haven't you? The daughter I raised never would have—"

"I'm still the daughter you raised, Mother. I'm the end product of all your years of tender, loving care. You can't imagine how much I learned from your example. You taught me exactly what kind of mother I don't want to be."

Elaine gasped. "I had hoped they could help you at Haven Home, but apparently they taught you that it's acceptable to be disrespectful to your mother. You have no idea how you disgraced me and J.B. and Mona when you pulled that stunt last year—going stark raving mad the way you did. That was bad enough, but then you had to check yourself into that place in Birmingham when you knew everyone in town would be aware of where you were. When I look at you right now, I don't know who you are, but you are not my daughter."

"If that's the way you feel, I'm sorry. But I'm not going to let you and J.B. or even Mona keep Seth from me and try to turn him into a carbon copy of Mark. He's my son, and he is his own person. I'll fight all of you to see that he has a chance to spread his wings and soar with the eagles."

"Soar with eagles. What are you jabbering about? You're talking nonsense again."

"No, Mother, I'm telling you like it is."

Cathy turned around and walked away, leaving her mother with her mouth gaping wide open.

Chapter Thirteen

The house on Madison was half the size of the parsonage where Cathy had lived with Mark and Seth. The church had provided them with a modern twenty-five-hundred-square-foot home that she had decorated in a simple, traditional style. Due to Mark's thriftiness, they had purchased inexpensive furniture, and only Cathy's flair for decorating had kept their home from looking like an assortment of yard-sale finds. Over the years, she had used her owner's discount at Treasures to buy a few antique items that had added a certain elegance to their home. She liked the idea of starting fresh now and being able to decorate this rental house without any input from other people, including her mother and mother-in-law. The movers had brought only the pieces of furniture she had chosen. She intended to sell the other items that were still in storage and gradually replace them with better pieces.

Ruth Ann had agreed to work at Treasures today, which she seldom did on Saturday mornings, so that Lorie could help Cathy instruct the movers and begin the grueling job of unpacking a slew of boxes. At one o'clock, Lorie had left to relieve Ruth Ann, and Cathy had taken a short lunch break, eating a pack of cheese and crackers and downing a diet cola.

After unpacking a box filled with bed linens, she carried an armload down the hall and into the kitchen, where the compact washer and dryer were stored in a small closet behind louvered doors. She put the sheets and pillowcases in the washer and laid the folded blankets and quilts on the floor to be washed later. Leaving the washer chugging away, Cathy strolled through the house, taking her time to explore each room. The twelve-hundred-square-foot house had been built in the early fifties and added on to in the mid-sixties. The exterior was a combination of dark red brick and wooden shingles that had recently been painted a muted moss green. One of the three bedrooms was tiny, only eight by nine. It would make a perfect studio/workroom for her. She could set up her drafting table and her sewing machine and add some bookcases along the back wall.

She intended to save the larger, twelve-by-twelve bedroom for Seth. The sturdy oak furniture that Lorie had helped her find through their connections with statewide antique malls and furniture outlets looked really good in there. Seth's old bedroom furniture, a gift from J.B. and Mona, had been some of the cheapest on the market because it was made from pressed wood. She'd sell the set for little to nothing or give it away.

The other bedroom, the one at the back of the house, was ten by twelve, and the only furniture in the room was an antique four-poster bed, a walnut chifforobe and a lady's writing table. All of the items had once graced the parsonage's small guest room, each item purchased with the money she had earned at Treasures. This was her bedroom. She intended to paint it a pale, creamy yellow. Mark had disliked yellow, which was her favorite color, so she'd never been able to use it in her home or even wear a yellow blouse.

Just as she headed toward the kitchen, intending to unpack the pots and pans and dishes and glassware, the doorbell rang. When she entered the living room, she caught a glimpse of her reflection in the mirror she and Lorie had hung over the sofa. A few stray tendrils of hair had loosened from her ponytail, and perspiration had erased most of her makeup. But she'd been too busy to worry about her appearance.

She peered through the viewfinder in the front door, smiled, opened the door and greeted her visitor.

"Hi there," Jack said.

"Hi," Cathy replied. "Please come in."

"Are you sure? I know you're moving in today, but when I drove by, I didn't see any other cars here, so I thought I'd stop and offer to help out."

"In that case, most definitely come on in." Cathy held open the door for him. As he eased past her, her breath caught in her throat.

He glanced around at the living room, which held a sofa and one chair and more than a dozen unopened boxes.

"Didn't the Wilsons used to live here?" Jack asked.

"The Wilsons? I don't remember them. I'm renting the house from a lady who lives in Chattanooga. Leslie McCafferty."

"She used to be Leslie Wilson," Jack said. "I dated her a couple of times back in high school. Nice girl."

"As I recall, you dated a lot of girls." Cathy grinned. "I knew who you were a long time before you knew I existed."

"I was a few years ahead of you in school and not into young, innocent girls." Jack reached out and tucked a flyaway strand of hair behind her ear. "In case no one has told you recently, you're even prettier now than you were at seventeen."

A flush of warmth spread through Cathy, a direct result of the compliment he'd paid her. Odd. She didn't remember Jack being the type to flatter a girl. He had been a moody, dark soul back then, and she suspected that in many ways he still was. But she liked seeing this side of him.

"So, did you really stop by to help me?" she asked.

"Absolutely. Point me in the right direction and issue orders."

"How about helping me unpack the kitchen stuff," she said. "I can't reach some of the upper cabinets without a step stool."

"Lead the way."

Three hours later, with the kitchen boxes unpacked and the items neatly stored, the bed linens washed, dried and put in place on the four-poster, Cathy led Jack into the small bedroom at the front of the house.

"I'm going to use this as my workroom," she told him.

He eyed the two large boxes pushed against the wall near the closet. "Want me to start with those?"

She nodded. "My portable sewing machine is in the smaller one. If you'll unpack it and set it on that desk"—she pointed to the rectangular pine desk painted white—"I'll take the packing tape off the larger one. My drafting table is in there. I haven't used it in years."

"Why didn't you go to college the way you'd planned and become an architect?" Jack asked.

Bent over the large box, her back to Jack, Cathy stiffened. She had known that it was only a matter of time before he started asking questions. Not that this question would be difficult to answer, but the reply would invariably lead to more questions. And the answer to those would require either several lies or a major confession.

She took the box cutter in her hand and ripped through the packing tape. Staying focused on the task at hand, she replied casually, "I got married instead. And I intended to eventually go back to school and get my degree, but Mark and I moved around quite a bit as he went from one church to another. And, of course, Seth kept me pretty busy."

Holding her breath, she waited for more questions. When Jack didn't say anything else, she glanced at him and found him busy removing her sewing machine from the box. She breathed a sigh of relief.

As he placed the sewing machine on the desk, he asked, "How about we order something for supper and I stay here and help you until I have to go to work?"

"What time do you have to go in?"

"Eleven," he replied. "I'm filling in for Tony Bradley. He's at the hospital with his wife, who went into labor at ten-thirty this morning."

"Are you sure you don't mind? I'd appreciate the help. Lorie mentioned coming back around six-thirty."

"We'll order dinner for three, my treat. Can you recommend a place that delivers?"

"Why don't I call Lorie and have her pick up something on her way here? And dinner is on me," she told him. "It's the least I can do to pay you back for helping me."

"Yes, ma'am." With a cocky, boyish grin on his face, he saluted her. "You call Lorie, and I'll set up your drafting table."

"Okay." Feeling relaxed and happy, she returned his smile. "How about Italian? Frankie's on Market Street has the best lasagna and a tomato pesto to die for."

"Any Italian cream cake?" Jack asked.

"Oh my God, yes. You can gain five pounds just smelling it."

He looked her over from head to toe and then leisurely made his way back up, stopping when their gazes met. "Why don't you order cake for all three of us? A few extra pounds won't hurt your figure."

Cathy felt almost giddy and couldn't hold back the laughter bubbling over inside her. After Seth was born and she'd been what some would have called pleasingly plump, Mark had helped her stick to a strict diet until she was at what he considered an acceptable weight. And over the years, he had kept a close eye on her eating habits. He had disapproved of her tendency to turn to food for comfort. And as J.B. had pointed out to her and Mona more than once, gluttony was a sin.

"I'll order two pieces," she said. "Lorie and I can split a piece and not feel too guilty for indulging."

Jack shrugged. "Suit yourself." He scanned the limited space in the small room. "Where do you want me to put the table?"

"There"—Cathy pointed to the area—"near the windows so that I can get a lot of natural sunlight during the day."

He nodded. "Sure thing."

She hurried out of the room, down the hall and into the bedroom, where she retrieved her phone from her purse. She hit the preprogrammed number for Treasures.

"Hey there. How's the unpacking going?" Lorie asked.

"Quite well," Cathy replied. "Especially since Jack showed up several hours ago and has been helping me."

"He can't seem to stay away from you, can he?"

"I don't know, but if that's the case, then I'm glad, because the feeling is mutual." She lowered her voice. "Just being around him makes me happy. I don't know exactly what it is about him, about us being together, but . . . I don't know how to explain it."

"You don't have to. Whenever I'm within twenty feet of Mike, all I want to do is reach out and grab him."

"Look, I didn't mean to get all soft and gooey on you. I'm actually calling to ask for a favor."

"You don't want me to show up tonight as planned."

"Yes, I do want you to come over, just as we'd planned, but I'd like for you to stop by Frankie's and pick up supper for three. Get the lasagna, Italian salad, bread sticks, tomato pesto and two slices of Italian cream cake."

"Are you sure you wouldn't rather be alone with Jack? I could have them deliver dinner for two."

"No, I don't think I'm ready for a romantic dinner, just

the two of us alone here at the house." Cathy simply couldn't handle more than friendship from Jack or any other man. Not yet.

"Okay, then. I'll see y'all around six-thirty. And I'll bring supper."

Although she had been expecting Griff's call, Nic nearly jumped out of her skin when her phone rang. She needed to hear his voice, needed to hear him tell her that he loved her and missed her as much as she missed him.

She hated the fact that in recent months she had become a jealous, insecure wife. Priding herself on being a strong, independent woman, Nic detested any weakness in herself. It had taken her a long time to completely trust Griff and even longer to trust the way she felt about him. Loving him had been the greatest risk she'd ever taken. She had gambled with her very soul, and now she was wondering if she'd made a mistake.

"Hello." Crap! Her voice sounded too soft, too vulnerable. "How's the trip going?" She forced a light, cheerful note into the question.

"I miss you," he told her and sounded damn sincere.

"I miss you, too."

"The next time I have to be away this long, you're going to have to come with me."

"You really do miss me, don't you?"

"More than you could ever know."

"Don't be so sure of that."

"Everything all right there?" he asked.

"Things are pretty much the way you left them. Holt Keinan arrived today, and Ben Trahern went back to Knoxville." The Powell agents rotated two-week stays at Griffin's Rest and while there were in charge of security. "And Maleah's here, too."

"Any special reason she's there?"

"No. I just wanted her here with me for a while. Any objections?"

"What's wrong, Nic?"

"Why do you think something's wrong?"

"I can hear it in your voice." He paused, waiting for her to reply. When she didn't, he added, "And your wanting Maleah to stay at Griffin's Rest is a dead giveaway."

"I need a friend sometimes. Someone who is just my friend. You have Sanders and Yvette and even Barbara Jean."

"They're your friends, too."

She didn't know how to respond. Yes, Barbara Jean was a friend, but her loyalty was to Sanders, the man she loved, and Sanders's loyalty was always first and foremost to Griff and to her only because she was Griff's wife. As far as Yvette was concerned, Nic accepted her share of the blame that they were not good friends. Early in her marriage, Yvette had reached out to her, and she had sensed that Yvette wanted them to be friends. She had to admit that it had been easier to consider Yvette a friend when she'd lived in London, half a world away from Tennessee.

"You're worrying me, honey," he said. "Do I need to fly home tonight?"

"No, of course not. I'm fine. Just missing you. But I'm glad you'll be home day after tomorrow."

He grunted. "That's the thing. I've run into a few snags, and it looks like I may be here awhile longer."

"How much longer?"

"Four or five days. A week at most."

"A week? Why, what's happened? I thought this was just a routine business trip."

"It's a business trip that's run into some problems that I have to fix."

She needed to tell him that there were a few problems here at home he needed to fix, but instead she said, "I may fly out to San Francisco and visit Charles David."

"Why don't you do that, honey, and take Maleah with you. I'm sure your brother would love to see you."

"Are the business problems you're trying to fix putting you in any danger?" Nic asked point-blank. She knew how he had acquired his vast wealth and the kinds of people he'd dealt with in his past.

"You shouldn't be so intuitive. Yes, there is a certain risk, but I'm working on eliminating any future problems."

"Who do you have there with you?"

"Luke Sentell. And a man from Cam Hendrix's firm, too. He's an expert in international law. I brought him along to work with the European lawyers I have to deal with on this project."

If Griff had taken Luke Sentell with him to act as his bodyguard, that meant he had anticipated trouble—big trouble. Sentell was a former Delta Force commando. "If you go and get yourself killed, Griffin Powell, I'll never forgive you."

Griff chuckled. "That alone is reason enough to stay alive."

"Does Yvette know what you're doing?"

Silence.

Then he took a deep breath and replied, "Yes."

"I see."

"No, you don't. What I'm dealing with right now concerns a part of the past that has come back to haunt me and Yvette and Sanders. That's the only reason they know more about this than you do. Believe me, honey, I want to protect you from—"

"When you come home, you'll tell me everything." She didn't add "or else," but she might as well have.

"I'll tell you everything I can. I promise."

Tears gathered in her eyes. Damn it, she hated women who cried at the drop of a hat. She'd never been the type. She cleared her throat and swatted away the pesky tears.

"Nic?"

"Come home to me, okay?"

"I will. I'll call you tomorrow night. And Nic—I love you. You know that. You're everything to me."

"Same here," she told him. "I love you."

Griffin Powell laid his phone on the table and walked away, his heart heavy. He hated himself for what this secrecy was doing to Nic, the person he loved more than life itself. But how could he tell her that the ghosts of a past he had thought dead and buried had suddenly reappeared and possibly threatened not only his life, but the lives of Sanders and Yvette and anyone they loved?

At this point, there were only rumors. Vague. Unsubstantiated. Underworld gossip. But if there was even a grain of truth in the vague reports he had received, he didn't dare ignore them.

Luke Sentell stood at the windows overlooking the Paris street below the fourth-floor apartment. "She's sleeping."

"Did you have to give her an injection?" Griff asked.

"Yes. She was too agitated to rest otherwise and finally agreed that she needed sleep. She'd been awake for more than forty-eight hours."

"I hate what this is doing to her."

"It's necessary."

Griff nodded.

"You should rest for a while, too," Luke told him.

"I will."

Griff left the parlor, intending to go to his bedroom and try to get a few hours sleep, but as he passed the guest room, he heard her moaning loudly. He eased back the partially open door. She tossed restlessly in her sleep, her arms flaying about as if she were fighting off demons.

Perhaps she was. He had no idea what vivid images appeared in her mind, even when she was asleep.

He walked quietly into the room and over to the bed.

When he reached down and pulled the wrinkled sheet and silk coverlet up and over her, she cried out, the sound chilling. And then she settled again, quiet and unmoving.

Griff stood by her bed and watched her sleep for several minutes. Meredith Sinclair's curly red hair looked like orange flames against the cream silk pillowcase. Without makeup on her round, freckled face, she looked young. Much younger than her twenty-nine years.

"I'm sorry, Meredith," he whispered. "I know what this is costing you. But Yvette understands that you could well be our only hope of finding out the truth. That's why she sent you with me."

Cathy made a pot of decaf coffee and served it with the Italian cream cake. Both pieces were enormous. Frankie's was known for its large servings. Jack and Lorie had cleared away the Styrofoam containers that had held their dinner and dumped them and the used plastic utensils into a large black garbage bag. When Cathy lifted the silver serving tray loaded with the coffee pot, three cups and saucers, a sugar bowl and a creamer, as well as three plates and plastic forks, Jack took the tray from her and carried it over to the small oak kitchen table. After he sat down, she distributed the cups, saucers, plates and forks and then poured the coffee. She hadn't been able to find her silverware, and the only dishes she had unpacked were her everyday Wal-Mart pottery. Thankfully, one of the first boxes she had unpacked had contained her coffee service, which she had bought several years ago using her Treasures discount.

"This cake looks delicious," Jack said. "I have a weakness for sweets, especially cakes."

Lorie surveyed his long, lean body. "Either you have a great metabolism or you work out like crazy to keep that great toned body."

Jack chuckled, but before he could comment, the doorbell rang.

"Are you expecting someone?" Lorie asked.

"No, I'm not." Cathy laid down her plastic fork and scooted back her chair. "If y'all will excuse me, I'll go see who it is."

"If it's a tall, dark, handsome stranger, invite him in," Lorie said. "And I'll take him home with me."

Cathy laughed as she left the kitchen. Despite all the hard work involved in moving and unpacking, Cathy had enjoyed the day immensely, in great part thanks to Jack. And the easy camaraderie that she and Jack and Lorie had shared this evening reminded her that this was the way life should always be.

When she reached the front door, she glanced through the viewfinder and smiled when she saw Seth standing on her porch. She opened the door without hesitation, ready to welcome her son, but suddenly she saw that he was not alone. Brother Donnie Hovater and his daughter were with Seth, and Missy held what appeared to be a potted plant of some sort.

"Hi, Mom," Seth said.

Donnie Hovater tapped his daughter's shoulder.

Missy cleared her throat, held out the plant that sported a small red bow and said, "Happy housewarming, Mrs. Cantrell."

Cathy accepted the gift and invited them into the living room. "Please come in. And excuse the mess. I'm afraid I've made only a small dent in the unpacking."

"That's quite all right," Donnie said as they entered the house. When he heard laughter coming from the kitchen, his brows rose quizzically. "Are we interrupting anything?"

"No, certainly not." Cathy shut the door and motioned to the sofa. "Please, won't y'all sit down?" She looked at Seth, puzzled as to why he was with the Hovaters. "If you'd like to see the house, feel free to look around." Then she turned back to Donnie. "I have decaf coffee. Would you care for some?"

He shook his head, then asked, "Do you have dinner guests?"

Right on cue, Lorie and Jack came out of the kitchen. Lorie answered for Cathy. "Just us," she said as she looked at Seth. "Hello, Brother Hovater. I'm not sure if you remember me. I'm Lorie Hammonds. We met a couple of months ago. Reverend Floyd introduced us."

"Yes, of course, Ms. Hammonds," he said. "How nice to see you again." He eyed Jack, who stepped forward and offered his hand.

"Jackson Perdue."

They shook hands.

"I'm Donnie Hovater, and this is my daughter, Melissa."

Cathy felt an odd tension in the air, and when she glanced at Seth, she realized he stood there ramrod straight, his gaze riveted to Jack.

"What's he doing here?" Seth asked.

"Seth, where are your manners?" She scolded her son as if he were a child, but then he was acting like a child.

"Sorry," Seth grumbled.

Cathy suddenly realized that she was fiercely clutching the potted plant, so she walked past her son and placed the plant on the mantel at the opposite end of the living room. "Jack is a friend. He and Lorie have been helping me unpack today, and we decided to order dinner from Frankie's."

"We probably should have waited before stopping by," Donnie said. "But I thought it would give you and Seth a chance to visit and for him to see your new home."

"Brother Hovater is taking Missy and me over to the community center for the Christian youth rally, and I asked him if we could stop by here on the way," Seth said. "If I'd known he was here . . . uh . . . that you had company, we wouldn't have bothered."

"Felicity and Charity Harper were going with us, but

their plans changed, so their dad's taking them," Missy explained.

"I hadn't heard anything about this youth rally," Cathy said, feeling like a stranger to her own son. "What sort of . . . ?"

"It's a community event and will be adequately chaperoned," Donnie told her. "If I thought it wasn't an appropriate event, I certainly wouldn't allow Missy to attend."

"Oh, I didn't mean to imply otherwise," Cathy assured him. "I'm afraid that since Seth is living with his grandparents for the time being, I'm out of the loop on his social life."

"This rally is one of Patsy Floyd's Uniting-Christians projects, isn't it?" Lorie asked.

"Yes, I believe so," Donnie replied. "However, I've been assured that it is a nondenominational event, and no Methodist doctrine will be included."

Cathy quickly glanced from Lorie to Jack. She noted the way Lorie's mouth twitched and how, with a broad grin, Jack glanced down at his feet.

"Seth, since you're here, would you like to see the rest of the house?" Cathy asked. "I can show you your room first and—"

"Not tonight," Seth answered coolly, glaring at Jack. "We don't have time." He looked pleadingly at Donnie. "We'd better get going, hadn't we?"

"Uh, yes, yes, I guess we had." Donnie seemed taken off guard by Seth's sudden need to leave. "I look forward to seeing you in church Sunday, Cathy." He glanced from Lorie to Jack. "And y'all are, of course, invited. Anytime. Anytime."

Before Donnie finished issuing his invitation, Seth was opening the front door. Cathy followed him out onto the porch, catching up with him and grabbing his arm.

"Why are you acting this way?" she asked him.

"What way?"

"I'm happy that you wanted to stop by to see me and our

new home. I wish you wouldn't rush off in a huff just because Jack is here."

"I don't like him." Seth pulled away from her and walked down the steps and into the yard.

Cathy followed. "You don't know him."

"Are you dating him?"

She groaned silently. "Is that the reason for your bad attitude? You don't want me to start dating because you think I'd somehow be disloyal to Mark . . . to your dad if I did?" She laid her hand on his shoulder, ignoring the fact that Donnie Hovater and his daughter stood on the porch directly behind them and possibly could hear their conversation. "Mark would not disapprove of my dating. He would want me to go on with my life."

"Dad would expect you to date someone like Brother Hovater." Seth looked her square in the eye. "Granddad says that Perdue guy is bad news, and he's a trained killer and all messed up in his head."

Cathy wanted to scream. Actually, she wanted to strangle J.B. How dare he say such things to Seth. And about Jack, of all people. *Count to ten. Say a prayer. Do something to keep from exploding and taking your anger out on your son.*

"Jack is a former Army Ranger," Cathy said as calmly as possible. "He's a decorated soldier. Your grandfather's choice of words implied something altogether inaccurate."

"Are you saying Granddad lied?" Seth demanded vehemently as he jerked away from her.

"Sorry to interrupt," Donnie said as he and Missy approached them. "And I certainly don't mean to interfere in what appears to be a family disagreement, but, Seth, son"—he patted Seth on the back—"your grandfather would expect you to show your mother the proper respect. And I'm sure she didn't mean to imply that J.B. lied. I believe she was trying to tell you that J.B. might have been misinformed about Mr. Perdue."

"So, he used to be a soldier," Seth said. "They train soldiers to kill, don't they? Dad didn't believe in killing. He believed in turning the other cheek, in loving your fellow man." Seth paused for half a second, and when Cathy simply stared at him, uncertain how to respond, he went on. "After what you've been through this past year, the last kind of guy you need right now is somebody who's got his own mental problems."

Seth had rendered her momentarily speechless. Who had her son become in the year she'd been away? Where was the compassionate, tenderhearted, caring young man she had raised? J.B. had done a good job of trying to turn Seth into a duplicate of Mark, and she hated him for doing it.

"You and I will talk tomorrow," Cathy said. "I'd like for you to have lunch with me."

"I don't know. I'll have to ask Granddad."

"I have an idea," Donnie interrupted again. "Why don't Missy and I take you and your mother out for lunch tomorrow after church? I'm sure your grandparents won't object."

"Yeah, sure, thanks. That would be great." Seth looked at Cathy, waiting for her to agree.

"Yes, thank you," Cathy replied.

Donnie spread his arms out, placing one around Seth's shoulders and the other around his daughter's waist. "Come on, kids. It's nearly eight o'clock. Y'all don't want to be late. This thing is from eight tonight until eight in the morning, right?"

"Yes, sir," Seth said.

"Yes, Daddy, eight to eight."

Cathy stood in the yard and watched Brother Hovater back out of the driveway. He threw up his hand and waved. She waved back at him and smiled.

Donnie seemed like a very nice man. He had certainly tried his best to act as a mediator between Seth and her tonight. She appreciated his offer to take them to lunch tomorrow, which would give them time to talk without J.B. being involved.

Jack came up behind her so quietly that he startled her when he spoke. "Are you all right?"

She gasped and jumped simultaneously.

"Sorry," he said.

She turned and faced him. "It's okay. And yes, I'm all right, but not happy about hearing my father-in-law's words come out of my son's mouth."

"All the more reason you should do everything you can to regain custody of Seth," Lorie said from where she stood on the porch.

"I hate that my being here tonight bothered your son so much," Jack said. "But you have to know that he's not going to approve of your dating, no matter who the guy is. No man will live up to his father. Not in his eyes."

Lorie and Cathy exchanged quick oh-my-God glances, and then Cathy looked directly at Jack. "That wasn't Seth talking tonight. That was J.B. Before I went away, before my breakdown, Seth and I were very close. He was my son far more than he was ever Mark's. Seth and Mark had a good relationship, but . . . I can't let this happen. I cannot lose Seth. I will not allow J.B. to manipulate him this way."

"I wish there was something I could do to help you," Jack said.

"There isn't, but thanks. I'll deal with this in my own way and in my own time."

"Come on, you two," Lorie called. "I'll put on a fresh pot of decaf and we can eat our dessert."

Jack slipped his arm around Cathy's waist. She felt his touch in every nerve in her body. A tingling warmth spread through her, an odd mixture of excitement and contentment. Side by side, the strength of his big body comforting her, they went up the steps, onto the porch and into the house.

* * *

Jack and Deputy Willis were holding down the fort to-night, and so far, more than four hours into their eight-hour shift, things had been relatively quiet. He glanced at the wall clock. It was already three-thirty Sunday morning. The night dispatcher had taken a total of five calls, and all of them had been easily handled by the night-shift patrolmen on duty. With little to do, he'd found himself thinking about Cathy. When he had returned to Dunmore and taken the job with the sheriff's department, he'd been at loose ends, uncertain what the future held. Now, here he was back home only a few weeks and he'd hired a contractor to restore his old home and he was pursuing a girl who'd dumped him for an-other guy nearly seventeen years ago.

Well, maybe he wasn't actually pursuing Cathy, just re-newing their old friendship and seeing where it went. And to be fair, he supposed he couldn't accuse her of dumping him. He'd been the one who had left her behind when his unit had been sent to the Middle East and he'd wound up spending months as an Iraqi prisoner of war. What had he expected her to do when he'd been reported missing in action?

Just as he lifted his coffee mug to his lips, Jack heard a ruckus at the front entrance, where Deputies Gipson and Dryer were escorting a group of teenagers into the building. He set the mug down on his desk and headed toward the of-ficers and a gang of grumbling youngsters. He counted seven in all, four girls and three boys. Two of the girls were crying, and one of the boys, a redhead, looked scared to death.

"My folks are going to kill me," one of the girls whined.

"Yeah, my old man will ground me for the rest of my life," the frightened redhead said.

"Ah, shut up pissing and moaning," said a stocky boy with a long, dark ponytail.

"You shut up," a tattooed girl with jet black hair and heavy purple eye shadow told him. "You're the reason we're in this mess. You promised that nobody would know if we slipped away for a while, just to smoke and drink a few beers. We didn't know you meant smoke marijuana."

Jack called out, "What have we here?"

"A bunch of stupid kids. The ones that were reported missing, the ones the police have been looking for," Deputy Dryer replied. "They didn't think anybody would miss them when they left the youth rally over at the community center. They were wrong."

"We just happened to find them a block away in the Piggly Wiggly parking lot," Gipson said. "They had three six-packs of beer that apparently one of them had stashed there earlier, and a couple of them were smoking pot."

"Miss Dagger Tattoo and Mr. Tough Guy were the two smoking," Dryer added.

"We didn't know it was marijuana," the tattooed girl said. "I swear we didn't."

Gipson rolled his eyes. "Yeah, sure, sure."

A tall, lanky boy with brown hair turned from where he'd been shielding one of the girls with his body. When Jack got a good look at the boy, he sucked in a startled breath.

Son of a bitch. There stood Cathy's son, Seth, a nervous yet defiant expression on his face. And the girl he'd been trying to protect was none other than Brother Hovater's daughter.

Chapter Fourteen

She woke to the smell of smoke and the realization that a hand covered her mouth. Acting purely on instinct, she tried to scream, but the sound came out a muffled whimper as her eyes flew open and she looked up into her mother's face.

"Stay calm," her mother told her. "Don't panic." She eased her hand away from Ruth Ann's mouth. "Get out of bed right now. The house is on fire, and we have to hurry before we're trapped."

Sleep-groggy, she jerked into a sitting position, her mind barely comprehending what she'd been told.

Her mother grabbed her arm and yanked her out of the bed. "If we run, we can make it out through the back door. The fire started in my bedroom, but it's spreading fast." She all but dragged Ruth Ann out of her room and into the smoky hallway. "We don't have much time."

Barefoot and wearing only a cotton gown, she glanced back over her shoulder as she ran with her mother down the hall and into the kitchen. Dark, heavy smoke followed them, allowing her only a glimpse of the fire quickly consuming their house. When they reached the back door, Ruth Ann hesitated half a second. Her mother screamed at her, jogging her into immediate action. They raced down the back steps and into the yard, stopping only when they were in the driveway, both of them slightly winded.

"What about Daddy?" Ruth Ann asked.

"It's too late for your father," Faye said.

She stared into her mother's cold, dead eyes and knew the truth. *Oh God in heaven.*

"We can't just let him die, can we?" Ruth Ann grabbed her mother's hands and squeezed them tightly. "It would be murder."

Faye pulled loose from Ruth Ann's fierce grasp and focused her gaze on the burning house. "No, it's not murder. It's retribution."

She didn't say anything else, not for a long while. Not when the neighbors came out of their homes to offer them solace and to watch the parsonage burn. And not even when the fire trucks arrived, along with the police and an ambulance. The paramedics pronounced that she was in shock, but she knew better. Stunned, perhaps. Feeling horribly guilty. Afraid to speak for fear she would say the wrong thing.

Tonight, she and her mother had killed her father. This secret would bind them together forever.

Ruth Ann woke suddenly and realized she had been dreaming again, dreaming about the night her father died. Turning over, she searched in the darkness for John Earl but found his side of the bed empty. Whenever she had one of her horrific dreams, he would always comfort her. She had come to rely on his steadfast love and kindness. If God had cursed her with a monster for a father, he had equally blessed her ten times over with a husband like John Earl.

She tossed back the covers, slid out of bed and slipped on her house shoes. Looking at the bedside clock, she saw that it was after four. Where on earth was John Earl?

When she opened the bedroom door and walked into the hall, she heard the soft murmur of a voice coming from the kitchen. The girls were at the all-night youth rally at the community center, leaving only John Earl, her mother and her in the house. Since her mother took a sleeping pill every night, she assumed the voice belonged to John Earl. Undoubtedly, he was on the telephone because there was some type of emergency with a parishioner. But why hadn't she heard the phone ring? Had she been that deeply asleep?

Pausing outside the kitchen, she listened for a couple of minutes.

"Yes, I understand, and I certainly appreciate your willingness to handle things this way," John Earl said. "Ruth Ann and I will be there as soon as possible."

With her heart hammering in her chest, she entered the kitchen. "What is it? What's wrong?"

John Earl, wearing only his pajama bottoms, snapped around and stared at her, his eyes blank. He shook his head, hung up the phone and then faced her. "First of all, both Charity and Felicity are all right. But they're in a bit of trouble. Especially Felicity. We need to get dressed and go to the sheriff's office right away."

"Lord have mercy, what's happened?"

"It seems that our girls, along with several other kids, slipped away from the youth rally tonight."

"What? Why would they—?"

"I don't know the answer to that," John Earl told her as he walked over and grasped her gently by the shoulders. "A couple of deputies found the kids in the Piggly Wiggly parking lot. They had beer with them, and one of the boys and Felicity were smoking pot."

"Oh God, no!"

He gripped her shoulders a little tighter. "It's going to be all right. That was Mike Birkett on the phone. Charity called me a few minutes ago. I thought for sure the phone would wake you, but it didn't. I came in here and called Mike back immediately. He's being very understanding about the situation. He says that we can pick up both girls tonight. Charity isn't being charged with anything. And the charges against Felicity—"

"What charges? Oh God, John Earl, will she have to go to jail?"

"No. Mike told me to contact a lawyer in the morning. Felicity will have to appear in juvenile court, but more than likely the sentence will entail a fine and community service."

Tears gathered in Ruth Ann's eyes. "I've failed her as a mother, haven't I? Where did I go wrong? Charity has never given us a moment's trouble, but Felicity . . . Oh dear. The whole town will know about this by the time Sunday school starts. How will this look—the minister's daughter arrested for underage drinking and smoking marijuana?"

"I'm not concerned about how this will look." He ran his open palms down her arms and grasped her hands in his. "People will either understand or they won't. Our only concern should be Felicity."

"Yes, I know. And poor Charity. I'm sure the only reason she was involved was because she was trying to look after her sister."

"Let's get dressed." He turned her toward the stairs and slipped his arm around her waist. "Our daughters need us to present a united front. We're in agreement that Charity will need reassurance that we don't blame her for any of this. And Felicity will need our love and support, but we have to make her understand how serious the situation is."

"Yes, of course, we're in total agreement. And we will certainly present a united front."

Jack had called Mike and explained that Deputies Dryer and Gipson had brought in seven teenagers, all but two under the age of eighteen. Six of the seven had slipped away from the Christian youth rally at the community center and been reported missing by the chaperones in charge. Both the local police and sheriff's department had been looking for them when two deputies had found the kids with several six-packs. And two of the seven were smoking pot.

"The nineteen-year-old is the real culprit," Jack had said. "My guess is he provided the beer and the marijuana. I'd nail his cocky ass to the wall. The others are probably good kids who got caught in a bad situation."

Mike had grumbled a few obscenities, as much a complaint about being awakened before dawn as a judgment on the situation.

"To complicate matters even more, you personally know four of the kids."

"Shit. Just tell me."

"Cathy's son, Seth. But he wasn't drinking or smoking, according to the others. Then there's the Harper sisters, whose father is the minister at First Baptist—"

"Lorie's cousin John Earl's daughters?"

"Yep. And Melissa Hovater, whose father is the Church of Christ preacher."

"I'll be there as soon as I can. I've got to call my mom and ask her to come over to stay with the kids. Have you let all of them contact their parents?"

"I wanted to talk to you first and see if we can't work something out so we can let these kids go home with their parents and maybe not charge them. Well, except Ricky, who provided the beer and the pot. And Seth has asked if he can call his mother instead of his grandparents."

"His grandparents are his legal guardians," Mike had reminded him.

"I know, but the boy's scared to death about how his grandfather will react. I thought Cathy could—"

"Hell, we'll work it all out when I get there."

It had taken Mike thirty minutes to arrange for his mother to babysit and for him to get dressed and make it to the office. That had been twenty minutes ago, and they were still trying to "work it out."

Neal Prater's parents were the first to arrive. His mother was in tears and his burly, blustering father was cursing a blue streak until Mike spoke to him privately. He calmed down instantly. Lacey Sims's mother, a divorcee who worked the night shift at the Tyson plant, sent Lacey's aunt to the station. Aunt Bree had accused them all of harassing her niece and bringing her in on trumped-up charges. Ricky had been booked, put behind bars and was waiting for his lawyer.

When Cathy arrived, she searched the crowd, looking for Seth. Jack went to her and took her aside for a couple of minutes.

"He wasn't drinking or smoking pot," Jack said. "I don't think Mike is going to charge him with anything, but he is going to talk pretty rough to all of them. The boy who brought the beer and pot is nineteen, and he's been arrested."

"Why would Seth do something like this? He's never—"

"I think he went along to keep watch over Missy Hovater," Jack said. "I got the impression he likes her."

Cathy glanced at the teenagers huddled together across the room, Seth with his arm around Missy's shoulders. Charity Harper was wiping the black mascara-streaked tears from her sister's face.

"Did you call J.B. and Mona?" she asked.

"No," Jack said. "Mike and I aren't in agreement on this, and he may call them yet, but Seth seems genuinely terrified of how his grandfather will react."

"J.B. doesn't allow for human frailties. He demanded perfection from Mark, and he expects no less from Seth."

"You realize your lawyer could use this incident against the Cantrells," Jack told her. "If you—"

"I'd never subject Seth to the humiliation. If Mike can find a way not to charge Seth . . . I know J.B. will have to be told. But it will be easier for Seth if he can tell him himself later and not have to face his grandfather here at the sheriff's office." She laid her hand on Jack's arm. "Thank you for letting him call me. Now I need to see my son."

Just as Cathy walked toward Seth, John Earl and Ruth Ann Harper arrived. The moment she saw her parents, Felicity ran straight into her father's open arms.

"Oh, Daddy, I'm sorry," she cried. "I swear I'll never do anything this stupid again. Please don't let them put me in jail. I just took one or two little puffs. I swear, I swear."

John Earl wrapped his arms around his younger child and whispered something to her. She laid her head on his shoulder and clung to him. Quietly, Charity came over to her parents and looked from one to the other.

"I tried to stop her," Charity said. "But she listened to Lacey and Neal, and when they all left, I couldn't let her go without me. And I couldn't tell on her." She glanced back at Seth. "Seth and I didn't drink anything or smoke anything. We just went along to keep an eye on Felicity and Missy."

John Earl offered his elder daughter a weak smile. "Thank you, sweetheart, for trying to look after your sister."

Ruth Ann wrapped her arm around Charity's shoulder. "This is not your fault, and I don't want you to worry that we blame you in any way."

Felicity raised her head, pulled out of her father's embrace and faced her parents. "It's all my fault. I'm the one who talked Missy into going. I told her Neal and Lacey were going to meet up with Ricky and wouldn't it be fun if we went, too. I'm sorry. I'm such an idiot."

"You certainly acted foolishly tonight," John Earl said.

"What are they going to do to me?" Felicity asked, a note of fear in her trembling voice.

"I don't know, honey," Ruth Ann said. "You're seventeen and were caught drinking beer and smoking marijuana."

Felicity burst into tears again.

Cathy walked over to Seth where he stood beside a subdued Missy Hovater, her head bowed, her gaze fixed on the floor. When he saw his mother, Seth stared directly at her, a silent plea for understanding in his blue eyes.

"I'm sorry about this, Mom."

"Are you all right?" she asked.

He nodded.

"What about you, Missy?"

When the girl lifted her head, Cathy saw tears in her eyes and remorse in her expression.

"Seth didn't do anything wrong. He tried to convince me not to go, but I wouldn't listen to him. He just went with me to make sure . . ." Her voice broke.

Cathy could tell from the imploring look in Seth's eyes that he wanted her to comfort Missy. She laid her hand on the girl's shoulder. "We all make mistakes. You've learned a valuable lesson tonight, and we're fortunate that Sheriff Birkett is trying his best to sort through the facts and keep most of you from winding up in juvenile court."

"I wish my father would see it that way. You're being so nice, and so are Felicity and Charity's parents." Tears streamed down Missy's face.

Cathy gave her shoulder a squeeze. "I'm sure your father will be disappointed in your actions, but I have no doubt that he'll be glad things didn't turn out much worse."

A voice called out from across the room. "Where's my daughter?" All heads turned to locate the source of the booming voice.

Donnie Hovater, in rumpled dress slacks and a white T-shirt, scanned the sheriff's department.

Cathy watched the play of emotions that crossed Missy's face, and she noted something that truly bothered her: terror. Not just plain fear, which was understandable, but genuine terror. Why would this sweet girl be so horribly afraid of her father?

Donnie made his way straight to Missy, who took a deep breath, squared her shoulders and faced him. Her hands trembled. Her face went chalk white. Cathy's first instinct was to stand between the preacher and his daughter, to protect the child from her own father.

Instead, she spoke to him in a calm voice. "She's all right. And Sheriff Birkett knows that, like Jack said, she's a good kid who got caught up in a bad situation."

"How could you have done this?" Donnie demanded. "What possessed you?" He glared at Seth. "Did someone talk you into—?"

"No, Daddy." Her voice trembled. "It's my fault, not Seth's. He . . . he didn't want to leave the rally." She dropped her head and swallowed her tears. "I'm sorry. Forgive me. Please . . . oh, please."

Cathy whispered to Donnie. "Your daughter needs your understanding right now. Can't you see she's scared?"

"Yes, yes, of course. You're right." Donnie practically shoved Seth aside as he reached out and wrapped his arms around Missy's shoulders. She tensed at his touch.

Cathy thought it odd that the girl didn't immediately turn into her father's arms to seek comfort.

Mike Birkett called for everyone's attention, and the room quieted instantly. "Okay, everybody, listen up. We've taken statements from all the kids brought in by Deputies Dryer and Gipson. Ricky Baker has been arrested. He provided the beer and the marijuana. Felicity, since you admitted to both drinking and smoking pot, I'm afraid we have no choice but to charge you, but since you're only seventeen and this is your first offense, I'll personally recommend a fine and community service."

"Am I going to jail?" Felicity asked.

"No, I'll release you into your parents' custody tonight. A date will be set for you, your parents and your lawyer to appear in juvenile court."

"What about the others?" John Earl Harper asked.

"Lacey Sims and Neal Prater will also be charged, since they, too, were drinking. And they'll have to appear in juvenile court. Charity Harper, Missy Hovater and Seth Cantrell will be released to their parents tonight, and no charges will be brought against them since everyone agreed that they were not drinking or smoking pot. But I warn all three of you"—his gaze moved over each of them—"let this be a lesson to y'all not to follow the crowd. You're getting off light this time."

Donnie grabbed Missy's upper arm. "Let's go, young lady."

"Yes, Daddy."

When Seth made a move toward Missy, Cathy clutched his hand. He glared at her. She shook her head.

Cathy wanted to say something, to somehow intervene, just as her son did, but she knew the relationship between Donnie and his daughter was none of her business. She had her hands full dealing with Seth, knowing that she had no choice but to involve his grandparents.

"Are you ready to go?" she asked.

"What's Brother Hovater going to do to Missy? She was really scared about how he'd react."

"Just as you're scared about how your grandfather will react?"

"Sort of, yeah, but the way she was acting, you'd think she believed he was going to beat her or something."

"She's a girl, and girls in general usually show their emotions in a way most boys don't," Cathy explained. "She's probably worried about disappointing her father, just as you are about disappointing your grandparents."

"I disappointed you, too, didn't I, Mom?"

"You'll disappoint me only if you don't learn from this mistake."

He nodded. "Can I go home with you?"

"Of course you can. But in a few hours, I'll have to call your grandparents and explain what happened. Then you'll have to face them."

"Will you go with me and stay with me while I talk to them?"

It was all Cathy could do to stop herself from hugging Seth the way she had when he'd been a little boy and had skinned a knee or cut a finger. "Of course, I'll stay with you. As a matter of fact, I'll ask J.B. and Mona to come to my house to talk. How's that?"

He swallowed hard. "That's great, Mom. Thanks."

As she and her son reached the exit, she glanced back at Jack, who stood nearby. Her gaze locked with his, just for half a second, but long enough for her to sense his concern. She offered him a fragile smile that said "Thank you."

He marched her straight to her bedroom and shoved her facedown across her bed. She wept and pleaded, but he didn't listen, didn't care.

Please, God, help me.

"I'm sorry. I promise I'll never—"

"Make all the promises you want, but they won't change what you did tonight, how you embarrassed me. You know I have to punish you."

She sobbed uncontrollably, knowing what was about to happen. Her body tensed when he reached under her and unzipped her jeans. She held her breath when he yanked her jeans down her hips to her knees, taking her panties down with them. With her bare buttocks exposed, she braced herself for the first blow. She clutched the bedspread.

The whiz of his belt as it came through the belt loops when he removed it from his slacks echoed in the silence. The first stinging hit was usually the worst. She knew he wanted her to cry out, and if she didn't, he would only inflict more pain with each strike.

I hate him. I wish he was dead.

He whipped her repeatedly, and because she muffled her

whimpers by burying her face in the bedspread, he struck her quicker and harder with each snap of his belt.

Give him what he wants. It's the only way to make him stop.

She cried loudly and begged for mercy. He enjoyed hearing her beg. And finally, after whipping her buttocks a dozen times, leaving her flesh burning and probably bleeding, he stopped.

The worst was yet to come.

"Oh, sweetie, your poor little butt. It's all red and swollen." He ran his fingertips over the welts he'd made with his belt. "Just lie still, and I'll make it all better."

No, don't. Please, please, don't.

He ran a series of soft, light kisses over the welts on her buttocks; then his tongue glided over each.

The snap of his slacks and the zing of his zipper warned her to prepare for what always came next. First the brutal spanking whenever she displeased him, and then . . .

With her face buried in the bedspread, her sore buttocks exposed, he lifted her up and yanked her to the edge of the bed. And then he probed inside her with his fingers, raking his thumb over her clitoris until her body softened despite her hatred of him and what he was doing to her.

She squeezed her eyes shut tightly and tried not to think about what was happening as he thrust inside her, deep and hard.

Chapter Fifteen

Seth had nibbled at the eggs and bacon Cathy had prepared for him. He looked as haggard and weary as she felt. Neither of them was looking forward to the upcoming confrontation with J.B. and Mona. Since they had been expecting Seth to return to their house sometime shortly after the all-night youth rally ended at eight this morning, she had telephoned them at seven-thirty. Keeping the facts to a minimum, she'd told Mona, who had answered the phone, that Seth was at her house, that he and some other teens had gotten into a bit of trouble last night and they needed to discuss the problem.

"There they are." Seth, who had been standing at the window waiting for his grandparents, turned to Cathy and grimaced. "Grandmother's with them."

Cathy groaned. She should have known that Mona would call Elaine and Seth's three grandparents would show up together. She sensed that in this situation, it was Seth and her against the world.

When the doorbell rang, Seth looked at her. "Mom?"

"You stay here. I'll let them in." She paused, glanced back

at her son and added, "It's going to be all right. We'll face them together. Just remember, they love you."

When she opened the door, her mother entered first and gave her a condemning glare. She refused to react in a defensive manner. Her mother couldn't intimidate her anymore. How often had she wondered if her father, who had died in an auto accident when she was twelve, had left them because he could no longer endure trying to live up to Elaine's impossible standards? Her parents had been separated for more than two years when Whit Nelson had died. What she remembered most about her dad was his loud, robust laugh.

Mona came in next, a sad half-smile curving her lips and a sympathetic expression in her eyes. She reached over and gave Cathy a quick hug before walking into the living room. By the time J.B. entered the house, both grandmothers were flanking Seth, who looked like a condemned man on his way to the gallows.

"You'd better have a good reason for this," J.B. said in a deep, gruff voice as he gave Cathy a stern, disapproving stare.

Ignoring J.B., Cathy turned to the others and said, "Why don't we all sit down. This is going to take a while."

Fifteen minutes later, after Seth had told them exactly what happened, without telling them that he had left the rally only to keep watch over Missy Hovater, the room fell into complete silence. All eyes turned to J.B., waiting for his judgment call.

God, how Cathy hated that her son had to endure having his grandfather act as his judge, jury and executioner. If only Mark were here to act as a buffer. Mark had respected J.B., but at the same time, he had, on occasion, stood up to him. He had certainly gone against J.B.'s wishes when he had married her.

"I'm very disappointed in you, Seth," J.B. said, his voice deceptively calm.

"Yes, sir, I understand."

"Do you, son?" J.B. focused directly on Seth. "There will be consequences. Except for church and your sports activities, you're grounded for the rest of the summer."

Seth stood straight as an arrow, his expression solemn as he nodded his head in agreement, taking his punishment like a man.

"And today, at church services, when Brother Hovater calls for sinners to repent, I expect you to go before the congregation and—"

"No," Cathy said adamantly. "Seth didn't commit a sin. It's ridiculous for you to expect him to stand up in front of the entire church and confess to something he didn't do."

"He disobeyed the rules. He violated my trust." J.B. glanced at Mona and Elaine. "Our trust. He shamed us and himself by his actions."

"He made a mistake," Cathy said. "He's not perfect. You can't expect him to never make a mistake."

"I expect him to live up to the high moral standards I've set for him, the same standards Mark would have set for him."

"If Mark were here, he would never ask Seth to—"

"How dare you presume to tell me what my son would and would not do," J.B. said, anger in his voice.

"And how dare you presume to make yourself the sole decision maker when it comes to my son," Cathy retaliated.

"Please, J.B." Mona laid her hand on her husband's arm. "Cathy, dear, this arguing isn't good."

J.B. jerked his arm away from his wife's gentle grasp and aimed his hard gaze at Seth. "You'll do as I say. Your mother has no authority over you whatsoever, legal or otherwise." He turned to Cathy. "Seth is leaving with us now. And if you try to interfere, I'll contact the police. Mona and I are Seth's legal guardians, not you."

Cathy had difficulty restraining herself from lunging at

J.B., claws out and teeth bared in defense of her child. But there was a better way to deal with this issue.

"You're right," Cathy said. "But I intend to reclaim my son. I had hoped we could come to some sort of agreement, but I know that's impossible. I've hired Elliott Floyd as my attorney, and I will take you to court if necessary. My days of rolling over and playing dead for you, J.B."—she glanced at her mother—"or anyone else are over." She looked back at her father-in-law. "Seth is my son. Today you may be able to force him to obey you, but that is going to change. And soon."

Seth had remained completely quiet during the entire exchange between her and J.B. She looked at him and smiled. He didn't return her smile, but she noted a hint of relief in his eyes.

"We're leaving." J.B. issued the decree and motioned to his wife.

Mona held her head down as she passed Cathy and followed J.B. to the front door. With her mouth puckered tightly, Elaine frowned and shook her head, her actions silently telling Cathy of her displeasure. Seth paused in front of Cathy, but didn't say anything.

She caressed his cheek. "I'll be at church today."

He leaned over and whispered, "I'll go talk to Mr. Floyd whenever you say." Then he hurried out the front door and caught up with his grandparents on the porch.

Bruce Kelley helped his wife dress. She had chosen a blue linen suit. He watched her while she struggled to hook her bra and then finally offered to help.

"Silly me, I'm all thumbs this morning." When she laughed, she sounded like herself, the Sandie he had known and loved most of his adult life.

If he could suffer this disease for her, he would; but then

if it were he and not she that had been afflicted, she would be the one condemned to watch the person she loved die by slow, pathetic degrees. They were both victims.

In the past, he had never understood how someone could choose to end their spouse's life when that lifelong partner was suffering unbearably. He'd been such a pompous fool. Arrogant. So smug in his safe, happy life. He had judged others so harshly, never once considering the love and sacrifice made by those poor spouses who could no longer bear to see their loved one suffer.

If not for his deep faith in God, in the Savior's benevolence, in a great plan for all mankind, Bruce wasn't sure he would have the strength to see this thing through to the end. Sandie still had good days, and even on the bad days she still had good hours. The worst was yet to come. But he was not in this hell on earth alone, as many were. He and Sandie had three fine children, all willing to do whatever was necessary to help him. But the last thing his sweet Sandie would ever want was to be a burden on anyone, least of all her children.

"I should wear my pearls with this outfit," Sandie said as she looked at herself in the vanity mirror. "But I can't seem to remember where my pearls are. Don't I have a jewelry chest?"

Bruce came up behind her and placed his hands lovingly on her shoulders. She glanced up at him from where she sat on the vanity stool and smiled at him.

Dear Lord, how he loved her smile.

There would come a day in the near future when she would no longer smile when she saw him, a time when she would not know who he was. Would he be able to bear it?

"Your jewelry box is in the closet," he reminded her. "You stay put, and I'll get your pearls."

"Thank you, darling."

Just as he walked away and headed toward the walk-in closet, she called to him, "Bruce, are the children ready for church? I can't remember if I packed everything in the diaper bag that little Kevin will need. He was so fretful last night. I'm afraid he's cutting a new tooth."

Bruce stopped dead still. His heartbeat accelerated. He closed his eyes and prayed for strength and courage. And the ability to see Sandie through to the end, no matter how long and difficult the path might be. She had no idea that her mind had wandered back more than thirty years to when their now-adult son had been an infant. This was not the first time it had happened, and heaven help them both, it would not be the last.

Faye Long stared at her reflection in the cheval mirror. She looked like an old woman, far older than her fifty-eight years. Guilt and regret weighed heavily on her shoulders. And fear.

Thirty-nine years ago, when she had married Charles Long, she had been a beautiful, desirable young woman. She could have had her pick from dozens of men, but she had chosen the man she believed worshipped the ground she walked on, the man who would be a good husband and father to their future children. Charles had been a handsome, dashing, charismatic young minister, and she had fallen under his hypnotic spell, never questioning what lay beneath the alluring façade he presented to the world.

She had made a horrible mistake by marrying him, and she had paid dearly for her stupidity. And she was still paying, as was her daughter and her granddaughters.

If only she could go back and redo her life, go back to the first time she met her future husband. She would run as far and as fast from Charles Long as she possibly could.

When Ruth Ann and John Earl had returned home a little after six o'clock this morning, with both Charity and Felicity in tow, she had known something was wrong. When she had gone to the kitchen earlier this morning at five-thirty, she had found Ruth Ann's note.

*John Earl and I have gone to pick up the girls.
There's been a slight problem. I'll call you if we aren't
home in a few hours.—Ruthie*

Ruthie. Her only child.

The spawn of the devil.

God, how she hated to think of her daughter in such a
way. Ruth Ann could no more help who her father was than
she could help the horrible things he had done to her. The
things he had done to both of them.

She often wondered what would have happened to the
two of them that night after fire had consumed their home
and killed her husband if it had not been for John Earl. At
the time, he and Ruth Ann had been dating for nearly a year,
and she'd known how much he loved her daughter. He was
such a good man, and she thanked the Lord every day that
both of her granddaughters were growing up in a home filled
with love and goodness.

But a shadow of evil hovered over all of them. Charles
Long's evil. Even now, after all these years, Ruth Ann still
had nightmares. And the emotional scars left by her father's
cruelty had created an emptiness inside Ruth Ann that af-
fected her relationship with both of her daughters.

No doubt Felicity and Charity's unfortunate escapade
would be the talk of the town by the time church services
began today. Poor John Earl. What an embarrassment for him.

But they would all hold their heads high this morning
when they arrived at church. Let the busybodies talk. No one
except she, Ruth Ann and John Earl knew that her granddaughters were predisposed to wickedness, that they had inherited a weakness for evil from Charles Long.

As soon as her mother and in-laws took Seth away, Cathy
knew what she had to do today. She could waste her time

crying and bemoaning the fact that J.B. and Mona had custody of her son. Or she could get ready, go to church and be there for the most humiliating moment of Seth's young life.

She showered, washed and dried her hair, chose one of two new outfits she had recently purchased on a shopping trip with Lorie and unpacked her makeup case. Only moments after she added the last touches—blush to her cheeks and a peach gloss to her lips—the doorbell rang.

Maybe it was Lorie, but she doubted it. She had phoned her best friend and filled her in on what had happened, everything she knew about Seth's misadventures and her confrontation with J.B. Lorie had offered to go to church with her this morning, but she'd assured her that it wasn't necessary.

"I know how much you'd hate it," Cathy had said. "You haven't been inside a church for worship services since you moved back to Dunmore."

"I'd do it for you."

"I'll be okay, and so will Seth, so don't worry too much. I have a feeling that God's on my side."

When she reached the front door, Cathy peeked through the viewfinder and gasped when she saw Jackson Perdue standing on her porch.

She opened the door. "Well, hello. What are you doing here?" She surveyed him from his neatly combed hair to his polished dress shoes. He wore khaki slacks, a white shirt without a tie and a blue blazer.

"I thought I'd go to church with you today," he said.

"Lorie called you, didn't she?"

"Yeah. She . . . uh . . . she thought you might need a little backup this morning."

"You don't have to do this, you know. I mean, it's not as if you and I . . . That is, this is my problem. Not yours. You—"

He gently shoved her backward into the house. With the front door still partially open, he cupped her face in his hands. Startled by his actions, she hushed immediately and stared up into his blue, blue eyes.

"Let's not analyze our relationship," he said. "There's been a lot of muddy water under the bridge. So, how about this—I'm here as a substitute for Lorie. She thinks you need a friend at your side this morning, and I agree."

"She thinks I need a keeper, doesn't she? She's concerned about what I might say or do without someone there to rein me in."

"Look, I wasn't around when you unraveled at the seams last year, so I don't actually know how bad it was for you. But having been there myself, I can imagine. Don't blame Lorie if she's worried about you."

"I don't blame her. I don't blame anyone for waiting to see if or when the crazy lady will go bonkers again. But that's not going to happen. I won't let it."

"Good for you." He looked her over. "Now get your purse and let's go. I believe Lorie said early morning services begin at nine, right?"

Cathy knew when to give in gracefully. Jack wasn't going to back down, and in all honesty, she didn't want him to. For more reasons than she dared admit, she not only wanted Jack at her side this morning, she needed him.

Cathy and Jack walked into the church three minutes before services began. They could have sat at the back, but when she saw Seth sitting in the front row beside J.B., she knew what to do. Jack didn't hesitate when she marched up the red-carpeted aisle and found a half-empty pew directly behind her son.

She and Jack got a lot of curious stares, which took the people's minds momentarily off the rumors that were no doubt circulating about Seth, Missy and the other teenagers who had been hauled into the sheriff's office before daylight this morning. Let them talk about her. She'd been fodder for the Dunmore gossip mill since the day Mark was murdered.

Poor Cathy, losing her husband so tragically.

Poor Cathy, having to raise her teenage son all alone.

Poor Cathy. You heard about her nervous breakdown, didn't you? She went completely off her rocker and wound up spending a year at Haven Home.

As soon as she sat, she leaned forward and placed her hand on Seth's shoulder. Startled by her touch, he jerked around and looked at her. His mouth formed the word *Thanks*. She smiled and patted his shoulder. Just as Seth glanced at Jack, J.B. turned around and glowered at Cathy. Seth looked back and forth from her to Jack and then turned around just as the song leader called out the number for the first hymn.

This church service was not going to be easy for any of them, but it would be pure torture for Seth. If only she could spare him from being on public display. If Mark were here . . . But he wasn't. Mark was dead. Seth had no one but her to protect him.

Jack reached between them and took Cathy's hand in his.

Was this a sign from God? Was the Almighty trying to tell her that she wasn't all alone?

Chapter Sixteen

Cathy had grown up attending church services every time the doors opened. Sunday school, Sunday morning services, Sunday night services, Wednesday night services, vacation Bible school and week-long gospel meetings. No one who knew Cathy's mother could say Elaine wasn't a devout Christian, but her single-minded obsession with religion bordered on fanaticism. To Elaine Nelson, anything that was too much fun, too enjoyable, had to be a sin. But by the time she was a preteen, Cathy had realized most members of their small Church of Christ in Dunmore were not fanatics but simply good people trying to live the best life they knew how by following the teachings of Jesus. As a teenager, she had become exposed to other Protestant religions through her school friends and learned that there were indeed people like her mother in all the various denominations.

At seventeen, she had begun feeling trapped by her mother's restrictions, so when home-on-leave Jackson Perdue had noticed her, she had been ripe for the picking. She didn't blame Jack, at least not now, and hadn't for a long time. He'd been twenty, almost twenty-one, and more than three years her senior, but a dozen years older in experience.

His bad-boy persona had intrigued her. He'd been moody and intense and drop-dead gorgeous. What teenage girl could have resisted him? She had fallen madly in love with him during their two-week whirlwind romance. And with dreams of happily ever after in her head, she hadn't hesitated to have sex with him.

Suddenly, when everyone in the congregation stood to sing and Jack tugged on her hand, Cathy snapped back from the past to the present, realizing that she hadn't heard one word of the last few minutes of Brother Hovater's sermon. The hymn was an invitation to sinners, both members and nonmembers alike. Members could come forward and ask forgiveness for their sins. Those who had not been baptized into the Church of Christ faith could confess their past sins, proclaim their belief in Jesus as the Son of God and be baptized. This plea to sinners was part of every church service.

Halfway through the chorus, Seth rose to his feet and stepped forward, extending his hand to Donnie Hovater. Missy, who had been sitting several rows behind them, also came forward and placed her hand in her father's. Both teenagers' movements were stiff, as if they were robots, their actions programmed into them.

"Please be seated." Donnie raised and then lowered his hands, emphasizing his instructions to the congregation.

He then took the two teenagers aside and spoke to each of them quietly, their conversations entirely private. Then he guided Seth and Missy to the front bench, where the song leader scooted down to make room for them. As soon as Seth and Missy were seated, Donnie faced the audience.

"Two of our beloved young people have come forward today asking for the Lord's forgiveness and mercy," Donnie said, his tone soft and filled with sympathy. "They were led astray by others and found themselves in bad company. They both deeply regret having made an error in judgment that has caused pain and embarrassment to their families." He bowed his head. "Pray with us as we seek God's loving goodness and ask Him to forgive Missy Hovater and Seth Cantrell and guide them in the paths of righteousness from this day forward."

The congregation hummed with whispers and a few louder comments ranging from "Bless them" to "Amen."

Tears threatened to choke Cathy. How many times had her heart bled for people who came forward during this phase of a church service to confess to some minor indiscretion that could hardly be called a sin. Not unless you considered everything that wasn't pure and holy a sin. Apparently, many people did. There had been a time, long ago, when she'd been a child, that she had lived in fear of not being good enough, worthy enough, of dying and going to hell. And even though she had been a minister's wife for more than fourteen years before Mark's death, she had done her best to raise Seth within the framework of a religion that was based on God's love and goodness and not on fear.

Just as she had been a product of her upbringing, so had Mark, but he had managed to become his own man despite his father's iron-fisted approach to fatherhood. And although he had often agreed with J.B.'s strict dogma, more times than not, he had disagreed. Mark had been far more his mother's son than his father's, for which Cathy had been exceedingly thankful.

The Sunday morning service ended with another hymn and a final prayer by one of the young deacons. J.B. headed straight for Seth, a satisfied expression on his face. Cathy didn't think she had ever despised her father-in-law more than she did at that very moment.

She leaned over and whispered to Jack, "I need to talk to Seth."

"I'll wait for you in the car." He glanced around at the horde of parishioners as if they were alien beings. Unless Jack had changed over the years, he was not a religious man.

"Okay." She squeezed his hand. "Thank you."

He grinned, then turned and walked away, doing his best

to avoid speaking to anyone on his rush up the aisle toward the vestibule.

Cathy smiled, nodded, and even shook hands with several people as she made her way to Seth. By the time she approached her son, Mona and Elaine had joined J.B., and the threesome surrounded him, providing a buffer between her and Seth.

Mona glanced at her, a plea for peace in her eyes. "Good morning, Cathy."

"Good morning. I'd like to speak to Seth privately, please."

"Say whatever you have to say to him in front of us," J.B. told her.

Seth stood tall and straight as he fixed his gaze on her. "Thanks for being here this morning, Mom."

"Where else would I be?" She totally ignored J.B. as she wedged herself between Mona and her mother so that she could touch her son. She put her hand on his shoulder. "I'd like for you to come to lunch with Jack and Lorie and me. We're going to the Cedar Hill Grill. You love their homemade yeast rolls and their chocolate pecan pie."

"Seth is going home with his grandmothers and me," J.B. said, his tone brooking no argument.

Cathy looked J.B. square in the eye. "Seth is old enough to think for himself. You can't force him to become a clone of Mark or, God forbid, a clone of you. He is his own person—"

"He thought for himself last night," J.B. told her. "And you see what happened. I think you need to remember that you no longer have any rights where Seth is concerned."

"I'm his mother!"

"You are an unfit mother."

Damn him!

Mona gasped.

"Mom is not an unfit mother," Seth said. "You shouldn't say such things about her."

J.B. snapped his head around and looked at Seth as if he'd

never seen his grandson before that moment. "You know better than to be disrespectful to me. That smart-mouth attitude is her doing, and I'll have none of it. Do you hear me, young man?"

Donnie Hovater hurried toward them, leaving his handshaking duties behind as he called to them, "Please, lower your voices. Remember you're in the Lord's house."

J.B. stiffened. "I apologize, Brother Donnie. I'm afraid I let my concern for my grandson—"

"We should go home, J.B." Mona curled her fingers around his forearm. "People are staring at us."

He nodded, then reached out and clutched Seth's wrist. "We're leaving. Now."

"I'm going with Mom," Seth said. "I'll be home later this afternoon."

"No, you will not go with her," J.B. said. "I forbid you to leave here with her."

"Perhaps we can reach a compromise." Donnie looked directly at J.B. "With your permission, Brother Cantrell, I'd like to invite Cathy and Seth to have lunch with Missy and me today, and then afterward I'll bring Seth home."

J.B. huffed loudly. Mona tightened her grip on his arm.

"That sounds like a perfectly reasonable idea, don't you think?" Mona's gaze begged her husband to agree.

"Very well," J.B. acquiesced reluctantly. "I'm entrusting him into your care, Brother Donnie." Without another word, J.B. marched off, leaving Mona and Elaine standing there. Both women forced halfhearted smiles.

"Thank you for acting as a mediator in this situation." Mona sighed heavily as she looked at Donnie.

Elaine grasped Cathy's upper arm, leaned over and hissed, "Keep this up and you'll lose Seth forever. Is that what you want?"

Acting as if she hadn't heard her mother's warning, Cathy turned to Seth. "I'd thought we might have lunch with Jack and Lorie, but I'm sure they'll understand why I'll have to cancel on them. I need to find Jack and tell him—"

"Why'd he come to church with you today?" Seth asked.

"He came with me as a friend, for moral support."

"Are we ready to go?" Donnie asked.

"Yes," Cathy replied. "I just need a few minutes to speak to Jack. He's waiting outside for me.

"Yes, by all means," Donnie said. "We'll meet you at my car. It's the silver Chevy Tahoe."

Cathy found Jack propped against the hood of his black 1999 Corvette, his arms crossed over his wide chest. When he saw her, he stood up straight and grinned.

"Ready for some of Cedar Hill's homemade yeast rolls?" he asked.

"I'm afraid there's been a change in plans," Cathy said, then went on to explain the situation. "I'm really sorry, but—"

"You don't need to explain," Jack told her. "Your son comes first. Besides, it's not like this is our only chance to have Sunday dinner together."

She stood on tiptoe and kissed his cheek. "Thank you."

"For what?"

"For coming to church with me today and for understanding about lunch."

"Stick to your guns, honey. Don't let anybody talk you out of fighting for your kid."

"J.B. Cantrell is a real son of a bitch," Lorie said.

Jack stared into his dessert plate, his thoughts a million miles away. Well, not quite a million miles, just a few miles away to wherever Cathy was. Whatever decisions she made about her life, especially those involving her son, were none of his business. He had no claims on her, despite their past.

What past? They had spent all of two weeks together,

sneaking around day and night, using Mike as a front so that Cathy's mother wouldn't figure out she was dating the town's former bad boy. So what if they'd thought they were in love? She'd been a starry-eyed seventeen-year-old and he'd been her first lover. And he'd been a horny, hungry-for-affection young man facing an uncertain future half a world away.

"Earth to Jackson Perdue." Lorie reached across the table and tapped him in the center of his chest.

"Yeah, what?" He stared at her.

"I said that J.B. Cantrell is a real son of a bitch."

Jack grunted. "Yeah, he is."

She studied Jack closely, a frown marring her smooth forehead. "Want to tell me what's going on with you? You show up in town for the first time in years. You move back, into a house you hated. You take a job that you're probably both unqualified and overqualified for, and you insert yourself into Cathy's life again at a time when the last thing she needs is another complication."

"Is that what I am to Cathy, a complication?"

Lorie drew in a deep breath, not answering immediately, and then she replied by turning his own question back on him. "Exactly what is Cathy to you?"

"An old friend."

Lorie snorted. "You and Cathy were never anything as simple as friends. You two were crazy about each other, couldn't keep your hands off each other."

"Yeah, sure, for two whole weeks."

"You left her, remember?"

"I was in the army. I had no choice. I thought she'd wait for me."

"She did."

"Not for long."

"You were reported missing in action, possibly a POW or worse—maybe dead."

"Yeah, and how long after that did she marry Mark Cantrell—a couple of months?"

Lorie shook her head, her thick, reddish-brown hair bouncing on her shoulders. "If you're pursuing her now in order to get some sort of revenge for—"

Jack laughed. "I haven't spent all these years pining away for Cathy any more than she has for me. Yeah, when I got out of the prison camp and came back to the U.S. and found out she'd married somebody else, I felt pretty raw about it. But that was a long time ago. Cathy and I are practically strangers now."

"Strangers who are still attracted to each other," Lorie said. "And I'm not saying that you wouldn't be good for each other. But I'm warning you—Cathy is the best friend I've ever had, and if you hurt her, I'll rip your head off."

Grinning, Jack reached over and took Lorie's hand. "She's lucky to have a friend who cares so much about her."

"I'm the lucky one. When I came back to Dunmore nine years ago, with my tail tucked between my legs, it didn't take me long to realize I was the town pariah. Even my own parents wouldn't give me the time of day. But Cathy reached out to me. She went against everyone, including her husband, to offer me her friendship. She was the only person in town who was willing to give me a second chance."

"What sort of man was Mark Cantrell?" Jack released Lorie's hand.

"He was basically a good man, considering the fact he was a preacher. And you should know that my opinion of clergymen in general is that half of them are sanctimonious hypocrites. Mark wasn't."

Frowning, Jack nodded.

"Not what you wanted to hear, huh?" Lorie said.

"Actually, I'm glad he was a good man. Cathy deserved somebody a lot better than me. I was pretty messed up back then." He let out a chest-deep chuckle. "Hell, I'm still messed up, but getting a little better every day."

"Mark was eight years older than Cathy and a lot more settled than guys her age. He'd been married before and lost his first wife. He was ready to get married again and to start a family. And that's what Cathy wanted."

"So she had a good life. She was happy."

Lorie grabbed Jack's hand and squeezed. "Yes, she had a good life. She was content. But . . ." She released his hand and leaned back away from him. "Damn, I shouldn't say this." She paused for a moment. "Cathy never forgot you."

Lorie's words hit him like a sledgehammer in the gut, knocking the air out of him. He sat there stunned and speechless for several seconds. But before he could react further, he felt a hand clamp down over his shoulder.

"Afternoon, Deputy," Mike Birkett said. "Is the blackberry cobbler good today?"

Jack scooted back his chair, stood and shook hands with his boss.

"Mama, you remember Jackson Perdue, don't you?" Mike said to the plump, silver-haired woman standing to his right.

"Sure do. How are you, Jack?" Nell Birkett smiled at him, and then she glanced past him at Lorie. Her smile vanished.

"Hello, Mrs. Birkett," Lorie said.

Nell hesitated before replying. "Hello, Lorie."

A rambunctious little boy with freckles and a stock of thick auburn hair tugged on his father's hand, and a shy, slender girl who was Mike's spitting image, dark hair, eyes and complexion, peeped out from where she stood behind him.

"Kids, I'd like y'all to meet Mr. Perdue." Mike pulled both kids in front of him. "This is M.J."—he ruffled his son's hair—"and this is Hannah."

"Hi." M.J. grinned.

"Hello, Mr. Perdue." Hannah smiled at Jack, and then glanced past him to Lorie. "Oh, hello, Miss Lorie."

Seeing Lorie, M.J. ran over to her. "You look mighty pretty today."

"Thank you, M.J." Lorie smiled at the boy and then glanced up at Mike.

"You two go on with your grandmother over to our table," Mike said. "I'll be there in a few minutes."

"But Daddy, we want to introduce you to Miss Lorie," Hannah said.

"Miss Lorie and I have been introduced." Mike bit out the words through partially clenched teeth. "Now go order dinner. I'll be right on over."

Nell grabbed both children's hands and hurried them away, but not before she glanced at Lorie, a rather sad look in her eyes.

"How is it that my kids know you?" Mike demanded, his cheeks slightly flushed.

Jack started to intervene, but thought better of it. Lorie wouldn't thank him for coming to her rescue. He sat back down, picked up his spoon and dipped into his cobbler.

"I've seen them at the interfaith socials a few times. Patsy Floyd has become a good friend, and she talked me into coming along with her to the monthly get-togethers."

"From now on, stay away from my kids."

"Why? You don't honestly think that my wickedness"— she held up her hands and shook them in a boogie-boo gesture—"will rub off on them, do you?"

Mike leaned down so that they were face-to-face and said in a calm yet harsh voice, "If you're using my kids to get back into my life, forget it. I'm not interested, and I never will be."

He turned and stomped off, leaving Lorie sitting there quietly, her face ashen and a sheen of moisture in her eyes.

"Are you all right?" Jack asked.

She nodded.

"Want to leave?"

She swallowed. "No. Finish your dessert."

"Mike was pretty rough on you. It's not like him to—"

"I hurt him something awful," she said. "Not just when I broke our engagement and went off to Hollywood thinking I'd become a big star, but . . ." She closed her eyes and rubbed her forehead, then looked up at Jack. "Mike's seen the spread I did for *Playboy* and that one porn movie I made, and he knows that three-fourths of the men in Dunmore have seen them, too. That's not something a man can forget or forgive."

Jack didn't know how to respond. He wanted to tell her that she was wrong, that given time, Mike would come around, that he would at least forgive her. But how could he tell her something he didn't believe? He had no idea how he'd feel if he were in Mike's place. He had to admit that in many ways modern man was as savage as his ancient counterpart and lived by the same double standard that his male ancestors had.

Erin McKinley always came away from the Sunday morning service feeling uplifted and inspired by John Earl's sermon. He possessed the unique ability to charm and to condemn, practically in the same breath. He taught the Word of God with enthusiasm, but with compassion and genuine understanding of human nature. Of all the ministers she had known during her life, even the ones she had loved with her whole heart, none of them compared to John Earl Harper. He was, without a doubt, her one true love. Unfortunately, he was completely in love with his wife.

Erin's first lover had been the youth minister at the Baptist church she attended as a teenager. She'd been fifteen and he twenty-five. When she had gotten pregnant, her lover had suddenly disappeared, supposedly going overseas somewhere on mission work. She had planned to give her child up for adoption but had miscarried in her fourth month.

At twenty-three, she had taken a job as the secretary for a large church in Athens. The minister had been a handsome, charming, silver-haired devil, and she'd fallen madly in love with him. Reverend Lester Yarbrough had been good to her, treating her with the utmost respect, and never once made any advances. But when his wife of twenty years and one of the church's deacons ran away together, she had seen her chance and taken it. Her affair with Lester had lasted six months, until his teenage son, Clay, had walked in on them while she was giving Lester a blow job.

There had been a few others, but none that she'd loved with all her heart. A couple of ministers, one church elder, two deacons and one church musical director. But now her heart belonged solely to John Earl—her heart but not her body. She would lie down and die for him. She would become his secret mistress. She would do anything he asked of her. But he saw her only as his secretary, only as one of his parishioners, only as a family friend.

Erin parked her Honda Civic in front of her duplex apartment, got out and rummaged in her shoulder bag for her house key. When she reached the front door, she noticed that it stood partially ajar. The door had not been jimmied, and the glass panes had not been broken. That meant only one thing—someone had unlocked the door. Only she and one other person had a key.

Smiling with anticipation, Erin eased open the door and walked into her apartment. After closing and locking the door, she tossed her purse onto the sofa as she made her way toward the bedroom. Lying there buck naked in the middle of her bed, Clay Yarbrough grinned at her as she stood over him, hands on her hips and a smirk on her face.

"What are you doing here?" she asked.

"What does it look like?" He thrust his hips up to show off his erection. "I figured after getting all hot and bothered over Reverend Harper at church this morning, you might need a good fucking. And if there's one thing I'm good at, it's playing substitute stud for Baptist preachers."

Without saying another word, Erin kicked off her shoes, unzipped her dress, removed it and tossed it on the floor. After easing off her pantyhose and stripping out of her bikini panties and bra, she crawled onto the bed and straddled Clay.

Gazing down into his rugged face, she said, "I'm actually very fond of you, you know."

Clay laughed. "Honey, you're fond of this." He grabbed his penis and rubbed it up and down between her feminine lips. "And I don't mind your calling me Lester or John Earl or whoever happens to be the minister of the month, just as long as I'm the guy who's screwing your brains out."

"Shut up, darling." She gently clutched his penis and inserted it into her body, then slid down over it, taking him completely inside her. "Make love to me." She closed her eyes and sighed. *Make love to me, John Earl. John Earl . . .*

"It would be my pleasure, my sweet Erin." He grasped her hips in his rough hands and set the rhythm for their frenzied mating. "Fuck me, baby. Come on. Give your John Earl a good fucking."

She went wild, clawing and scratching, moaning and screaming until she climaxed. While she melted around him, he flipped her over on her back and lunged deeper and harder until he came.

Ten minutes later, Clay was gone. He had dumped his condom in the bathroom wastepaper basket, washed, put on his clothes, kissed her on the forehead and left.

Erin lay there, naked, her body slightly bruised and completely sated in a physical way. But emotionally, she felt empty. For a few glorious minutes, she had been able to pretend the man giving her pleasure was John Earl, just as, years ago, after Clay's father had ended their affair, she had been able to pretend the seventeen-year-old Clay had been Lester.

She was alone, so alone. When she loved, she loved completely. She gave her all and got so little in return. As much as she had loved the men in her life, she had also hated them.

Why couldn't John Earl look at her just once and see her for who she was? His soul mate. The woman meant to be his wife.

No, she wasn't perfect. She wasn't without sin. But then neither was he. For all his goodness, John Earl was as human as all clergymen were. He made mistakes. He sinned. And he, like all others, would one day be rewarded for his goodness and punished for his sins.

Erin curled into a fetal ball and wept.

Chapter Seventeen

Seth had left Sunday night services with his grandparents, and Missy had gone home with a girlfriend, the daughter of a church deacon, for a sleepover. Since Cathy had spent the day with Donnie, Missy and Seth, she didn't have a way home tonight and had gladly accepted Donnie's offer to escort her. Otherwise she would have been forced to either walk or allow her mother to drive her home.

The day that had begun so badly had actually ended on a positive note. A couple of hours before Sunday night services, Donnie had persuaded Cathy to go with him to talk to J.B. and Mona. She had agreed reluctantly, but much to her surprise, the visit had gone much better than she had anticipated.

"I believe you're a miracle worker," Cathy told Donnie.

When he smiled, shallow dimples appeared in his round cheeks. He was an attractive man in a cute, boyish way. He was one of those people who would look the same at sixty as he had at six, simply older. But what his face lacked in strength and maturity, it made up for in a gentle attractiveness.

Donnie turned to her there in the semidarkness inside his car and smiled. "You give me too much credit. All I did was intervene between the two of you. I reminded Brother Cantrell that in his zeal to protect Seth, he cannot forget that you are Seth's mother and you love him."

"And you reminded me that even if I disagree with J.B., which I do, that I owe him and Mona a debt of gratitude for taking good care of Seth while I was ill."

Donnie spread his arm across the back of Cathy's seat and leaned toward her, his gaze connecting with hers. "We made progress this afternoon when we stopped by the Cantrells. You showed Seth that you're willing to meet his grandfather halfway, that you and J.B. don't have to be enemies."

"I hate the thought of making Seth choose between his grandparents and me," Cathy said. "But I felt that J.B. was giving me no choice but to take them to court to regain custody."

"And now?"

"Now, thanks to you, I'm willing to wait a little while longer in the hopes that J.B. will see reason and I won't have to take drastic measures."

"It could take weeks, even months," Donnie told her. "You must be patient. I'll talk to J.B. again."

"In the meantime, I want Seth to be able to spend the night at my home whenever he wants to while we're trying to settle this problem out of court."

"Why don't you let me continue talking to J.B.? I can suggest that he allow Seth to join you and Missy and me for dinner and a movie this Friday night. And if he's in agreement, I'll see if he'll consider allowing Seth to spend the night with you."

Cathy's heart soared with hope. This morning, she had been certain that she had no other alternative than to take her in-laws to court. But tonight, she thought there was a possibility that J.B. might eventually see reason. She was willing to wait, just not forever. Seth had all but said that he had changed his mind and wanted to live with her, but he'd been adamant about not wanting to hurt his grandparents.

"I'm all Nana and Granddad have now that Dad's gone," Seth had said.

"You're all I have, too," she'd reminded him.

"I know, Mom, but you're young, and you'll probably get married again and have more kids."

Surprised by his comment, she had questioned his reasoning. She knew, before he confirmed her suspicions, that he had simply repeated exactly what J.B. had said about her.

Donnie cleared his throat, which immediately drew her back into the present moment. She smiled at him. He looked at her longingly, as if he wanted to kiss her. All she had to do was respond. But did she want him to kiss her? She was sure the experience would be pleasant, but in all honesty, she wasn't attracted to him in a sexual, man-woman way. How could she tell him without hurting his feelings, which she would never do, not for anything in the world. If he kissed her . . .

Suddenly he moved back and away from her. He cleared his throat again. "I should walk you to your door and then go home. I need a good night's rest tonight. I'm working all day tomorrow at the community food bank, from seven in the morning until six in the evening."

"I appreciate the ride home, but you don't have to walk me to the door."

"Of course I do. What kind of Southern gentleman would I be if I didn't escort you safely to your front door?"

They both laughed.

By the time Cathy opened the car door and stepped out onto the driveway, Donnie was there with his hand extended. She took his soft hand and smiled when he clasped hers tenderly.

There was something about Donnie that reminded her of Mark. Not so much his physical appearance as his demeanor. He seemed to possess a similar easygoing charm and sweet gentleness. And he was a minister of the gospel, a man dedicating his life to helping others. If she were dating

Donnie, her in-laws and mother would approve. But if she encouraged a relationship with him, it would be for all the wrong reasons.

He waited with her on the porch while she unlocked the front door. Then, when she eased open the door, she turned to him. "Would you like to come in for some decaf or a glass of iced tea?"

He smiled. "Not tonight, Cathy. Perhaps another time."

"Certainly." She kissed his cheek, a simple act of gratitude. "Thank you for trying to help me with J.B. and Mona."

His round face flushed a light pink. "I'll continue doing all I can to help you and Seth and the Cantrells."

Cathy stood in the open doorway and watched Donnie until he got in his SUV. Then she went inside and closed and locked the door. She felt a sense of hope wash over her. A day that had started off with a trip to the sheriff's office was ending peacefully. Thanks to Brother Donnie Hovater, she felt that it might be possible not only to reclaim her rights as Seth's mother without involving lawyers, but to salvage her relationship with her in-laws.

In all the years they'd been together, Bruce Kelley had never lied to his wife. But today, not only had he lied to her, so had their three children. However, the deception had been for her own good. If they had told her Mirabelle Rutledge would be living with them as her companion and jailer, Sandie would have protested. She wouldn't have understood. In her lucid moments, she tried to deny her illness. And in her incompetent moments, she was incapable of understanding.

"I met Mirabelle when I visited Bright Side recently, and I really liked her," Kira had said shortly before Kim and Mirabelle arrived. "She's such a dear, sweet person. I think you'll just love her."

"This arrangement will be good for you and Dad and for

Mirabelle," Kevin had told his mother. "She needs a home and—"

"Of course we'll give the poor child a home," Sandie had said without hesitation. "Your father and I have worked with foster children in the past, so this won't be very different, except that Mirabelle is a grown woman with a child's mind."

"Actually, she's quiet intelligent," Bruce had said. "I believe she's simply a little slow." He had reached over and squeezed Sandie's hand. "She'll want to stay with you all the time, you know, the way a child would with her mother."

Sandie had smiled. "And I'll do my very best to be a mother figure for her."

Later in the afternoon, before Kim left, she had reinforced his earlier comments. "Mirabelle will want to stay right with you whenever Dad's not around. She doesn't like to be alone."

As Bruce looked down on a sleeping Sandie, her lovely face peaceful, her slender body covered only by a sheet and lightweight blanket, he swallowed his tears. An hour before bedtime, she had become disoriented and for a few moments hadn't known where she was. As happened occasionally, this evening her mind had wandered back to a time in her own childhood, and oddly enough she had thought Mirabelle was her mother.

The sweet, gentle young woman had helped him with his wife, taking over with an ease that surprised him. She had aided Sandie with as much patience and tender care as a mother would have taken with her own child. And when Mirabellele tucked Sandie into bed and kissed her on the forehead, Bruce had known that bringing this girl into their home had been the right decision. Indeed, it seemed to be a blessing.

"I will stay here," Mirabelle told him. "You mustn't worry, Mr. Bruce. I won't leave her. I will sleep beside her. It's all right that she doesn't know who I am. She's happy because she thinks I'm her mother."

He patted Mirabelle on the shoulder. "Yes, she did go to sleep happy, didn't she. I'll be in the guest room across the hall. If she wakes in the night or if you should need me . . ."

"I'll come and get you, Mr. Bruce."

He gazed into the girl's warm brown eyes and saw beyond the slow mind and into the loving heart. Abruptly, he turned and walked out of the bedroom just as the tears he could no longer control trickled down his cheeks.

The room is dark and quiet. Lying on my back staring up at the ceiling, I see only a glimmer of moonlight creeping through the closed blinds. I feel as if I'm floating on a peaceful black sea. Safe in God's hands. Nothing bad can happen to me. No one can hurt me. I am surrounded by a cloak of holy protection.

What is that tune humming inside my head? Oh, yes, it's a beautiful hymn that I learned as a child. My earliest memories are of being at church, inside the blessed sanctuary for the righteous, each service a haven for God's true children.

That's what I am—one of God's true children. I am not like so many who profess to be brothers and sisters of Christ and yet prove themselves unworthy of the name Christian.

"The Lord is my light and my salvation; whom shall I fear? The Lord is the strength of my life; of whom shall I be afraid?" The words of Psalm Twenty-seven echo inside my heart. "When the wicked, even mine enemies and my foes, came upon me to eat up my flesh, they stumbled and fell."

With my eyes closed against the ugliness of the world, I am so blessed to be able to recall the Holy Scripture. King David's psalms are some of my favorite passages from the Old Testament. "When my father and my mother forsake me, then the Lord will take me up. Deliver me not over unto the will of mine enemies: for false witnesses are risen up against me, and such as breathe out cruelty."

The world is filled with evil and cruelty, with those who

profess to love the Lord and do His work. But some are false prophets. Those are the ones God commands me to punish.

I'm listening, Lord. I know who You have chosen next to receive Thy swift and harsh punishment. Give me the time and day of his death, and I will do Thy bidding. I am Your humble servant, Your avenging angel of death.

Knowing she had a busy day tomorrow, even with Treasures closed, Cathy took a shower and prepared for bed earlier than usual. She and Lorie were in charge of the Lansdell Estate sale, which was scheduled for two weeks from yesterday. They would have to begin clearing the junk from the old house and preparing the furniture and the saleable contents to be displayed and priced. As she towel-dried her hair, she debated whether to use the blow-dryer or simply let it dry naturally overnight. After hanging the towel across the shower curtain rack and running a comb through her wavy, damp strands, she put on her floor-length cotton gown and padded barefoot into the bedroom.

The sound of the doorbell at—she glanced at the bedside clock—nine-thirty on Sunday night surprised her. She certainly wasn't expecting anyone. By the time she'd found her house slippers and lightweight cotton robe, her visitor had rung the doorbell again.

She rushed down the hall, through the living room and to the front door. When she peered through the viewfinder, she sucked in a deep breath. What was Jack doing on her doorstep at this time of night?

Without hesitation, she unlocked and opened the door. He stood there with a peculiar expression on his face.

He looked her over from head to toe. "Were you already in bed? I didn't wake you, did I?"

"No," she replied. "It's been a long, tiring day, which started pretty early this morning, and I have a busy day tomorrow, so I thought I'd try for an early bedtime tonight."

"I guess I should have called first."

"It's all right." When he kept staring at her so oddly, she asked, "Is something wrong?"

He glanced from side to side. "Mind if I come in? I'd rather not include your neighbors in our conversation."

"Oh, of course." She stepped aside to allow him entrance. "Please come in."

After he entered, she closed the door and turned to face him. He was close. Too close. Only inches separated their bodies. Jack was a good nine inches taller than her height of five-five, and the lanky young guy she'd fallen in love with years ago was now broader and more muscular but equally lean and fit. She stared up into his blue eyes, eyes she had never been able to forget. A shiver of pure sexual awareness rippled along every nerve in her body.

Jackson Perdue was the only man who'd ever been able to light up her insides like a glowing Christmas tree by doing nothing more than looking at her. No matter what else had changed in her life and in their relationship, that one fact remained the same.

His gaze devoured her. "Cathy . . ."

The way he looked at her and the way he said her name brought back memories of a time in her life she had tried to put behind her.

She couldn't allow her traitorous body to dictate her actions. She couldn't do this. She couldn't! She wasn't ready.

Easing away from him, putting some safe distance between their bodies, she took several steps into the living room. "Please come in and sit down. I'll get us some iced tea."

She watched as his chest moved with the force of the deep breath he sucked in and released, and she knew that he felt the magnetic force vibrating between them as intensely as she did.

"No iced tea for me," he said as he followed her.

She indicated the sofa. He sat down first, and then she sat on the opposite end of the sofa. "Why are you here, Jack?"

"I'm not sure," he admitted as he rubbed his open palms up and down his thighs. "I guess I thought maybe you'd call me and tell me how things went today, you know, with you and Seth and—"

"Oh, I didn't realize you expected me to call you."

"I don't expect anything from you," he told her. "I just thought that maybe you might want to talk, but I guess you've got Donnie Hovater to talk to now."

She caught the hint of censure in his voice and realized that he either disapproved of her budding friendship with the minister or was jealous.

"Donnie is a new friend, and that's all he is—a friend. He's trying to help me work out something with J.B. and Mona so that I don't have to take them to court to regain custody of Seth."

Jack cocked an eyebrow, the action expressing doubt. "If he can accomplish that, more power to him. But I'd hate to see you get your hopes up for nothing."

She forced a smile and then changed the subject because there really wasn't anything else to say about the matter. "How was your lunch at the Cedar House Grill? Did you take Lorie?"

"Yeah, I took Lorie. Why do you ask? Are you jealous?" he asked, a quirky grin on his face.

"No, of course not. What a thing to say. You and Lorie aren't . . . Are you?"

Jack laughed. "Hell, no."

"She's still in love with Mike, you know."

"Warning me to stay away from her?"

"You and Lorie are free to—"

"I'm not interested in playing second fiddle. Like you said, she's still hung up on Mike."

Cathy sighed softly. "And it's pretty much hopeless."

"Yeah, she filled me in on the situation. I like Lorie. I always did. She and Mike were great together, way back when. But I can see his side of things. It would take a pretty big man to get past what she did."

"She made some mistakes. We all make mistakes. Are you saying that we shouldn't find a way to forgive the people we love?"

"Don't put words in my mouth, honey. All I'm saying is that Lorie bared all in *Playboy* and had sex with several partners, on film, and Mike's a proud man and in many ways a very old-fashioned man."

"If he loved her . . ."

"Damn, Cathy, you and I know that sometimes love isn't enough."

She stared at him, her eyes wide, her heart hammering inside her chest. "I did love you," she said in a whisper.

"Did you?"

"Yes. With all my heart." *Please, God—please don't let him ask me why I married Mark if I loved him so much.*

He nodded. "We were a couple of kids with raging hormones. I was horny as hell, and you were in love with love." He shot to his feet unexpectedly.

Cathy looked up at his back, a sick feeling hitting her in the pit of her stomach. How many times during those two weeks they had shared had he told her how much he loved her?

Only a few times—when they had been having sex.

Maybe that's all it had been for him. Just sex.

She stood, walked over to him and laid her hand on his back. "Are you saying that you didn't love me?"

He turned so quickly that if he hadn't reached out and grabbed her, he would have knocked her down. His hands tightened on her arms.

"I'm not sure I've ever known what love is, not the kind of love you're talking about. But if you're asking did I want you, did I need you, did I think about you all the time, did I want to make you happy, then the answer is yes. If that's love, then I think you're probably the only woman I've ever loved."

Of all the things he could have said to her to dissolve her resistance, he had chosen the one argument that no woman could resist. And before she had a chance to assimilate the information and separate her thoughts from her feelings, Jack cradled her face with his big hands and then leaned down and kissed her. Gentle at first, the kiss soon became a ravenous mating of mouths and tongues.

Breathless and shaken when Jack ended the kiss, Cathy shoved against his chest. "Oh God, Jack. God . . ." Tears misted her eyes.

Slowly, reluctantly, he eased his hands away from her face. "I guess it's obvious that I still want you."

She nodded.

"If you'd let me, I'd take you to bed right now. But I'm in no position to make you any promises, and unless I miss my guess, you're still the kind of girl who's got love and sex all tied up together."

"I—I want you," she told him. "That's the honest truth. But my life is far too complicated already to have to deal with an affair with you or anyone else."

"Not even Donnie Hovater, whom I'm sure your mother and your in-laws approve of?" Jack cursed under his breath. "Forget I said that, will you? If you want the honest truth, then I'll admit that I'm jealous of the guy."

"I'm flattered that you're jealous of Donnie, but you have no reason to be. As I told you, he's a new friend and that's all. And you and I are friends, and that's all I can handle right now. So if you want to date someone else, I'll understand. I won't like it, but I'll understand."

"Yeah, sure." He nodded toward the front door. "I guess I'd better go and let you get some sleep."

She walked to the door with him and then out onto the

porch, not caring what her neighbors thought if they saw her standing there in her robe.

"I should have some preliminary plans for your house ready by the end of the week," she said. "How about lunch on Friday?"

"Sure thing. Call me with the time and place."

"I will."

"Good night, Cathy."

"Good night."

She stood on the porch and watched as he drove away. Her body ached for him. It would have been so simple to have taken him to her bed and made love with him all night.

Simple? Was she crazy? Nothing in her life was simple these days, least of all her relationship, past and present, with Jackson Perdue.

Chapter Eighteen

While working with the Fire and Brimstone Killer task force, comprised of local, regional and state law-enforcement officials, Jack had come to respect Derek Lawrence. Heck, he was beginning to like the guy, something Maleah wouldn't want to hear. Yeah, sure, the man could rub you the wrong way with his cockiness, but once you got past that character flaw, you had to admire his brilliant mind, his great sense of humor and his keen insight into human nature. It wasn't that he and Derek had become good friends. A relationship like that was built over time and required a foundation of trust that had to be earned. But they had reached the drinking-buddies stage, and each night this past week, they had grabbed a quick bite and a few beers together before heading their separate ways. Last night, Mike had joined them and they had talked business before their minds wandered off in a different direction after a couple of rounds. The subject had changed from how to catch a serial killer to the bra size of the bosomy waitress and bets on whether or not she had implants.

This morning, Jack needed caffeine. He poured himself

another cup of the office sludge that vaguely resembled coffee and tasted more like thin tar. Having had way too much on his mind at bedtime, he hadn't drifted off to sleep until after two this morning, and then he hadn't slept worth a damn. A war-related nightmare that he preferred not to think about in the hard, cold light of day had interrupted his four hours of on-and-off sleep. And right now, he was feeling the aftereffects. He placed his mug on the desk, pulled out his chair and sat. After taking a couple of sips of the strong, hot brew, he put the mug aside and stared at the stack of file folders beside his computer.

The task force was no closer to finding their killer than when the investigation first started. Without any witnesses and with no definitive evidence linking the three murders to a specific person, they were pretty much spinning their wheels. Out there somewhere, possibly living in Dunmore, was a murderer who, according to Derek, probably seemed relatively normal. He or she could be anyone's next-door neighbor, a regular guy or gal, someone who, on a day-to-day basis, looked and acted like everyone else. But a monster existed inside this killer.

"You've got to be a really sick bastard to be able to set another human being on fire," Lieutenant Wayne Morgan, the ABI agent who headed the Fire and Brimstone task force, had said during their most recent meeting. His statement had been a consensus of the others on the task force.

So, how did you recognize a monster if he or she didn't have horns and a tail? If this person spit fire, had glowing red eyes or their head twirled around and around, it would make law enforcement's job a lot easier.

If their killer stayed true to form, he or she wouldn't kill again for a good while. Mark Cantrell had been killed more than eighteen months ago, and then, six months later, Charles Randolph had met his maker. Father Brian Myers had become the third victim, murdered almost a year after the second clergyman's death. Would the killer wait six months or even a year before striking again? Derek seemed to think that it would be a lot sooner.

"Call it gut instinct," Derek had told them, "but I believe there will be another similar murder sometime in the next few months."

"There was six months between the first two murders, then nearly a whole year before the killer struck again," Huntsville police detective Jeremy Vaughn had said at yesterday's meeting. "What makes you think he's going to strike again so soon?"

"Other than going by my instincts, you mean? Nothing, really. Just an educated guess. There's a fury inside our killer that is bound to intensify as time goes by. All that's needed is the right incentive, and he or she could go into a killing frenzy."

A killing frenzy!

Jack knew all about killing. When he'd been in the Rangers, he had not only witnessed horrific murders more times than he could count, but he, too, had killed—numerous times. It was all a part of being a soldier, part of being at war. It was kill or be killed. And although he was no longer a soldier, no longer living in a war zone, he was now a member of a select group of men and women who fought crime on a daily basis.

The one thing everyone on the task force agreed about was the fact that another murder was imminent. Jack couldn't help wondering how Cathy would react when another clergyman was killed.

Damn! He didn't want to think about her so much, but she'd been on his mind all week. Although he hadn't seen her since Sunday night, she had phoned yesterday to tell him she had finished the preliminary plans for renovating his house. The call had been brief and to the point. They were meeting for lunch today, a strictly business lunch. Yeah, sure.

He didn't for one minute believe that anything could ever be strictly business between Cathy and him.

My life is far too complicated already to have to deal with an affair with you or anyone else. He had replayed her words over and over inside his head for the past five days and knew he had to accept the fact that she meant what she'd said. But God in heaven, the way she had responded to his kiss told him that her body was more than ready to take a lover. And he wanted to be that lover.

You and I are friends, and that's all I can handle right now. So if you want to date someone else, I'll understand. I won't like it, but I'll understand.

He had gotten along just fine without Cathy in his life for the past seventeen years. He might want her, but he didn't need her. He just needed a woman. Any woman would do.

Okay, if that's the way you really feel, why aren't you dating someone else? he asked himself. *Why haven't you gone out and gotten yourself laid?*

Damned if I know.

Cathy told herself that she had bought a new dress because she needed to gradually replace old clothes with new. But if she were completely honest with herself, which she tried to be these days, she'd have to admit that her lunch date with Jack had influenced her decision to purchase a new outfit.

After she emerged from her car, she adjusted the navy bolero jacket she wore over her red and white striped sundress. The navy purse and shoes were stock items that had been a part of her wardrobe for several years, as were the small gold hoop earrings. But the five inexpensive little red, white and blue bangle bracelets were a recent purchase. She could tell herself that she simply wanted to look nice for a client, but that would be a half-truth. Of course, she always wanted to look her best, but she had gone to extra trouble and expense to impress Jack.

Sighing heavily because she knew that she was sending him mixed signals, Cathy squared her shoulders and walked toward the restaurant entrance. If she was smart, she would sever her ties to Jack. After today, she should turn the house-renovation project over to Lorie and tell Jack that they couldn't date. She'd been a fool to think she could keep him at arm's length, not when she still had feelings for him. What if they fell in love again? How would that affect Seth?

With her portfolio containing all the renovation plans she had worked on every night this week tucked under her arm, Cathy entered the restaurant. The Cedar Hill Grill, which had opened only a couple of years ago, was the nicest place in town and was locally owned and managed by Patsy and Elliott Floyd's twenty-five-year-old son, Drew.

An attractive young hostess with a pleasant smile met Cathy. "Table for one?"

"No, I'm meeting someone. Mr. Perdue. I'm probably a little early."

"Not at all. Mr. Perdue is already here." The hostess, whose name tag read Krista, led Cathy straight to a secluded back booth, where Jack sat with a glass of iced tea in his hand.

The moment he saw her, he set the glass down, slid out of the booth and stood to greet her. Wow! He looked great, all six-two of him, with his sun-streaked hair and piercing blue eyes. Having a tall, muscular build, he was the type of man who looked good in a uniform, even the standard sheriff's department brown slacks and shirt.

He smiled. She smiled.

She could tell that he wasn't sure whether to shake her hand or give her a quick hug. She made the decision for him. After propping her portfolio up against the back of the booth, she gave Jack a brief, friendly hug. Perhaps it hadn't been a smart move, not if she intended to end their new relationship before it went any further, but hugging him seemed the natural thing to do.

After she slid into the booth and picked up the menu lying on the table between them, Jack sat down across from her.

"Lunch first or business?" he asked.

"Lunch, please. I'm starving. I skipped breakfast this morning." She kept her gaze fixed on the menu. "Yum, everything looks good."

"I've narrowed my choices down to either a cheeseburger and fries or a rack of ribs."

"I love ribs, but they're awfully messy." The last thing she wanted was to accidentally drop barbeque sauce on her new dress.

Their waitress came over to the booth and asked Cathy, "What would you like to drink?"

"Sweet iced tea with lemon, please."

"Yes, ma'am. Are y'all ready to order?"

Jack looked at Cathy, who replied, "Yes, I am. I'd like the half sandwich and cup of soup—club sandwich and vegetable soup."

The waitress turned to Jack.

"A rack of ribs," he said. "With fries. And more tea."

"Be right back with your drinks."

Alone again, Cathy and Jack looked at each other. She realized he was as nervous as she was. One of them had to say something about what had happened this past Sunday night. The kiss they'd shared had dominated her thoughts all week. As much as she wanted Jack, more now than she had as a teenager, she couldn't risk making a mistake by falling in love with him all over again. It had taken her such a long time to stop loving him, to put him in the past where he belonged and move on with her life. Thank God when she and Mark had married, he'd still been in love with his first wife, so he had understood her feelings for Jack. In the early days of their marriage, they had talked to each other about their lost loves, but all that changed after Seth was born. Oddly enough, Seth had been the glue that cemented their marriage and continued to be the glue that held them together until the day Mark died.

"Penny for your thoughts," Jack said.

Slightly startled, Cathy snapped out of memory land and came back to the present moment. She smiled. "I was thinking about Seth." It was a half-truth.

"How's he doing?"

"I haven't seen him since Sunday, but we've talked on the phone every day. J.B. has kept Seth grounded, and I don't entirely disagree with him doing that."

"Do you still plan to put off taking your in-laws to court?"

"Yes. I prefer to settle the custody matter out of court, if at all possible. For Seth's sake."

"Do you really think your father-in-law will eventually hand Seth over to you without putting up a fight?"

Cathy sighed. "I hope so. Donnie believes that, given time, J.B. will see reason."

"And you think Donnie Hovater has all the answers, that he knows J.B. Cantrell better than you do, even though he's known him for less than a year and you've known the old goat for what—more than sixteen years?"

Cathy laughed. "Old goat, huh?"

"I could have been really blunt," Jack said. "I'm sure I could have come up with more explicit words to describe your father-in-law."

"Actually, old goat is fine." She glanced down at the table, avoiding Jack's steady gaze. "J.B. isn't a bad man. He's not cruel or evil, not the way—" Cathy stopped midsentence, realizing what she'd been about to say.

"Not like Nolan Reaves." Jack finished the sentence for her. "J.B. didn't physically abuse his wife and kids. He didn't make life a living hell for people he professed to love. That makes J.B. a better man than my stepfather, but it doesn't make him a good man. I get the feeling that your husband's father has committed his share of mental and emotional abuse, at least to some degree."

"Maybe." Cathy hated to admit the truth. "Yes, okay. J.B. isn't a saint. And he's almost as good at emotional manipulation as my mother is. But it's not as if he consciously intends to harm anyone."

Jack lifted his brows in a manner that expressed his doubts. "I realize how you live your life is none of my business, and I have no right to tell you what to do or influence what decisions you should make about your son. But you have to know that your father-in-law has spent the past year manipulating Seth. Don't you want to put a stop to that as soon as possible?"

"Like you said, my life and my son are none of your business," Cathy snapped.

"Is your life any of Donnie Hovater's business?"

Cathy's gaze met Jack's head-on just as the waitress returned with their drinks. As soon as she placed their glasses on the table and left, Cathy took a deep, calming breath before responding to Jack's question.

"I didn't meet you for lunch today to discuss Seth or J.B. or Donnie," she reminded him. "I'm here as your design consultant." She patted the large portfolio propped beside her against the back of the booth. "And your amateur architect."

"And as a friend?" he asked.

"Yes, of course."

"If I promise to keep my nose out of your personal business, will you go to dinner and the movies with me tonight? We could drive over to Huntsville and—"

"I already have plans."

"Do you really have other plans, or is that your way of telling me to back off?"

"If we can have dinner and go to the movies as friends only, I'll be free next weekend," she told him. "Tonight, I do have plans with my son. He and I are going for dinner and then bowling with Donnie and Missy. And J.B. has agreed to let Seth spend tonight and tomorrow night with me."

"That's great, honey."

"No comment about my spending time with Donnie?"

"Your life, your business."

She smiled.

"How about I call you midweek next week and we'll make plans." He added, "As friends."

They ate in relative silence. Cathy felt the tension between them dissipate slightly during their shared meal, but that live-wire sexual connection couldn't be severed. It was far too strong, and there didn't seem to be a damn thing she could do about it.

As they sipped coffee, which they had ordered in lieu of dessert, Cathy lifted the portfolio, laid it on the table and opened it to reveal her handiwork. "Let me show you what I've come up with for the exterior first. I've included a porch gazebo that I think you'll like."

"If you like it, I'm sure I will."

"Helping with the restoration of an old Victorian home is a wonderful experience for me. I may never have my dream home, but doing something like this comes in a close second."

"Have you thought about going back to school and getting your degree?" Jack asked as he flipped through the professional-looking plans she had drawn for his house. "These are good, honey. Really good."

"Thank you. And funny you should ask about my going back to school. I'm definitely considering it. But not until I have the situation with Seth worked out. Who knows, when he goes to college, I may go with him."

They both laughed, and for the first time since she had arrived at the restaurant, Cathy relaxed.

That afternoon, when Mike had invited Jack to go along with him and his kids to Dutton's Bowling Alley that night, he had declined. He figured the last thing he needed was to run into Cathy and Preacher Hovater. But before his shift ended, he told Mike that he'd changed his mind. What difference did it make if he and Cathy were at the same place at the same time? They weren't even dating, at least not officially. And she'd made it perfectly clear that she wasn't ready for anything more than friendship from him or any other man.

"Great. Meet us around seven and we'll grab a bite there," Mike had said. "They've got halfway decent burgers and dogs and the best greasy onion rings in the county."

Jack had considered trying to find a date to take with him, but realized that since returning to Dunmore there had been only one woman on his mind. His female acquaintances were limited. He knew the two female deputies, but one was married and the other had a steady boyfriend. And he knew Lorie, but considering her long-standing friendship with Cathy, she was off-limits. Besides, Mike wouldn't appreciate him showing up at the bowling alley with his old lover.

Five minutes into their meal, with Hannah seated at the booth alongside Mike and M.J. beside Jack, Mike's gaze fixed on something or someone behind Jack.

"Did you know Cathy would be here tonight?" Mike asked.

"Who's Cathy?" Hannah looked up at her father.

"Yeah, she mentioned it when we had a business lunch today," Jack replied.

Looking squarely at Jack, Mike answered his daughter. "Cathy is Mrs. Cantrell. She's an old friend of Jack's and mine."

"Oh, like Miss Lorie," Hannah said.

"Sort of," Mike mumbled.

"Hey, it's a free country," Jack said. "Why should I have missed the chance to spend a fun evening with you, Hannah and M.J. just because my path might cross with Cathy and her date?"

Mike's eyes widened. "She's dating the preacher who took over her husband's congregation?"

"They're just friends."

"Hmm . . . Apparently." Mike chuckled. "Most people don't take their teenage kids along with them on a date." Suddenly an odd expression crossed Mike's face. He lowered his voice. "Don't look now, but here they come."

"Huh?" Jack turned around at the exact same moment Cathy walked by with her date and their kids.

Cathy paused, a startled look in her eyes. "Good evening." She glanced from Jack, who rose to his feet immediately, straight to Mike. "This is a popular place tonight." She smiled. "How's the food?"

"Not half bad," Mike said as he stood.

"Evening, Deputy." Donnie Hovater extended his hand. "Good to see you again."

Jack nodded, shook the preacher's hand and sat back down.

He didn't like this guy. Yeah, sure, he resented Cathy spending time with a man who had to remind her of her dead husband. But it was more than that. Jack's gut instincts picked up some weird vibes from the preacher man.

"Enjoy your evening," Cathy said, deliberately avoiding eye contact with Jack.

"Yeah, you, too," Mike said when Jack remained silent.

As soon as the foursome was out of earshot, Mike sat down, his face crunched in a disapproving frown. "That went well, don't you think?" he said sarcastically. "Why didn't you just sock the guy in the jaw instead of shaking his hand?"

"Why should Jack have hit Brother Hovater?" Hannah asked.

"Yeah, you told us to never start a fight," M.J. added.

"Jeez," Mike grumbled under his breath. He pulled out a ten from his wallet and handed it to his son. "Take Hannah with you and y'all go get ice cream for dessert."

As soon as his children headed off toward the nearby concession stand, Mike leaned forward and said, "What's going on between you and Cathy?"

"Nothing."

"Don't give me that. The vibes between you two were so intense, I'm surprised—"

"I want her. She wants me. But she's not ready for anything more than friendship." Jack slid out of the booth and stood. "I think I'll pass on the bowling. Thanks for inviting me."

"Running away won't solve your problem."

"A smart soldier knows when to retreat and work on new battle plans."

Mike shook his head. "Is that how you think of your relationship with Cathy, as a battle? You think Donnie Hovater is your enemy?"

"I think he wants Cathy," Jack said. "And I damn well don't intend to let him have her."

Jack didn't wait around to hear what else Mike had to say. He walked out of the bowling alley and went directly to his car. After sliding behind the wheel, he sat there and stared through the windshield into the dark night sky.

What the hell was the matter with him? Hadn't he decided, just this morning, that what he needed was to get laid? Cathy Nelson Cantrell was not the only woman in the world, not even the only woman in Dunmore, Alabama. If all he wanted was a one-night stand, he could go to any bar in Dunmore or nearby Decatur, Athens or Huntsville and probably have his pick.

As for Donnie Hovater, if Cathy preferred his type—Mark Cantrell's type—then who the hell cared? He'd never fought for the rights to a woman, had never known one worth fighting for, except maybe his mother and definitely his sister. So why did he want to beat the living daylights out of the preacher, stomp him to the ground, walk over him and claim his prize?

Jack slammed both fists down against the steering wheel. Cathy would sure as hell love being thought of as a prize, wouldn't she?

That woman has turned you inside out and tied you into knots.

But he couldn't blame her. It wasn't her fault. Some people just had an undeniable chemistry that made it difficult for them to keep their hands off each other. It had been that way for Cathy and him seventeen years ago. It was still like that for the two of them.

Jack inserted the key into the ignition, started his Corvette and headed toward Huntsville. It was Friday night, and the bars would be open well into the morning.

The house was deadly quiet as she slipped out of her bedroom at eleven-thirty. No one would miss her. Even if her bed was empty, it would be assumed that she was outside in the gazebo where she often went at night when she couldn't sleep. No one bothered her there while she sat alone in the darkness. It was her only refuge on earth.

The doctors had given her a prescription for non–habit-forming sleeping pills, and for a while she had pretended to take them. Finally, she had admitted that she didn't want to take drugs. Her body was a temple, not to be abused or defiled.

"Know ye not that your body is the temple of the Holy Ghost which is in you, which ye have of God, and ye are not your own. For ye are bought with a price: therefore glorify God in your body, and in your spirit, which are God's."

She knew her Scriptures, had learned chapter and verse from her earliest childhood. God's holy words about the sanctity of the body were found in I Corinthians 6:19-20.

Drugs were of the devil.

The devil lived in and worked through human beings, even those who professed to be His prophets and teachers of

His divine word. God despised wickedness. He punished those who sinned against Him. But blasphemers were the most despised of all sinners, those who set themselves up as pure and holy, pretended to be doers of good deeds when in truth their hearts were black with sin.

She clutched the car keys in her hand. Since the houses were relatively close together, the sound of a car starting would go unnoticed. Cars came and went at all hours, especially on weekend nights. If anyone did discover that she was not at home in bed asleep, she would have no trouble convincing them that she had been restless and hoped taking a drive would relax her. Even if there were consequences, she would deal with them. All that mattered tonight was for her to accomplish her goal.

She was on a mission for God.

The drive to Decatur, to the Kelley house, would take approximately thirty minutes. She shouldn't be there longer than ten minutes, fifteen at the very most. And then the return drive would take another thirty minutes. She should be back home and in bed again by one o'clock.

As she eased the car out of the driveway and onto the street, she prayed for guidance and protection. If the Lord wanted her to continue her work, to destroy more of the world's most vile sinners, then He would keep her safe. He would watch over her and never deliver her into the hands of His enemies.

As the miles passed by, she alternated between planning and praying. The gasoline can was in the car trunk, and the Pocket Torch lighter was in the glove compartment.

"Help me, merciful God, my loving heavenly Father. Guide my hand in Thy service. I will do Thy will."

If Reverend Kelley came to the back door tonight, it would be a sign from on high. If someone else answered her knock, she would stay hidden in the shadows and know that tonight was not the night.

Chapter Nineteen

Bruce stood in the doorway watching Mirabelle as she sat on the side of Sandie's bed, soothing her with a tender touch and soft words. He had never felt as helpless in his entire life as he did now. During the brief time Mirabelle had been living with them, she had become his wife's surrogate mother, sister, child and friend. In her lucid moments, Sandie treated Mirabelle as the half child, half woman she was. Bruce knew *that* Sandie, the woman he had loved for most of his life. In other moments, when his wife teetered on the brink and was often confused and occasionally hostile, Mirabelle became her friend, the girl's sweet innocence seeming to somehow relate to the lost child in Sandie. And in the worst moments, when Sandie crossed over into a realm where she didn't know who he was, who her own children were, she looked at Mirabelle and saw her mother and occasionally her sister, Allison, both women long dead.

Tonight had gone well. Sandie had been herself during dinner and for several hours afterward, but shortly before ten, she had become disoriented. For the past two hours, he and Mirabelle had done whatever they could to keep Sandie calm and reassured as they prepared her for the night. As much as he hated sedating his wife, he now knew when it was best for her—and, yes, for him, too—to be given medication to help her rest. At eleven-thirty, he had prepared a glass of chocolate milk for her and doctored it with a sedative. Mirabelle had taken the milk to her and smiled triumphantly when she'd brought the empty glass back to him.

With the medication taking effect now and Mirabelle at Sandie's side, Bruce allowed himself to breathe a free, relaxed breath, but he couldn't bring himself to leave the doorway. Not yet. Not until Sandie was asleep. Not until he felt certain that Mirabelle would be all right on her own.

Once he felt reassured that all was well, he would go to the guest bedroom where he now slept and read for a while until God blessed him with a few hours of uninterrupted sleep.

The ting of the doorbell surprised him, the sound echoing up the staircase from the ground floor. At first he hadn't been sure what the sound was, but when the bell rang again several times, he realized exactly what it was. But who would be at their door this time of night, at midnight?

Mirabelle looked his way, and their gazes met, hers silently repeating the question he had just asked himself about who their midnight caller was.

Using hand motions, he told her he was going downstairs. She smiled and nodded her understanding.

Even though it was midnight, Bruce still wore the khaki slacks and short-sleeved plaid shirt he'd worn all day. He made his way down the stairs, across the foyer and to the front door. He turned on the porch light and opened the door, leaving the storm door locked.

There was no one there. The porch was empty.

Odd. Had some teenager playing a prank rung the doorbell and run away? He heaved a hard, weary sigh and closed the door.

The doorbell rang again.

He opened the door. No one there.

He closed the door and turned off the porch light.

Then it hit him that the back door also had a doorbell, one that was seldom used because visitors always came to the front door. Perhaps a neighbor had a problem and for some reason had chosen to go to the back of the house. Bruce trekked down the hall, through the kitchen and into the mud room. He turned on the outside lights, one on either side of the door, and peered through the half-glass back door. He saw no one.

He needed to get to the bottom of this. If someone was deliberately harassing them, he had to put a stop to it immediately. He couldn't risk anything disturbing Sandie. Hesitant to unlock the back door, Bruce reminded himself that a burglar would hardly ring the doorbell.

With a slightly shaky hand, he unlocked and opened the door. "Is anyone there?" he called in a confident, no-nonsense voice.

No response.

"Hello, is someone out there? Do you need help?"

Except for the soft rustle of a warm June breeze rippling through the trees and shrubbery, the backyard was eerily quiet. Bruce took several tentative steps out onto the wooden deck. He glanced right and left and then out into the dark yard but saw nothing out of the ordinary, not even a stray animal.

Just as he turned to go back inside, he caught a glimpse of movement in his peripheral vision. Jerking back around, he spied a dark form hovering near the old magnolia tree a good ten feet away and to his right.

"Who's there?"

"Help me," a quavering female voice whispered.

Bruce moved forward until he reached the edge of the deck, all the while keeping his gaze on the small shadow of the woman in his yard.

"Who are you, and what can I do to help you?" he asked.

"God has sent me to you," she said, her voice whispery and fragile.

A frisson of uncertainty crept up Bruce's spine. Was the woman someone he knew, or was she a stranger, perhaps a deranged person who had sought him out because he was a minister? Could she be the Fire and Brimstone Killer?

"Show yourself," he said, doing his best to keep his tone compassionate despite his wariness. "We'll go inside and talk. I'll do whatever I can to help you." He held out his hand. "Whatever you need, I'll do my best to provide it."

Without saying a word, she emerged from the shadows and walked slowly toward the deck. When he saw her more clearly, he sighed and relaxed. She appeared quite normal, although her expression hinted at an inner anguish.

Bruce stepped down off the deck and walked toward her. As she approached him, he noticed that she carried something held halfway behind her. A suitcase or knapsack, perhaps? Was she homeless? She appeared to be neat and clean. When she was within a few feet of him, he realized her other hand was knotted into a fist, as if she held something small hidden inside her tight grasp.

"Hello, I'm Reverend Bruce Kelley," he told her. "And you are?"

"I am the Lord's chosen," she said.

A hard knot of apprehension clutched Bruce's gut. Who was this peculiar woman? "Can I call someone for you, someone who will be concerned about you?"

When she smiled, her lips curving upward in a closed-mouth grin, Bruce looked directly into her eyes and saw sheer madness. *Merciful Lord, is she dangerous?* His heartbeat accelerated at an alarming pace. Real fear swelled up inside him.

He took a cautious step backward, away from his late-night visitor, but he kept focused on her face, on the wild look in her eyes.

Still smiling, she stared at him but said nothing. Her sudden silence seemed to issue a warning. Danger. Beware.

Before he realized what she intended to do, she brought what he'd thought was a small red suitcase out from behind her, lifted it into the air and flung something wet and foul-smelling on him. It took him a good ten seconds to grasp the fact that she had dropped the object in her hand—a square red can and not a suitcase—and that she had doused him with whatever had been inside the can.

His mind sped from the reality of the moment to several different scenarios, but too late he knew what was happening.

She uncurled her fist, held the small metal lighter in her hand, and flicked the ignition. Bruce froze to the spot.

Run! Get away from her! Do it now!

Just as he turned to flee, she tossed the lighter, the flame locked, onto his back. Instantly, the gasoline she had tossed on him ignited and quickly turned him into a human torch. As the flames ate away at his clothing, he ran in a blind panic and then realized, even through the haze of agony spreading through his body, that in running he was simply feeding the flames. He dropped to his knees as the fire and pain engulfed him.

Help me, dear God. Help me!

He managed to roll over a couple of times, not recognizing the screams he heard as being his own. Before the unbearable anguish consumed him, blessed unconsciousness came as the answer to his prayer.

She stood there for a few seconds and watched the magnificence of her handiwork. Bruce Kelley was being punished for his sins, for professing to be a man of God and yet harboring Satan's own evil within his heart.

After picking up the hot, lighter from the ground, she slipped it into her pocket and, clutching the handle on the gasoline can, turned and walked away. She hurried out of the backyard and into the alleyway where she had parked her car. Once she had stored the can in the trunk, she opened the door and slid behind the wheel. As she slowly drove down the alley and toward the street at the end of the block, she recited an appropriate Biblical passage to herself. Her lips were silent, but her heart shouted.

"For behold the Lord will come with fire, and with His chariots like a whirlwind, to render His anger with fury, and His rebuke with flames of fire. For by fire and by His sword will the Lord plead with all flesh: and the slain of the Lord shall be many."

Isaiah 66:15-16.

At first Mirabelle wasn't sure if the screams she heard were real or perhaps coming from a television program. Had Mr. Bruce gone downstairs to watch TV? No, surely not. Every night after he helped her with Miss Sandie, he went to his room, and unless she needed him during the night, she didn't see him or hear anything from him until the next morning.

That meant the screams she heard were real. Someone outside was screaming as if they were hurting something awful.

She glanced down at Miss Sandie, who had fallen sound asleep only moments ago.

She'll be all right for a little while.

Mirabelle left the bedroom, walked down the hall and saw that Mr. Bruce's bedroom door was open and the bedside lamp was on, but the room was empty.

Without hesitation, she went down the back stairs that led to the kitchen. The back door stood partially open, and the outside lights were on. She thought it odd that Mr. Bruce would have gone outside this late at night, and she didn't like the idea of going outside in the dark by herself. But she needed to find Mr. Bruce and tell him about the screams that she'd heard.

When she walked out onto the deck, she didn't see Mr. Bruce. But as she reached the steps, she saw something lying on the ground. Was it the person who had rung the doorbell? The grass around the unmoving man—at least she thought it was a man—looked very dark, as if someone had painted it black.

"Mr. Bruce, where are you?" she called.

No one answered.

She didn't want to get close to the strange body lying near the steps. Whoever it was, he looked dead.

"Mr. Bruce," she screamed. "Help, help, there's a dead body in the yard!"

Mirabelle kept calling for help. She didn't know what else to do. Then suddenly she remembered what they had taught them at Bright Side.

In an emergency, dial 911.

Just as she started to go back inside and make the call, she heard voices saying her name. When she looked over her shoulder, she saw two people she recognized, Judy and Bob Calhoun, who were the Kelleys' neighbors, both of them nice people.

"I have to call 911," she told them as they halted when they saw the body. "I can't find Mr. Bruce to tell him about the screams I heard and about this dead person in the yard."

If Jack hadn't put his phone on vibrate as well as ring, he would have missed the call. He'd spent the past few hours at the Purple Mustang Club in Huntsville, and the noise level was off the charts. He'd drunk a couple of beers, danced with three different women and had finally narrowed down his choice to the sassy little brunette curled up in his lap.

"Why don't we get out of here and go to my place?" She licked a circle around his ear.

"We will," he told her as he lifted her off his lap and set her back in the chair beside him. "I need to get this first." He pulled the phone off his belt loop, put it to his ear and covered his other ear with his hand to block out some of the noise. "Yeah, Perdue here."

"Jack, it's Mike. Did I wake you?"

"No. I'm awake. So, what's up?" Jack asked.

"Where the hell are you? I can hear some pretty loud background noise. I figured you'd be in bed at this hour."

"I'm out of town. What time is it anyway?"

"Nearly two o'clock," Mike answered. "Wherever the hell you are, get yourself over to Decatur pronto and meet me at police headquarters—that is, if you're not too drunk to drive. We've got ourselves another Fire and Brimstone murder."

"Son of a bitch. Who was it this time?"

"A Presbyterian minister by the name of Dr. Bruce Kelley."

"I'm not too drunk to drive. I'll be there as soon as possible." He glanced at the woman beside him and noted her pouting lips. He'd been looking forward to finding out just what those lips could do to him tonight.

"Derek was right," Mike said. "Our killer didn't even wait a whole month before killing again."

Jack slipped his phone onto the belt holder and scooted back his chair. His companion stood, wrapped her arms around him and rubbed her body against his.

"You're not really leaving me, are you?"

"Sorry, honey. Duty calls."

Frowning, she backed away from him. "If I give you my number, will you get in touch later?"

"Sure."

She recited the number and then frowned when he didn't make any attempt to write it down.

"I've got it memorized," he told her as he walked away.

By the time he reached his car in the side parking lot, he

had forgotten her number. But that was just as well, because he couldn't remember her name, either. Knowing that the Fire and Brimstone Killer had struck again, the only name that mattered to Jack was Catherine Nelson Cantrell, the woman whose life would be turned topsy-turvy by the news that her husband's killer had struck again.

Chapter Twenty

"Reverend Kelley is still alive," Mike said as he met Jack outside Chief Richard Donaldson's office at Decatur police headquarters. "Just barely."

"What kind of shape's he in?" Jack asked.

"From what I've been told, he has third-degree burns over seventy-five percent of his body, his neck and the back of his head. He's unconscious, and the odds of him living twenty-four hours are slim to none."

"Then there's no way to question him?"

Mike shook his head. "The only reason he's alive is because neighbors heard him screaming and then heard his wife's caretaker screaming. They got to him pretty fast right after it happened and called 911. He was airlifted from Decatur General straight to Vanderbilt. They're a Level One Trauma Center with a top-notch burn center."

"Did any of the neighbors see anything, see anybody?"

"Nope. But they thought they heard a car in the alley, so the entire alley is being considered part of the crime scene."

"Have you contacted Wayne Morgan?" Jack asked about the ABI agent who headed the Fire and Brimstone Killer task force.

"He's got a unit on its way to the crime scene right now." Mike inclined his head toward the exit. "Leave your car here and ride over to the reverend's house with me. Chief Donaldson's given us the green light since two of the four murders occurred in our jurisdiction and you're on the task force."

"We both know that I wouldn't be anybody's top pick to represent your department on the task force. It just worked out that way because you'd put me in charge of your cold cases."

"You're as qualified as any man on my force," Mike corrected him. "I don't kid myself about my people or myself. We're a group of honest, down-to-earth country folks who seldom have to deal with murders and certainly not serial killers."

Jack shrugged. Mike was right. It wasn't as if anyone on his team had ever dealt with a serial killer. And only the ABI guys were actually trained, at least to a certain extent, to deal with this type of crime.

"Reverend Kelley's death is bound to be on the local early morning news," Jack said. "Don't you think somebody should contact the families of the previous victims?"

"Do you want to contact Cathy and tell her?"

"Yeah, I do. This is going to hit her hard. She managed to hold it together when the Catholic priest was murdered, but . . . Maybe we should call Lorie and have her go over to Cathy's."

"Sure. As soon as we get on the road, go ahead and call Lorie." Mike pulled keys from his pocket and headed for the exit. Jack followed. "Ask her to contact Cathy and then inform Cathy's in-laws."

Once settled in Mike's SUV and en route, Jack checked the stored numbers in his cell phone. But before he could dial the first number, Mike asked him a pointed question.

"Where were you when I called?"

"Some dive called the Purple Mustang in Huntsville."

"Please tell me you didn't drive here under the influence."

"I had two beers," Jack said. "It would take more than a six-pack for me to feel the effects." When Mike gave him a skeptical glance, Jack added, "Believe me. I've built up a tolerance over the years. I know when I've had my limit."

"What were you doing at the Purple Mustang—trying to drown your sorrows?"

"Something like that."

"Looking for a little TLC?"

"Yeah, why not?"

"Did you find any?"

"What is this, the frigging third degree? You're not my father, and I'm not some disobedient kid who needs reprimanding."

"Call Lorie," Mike said, letting the matter drop.

Jack brought up her number on his phone, hit SEND and waited for her to answer. Considering that it was close to three in the morning, he was surprised she picked up the phone after the second ring.

"Jack?" she asked in a sleep-hoarse voice.

"Yeah, it's me. Sorry to wake you, but I need you to go over to Cathy's as soon as you can."

"What's happened?"

"Our Fire and Brimstone Killer has struck again, this time in Decatur. The victim is a Presbyterian minister named Kelley, and for now he's still alive."

"Oh God! Can he ID his attacker?"

"He's unconscious, and that's all I can say."

"Yeah, sure. I understand. Are you calling Cathy or do you want me to tell—?"

"I'll call her," Jack said. "But you get your cute little butt over there ASAP. She's going to need you. And call her in-laws later, before the news hits the airwaves."

"Okay. I'll handle calling the Cantrells. And I'll take care of Cathy."

"Thanks."

"Jack?"

"Huh?"

"I know you're going to be busy with the task force, but . . . Cathy might need you. She might—"

"If she needs anything from me, just call."

"I will."

As soon as he finished his conversation with Lorie, he phoned Cathy. God, how he wished he was back in Dunmore so he could be there to comfort her when he gave her the bad news.

The jarring ring of the telephone on the bedside table brought Cathy out of a deep sleep. Reaching from beneath the sheet and light blanket covering her, she grabbed the phone but somehow managed to knock the base off and onto the floor. As she hit the TALK button on the portable handset, she didn't even bother looking at caller ID. Instead, she glanced at the digital alarm clock. Who would be calling at 2:56 in the morning? If it wasn't a wrong number, it had to be an emergency.

"Hello."

"Cathy, this is Jack Perdue."

She shot straight up in bed. "Jack? What's wrong?"

"Listen to me," he said in a consoling voice. "Lorie's on her way there as we speak, so you won't be alone."

"I'm not alone. Seth's here. He's spending the weekend." Whatever it was, it had to be bad if he'd called Lorie first. "Just tell me, please." But she knew. Oh God, she knew.

"The Fire and Brimstone Killer has struck again."

Cathy swallowed hard. "Who?"

"A Reverend Kelley, from Decatur. It happened just a few hours ago."

"Bruce Kelley?"

"Yeah, that's the name. Why, do you know him?"

"I'm acquainted with the family," Cathy said. "One of his daughters is the director of Bright Side, a school and help center for the mentally challenged. It's located here in Dunmore."

"Damn," Jack mumbled under his breath.

"I'll wait until morning to tell Seth and call J.B. and Mona."

"You'll have to tell Seth, but Lorie will call the Cantrells. I'm sorry that I can't come straight over there, but—"

"I'll be all right. You do your job and help find the person responsible for these murders."

"We're doing all we can, honey."

"Yes, I know . . . I know."

"I'll see you later, okay?"

"Okay."

She had no more than said good-bye and turned on the bedside lamp when she heard footsteps in the hallway. She got out of bed and picked up the phone base lying on the floor. By the time she had set it back in place, Seth called out to her from the doorway.

"Who was on the phone?" he asked, as he entered the bedroom.

"Jack Perdue."

Surveying her face and apparently sensing the worst, Seth said, "Something terrible has happened, hasn't it?"

"There's been another murder."

"The Fire and Brimstone Killer?"

Cathy nodded. "Reverend Bruce Kelley from Decatur. I know his daughter, Kim Randall. She's the director at Bright Side."

"Oh, Mom."

Looking at Seth, she saw a sad, vulnerable boy who had lost his father to an insane killer, a boy badly in need of comfort. When she held open her arms, he didn't hesitate. He went straight into her embrace. She held her tall, teenage son in her arms and asked God to give her the strength to help them both. The memories of Mark's brutal murder, his funeral and the days that followed came rushing back, front and center, for both of them. First she had to fight her own demons, and then she could help her son vanquish his.

The neighbors stayed there at the house with her mother and Mirabelle, allowing Kim and her siblings to drive to Nashville, where their father was being treated for life-threatening burns. When they arrived at the Burn Center, located on the fourth floor of the main hospital, the morning nurse in charge of the ICU, Susan Bolden, came out and spoke to them.

"The first forty-eight hours after a burn injury are the most critical," she explained. "Our immediate concerns are to prevent fluid loss and to do all we can to prevent infection."

"When can we see him?" Kim asked.

"Right now, the staff is working with him. He's been given a tetanus vaccination and is receiving fluids, electrolytes, antibiotics and pain medication through an IV. He's also been catheterized."

"Is he in horrible pain?" Kira asked, tears dampening her face.

Nurse Bolden grimaced. "He is in considerable pain, but the medication is helping him."

"Is he going to die?" Kevin asked.

"I can't answer that," Nurse Bolden replied. "Dr. Cummings will speak to you sometime later today. But in the meantime, rest assured that we're doing everything possible for your father."

"Will he need skin grafts?" Kim asked.

Nurse Bolden glanced away as if she couldn't bear to look at them, but she recovered quickly and replied, "It's too soon to know what type of treatment will be required. For now, that's all I can tell you. We have a visitor's lounge on the eleventh floor for the families of our patients. It will probably be during the one o'clock visitation time before y'all can see Reverend Kelley. You might want to have breakfast in the cafeteria or drive to a nearby restaurant. Leave your cell numbers, and someone will contact you if there's any significant change in your father's condition."

With that said, Nurse Bolden disappeared into the intensive care unit. Kim looked at Kevin, who stood there with his shoulders slumped and head bowed. She knew he was praying. When she glanced at her sister, Kira immediately burst into tears and hurled herself into Kim's arms.

"Daddy's going to die, isn't he?" Kira trembled as she cried.

Kim stroked her sister's back and wished she could promise her that their dad would live. She couldn't. From what the Decatur police officers had told them, their father had been doused with gasoline and set on fire. Just like the other three clergymen. Mark Cantrell had been the first. Kim knew his wife, Cathy, who had been a volunteer at Bright Side. It didn't seem possible that the same deranged killer who had murdered Cathy's husband, an Athens minister and a Catholic priest had now tried to kill her father. Why hadn't that monster been caught and put behind bars?

By seven that Saturday evening, it seemed to Cathy that half the world had stopped by her house during the day. Of course, that was a huge exaggeration. Lorie had been the first to arrive. Cathy was thankful that she'd stayed all day and planned to stay with her and Seth tonight. Lorie had served as a buffer between Cathy and the numerous concerned visitors, and she had taken over the dreaded task of contacting J.B. and Mona with the news of Reverend Kelley's condition. Her in-laws had shown up before breakfast, with her mother in tow, and the three of them had stayed until midafternoon. J.B. had wanted Seth to go home with them, but he had adamantly refused.

"Mom needs me to stay with her," Seth had told his

grandfather. "It's what Dad would want me to do. I'm not leaving her."

J.B. had backed off reluctantly.

Donnie and Missy had come by twice, once in the morning and then again only an hour ago. John Earl and his daughters had visited briefly, and Ruth Ann had stopped by on her way home after having worked at Treasures all day. Patsy and Elliott Floyd had been among the many visitors, along with at least a dozen members of Cathy's church.

"You two have to be hungry. I don't think either of you has eaten a bite all day," Lorie said. "I'm going to fix some sandwiches, and I expect both of you to eat."

"I'll help you," Seth said as he followed Lorie toward the kitchen. He paused, glanced over his shoulder and said, "Mom, why don't you sit down or even lie down for a little while and try to relax while no one else is here. I'll come get you when the sandwiches are ready."

"Okay, I'll do that." To humor her protective son, Cathy sat on the sofa, kicked off her shoes and folded her legs at the knees as she pressed her back against the padded armrest.

She was physically, mentally and emotionally exhausted, as much from the parade of well-meaning friends and acquaintances as from the knowledge that Mark's killer had struck again. But she had to admit that having had to deal with company coming and going all day had actually been a blessing, keeping her too busy to allow depression to take hold. Whenever she had gone off by herself, even for a few minutes, either Seth or Lorie had come after her. She hadn't missed the worried look in their eyes and the concerned glances they had exchanged.

The only way she could convince her son and her best friend that she was not going to fall apart was simply not to do it. Yes, whenever she had a quiet moment, such as now, memories of the day Mark had died bombarded her. Unless a person had experienced it, no one could imagine the horror of seeing someone you loved die in such an agonizing way. Mark had gone into shock, and that had lessened his chances for survival. The shock combined with the extent of the third-degree burns covering his body had made recovery impossible. Even now, Cathy asked herself if there was anything she could have done to save Mark.

His death is not your fault. There was nothing more you could have done. Even the paramedics who treated him for shock had been unable to save him.

Tears burned her eyes and tightened her throat. She had needed to cry all day, but had kept her emotions in check, as much for Seth's sake as to prove to herself that she was in control.

When the doorbell rang, she hesitated. Please, God, not more company, not now when she was on the verge of crying her heart out.

As she swung her legs off the sofa and stood, she called out to Lorie and Seth, "I'll get it."

Barefooted, she padded to the front door. The moment she peered through the viewfinder and recognized her visitor, she swung open the door. Jack Perdue stood on her porch, a five o'clock shadow darkening his face.

"Hi, honey. How are you?"

"Holding it together," she replied.

"I can't stay long. The task force is meeting for a big powwow in about an hour, but I wanted to come by and check on you."

She stepped back, allowing him room to enter. The moment he closed the door behind him, he reached out and ran his hand over her cheek. She gasped at his touch, his gentleness breaking the dam that had held her emotions in check all day. Tears seeped from the corners of her eyes. Jack swiped the tears away with his fingertips.

"Ah, babe, don't do this to yourself."

She swallowed her tears as she stared up at him.

Without saying another word, he pulled her into his arms

and held her firmly against him. She wrapped her arms around his waist and laid her head on his chest. Odd how comforting his embrace felt.

He rubbed her back as he kissed her temple. "If you need to cry, go ahead and cry. I'll hold you. You're safe. I won't let anything bad happen to you. Not ever again."

His words were her undoing. She wept in his arms, her body trembling as she released the pent-up emotions that so desperately needed release.

"Mom, who was at the—?" Seth's question died on his lips the moment he saw Jack.

Cathy lifted her head and looked at her son, but Jack held fast, refusing to release her.

"Uh, the sandwiches are ready," Seth said. He looked right at Jack. "We've got more than enough if you'd like to eat with us, Mr. Perdue."

A sense of overwhelming relief spread through Cathy. Her son's cordial invitation to Jack had surprised her. Was it possible that he was finally accepting the fact that she and Jack were friends and her relationship with Jack or any other man was not a betrayal of her marriage vows to his father?

"Thanks," Jack replied. "I haven't had anything since a quick bite of breakfast late this morning when Mike and I stopped by McDonald's."

Cathy eased out of Jack's arms and grasped his hand. "Come on. Let's eat. I suddenly feel very hungry."

Chapter Twenty-one

The Harper family left the courthouse with uplifted spirits and thankful hearts. John Earl gave God the credit for
their good fortune. Judge Stevens had taken many things
into consideration, including Felicity's genuine regret and
promise to stay out of trouble in the future, before announc-
ing his decision in the juvenile court proceedings. Of course,
Sheriff Birkett putting in a good word for Felicity hadn't
hurt. The judge greatly respected Mike's opinion.

After they all piled into the family's SUV—that "all" included not only Ruth Ann and both of their daughters, but
also his mother-in-law and his secretary, Erin McKinley—
John Earl asked for a moment of silence in which to pray. He
kept his words to a minimum.

"Merciful heavenly Father, hallowed is Your name. I, Your
humble servant, come to You with a grateful heart. I ask that
You look down upon my younger daughter, Felicity, and help
her in her efforts to atone for her misconduct by doing the
community service appointed to her by Judge Stevens. Let
her learn from this experience. We all thank You for taking
care of Felicity and helping her to see the error of her ways.

Bless us, oh Lord, and may we always strive to do Your will. In Jesus' name, amen."

Ruth Ann said softly, "Amen."

Before he started the engine, he glanced from his mother-in-law to his secretary. "Would either of you like to go home?"

"I'm rather tired," Faye said, her hands folded securely in her lap. "It's been an exhausting afternoon."

"Aren't you feeling well, Mama?" Ruth Ann asked.

"I'm quite all right, just tired," Faye replied.

"Perhaps John Earl should take you home."

"No, no, that won't be necessary," Faye said. "I should go to the prayer vigil. Every prayer is important."

"If you don't feel up to it, I can easily drop you off at the house on our way," John Earl said. He didn't love his mother-in-law, didn't even especially like her, but he put up with her for Ruth Ann's sake. And also because it was his Christian duty.

"Please don't make such a fuss over me. I want to go to the prayer vigil."

After a few moments of silence, Erin said, "I'd very much like to accompany y'all, if you don't mind my tagging along."

"Of course we don't mind," John Earl assured her. "The more people asking God to help Reverend Kelley, the better. There is great strength in numbers. Having so many voices rising up to heaven will certainly gain the Lord's attention."

Ever since the Decatur minister had been set on fire four days ago, the citizens of Dunmore and the surrounding small towns and the cities of Athens, Decatur and Huntsville had been praying for his recovery. According to reports on Bruce Kelley's condition, the poor man's every breath was drawn in agony. And although all clergymen and their families had become wary and vigilant, John Earl and many others had stood at their pulpits this past Sunday and proclaimed that

God would protect them and that the monster who had killed four innocent men would soon be caught and punished by man's laws.

This evening at six o'clock, before Wednesday night services at their own churches, the good Christians of Dunmore would meet at the black Baptist church, where Reverend Phillips would lead them in a thirty-minute prayer vigil. Patsy Floyd had phoned John Earl yesterday morning, and they had discussed the matter.

"Dewan Phillips came by to see me quite early," Patsy had said. "He would like to invite all the area churches to join his congregation Wednesday evening for a prayer vigil for Bruce Kelley. I was wondering if you'd help me get the word out as quickly as possible."

He had, of course, agreed, and when he had telephoned other clergymen, not one had declined the offer. John Earl expected the small black church to be filled to capacity, possibly overflowing.

Tasha Phillips stood on tiptoe and wrapped her arms around her husband's neck. She loved him with her whole heart. He and their unborn child were her reason for living.

Dewan lowered his head and kissed Tasha, his mouth warm and moist, great tenderness and love in his actions. He cupped her buttocks and held her close.

"Are you ready for this?" she asked him. "I've looked out into the sanctuary. It's nearly full, and it's only twenty till six. I never imagined so many people would actually show up here this evening."

"Why?" he asked, a soft smile curving his wide, full lips. "Because I'm a black minister and this is a black church?"

"There would have been a time when—"

"Things change. Slowly and with great difficulty, but they do change. The people of this town are coming together to pray for a man of God. A good man who has devoted his life to others. Any petty differences and age-old prejudices are being set aside for a greater good."

Tears misted her eyes. "I love you, you know. You're my husband, my lover, the father of my child"—she glanced down at her belly—"and my hero."

"Don't put me up on too high a pedestal," Dewan warned her. "After all, I'm only human." He pressed his cheek against hers. "And later tonight I'll show you just how human."

Tasha giggled softly. He kissed her again and then shoved her gently backward as he slid his hands down her arms and grasped her hands in his. "I need a few moments alone to talk to God and prepare myself."

"I'll be sitting in the front row," she told him as she eased her hands out of his. "I'm so very proud of you."

Tasha left him alone in the small study at the back of the church. She opened the door to the sanctuary and paused before entering, amazed that the church was now almost filled to capacity and the deacons were bringing in folding chairs to place in the aisles.

She didn't know Reverend Kelley, but she had met his elder daughter, Kim Randall, through her community service, and her heart went out to the Kelley family. The life of every clergyman in the region was at risk, including Dewan's life, a thought she could hardly bear. But everyone had to be wondering who the killer would target as his next victim.

With her head held high and a brave expression on her face, she entered the sanctuary and found her spot in the front row between Deacon Fuqua and his wife, Dionne.

She leaned across and spoke to the deacon. "Should someone adjust the air-conditioning? With so many people packed inside the church, it's bound to get hot."

"It's being done," Deacon Fuqua told her. "Can you believe this crowd? I see God's hand in this prayer vigil that Dewan organized."

"God's hand is in everything my husband does," she said.

A flurry of activity up on the podium at the front of the sanctuary gained Tasha's attention. The members of the choir, decked out in their white and gold robes, were taking their places and preparing to sing God's praises. She closed her eyes, her every thought a prayer for all those whose hearts were heavy tonight.

Patsy and Elliott Floyd had arrived in time to find seats in the middle aisle, a few pews from the back of the building. As she glanced around, Patsy was pleased to see so many of her parishioners here this evening. She had sent out e-mails to the entire congregation and made numerous personal phone calls. Tonight's prayer vigil was of great importance on several different levels. First and foremost, Bruce Kelley needed the combined strength of this type of group praying. Second, holding this vigil at the black Baptist church went a long way toward bridging the gap between black and white Christians in the area. Third, this was an example of how all churches, regardless of their doctrine, could support one another. And coming together to pray for one of their own would bring strength and comfort to the ministers and their families who were living each day with fear in their hearts.

As they sat quietly side by side, Elliott reached between them and took her hand in his. They had been married for nearly thirty years, and they had stayed together through thick and thin. They had argued often in the early years, mostly because Elliott had never been at home and she'd been trapped there with two toddlers. She had not been as understanding as she should have been. After all, Elliott had been holding down a part-time job and putting himself through law school. The bills had piled up, and even a new tube of lipstick had been too expensive for their tight budget. Seven years into their marriage, she'd had an affair which had nearly destroyed their union. But because of the two children they shared, they had stayed together. And they'd both been miserable.

Then, twenty years ago, Patsy had experienced a minor epiphany and realized that she had been called to preach. It had not been some miraculous moment when God spoke directly to her in a loud, commanding voice. Actually the exact opposite had happened. In her efforts to bring her children up in the religion in which she'd been raised, Patsy took her son and daughter to church every Sunday, and one Sunday a visiting missionary spoke to the congregation about her years of service to the Lord. In the quiet corners of her heart, Patsy had sensed that she, too, should be spreading the gospel and giving aid to the less fortunate.

Oddly enough, Elliott, who had not been inside a church since he was a teenager, encouraged her to pursue her goal. He had supported her in a way that she had never supported him, and as the years went by, she found herself falling in love with her husband all over again. He was her rock, her helpmate, the love of her life. And she thanked the Lord for their marriage every day of her life.

As she squeezed Elliott's hand, she turned to him and smiled. When he returned her smile, she mouthed the words "I love you."

Cathy had ridden to the prayer vigil with Lorie, and they had found empty spots on the last pew, several rows behind Patsy and Elliott Floyd, and on the same bench with Seth, her mother and her in-laws. Shortly after Donnie and Missy arrived, Missy managed to squeeze in beside Seth, who sat in the middle of the pew between his grandparents. Donnie dragged a folding chair up directly behind Cathy, who sat at the end of the pew. When he reached out and gently clamped his hand down over her shoulder, she turned and smiled at him.

"Great turnout," he said. "Must be a quarter of the town here tonight."

"I doubt anyone from our church would be here if you hadn't encouraged them to see this not as a religious service, but as a community event."

"It is a community event," he said. "It's a community prayer vigil that just happens to be taking place inside a church building."

The choir leader came to the microphone and announced that before Reverend Phillips spoke, they wanted everyone to join them in one hymn. Within minutes the chorus and the visitors joined together to sing an old spiritual that had been popular for generations, "Sweet Hour of Prayer." Halfway through the song, Cathy caught a glimpse of someone in her peripheral vision, someone who had set up a folding chair alongside the end of the pew, right beside her. When she turned to see if she knew the person, her heart skipped a beat. Jackson Perdue, still in his deputy's garb, smiled at her.

Although he had called her a couple of times every day, she hadn't seen him since Saturday night, when she had wept in his arms. She understood that he'd been working night and day with the task force, trying his best to find a killer who seemed to be unstoppable. And until this very moment, she hadn't realized how much she'd missed him and how badly she'd wanted to see him.

She knew that Seth and her in-laws expected her to leave here and go directly to Wednesday night services with them, and that had been her original plan. But now she wished she could slip away with Jack.

She listened as Reverend Dewan Phillips spoke to the crowd. The man was a spellbinding orator, the type who could charm the birds from the trees.

But he was full of himself. A blowhard. He claimed to

give God all the praise, but she knew he lied, knew that in his heart all he cared about was himself. Since it was so obvious to her that this man possessed an evil heart, she didn't understand why everyone couldn't see him for what he was.

Is he to be punished next, Lord? Guide me so that I will know Thy will.

Taking the opportunity to search the crowd while the audience was mesmerized by this silver-tongued devil, she sought out the visiting clergymen and was surprised to see so many different denominations represented. Even Rabbi Tischler and Father Benedict were here. Black and white, Jewish, Catholic and Protestant, the clergymen—and clergywomen, counting Patsy Floyd from the Methodist Church— of Dunmore had come here tonight to pray for the life of Bruce Kelley. Didn't they know that they were praying for a soul already lost to Satan? There was a special place in hell for people such as he, and very soon he would join Mark Cantrell, Charles Randolph and Brian Myers for the eternal punishment he deserved. They had all been false prophets, men professing to do good works, proclaiming they were chosen of God.

Liars! Blasphemers!

The Bible said, in the seventh chapter of Matthew, *"Beware of the false prophets, which come to you in sheep's clothing, but inwardly they are ravening wolves."*

Her gaze fell on Patsy Floyd, an attractive middle-aged woman who exuded warmth and caring. But was she truly the saint people believed her to be?

Show me the way. Point out the evil ones among us.

There were others besides Dewan Phillips.

A voice inside her head whispered a name. She scanned the audience so others would not suspect anything out of the ordinary when her gaze settled briefly on the demon sitting at the back of the church in one of the many folding chairs.

Yes, of course. It was quite obvious to her now who the next false prophet was that God wished for her to punish. A man who committed the most grievous sins, a man she should have already sent straight to the fires of hell.

How many unholy men of God were rapists? Pedophiles? Adulterers? Far too many. All of them needed to be wiped from the face of the earth. It was her duty to act on God's behalf as His angel of death and execute the wicked.

I am blessed to have been chosen.

My life should have been an abomination, and if not for Thy great benevolence, it would have been. But in choosing me as an instrument of Thy punishment, I have been saved.

The prayer vigil ran over by a good fifteen minutes, which left the visitors who attended Wednesday night church services elsewhere approximately forty-five minutes to make their way through the crowd, get to their vehicles and drive to their own churches. Since she was sitting on one of the back pews, Cathy surmised that she should be able to exit the building fairly quickly, but once she stood and looked behind her, she saw dozens of people standing up, all the way from the final pew to the open doorway. And the crowd spilled outside onto the front steps and into the churchyard.

"There must be at least four or five hundred people here," Jack said as he cupped Cathy's elbow. "Did you drive or ride with Lorie?"

"I rode with Lorie."

"I could give you a ride home."

"Thank you, but I'm going from here to Wednesday night services," she told him. "I'd planned to ride with Seth and his grandparents."

Jack nodded.

"If you'd like to go to church with me . . ." she offered.

"I'll pass." He eased his hand away from her arm.

Donnie Hovater spoke directly to Jack. "Hello, Deputy Perdue. Good to see you and Sheriff Birkett and the other lawmen here tonight."

Jack didn't reply, just nodded again.

"Cathy, would you and Seth like a ride to church?" Donnie asked.

"I . . . uh . . ." She glanced at her son, who had his arm draped around Missy Hovater's shoulders. "Yes, thank you. I'm sure that will be fine with J.B. and Mona."

"We'd love to see you at church again," Donnie said to Jack.

"Yeah, sure. You never know when I might show up."

Cathy wondered if she had imagined the competitive glare the two men had exchanged.

"Are there any updates on the case?" Cathy asked, hoping to defuse any tension between Jack and Donnie.

"None that I can discuss," Jack replied.

"I'm sure y'all are doing everything you possibly can," she said.

"I don't mean to interrupt," Donnie said. "But we really should get going. I imagine, considering this crowd, that traffic is going to be a nightmare leaving here."

"Call me," Cathy told Jack, her voice little more than a whisper. A part of her longed to go with him, to forget about everything and everyone except Jack and the way she felt about him.

"Yeah, sure," Jack said before he walked away.

Donnie came around from the back of the pew and called to his daughter. "Missy, honey, Seth and his mom are riding with us." Then he turned to Cathy. "Are you ready?"

"Yes."

She fell into step alongside Donnie, but she kept track of Jack as he made his way through the horde of people ahead of them. Before they reached the front steps, she saw Jack walking across the road to where his car was parked. He didn't look back, not even once.

Was he angry with her? Disappointed? Hurt? It was difficult to tell exactly what Jack was thinking or feeling.

Jack shouldn't matter so much to you, she told herself. *You have enough problems to handle without adding a love affair with Jackson Perdue into the mix.*

After an hour-and-a-half church service, followed by the congregation's own prayer vigil for Bruce Kelley, Seth left with his grandparents, and Donnie insisted on driving Cathy home. Missy had remained in the car while he walked Cathy to her door, and she'd been sure he would have tried to kiss her if his daughter hadn't been with him. If only she could feel half the attraction for Donnie that she felt for Jack, it would make her life far simpler. J.B. and Mona would approve of Donnie. Even now they were beginning to think of him as an honorary member of their family. And she suspected that Seth would approve of her dating Donnie solely because he reminded them both of Mark. Not that the two men were by any means identical, just similar.

Perhaps, in time, she could learn to care for Donnie. After all, when she'd married Mark, she hadn't been in love with him, nor had he been in love with her. She had learned to love him, and they'd had a good life together.

But could she settle for less than being passionately in love for a second time in her life?

No, she couldn't. She wouldn't. She deserved more.

Even if she lived the rest of her life alone, it would be better than settling for less than real love.

As she unbuttoned her lavender silk blouse, Cathy kicked off her black sandals in the bedroom before walking into the bathroom. She placed the blouse in the dry-cleaner pouch she kept hanging on the back of the door. Then she stripped out of her dress slacks and peeled off her bra and panties. Feeling hot and sticky, she looked forward to a nice lukewarm shower, something to relax her and cool her off before bedtime. Temperatures were already in the low nineties, and the humidity was horrendous for this early in June. It wasn't even officially summer, but in Alabama, summertime weather often hit in late spring.

Twenty minutes later, scrubbed clean, her hair damp and her pajamas on, Cathy headed for the kitchen. During her marriage to Mark, she had adhered to his teetotaler philosophy, but while living in Birmingham during her recovery, she had discovered the pleasures of a glass of good wine. Although not a connoisseur by any stretch of the imagination, she knew what she liked. She loved a crisp, white Zinfandel and happily poured a glass from the bottle she kept in the refrigerator.

When the doorbell rang, she glanced at the wall clock. Ten-thirty. Not late by most people's standards, but certainly past the hour for visitors. Had Donnie taken Missy home and returned? She hoped not. The last thing she wanted to do was hurt his feelings, but she couldn't encourage him.

She set her glass on the kitchen table and ran through the house to the bedroom. After grabbing her housecoat off the foot of her bed, she slipped into it, rushed to the front door and flipped on the porch light. The moment she recognized her visitor, she opened the door to him, her heart doing a crazy little rat-a-tat-tat number.

"Evening." Jack stood on the porch, the overhead lamp turning his light hair to burnished gold.

"You're stopping by sort of late, aren't you?" *Dear God, Cathy, was that the only thing you could think of to say?*

He looked her up and down, taking in her damp hair and her sleeping attire. "I guess I should have called first."

"No, it's all right. Really." She eased back a couple of feet and invited him in with a sweeping hand gesture.

"I could have phoned you with the news, but . . . well, I thought it best to tell you in person." He stepped over the threshold.

Cathy's heart stopped for a millisecond. "What's wrong?"

He closed the door behind him, then looked her square in

the eye. "Mike called me about ten minutes ago. Reverend Kelley died tonight, less than an hour ago."

"Oh God, no." Emotion welled up inside her. How foolish of her to believe that a prayer vigil attended by hundreds of people could actually keep Bruce Kelley alive.

"It's probably better this way," Jack said. "The guy was in horrible shape. He couldn't have made it much longer, and he was suffering in the worst way."

Cathy swallowed. "Mark suffered."

"Ah, honey, don't."

When Jack reached out and pulled her into his arms, she went without protest, gladly letting him hold her close. Encompassed within his strong embrace, she felt safe. Her every instinct told her that this was where she belonged. With Jack, the man she had once loved more than life itself.

Chapter Twenty-two

Jack wasn't sure if his motives for coming here tonight to tell Cathy about Bruce Kelley's death were totally unselfish. Maybe somewhere deep inside him, he had believed that she'd need a shoulder to lean on; maybe he'd hoped she would turn to him for comfort. Hell, he wasn't sure of anything except at this precise moment, there was nothing more important to him than the woman he held in his arms. Cathy. His Cathy.

Damn it, man, she hasn't been your Cathy in nearly seventeen years, if she ever was, even back then.

She's mourning the man who replaced you in her bed and in her heart. She's crying for Mark Cantrell. She's hurting because she's remembering how much he suffered before he died.

Jack couldn't move, could barely breathe. All he could do was hold her and let her cry it out. While she trembled, sobs racking her body, he rubbed her back soothingly and pressed his cheek against the top of her head.

God damn it, he hated seeing her like this.

He wasn't sure how long they stood there, just a few feet from the front door, Cathy secure in his arms. Finally, she lifted her head from his chest and gazed up into his eyes. His body tightened. His gut clenched painfully.

"You loved him a lot, didn't you?" Jack didn't know why the hell he'd asked her such a stupid question. Wasn't the answer obvious?

"No." The one word erupted in a hoarse gasp. She shook her head gently and lowered her gaze.

He cupped her chin between his forefinger and thumb and tilted her face so that she couldn't avoid looking right at him. "Want to tell me about it? Why you married him, why you had a nervous breakdown six months after he died, why you're still mourning him?"

"Does any of that really matter?"

"Apparently it does, at least to you."

"I don't want to talk about any of that. Not tonight. And I don't want to discuss Mark with you. It's not fair to you or to his memory. He was a good husband, a good father, a fine human being. It wasn't his fault that . . ." She turned her head and pulled away from Jack.

He followed her as she fled, catching up with her when she stopped abruptly in the middle of the living room. He came up behind her, mere inches separating their bodies, but he didn't touch her.

"You've got to know that I don't want to hurt you," he told her, his voice low and husky. "I heard somebody say once that when a man wants to fuck a woman and wants to protect her at the same time, then he's in love. I don't know if that's true or not, but it sure is how I feel."

She whipped around and faced him, her eyes wide, her expression filled with longing. "I haven't been with anyone. Not since Mark died."

"If you're still not ready . . . if the time isn't right, I'll understand. But I swear, honey, I'm about half out of my mind wanting you."

"Oh, Jack."

She all but flung herself at him, flying straight into his

waiting arms. "I don't care anymore if it's the right time, if I'm ready, if I'll regret it in the morning, if all you want is sex. I just plain don't give a damn."

Her face glowed with the brightness of her smile, and that beautiful smile lit up his whole world, a world that had shrunk to include only the two of them.

Jack lifted her off her feet and up into his arms. He practically ran toward her bedroom. The door stood wide open. A single bedside lamp glowed dimly. The covers had been turned down, and her bed welcomed them.

When John Earl went into the kitchen for a late evening snack, intending to cut himself a piece of Ruth Ann's homemade pecan pie, he was surprised to find his mother-in-law sitting at the table, a mug of hot tea cupped in her hands. She glanced up at him as he entered the kitchen, and they exchanged weary smiles. Faye knew that he tolerated her presence in their home for Ruth Ann's sake. He tried not to blame her for what had happened to Ruth Ann, but if Faye had stood up to her husband . . . If, if, if.

"You're up late," John Earl said.

"I was restless," Faye replied. "Those sleeping pills don't help much any more. I thought some tea might help. What about you? I thought you and Ruth Ann went to bed right after we got home from church."

"She did. She's been asleep for more than half an hour. But I couldn't get that delicious pecan pie off my mind, so I sneaked back down here for a piece."

"Why don't you sit down and let me get you some pie and fix you a cup of tea to go with it?" Faye suggested.

"Thanks. That would be nice."

Just as Faye downed the last drops of her tea and scooted back her chair, the sound of agonized screams echoed down the back stairs and into the kitchen.

"My God, that's Ruth Ann." Faye started toward the stairs.

John Earl moved quickly and dashed ahead of her. He took the steps two at a time and reached the partially open bedroom door before Faye was halfway up the stairs.

John Earl flung open the door and ran into the room. There in the semi-darkness he saw Ruth Ann thrashing about in their bed, her eyes closed, her dark hair disheveled, her arms flinging back and forth as if she were fighting off an attacker. *Dear Lord, help her.* His poor, sweet Ruth Ann could not escape the nightmare that had haunted her all their married life. It had taken years for the nightmares to subside from a few times each week to only occasional unwanted visits. But recently, with two more clergymen murdered—burned to death—those old dreams had resurfaced.

John Earl hurried to his wife, called her name as he sat on the edge of the bed and reached down to pull her gently into his arms. "Wake up, Ruth Ann. It's all right. You were only dreaming."

She beat on his chest, whimpering incoherently.

"It's John Earl, sweetheart. Open your eyes. You're safe. No one can hurt you."

When he heard movement behind him, he glanced over his shoulder and saw Faye standing just inside the doorway. He shook his head.

"Can you understand what she's saying?" Faye asked, a concerned look in her sad eyes.

"No, not this time." He gave his mother-in-law a warning glare, silently cautioning her. The three of them knew the truth, knew what Ruth Ann had endured at the hands of her cruel father. If not for their daughters overhearing her and asking questions, it wouldn't matter what she said in the throes of her subconscious nightmare memories.

"I'll go to my room and leave her to you," Faye told him. "In the past, whenever I've tried to calm her, I've only made matters worse. She needs you. Only you."

He ignored Faye's final comments and focused all his attention on his wife. It took several more tries, with him saying her name and reassuring her that she was safe, before she opened her eyes and recognized him. When she did, she gazed at him like a lost child, tears trickling down her cheeks.

"I'm having those dreams more often," she said. "They're getting worse. And they seem so real. It's as if I'm reliving what happened over and over again."

He took both her hands in his. "I wish there was something I could do. But I can't change the past, and I can't stop the Fire and Brimstone Killer. Even the police seem unable to stop these brutal murders."

She squeezed his hands. "Oh, John Earl, don't you see? In my heart I know that I'm as guilty of murder as the person who killed Mark Cantrell and the others."

"Don't talk nonsense, sweetheart. There is no comparison whatsoever. You were the victim, not the perpetrator."

Ruth Ann closed her eyes as if she could block out the memories by shutting out the light. "He didn't scream, you know. He didn't make a sound. He was asleep, a drugged sleep. And the house burned down around him."

"I know. I know."

She opened her eyes and stared right at John Earl. "If I had it to do over again . . . That's the terrible part. I don't think I would do anything different. I would still let him die. God forgive me."

A soft, quiet voice calling to him alerted John Earl that Ruth Ann's screams had awakened their elder daughter.

"Daddy, is Mama all right?" Charity asked.

"Oh mercy," Ruth Ann whimpered. "Go talk to her, explain that it was just a stupid nightmare."

John Earl eased her backward until her head rested on the down pillow. Then he rose to his feet and turned to face his daughter. Correction, his daughters. Felicity stood directly behind her older sister, both girls peering into the room, their eyes filled with questions and concerns.

He walked out into the hall, shooing them back as he closed the bedroom door. "Your mother had a nightmare. She's all right now."

"She's been having a lot of nightmares lately," Felicity said.

"She used to have them all the time when we were little," Charity said. "You just don't remember."

"You two go back to bed. Everything is all right," he told them as he moved in between them and placed one arm around Charity and the other arm around Felicity.

"She's worried about something bad happening to you, isn't she?" Felicity asked. "She's afraid the person who killed all those other preachers might try to kill you."

"Yes, I'm sure that's it," he agreed. "You know what a worrier your mother is."

"You need to convince her that nothing bad is going to happen to you, not like what happened to those other men," Charity said. "You're a good man, Daddy. God will take care of you."

He leaned over and kissed Charity's forehead. "Yes, He will. And He'll take care of your mother, too. So stop worrying. Go to bed and get a good night's rest. Everything will be better in the morning."

John Earl wanted to believe what he'd said, but if Ruth Ann continued to have the old nightmares, things would get worse instead of better.

Jack set Cathy on the edge of her bed, leaned down and slowly pulled her pajama top up and over her head. She lifted her arms, closed her eyes and savored the moment as the cool air touched her nipples and hardened them to tight buds. When she heard his indrawn breath, she opened her eyes and found him kneeling in front of her, his gaze on her throbbing breasts. She wanted to scream "Touch me," but she couldn't get the words past the knot in her throat.

Mark had wanted her to talk during sex, something she found difficult because she'd been so afraid she would call out Jack's name. She couldn't stop herself from thinking about Jack and the way she'd felt when they had made love.

Don't think about Mark. What I had with him has nothing to do with what's happening now. This is all about Jack and me. I don't have to dream that it's Jack making love to me. The dream has become a reality.

When she reached for him, intending to unbutton his shirt, he grabbed her hands, brought them to his lips and kissed them. She shivered. And before she realized what he was doing, he had unbuttoned his shirt halfway and then dragged it up over his head and tossed it on the floor.

"Might as well get a good look now, honey. It's not a pretty sight." He turned slowly so that she could see his chest, his side and then his back. "The scars from Nolan's beatings are nothing compared to what that explosion did to me."

He knelt in front of her, his gaze cast downward at the scars covering the right side of his body from shoulder to waist.

As she looked at the thick, discolored scar tissue, she sucked in her breath. "Oh, Jack . . . Jack." With an unsteady hand, she reached out and skimmed her fingertips gently over his chest. "It must have been horrible. The pain had to be excruciating."

He covered her hand where it lay in the center of his chest. "It's pretty repulsive, isn't it? I wouldn't blame you if—"

She leaned forward and pressed her lips against his shoulder, then carefully, tenderly, distributed kisses over his battle scars.

Jack closed his eyes and clenched his teeth.

When she lifted her head, she reached out and unbuckled his belt. He opened his eyes, looked up at her and smiled. Then he rose to his feet, unzipped his pants and kicked them off. He stood before her in his brown and black striped briefs, his hairy legs powerful, his scarred chest broad and muscular, his arms large and strong.

"You've filled out nicely," she told him, a teasing smile twitching the corners of her mouth.

"So have you, honey." He opened his hands and covered the undersides of her breasts, lifting them gently as he lowered his mouth to her left nipple.

She whimpered the moment his warm, moist mouth made contact with her hot flesh.

"You like that?"

"Yes," she replied on an indrawn breath.

He switched to the other breast. She cupped the back of his head with one hand, encouraging him to continue, and clamped her other hand over his shoulder to brace herself.

While he laved her nipples, moving back and forth from one breast to the other, he slipped both hands inside the waistband of her pajamas and slid them under her buttocks, lifting her enough to maneuver the bottoms down her hips. She cooperated fully and helped him strip her naked.

Jack pushed her farther back in the bed and then came down over her, straddling her, his knees on either side of her thighs. She reached up between them and caressed his straining sex through the thin barrier of his cotton briefs.

He pushed her hand away as he licked a path from her collarbone to her belly button. Cathy trembled with sexual longing. When he parted her legs and touched her intimately, her buttocks tightened and her body instinctively thrust upward. He moved lower through the thatch of curls, and his tongue found her clitoris and began stroking gently. She whimpered and moaned and latched on to his shoulders as he increased the depth and strength of his laps.

While his mouth worked feverishly, he kept one hand

under her butt and brought the other up to caress her nipples. Within minutes, Cathy became mindless, her entire being centered on achieving pleasure. Her body arched higher. Jack licked and sucked and lapped with an intensity that brought Cathy to the brink and then tossed her headlong into an explosive orgasm.

While the aftershocks of her climax rippled through her, Jack rose to his feet, leaving her for a couple of minutes. When he came back to her, he kissed her long and hard and deep, and she tasted the damp muskiness of her own body on his lips.

He reached between them, took her hand and brought it to his erect penis. When she circled him, she felt the thin condom sheathing his impressive erection.

Without saying a word, he lifted her hips and plunged into her, deep and hard. She gasped as he filled her. With a shared single-mindedness, they came together in a wild frenzy, her body responding feverishly as he hammered into her. He came first, shaking and groaning and then kissing her repeatedly while she climaxed again. Sated completely, he sprawled on top of her for a couple of minutes, and she stroked his back and buttocks. When he rolled away from her and onto his back, he slipped off the full condom and dropped it on top of his briefs lying on the floor. Then he slid his arm beneath her, pulled her up against him and brushed soft, tender kisses down the side of her face from temple to chin.

I still love you, Jack.

The words filled her mind. But she didn't say anything. She lay there in his arms, happier and more fulfilled than she could ever remember.

Jack grabbed the edges of the blanket and sheet, pulled them up over their damp bodies and kissed Cathy. They fell asleep wrapped in each other's arms.

Chapter Twenty-three

Jack and Cathy didn't get much sleep, only taking short naps between lovemaking sessions. They made love as if there were no tomorrow. Each took pleasure and gave it in equal amounts. And when morning came, they showered together and made love again. Cathy tried not to think about the past and tried even harder not to wonder about the future. She wasn't a seventeen-year-old kid with her head in the clouds and a bunch of foolish dreams in her heart. She was thirty-four, widowed and the mother of a son who would soon turn sixteen. She had somehow survived her husband's horrific murder, a mental breakdown that nearly destroyed her and a mother and in-laws who had been determined to keep her son from her. Maybe she had been weak and helpless. Maybe she had needed a trial by fire, so to speak, to harden her into a mature woman. All she knew was that she would never again allow other people to make her decisions and tell her what to do. Whatever she had with Jack this time around, be it sex or love or a combination of the two, she wanted it. If their relationship turned out to be a short affair, so be it. And if it became more . . .

Jack came up behind her, wrapped his arms around her waist and kissed her neck. She squirmed against him.

"Go sit down," she told him. "The pancakes are almost ready."

"How about I pour us both a cup of coffee?" He released her and reached out to retrieve two mugs from the overhead cupboard.

"Thanks. And while you're being my helper, get the syrup out and put it on the table. I've got two kinds. Plain pancake syrup and blueberry flavored. The blueberry is Seth's favorite."

"How about that. It's my favorite, too. One more thing your son and I have in common."

Cathy flipped the four large pancakes on the griddle before replying. "What else do you and Seth have in common?" She tried her best to keep her voice calm and even.

"You," Jack replied. "You're important to both of us. You're his mom, and you're my . . . You're my what? Girlfriend? Lover?"

Cathy breathed a sigh of relief. "I like the sound of both. How about girlfriend in public and lover in private?"

"So you're okay with my referring to you in public as my girlfriend?" He popped her on the butt before he poured their coffee.

"Yes, I'm okay with it, just as long as I can call you my boyfriend." She giggled. "God, we sound like a couple of kids, don't we."

He set their full mugs on the table, and then searched the cupboards for the syrup. "How do you think your in-laws will feel about your dating me?"

"I'm sure they'd prefer that I date Donnie Hovater."

"Yeah, I'm sure they would."

Cathy flipped the pancakes onto two plates, turned off the griddle and carried the plates over to the table. "I prefer you." She set the plates on the table. "I like Donnie, but he doesn't put butterflies in my stomach or make me shiver when he touches me or—"

Jack yanked her into his arms, nuzzled her neck and then he lifted his head and stared into her eyes. "In case there's any doubt in your mind, I'm crazy about you, honey."

She wrapped her arms around his neck, stood on tiptoe, gave him a quick kiss and said, "I'm crazy about you, too."

His smile vanished. "Sooner or later, we'll have to talk about it, you know. About the past. Our past together and our separate pasts."

"Not now. Not yet."

"No, not yet, but someday soon."

Yes, someday soon, she would have to tell him why she had married Mark Cantrell. But did she dare tell him the truth?

Seth stopped outside the kitchen when he heard his grandmother mention his mother's name. What was she doing here so early in the morning? Grandmother lived nearby and often dropped in unexpectedly, but seldom for breakfast. He stood quietly by the closed door and listened.

"You seem terribly upset, Elaine," Mona said. "Why don't you sit down and let me get you some coffee."

"Didn't you hear me? I just got off the phone with Gayle Laney. She lives across the street from Cathy."

"Yes, dear, I heard you, but when I asked if Cathy was all right, you said that she was, so why are you so upset?"

"Where's J.B.?"

"He's shaving."

"I don't know if we dare tell him about this."

"About what?"

"Gayle was doing what she believed was her Christian duty," Elaine said. "She's not a busybody, and she even said it was none of her business, but she thought, as Cathy's mother, I should know."

"For goodness sakes, know what?"

"That there was a strange car—a Corvette—parked in Cathy's driveway all night."

"Was there?"

"You don't seem shocked."

"Should I be?"

"Yes, you should be. The car belonged to Jackson Perdue. Of all men, Jack Perdue!"

"Lower your voice," Mona suggested. "I think you're right about our not telling J.B. It would only upset him."

"Aren't you upset? I certainly am. By lunchtime today, the whole town will know that Cathy had an overnight visitor. I don't think we can keep this from J.B. for very long."

"Perhaps not, but I'd prefer you let me tell him when it becomes necessary," Mona said.

"I don't know where I went wrong with that girl. I did my best to bring her up the right way, but—"

"This Jack Perdue, he's the boy Cathy was in love with when she was a teenager, isn't he?"

Silence.

Seth needed to hear his grandmother's answer.

"Yes," Elaine said so quietly that Seth barely heard her. "He was wrong for her then, and he's wrong for her now."

"That isn't your decision to make, is it?"

Elaine gasped. "You can't possibly approve of—"

"It's not my place to approve or disapprove of Cathy's decision."

"Don't you think her having an affair with Jack Perdue will adversely affect all our lives, especially Seth's?"

"Seth is nearly sixteen. He's not a child. He has to know that it would be wrong for Cathy to spend the rest of her life mourning Mark."

"You're far more understanding of my daughter's human frailties than most mothers-in-law would be."

"I love Cathy. She was very good to my son and . . . and she gave us a grandchild when I'd given up hope of ever . . .

Elaine, if she loves this man, she has every right to be with him."

His mom had been in love with Jack Perdue when she'd been a teenager, before she'd married his dad. And now she might be in love with him again. Seth wasn't sure how he felt about his mom being with another man. He'd thought maybe she would start dating Brother Hovater. He kind of reminded him of his dad. He guessed it was selfish of him to wish that his mom wouldn't date anybody, that she'd stay true to his dad forever.

Yeah, that was stupid. His father was dead. His mother was still a fairly young woman. It was only natural that she'd want to get married again and maybe have more kids.

But why did the guy have to be Jackson Perdue?

Why not? What was wrong with Jack?

"Since we don't seem to be very busy this morning, I'm going to take my break," Lorie told Cathy. "And unless we're swamped with customers, I may try to catch up on the book-keeping."

"Go ahead," Cathy said. "I think I can hold down the fort." She glanced around at their entirely empty shop.

Lorie laughed. "Are you sure you have the energy to even stay awake?" She lowered her voice. "Going at it hot and heavy all night with the golden god had to have taken a lot out of you."

Grinning shyly, Cathy motioned for Lorie to hush. "Stop that. You don't know who might walk in and overhear you."

"Oh, sweetie, if you think half the town doesn't already know that Jack's Vette was parked in your driveway all night, then you're far more naive than I thought you were."

Cathy huffed, hating to admit that Lorie was right. "I know, and I'm dreading having to deal with what my mother is going to say and how J.B. and Mona will react."

"It's none of their damn business. Tell them that."

"I just might do it. But if Seth finds out that—"

The tinkling chime hanging over the front door jingled, alerting them that a customer had just entered the store. Both of them glanced at the door. Cathy's heart sank.

"I'll leave you two alone," Lorie whispered and hurried off toward the back storeroom.

Cathy faced her son. She could tell just by looking at him that Seth was upset, and she had a pretty good idea why.

"Good morning. I'm surprised to see you here. I thought you were still grounded," Cathy said.

"I am, but Nana gave me permission to come see you. She dropped me off and told me she'd pick me up when I called her."

"That was very nice of Mona."

"Is it true?" Seth demanded.

"Is what true?"

"Did Jackson Perdue spend the night with you?"

This was what she had dreaded far more than a confrontation with either her mother or her in-laws. Despite being six feet tall and thinking he was grown, Seth was still just a boy on the verge of manhood. As far as she knew, he was still a virgin. Actually, she'd bet money on it. How could she explain to him about his mother having sex with a man who wasn't her husband?

An old adage instantly came to mind. Honesty is the best policy.

"Yes, Jack spent the night with me."

"You do know that everybody in town is talking about it, don't you? Some neighbor of yours called Grandmother this morning, and she couldn't wait to come over and tell Nana."

"Gossip travels fast, especially juicy gossip."

"I don't like my mother being gossiped about that way."

"I'm sorry if Jack spending the night with me has caused you any embarrassment, but what I do in my personal life is nobody's business."

"It's my business. You're my mother."

"Yes, I'm your mother and I love you, and because of those two facts, I'd prefer to have your approval. Jack and I are going be seeing a lot of each other. We're officially dating."

"Dating. Is that what you call it? He spent the night."

"Yes, he did."

"You had sex, didn't you?"

"Yes, we did."

Groaning, Seth shook his head, then turned from her and forked his fingers through his thick brown hair. "What if I said that I don't want you seeing him again?" He lifted his gaze hesitantly.

She looked right at him. "I love you more than anything, Seth. I'd do anything for you, but you're a fifteen-year-old boy. You're the child, and I'm the adult. I have no intention of allowing you to issue orders to me, to tell me who I can and cannot date."

"Yeah, well, go ahead and date whoever you damn well please, but don't expect me to like it. I thought I wanted to come live with you, but if he's going to be around all the time, I might change my mind and stay with Granddaddy and Nana."

So there it was, the thing she had feared the most. Her own son was blackmailing her to get his way. The thought of losing him to his grandfather unnerved her, but she could not allow him to get away with bullying her. She had walked that path with her mother and her father-in-law and even sometimes with Mark. She wanted her son to be a better person, to be the man she knew he could be.

"I want you to live with me," she told him, keeping her voice far calmer than she felt. "But if you prefer to stay with your grandparents, then that's what you should do. Jack and I are going to be seeing quite a bit of each other. I don't know what the future holds for us, but he and I have a right to find out." She searched Seth's eyes, hoping to see even a glimmer of understanding. "I have a right to be happy, don't I?"

"Does he make you happy?"

"Yes, he does. He makes me very happy."

"I heard Nana ask Grandmother if he was the guy you were in love with when you were a teenager. Grandmother said he was and that he was wrong for you then and he's still wrong for you. Were you in love with him before you married Dad?"

"Yes. Jack was my first love." *And my first lover.*

"Did you love him more than you loved Dad?"

"Oh, Seth."

"Did you?"

"I loved Mark in a different way."

"Did Dad know about him?"

"Yes, Mark knew all about Jack, just as I knew all about his first wife. Your father and I didn't have any secrets from each other."

Seth stood there, sulky and quiet, his eyes wide and an angry flush on his cheeks. "Does Jack Perdue mean more to you than I do?"

"No one means more to me than you do. Don't you know that?"

"But you do love him, don't you?"

"I don't know. Maybe. We're just getting to know each other again."

"Does he love you?"

"I don't know. I don't think even he knows for sure."

"He could wind up hurting you. He could break your heart."

"Yes, he could. And I could break his heart, too." *We did that to each other years ago, and there are no more guarantees now than there had been then.* "It's a risk you take when you go into a relationship, when you open yourself up to care about someone. I think maybe you might know a little something about that."

"Huh?" He looked at her with a puzzled expression on his face.

"Am I wrong about your liking Missy Hovater?"

"Jeez, Mom, Missy and I are just friends."

"But you'd like for there to be more between you, and if it doesn't work out and she starts dating someone else, it's going to break your heart just a little, isn't it? You're taking a chance by liking Missy. That's what I'm doing with Jack. I'm taking a chance that in the end, we'll feel the same way about each other."

Seth stared at her, and for a moment she wasn't sure she'd gotten through to him. Then suddenly she noticed a change in his expression.

"You don't care that everybody knows?" Seth asked. "I mean, you were a preacher's wife and here you are having sex outside of marriage. Granddad's going to call that fornication."

"Granddad can call it whatever he wants to call it," Cathy said. "And no, I don't care if everybody in town knows that I'm sleeping with Jack Perdue. Who I have sex with is no one else's business. Not even yours."

Seth swallowed. "Yeah, maybe you're right. I don't know. It's just that I wish . . . I wish . . ." He turned from her, and she knew he was on the verge of crying.

She walked over to him, placed her hand on his shoulder and asked, "What do you wish?"

"I wish my dad were still alive. I wish he hadn't died. I wish we were still a family. How stupid is that? Wishing for the impossible."

Cathy wrapped her arms around her son and hugged him. "It's not stupid at all. And if I could bring Mark back to us, I would. But I can't. And we both have to find a way to go on without him. We have to build a new life for ourselves."

"And that new life includes Jack Perdue, at least for you."

"Maybe. And if that happens, I hope you'll give Jack a chance to be a part of your life, too."

Seth pulled away from her. "I'm not making any promises."

"I don't expect you to. Just be the wonderful, kindhearted and caring young man I know that you are. That's all I ask."

"If he hurts you, he'll have to answer to me."

Cathy barely managed to stop herself from smiling. How very sweet that Seth saw himself as her protector. Her heart sighed. She hadn't lost him. He was still her son.

And in time . . .

Chapter Twenty-four

Maleah had enjoyed the time that Nic and she had spent with Nic's brother in San Francisco, where he lived and worked as an up-and-coming young artist. His paintings had in the past few years garnered numerous wealthy patrons, including Nic's husband, Griff. Of course, Maleah couldn't afford the price of even one of Charles David's sketches. She'd been surprised when, several evenings ago, he had asked her permission to sketch her and then only this morning had presented the sketch to her as a farewell gift.

If Nic's brother wasn't already involved with a very lovely woman—almost twice his age—Maleah might have fallen for him. He was handsome, intelligent and talented as well as kind and sensitive. Why were all the good ones unavailable?

While Maleah had filled her days with sightseeing, shopping and indulging in sleeping late and eating too much— she'd probably gained five pounds since they'd been here—Nic had simply put on a happy face. Each time Nic had spoken to Griff, she had come away from his phone call moody and depressed. It seemed that his business trip to Europe, which had been supposed to last only a few days, had required him

to stay much longer than he'd intended. When he called yesterday and told Nic that he was coming home via San Francisco to pick up her and Maleah, you'd have thought that the
news would have made Nic happy. It hadn't.

"As long as he was out of the country, I could halfway
pretend everything was all right," Nic had said. "But once
we're face-to-face again . . . He's keeping secrets from me,
secrets that have to do with his past. Something's happened
in Europe, something I think Yvette and Sanders know
about, but Griff hasn't shared with me."

Maleah understood her friend's frustration. If her husband shared a mysterious past with another woman, she'd
probably be as jealous as all get-out. And if he shared things
with that woman he didn't with her, and if that woman knew
more about what was going on with him than she did, she'd
be pissed enough to contemplate cutting off his balls. By nature, Maleah wasn't a violent person, but by God, she had
learned that if you didn't stand up for yourself against the
bullies of this world, they would knock you down and walk
all over you. Not that Griff was by any means a bully. Not
the way her stepfather had been. Nolan Reaves had been
downright mean.

For the most part, she didn't think about her stepfather.
And that was one reason she would never go back to Dunmore to live. She wondered how in the world Jack could not
only return to their hometown but actually move into the
house of horrors where they had grown up under Nolan's
cruel domination.

Because Jack's tougher than you are. He always was.

She didn't like to think about what her brother had sacri-
ficed for her, how many beatings he had taken in order to
spare her Nolan's wrath. The verbal lashes, the mental and
emotional torment he'd put them all through year after year,
had been bad enough. No one could have stopped that, not
even Jack. Being a cruel tyrant had been who Nolan was,
and no amount of threats could have changed his basic per-

sonality. Only when Jack got old enough—and big enough—
to pose a physical threat to the old bastard had he stopped
beating Jack.

Yeah, she might be a tough broad, but she was a marsh-
mallow compared to Jack. And yet there he was in Dunmore,
facing down his demons, rebuilding his life and rekindling
an old romance. She hoped that this time he and Cathy got it
right. After all, if Jack didn't get married and produce a few
kids, the Perdue line would die with the two of them. She
sure as hell had no intention of ever getting married, of tying
herself to some man who would expect to tell her what she
could and couldn't do. Yeah, yeah, so there were marriages
that actually worked, where the husband and wife were equal
partners. She'd thought that was the kind of marriage Nic
and Griff had. Apparently, she'd been wrong.

It wasn't that she didn't like men. She did. And she loved
sex, at least she had with a couple of partners, both now part
of her past. One had been her college boyfriend. But when
he'd asked her to marry him, she'd ended things. And then,
several years ago, she'd gotten involved with a fantastic guy
who had a truly liberal attitude about women. Their love affair had lasted nearly two years until he, too, had brought up
the idea of their getting married.

Maleah stuffed the remainder of her recent purchases into
the oversized duffel bag she'd bought just to hold these
items. Griff was due to arrive within the hour, and after a
brief visit and lunch here at Charles David's loft, they'd fly
home to Knoxville this afternoon. Considering the inevitable tense atmosphere on the trip from California to Tennessee, Maleah was not looking forward to being trapped on
the private jet with the feuding Powells.

With the death of the Fire and Brimstone Killer's fourth
victim, the head of the task force, ABI agent Wayne Morgan
had called a meeting for today and was using Mike Birkett's

office as the force's headquarters. The first thing he'd done when he arrived twenty minutes ago was inform the ten-man group that he was cutting the force back to five members.

"Every law-enforcement agency in northern Alabama will be kept informed of what we're doing and any new information we unearth," Morgan had said. "But in order to be more effective, we need to streamline this operation. And if it becomes necessary to call in the Feds, my cutting the numbers will save them the trouble."

"Have you contacted the FBI?" Derek Lawrence had asked.

"Yes, I've spoken to Jeff Ballard, the AIC at the Birmingham office. He's been very cooperative, but no one is going to come in and take over the investigation at this point. Not without an invitation."

A couple of the guys grumbled about being cut from the task force, but Jack figured that was more for show than their actually being pissed about the matter. It wasn't that he didn't have great respect for local policemen and deputies, but for the most part, as Mike had pointed out, they were just good old boys with high school diplomas and a desire to keep law and order in their towns and counties. Most of them were no more equipped with knowledge or experience than he was to deal with a serial killer. And in this case, a killer who had gotten away with four murders and left behind no substantial evidence that would link him or her to the crimes.

"I've ordered lunch for the five of us," Mike Birkett told Morgan. "If we make this a working lunch, I figure we can wrap things up sooner."

"Good idea." Morgan nodded and then glanced at Derek. "Why don't we start with you, Lawrence? You're the big-time expert."

Derek grinned. "I know you boys are counting on me to solve these murders for you, but you're going to have to provide me with a little more to go on than four corpses."

No wonder people assumed Derek was a cocky SOB. Actually, he wasn't, but he sure put a great deal of effort into presenting himself as one. During their brief acquaintance, Jack had gotten to know the real Derek, at least to some degree. Yeah, he could be a bit cocky, but in his shoes, who wouldn't be? He was rich, brilliant and handsome.

"We've shared more than four corpses with you," Mike said. "You've been given access to everything we have."

"Which is zip," Derek replied. "No witnesses. No clear fingerprints. No hair or fibers. No DNA. Some Pocket Torch lighters that can be purchased almost anywhere. And the shoe and tire prints at the scenes were too numerous to link them to the crimes. Even the weapon of choice—in this case, fire—can't be traced. Gasoline is readily available. And the only thing our killer needed to ignite it was an open flame— the torch lighters that feature a flame lock. There was no gasoline can left behind, so that means our killer took it with him . . . or her. And my gut says our killer is female."

"Are you basing that on the state M.E.'s findings?" Sergeant Jeremy Pritchett, a husky, middle-aged black man, asked. "Wasn't it just an educated guess on his part that the killer was shorter than the victims, thus assuming the killer was probably female?"

Pritchett was a seasoned cop from Huntsville. He had fifteen years of police work under his belt, so Jack could see why Morgan had kept him on the task force. Actually, he knew why the other three had also been chosen. But why he hadn't been eliminated was a puzzle to him. Of everyone present, he was the least qualified.

"Sometimes educated guesses are all we have." Karla Ross, the lone female member of the force, turned her sharp gaze on Pritchett.

The lady was all business, a real no-nonsense type who wore her hair severely short, didn't bother with makeup and walked with a swagger to balance the chip on her shoulder. She was a woman climbing the ladder of success in a man's world, and she was damned and determined to prove something to every man she met. She had the "I'm as good as you, probably better" attitude written all over her.

"Ross is right," Derek said. "A great deal of profiling involves educated guesses and just plain old gut instinct. It's not by any means an exact science, nor is it a mystical art. It's a skill—nothing more, nothing less. And we make mistakes, God help us."

Agent Ross studied Derek with newfound respect, and Sergeant Pritchett nodded in agreement with Derek's self-assessment, with his admission of being fallible.

A knock on the half glass door gained everyone's attention. Mike motioned for the young deputy to enter.

Clint Willis opened the door and stuck his head in. "Lunch is here. Want me to send the guy in with it or . . ."

"Send him in," Mike said. "And see if somebody will put on a fresh pot of coffee."

"Sure thing." Clint hesitated.

"Is there something else?" Mike asked.

"Yes, sir. Uh, there's a kid out here who says he wants to talk to Jack."

Mike lifted his brows. "This kid got a name?"

"Yes, sir. He's Seth Cantrell."

Mike and Jack exchanged quick, questioning glances.

"You probably need to take care of that," Mike told him.

"Yeah, thanks." Jack came out of the corner where he'd been standing observing the others during the meeting and walked into the outer office.

He saw Seth at the far end of the room, alone and looking nervous. Not for the first time, he noted how much Cathy's son resembled her. Of course, Jack had never met Mark Cantrell, even though they'd lived in the same town for a number of years, so he had no idea if Seth looked anything like his father. When he approached the boy, he sensed frustration and anger.

"You wanted to see me?" Jack asked, doing his best to keep his tone friendly.

"Yes, sir, I did."

"What can I do for you?"

Seth shifted nervously. His face flushed. "You can promise me that you won't hurt my mother."

"What?"

"I said—"

"I heard what you said, but I think you need to be a little more specific."

"If you hurt my mother, you'll have to answer to me. Is that specific enough for you, Deputy Perdue?"

The boy had balls. Not many fifteen-year-old kids would confront a man twice their age and a great deal larger, who also happened to be a deputy. It was obvious that Seth Cantrell saw himself as his mother's protector, and damn if Jack didn't admire the boy for it. Over dinner that evening, he debated whether to tell Cathy about Seth's visit to the sheriff's office that morning.

"Don't you like smoked pork chops?" Cathy asked.

"Huh?" Jack had been so deep in thought that the only words he'd caught were pork chops. "They're delicious." He reached over on the platter, pierced another juicy, tender chop and laid it on his plate.

Cathy eyed him quizzically. "Want to tell me what you're thinking about so hard that you stopped eating?"

The chop was so tender he was able to slice it with his fork. After eating a couple of large bites, along with some mashed potatoes and butter beans, he rinsed it down with iced tea.

"Seth stopped by the office today," Jack told her.

"Did he say or do anything that he shouldn't have?"

"Get that worried mother-hen look off your face. Seth behaved himself."

She sighed.

"He told me that if I hurt you, I'd have to answer to him."

Cathy's eyes widened. "He didn't." The corners of her mouth tilted upward in a hint of a smile.

"Oh, he did. You'd have been proud of him."

"I am. It's just—"

"He knows about us, about the fact that I spent the night here last night."

Cathy's lips curved into a closed-mouth smile. "Oh, yes, he knows. My guess is that everybody in Dunmore knows. It seems I have at least one nosy neighbor who thought it was her Christian duty to call my mother this morning and tell her."

"Son of a bitch," Jack grumbled. "Did you have to deal with your mother today?"

"Sort of. She stopped by Treasures, and before she opened her mouth, I told her, in front of several customers, that I was thirty-four years old and that my personal life was no one's business but my own, and that included her."

"Have you talked to Seth?"

"He came to see me this morning. I'm pretty sure that's why he confronted you. You see, I told him that you and I are going to be seeing quite a bit of each other and that I didn't know what the future held for us, but we had a right to find out."

Jack released a long, low whistle. "So how'd that go over?"

"He wasn't thrilled," Cathy admitted. "About our dating or . . . or about our sleeping together."

"You admitted to him that we—"

"He's fifteen, Jack, not five. He knew you spent the night. Besides, I told him that who I have sex with is no one else's business and that I don't care if everybody in town knows you and I are lovers."

Jack let out a loud, guttural laugh. "Damn if I don't know where your son gets his brass balls. Lady, you amaze me.

What happened to that sweet, shy, people-pleaser you used to be?"

"She grew up. And like you said, she grew a set."

Jack shoved back his chair so quickly that he almost toppled it over. He rounded the small kitchen table where they'd been eating the delicious meal Cathy had prepared and yanked her out of her chair. Startled by his sudden, unexpected actions, she shrieked, but when he hauled her up against him and gave her a resounding kiss, she kissed him back.

They broke apart, both of them laughing.

He tugged on her hand and nodded toward the door.

"But I made banana pudding for dessert," she told him.

"It'll keep. We can have it for a midnight snack."

"Midnight snack? But it's only seven o'clock. Do you plan to keep me in bed for the next five hours?"

"Yep. We'll make love for five hours, take a break and eat banana pudding, then make love again."

She didn't hesitate another second. She followed him out of the kitchen, down the hall and straight to her bedroom.

Chapter Twenty-five

Griff had handled this situation all wrong from the very beginning. He had kept the truth from Nic, telling himself that he was protecting her. That had been as good an excuse as any, and a partial truth. He did want to protect Nic. She was the most important thing in the world to him. He'd kill to protect her. He'd die to protect her.

His first allegiance should always be to his wife, but . . .

Nic had known when she married him that secrets from his past haunted him, that he had shared only a small portion of the truth with her. There were things he never wanted her to know, things that he would pay any price to forget. And he had sworn an oath to Yvette and Sanders, as they had to him. He was bound by that oath, as they were, and only when the three of them were in complete agreement were they free to share any portion of their traumatic past with anyone outside their survivor's trinity.

Yvette and Sanders had allowed him to tell Nic the bare facts of the ordeal they had endured as Malcolm York's captives. He had even warned Nic that the brutal savage York had turned him into during his years on Amara still existed inside him. And now more than ever, that knowledge worried Griff, because he knew how easily he could revert to the inhuman beast he had once been.

If it turned out that the rumors whispered in certain sections throughout Europe had any basis in fact, they were all in mortal danger: he, Sanders, Yvette and anyone they loved. Nic would be in great danger, and just the thought ignited a fierce anger inside him that he hadn't felt since she had almost died at the hands of serial killer Ross Everhart.

He had chartered a plane for Meredith Sinclair and Luke Sentell, who was acting as her bodyguard and keeper, and they had returned to Griffin's Rest before Griff. He had taken his brief stopover in San Francisco to pick up Nic and Maleah into account when planning for Meredith to return to Tennessee ahead of him. Nic would have asked far too many questions had Meredith and Luke accompanied them, questions he wasn't prepared to answer. Not yet. Not until it was absolutely necessary.

Griff had hated using Meredith the way they had, but she had cooperated of her own free will, even though they all knew that she'd done it only out of obligation to Yvette. The poor girl was cursed with an amazing ability even greater than her mentor's, an ability that a man such as York would have used in the most diabolical ways. But in this case, she was working against the kind of evil Malcolm York had inflicted on the world.

As he stood by the balcony doors, Griff glanced back at Nicole as she lay sleeping peacefully in their bed. He worshipped the ground she walked on. He had never loved anyone the way he loved her. She was his life. But because of the secrecy surrounding his actions recently, she had begun pulling away from him. And she blamed Yvette and even suspected Yvette of coming between them. How could she ever think that he would betray her with another woman, even Yvette, whom he also loved? But his love for Yvette was that of a comrade, a fellow soldier who had survived the same grueling war. She and Sanders were his best friends.

They were his sister and brother of the soul. He owed them his life, and it was a debt that he intended to continue repaying for as long as he lived.

Trust me, Nic. Believe in our love. Know that whatever I do, I do to protect you.

The Ice Palace ice-cream parlor on the corner of Main and Fourth Streets in downtown Dunmore had become one of the favorite family hangouts on weekend nights, especially during the summer months. But even in the coldest weather, residents often stopped by after dinner or a movie or bowling for a cup of gourmet coffee, delicious lattes and to-die-for hot chocolate. And their home-baked desserts were favorites of adults, teens and children. This Friday night appeared to be no exception, and even with summer weekend hours extended to make closing time at eleven, there was still a line to get into the parlor.

"If they didn't have the most delicious caramel ice cream this side of heaven, I wouldn't wait in line." Lorie shifted from one foot to the other. "My feet are killing me."

"If you hadn't worn four-inch heels tonight, your feet wouldn't be bothering you," Cathy said. "You're the only woman I know who wears heels to the movies."

"I'm short, but in heels I'm tall." She sighed, and then admitted, "Well, in heels, I'm not as short."

"We could get ice cream over at the Dairy Dip a lot faster," Seth said, then looked at Cathy. "Would you let me drive? I promise that I'll be very careful. Please, Mom."

"We're not going to the Dairy Dip," Cathy told him. "Not after we've already stood in line for fifteen minutes to get in here. But maybe I'll let you drive when we leave."

"Thanks, Mom. You're the greatest."

Having gotten what he wanted, Seth scanned the waiting crowd, and his attention was quickly captured by two teenagers near the back of the long, half-block line.

"Hey, I see a couple of guys I know," Seth said. "I'm going back there to say hi." He glanced at the front door of the parlor and realized they were next in line to be seated. "It'll just take a sec. Promise."

As soon as Seth headed toward his friends, Cathy lowered her voice and asked Lorie, "So, what's the real reason we're here?"

Putting on a fake I'm-totally-innocent face, Lorie replied, "I don't know what you're talking about."

"I don't remember your having a passion for caramel ice cream or for any flavor of ice cream for that matter, and yet you insisted we stop by here after we left the theater. Why?"

The hostess called out "Cantrell," and when Lorie and Cathy approached, she checked the name off her list and showed them to a round table near the row of booths that circled the soda-fountain counter.

"My son is with us," Cathy said. "Seth Cantrell. He'll be joining us in a couple of minutes."

"Yes, ma'am."

Suddenly Lorie's motives for insisting on showing up at the Ice Palace tonight became abundantly clear. Mike Birkett and his two children sat in a booth almost directly across from their table. When Cathy saw Mike, she smiled and spoke. He lifted his eyes from his banana split and returned Cathy's warm smile. Then, when he noticed her companion, his smile vanished.

As soon as they took their seats at the small round table, Cathy leaned over and said softly, "You knew Mike would be here, didn't you?"

"Guilty as charged."

"Oh, Lorie, why do you do these things to yourself?"

"I'm a glutton for punishment. I'm a masochist. I like getting my teeth kicked in on a regular basis."

"Mike's not the only man in the world, you know."

"Yeah, sure, Ms. I-think-I'm-falling-in-love-with-Jack again.

Easy for you to say when the man of your dreams has slept in your bed and curled your toes the past couple of nights."

"It takes two," Cathy reminded her. "Jack's a willing participant. Mike's not. And I hate to see you keep pining away for him when it's obvious he's—"

"Shush. Here comes Seth, and he's not alone."

"What?" Cathy turned her head to see which one of his young friends Seth had invited to join them and was beyond surprised to see Jack walking alongside him.

And Seth didn't look angry or upset.

"Good evening, ladies," Jack said. "Mind if I join y'all?"

"I ran into Mr. Perdue outside, and I invited him to sit with us," Seth said as casually as if he'd said it was warm outside tonight.

"We'd love for you to join us." Lorie grinned at Jack.

"Yes, please sit down." Cathy glanced from Jack to Seth. "Both of you sit."

"Nice night." Jack sat in the chrome and vinyl diner chair to Cathy's left.

"I was out taking an evening walk and happened to notice the long line outside this place, so I stopped to see what was going on."

"That's when I saw him," Seth said. "I figured tonight was as good a time as any to show everybody that I'm okay with you two dating."

"You are?" Cathy stared at her son. "I thought you didn't approve of my seeing Jack, that you were concerned about what people might say."

Seth looked directly at Jack. "Mr. Perdue and I had a talk, and he knows how I feel about things."

"I see. Since I'm your mother, would you mind sharing how you feel with me?"

"Nobody has the right to tell you who you should date, not even me. My dad's dead, and neither of us can change that fact. You were bound to start dating sooner or later, and

I'd be a selfish brat if I expected you to spend the rest of your life alone."

Cathy reached over and squeezed Seth's hand. "When did you grow up into such a wonderful young man? The last time I looked, you were just a little boy."

He eased his hands out of Cathy's, all the while glancing around to see if anybody noticed his mother holding his hand. He was a typical teenage boy in that respect.

On the verge of crying happy tears, Cathy laughed.

Just as the waitress came to take their order, Jack said, "How about you call me Jack from now on? Mr. Perdue sounds a bit formal to me."

"Yes, sir," Seth replied in a not overly friendly but a respectful manner.

Cathy felt as if she were dreaming. Seth had shown an amazing maturity in his about-face concerning her relationship with Jack. And so quickly. She had been concerned about her son's attitude, afraid that she might lose him if she stood her ground and continued seeing Jack. But what good was her hard-won independence if, when confronted with her first extremely difficult choice, she reverted back to pleasing others instead of herself, even if that other person was her own son?

"What'll it be folks?" asked the forty-something blond waitress wearing fifties-style blue jeans, white shirt and ponytail.

"A double scoop of caramel ice cream in a waffle cone," Lorie said without a moment's hesitation.

"Just a Cherry Coke for me," Cathy said.

"Hot-fudge sundae," Jack and Seth replied simultaneously.

Jack grinned. "With extra walnuts."

"Yeah, me, too," Seth told the waitress.

Cathy forced a smile. "I've changed my mind. Make that three hot-fudge sundaes with extra walnuts."

Seth looked at her questioningly. "I didn't think you liked walnuts."

"Oh, you're right. Sorry. Make that pecans."

"Yes, ma'am." The waitress repeated the order and then asked Cathy, "You still want the Cherry Coke, too?"

"No, thank you."

Think of something to say to avert either Jack or Seth from commenting on what a coincidence it was that they both loved hot-fudge sundaes with walnuts.

She knew it was silly of her to worry about such a mundane matter. After all, millions of people loved hot-fudge sundaes, didn't they?

"This has to be the most popular place in town." She glanced around at the full-to-capacity interior. "I see quite a few people I know."

"Yeah, ever since it opened last summer, it's been *the* happening place," Lorie said a bit too enthusiastically. "Even the local ministers hang out here." She laughed, the sound slightly shrill. "Look over there." She lifted her hand and waved. "There's Patsy and Elliott."

"Isn't that Reverend Phillips and his wife?" Seth asked, and they all followed his line of vision to where the black Baptist minister and his wife sat on bar stools at the counter.

As his gaze surveyed the room, Jack paused when he saw his boss. "There's Mike with M.J. and Hannah." Jack threw up his hand and waved. Mike motioned to Jack. "If y'all will excuse me for a minute, I'll go over to say hi."

As soon as Jack left the table, Seth stood and said, "I think I'll choose some tunes on the jukebox. Lorie, have you got a preference?"

"Just something loud and fun," Lorie told him. "Something that'll make us want to shake our booties."

Seth laughed. "I'll see what I can do."

"What about your mom? Aren't you going to choose something for her?"

"I already know what Mom will want to hear. She used to

play it a lot when I was a kid." Not waiting for a response, Seth made his way through the crowded tables to the juke-box, a modern replica of the type popular in the fifties.

Cathy wanted to call Seth back, to ask him not to choose that particular song, but how could she explain to him why, tonight of all nights, she didn't want to hear what he knew was her heart's choice?

"You've got an odd look on your face." Lorie studied her closely. "You're not still concerned about Jack and Seth ordering the same dessert, are you?"

"Goodness, no. A lot of people love hot-fudge sundaes. It's not as if preferences in food are considered hereditary."

Lorie nodded. "Yeah, you're right." She glanced to where Jack stood by the booth across from their table, he and Mike talking and laughing. "I need to find myself a boyfriend. Somebody big and strong and good-looking. Somebody who doesn't give a damn about my notorious past."

"Before you start boyfriend hunting, I suggest you stop drooling over Mike Birkett. You might find a man who doesn't give a damn about your notorious past, but I doubt you'll find one who's willing to play second fiddle to the sheriff."

"The right man could make me forget Mike."

"Maybe."

"Did Mark ever make you forget Jack?" Lorie cursed under her breath. "Sorry, I had no business asking you. I know you and Mark had a good marriage."

"We did. And I don't regret marrying him. But to answer your question, no, I never forgot about Jack."

"Of course you didn't—not with the constant reminder you had."

Before Cathy could respond, the next song on the jukebox began playing. For a half second her heart stopped as Whit-ney Houston's amazing voice rose above the clatter inside the Ice Palace.

Cathy closed her eyes as the song her son had chosen for her took her mind back nearly seventeen years. The incredi-

ble Ms. Houston sang "I Will Always Love You," the song
that was playing on the car radio the November night Seth
had been conceived. As the mournful words enveloped her,
Cathy opened her eyes, and her gaze sought and found Jack.
He stopped talking to Mike, turned and looked directly at
her. He, too, was remembering the last night they had spent
together, the day before Jack left Dunmore to return to active
duty.

She knelt in prayer. If anyone noticed her, they would
think nothing of seeing her inside the gazebo alone and obviously beseeching God for His help. No one must ever suspect the truth: that she was God's angel of vengeance. Her
holy mission was a secret pact between her and the Almighty. If anyone discovered her identity, they would put an
end to her righteous executions.

Only God knew what was in her heart. What she did, she
did for the good of all mankind. If only someone had taken
up the task of separating the wheat from the chaff years ago,
not only would she have been saved from the agony she endured, but many others would have been, too. But it was not
her place to question God's reasons for allowing these so-
called ministers and priests and professed do-gooders to
spread their evil. No, her place was to follow God's instructions and mete out punishment to the wicked blasphemers.

She lifted her face upward toward heaven and respect-
fully closed her eyes. Her prayers were spoken now in silence, as she suffered in silence. No one could help her. No
one could change the past. But she had the power to change
not only her future, but the future of others. She must be the
protector of the weak and defenseless, those without the
power to overcome their oppressors. By slaying those who
did not deserve to live, she could wash away her own sins,
the sin in which she had been born. ·

"Speak to me, Lord. Tell me who You have chosen for

Your righteous judgment. Lead me along the right path, direct me to his doorstep. Whisper his name in my ear."

God had already shown her that Patsy Floyd was to be spared, that indeed she could erase all female clergy from her mental list of chosen ones. Only men were capable of the kinds of carnal evil that required death by fire. Although not blameless, women were to be spared until the final day of judgment. She accepted His decision without question.

"Will I visit Dewan Phillips next?" she asked. "Or is it time to strike against Donnie Hovater? Speak his name, Lord. Is it either of them, or have You chosen someone else?"

She prayed in earnest until her knees ached and tears streamed down her face. And finally, God spoke to her. Softly. Quietly. As gentle as the rustle of the wind. But she heard him.

"Yes, of course. I knew in my heart that he would be next. And yes, I will not wait. I will mete out his just punishment tomorrow night."

How fitting that God had chosen the night after Bruce Kelley's funeral to strike down yet another wicked blasphemer.

Chapter Twenty-six

This was the last place on earth Cathy wanted to be, but here she was at Bruce Kelley's funeral. A special section of the Decatur Presbyterian Church had been roped off for the family members of the other Fire and Brimstone Killer's victims. And since Mark had been the first victim, at least as far as the authorities knew, that made the Cantrells sort of the first family. Seth had been as disinclined to attend as she had been, but his grandparents had persuaded him that this was the right thing to do. Cathy had come here solely because of her son. He didn't need to go through the ordeal without her. It had been so difficult for him at Mark's funeral. A boy barely fourteen who had loved and admired his father, Seth had put on a brave front in public, being the man his grandfather had expected him to be. But in private her son had wept in her arms.

She looked at him today, sitting between her and his grandfather, and saw the man he would become instead of the boy he had been. He was on the precipice of manhood, a mixture of man and boy, testing his wings to see if he could safely fly away from the nest. He was tall at six feet, and she suspected he would grow another couple of inches in the next few years. Although he had inherited her brown hair, her smile, her bone structure and even her nose, he possessed his father's beautiful blue eyes and lanky build. Wearing his navy blue suit and red and gray striped tie, with his Bible resting in his lap and sitting shoulder to shoulder with J.B, he looked every inch Mark Cantrell's son. And for all intents and purposes, that was exactly who Seth Nelson Cantrell was, who he had been since the day he was born and Mark had claimed him as his own. But in quiet private moments within her heart, the truth still existed. And oddly enough, today of all days, when she looked at her son, so much Mark's son, she saw neither Mark nor herself, but the twenty-year-old soldier who had been her son's biological father.

Jackson Perdue never knew that during their brief, passionate romance, they had created a child together.

"Mom, are you all right?" Seth asked.

"Yes, I think so. But I wish the service would start soon. This must be an especially difficult ordeal for the Kelley family, considering Mrs. Kelley's mental state."

"Yeah, she's kind of pitiful, isn't she? She acts like she doesn't even know where she is or who her kids are."

"Alzheimer's is a horrific disease."

"Thanks for coming here today," Seth said, keeping his voice low. "I know you did it for me."

"And you're here for your grandfather."

He leaned closer and whispered, "I think I should stay with Granddad and Nana the rest of this weekend. Is that okay with you? I know my weekends are supposed to be with you, but—"

"It's all right, honey. I understand. And I'm so very proud of you."

Seth's eyes misted.

The church's choir took their places quickly and then sang the first of six songs that were dispersed throughout the service. With her hands folded in her lap, Cathy let her gaze sweep over the audience in front of them and on either side.

She recognized numerous faces. Edith Randolph, the second victim's wife, sat directly in front of her, along with the Lutheran minister's children and teenage grandchildren. She assumed the three Catholic priests to their left were here on behalf of Father Brian. On the other side of the church, not part of the reserved seating for the victims' families, she caught a glimpse of Patsy and Elliott Floyd as well as Brother Hovater, although he seemed to be alone. Undoubtedly, he had allowed Missy to skip the funeral, which in Cathy's estimation made him a good father. Reverend Phillips and his wife sat with several other black couples who Cathy assumed were members of his church.

She couldn't help wondering how many area clergymen were attending today, each one thinking "But by the grace of God . . ." No one knew who would be next. And no one knew how the killer chose his victims. Of all people to target, why men of God?

Anyone who had known Mark had known what a fine Christian man he was. A good husband. A good father. How could anyone have thrown gasoline on him and set him on fire?

Cathy shivered as the memories of that day zipped through her mind, moment by moment of that terrible afternoon replaying vividly inside her head like some eerie slide show. She heard his screams, saw him on fire, his clothing and the body beneath burning. She could still smell that distinct scent of gasoline and charred flesh. A tight knot formed in her belly.

"Mom? Mom?"

Seth grasped her arm and shook her gently. She stared at him through a haze of tears.

"You shouldn't be here," he told her. "You shouldn't have come."

"Neither should you."

"I'm okay. I—I wasn't with Dad when he died. You were."

She nodded, glad that her son understood how her memories of that fateful day were tormenting her.

"Go home," Seth said.

"I think I should leave." She kissed his cheek. "Call me this evening, okay?"

"I will."

She quietly rose to her feet and made her way out of the pew, exiting on the opposite side from the Cantrells and her mother. She knew people were watching her, some whispering about her, but she didn't care. Just as she made it to the open sanctuary doors, the first minister walked up to the podium and requested a moment of prayer.

Cathy rushed into the crowded vestibule, overflowing with people who hadn't been able to find seating in the huge church, neither upstairs nor down. When she finally managed to make her way through the horde of mourners and emerged on the church steps, she stopped dead still when she realized the churchyard was overrun and that apparently outdoor loudspeakers had been set up to carry both the choir's songs and the eulogies and addresses by various clergymen and friends.

By the time she reached her car, Cathy was trembling so badly that she dropped her keys on the pavement. And once inside her car, it took her three tries to get the key into the ignition. She beat her fists against the steering wheel in an effort to vent her frustration, but within minutes grief overcame her and she laid her forehead against the steering wheel and wept.

Jack had spent a couple of hours this morning with his contractor, Clay Yarbrough. Reconstruction efforts had begun on the upstairs of the house, with his mother's bedroom the first room to be renovated. He had told Clay that he wanted Cathy's plans followed to the letter and if there were any questions concerning even the smallest matter, he wanted to be notified. He didn't want Clay going to Cathy. Hell, he didn't want the guy anywhere near her. Call him old-fashioned, but he was proprietary when it came to Cathy. Maybe he didn't have a right to be, but he was.

They hadn't made each other any promises of undying love or forever after, and for now that was what they both wanted. But that didn't mean Cathy wasn't his. For two nights, he had claimed her in the oldest, most primitive way a man can claim his mate. Yeah, sure, sex wasn't love, and it never had been with any other woman; but Cathy was different. The way he felt about her was different. It had been seventeen years ago and it was now.

The June sun grew hotter the closer it drew to two o'clock, so Jack removed his shirt, tossed it on the back fence and then picked up the weed eater he'd laid on the ground. He'd thought about hiring someone to do the yard work, and in the future, he still might. But for now, when he needed to vent some sexual frustration, manual labor was the best solution. After two nights in Cathy's bed, he had felt deprived sleeping alone last night. Actually, he hadn't gotten much sleep. He'd had way too much on his mind. He had thought about Cathy, of course, and her son. He'd thought for sure he'd have to fight the boy tooth and nail, but Seth had surprised him at the Ice Palace last night when he'd all but given Cathy and him his blessing to date.

Then he'd gotten to thinking about renovating this old house and eradicating every bad memory from the place. He liked the plans Cathy had drawn for the interior and exterior, her work equal to any professional's. Around midnight, he had admitted to himself that he'd been envisioning Cathy living here with him.

If he'd never been sent to the Middle East seventeen years ago during the Gulf War and wound up as a POW, and if Cathy had waited for him instead of marrying Mark Cantrell, how different their lives would be now. He figured they would be married and have a couple of kids, but they wouldn't be living here in Dunmore.

As the night had worn on, he'd slept on and off, until a

bomb had exploded in his nightmares and he'd found himself sitting straight up in bed and drenched in sweat. Damn, would those reenactment dreams never end?

Jack was so engrossed in his thoughts and with the weed eater's loud motor drowning out every other sound, he wasn't aware that a car had pulled into the driveway until he caught a glimpse of movement out of the corner of his eye. Instinctively, he snapped his head around to search and find what he'd seen in his peripheral vision.

Cathy, in a neat black dress and black patent-leather heels, emerged from her old Jeep Cherokee. The first thing he noticed was the necklace of stark white pearls caressing her throat and lying against the black bodice of her dress just above her breasts. When he'd called her this morning, she had told him that she was meeting Seth, the Cantrells and her mother in Decatur at Bruce Kelley's funeral and would probably spend the afternoon with her family. A part of him hated that she still thought of Mark Cantrell's parents as family, especially considering the hell J.B. Cantrell had put her through since her return to Dunmore.

She walked toward him, eagerness in her step, and he realized that something was wrong. He turned off the weed eater and laid it on the ground. As she approached, he pulled a rag from the back pocket of his jeans and used it to wipe the sweat from his face and chest and the dirt from his hands. After tossing the rag on the ground, he took several long, quick steps to meet her.

"Hi," she said, her gaze fixed on his face.

"Hi." When she just stood there looking as if she might faint, he grasped her upper arms. "What's wrong, honey? Are you all right?"

She pushed herself against him, her pretty black silk dress absorbing the moisture still clinging to his bare chest.

"Hold me, Jack. Please hold me."

Without hesitation, he wrapped his arms around her. "What happened? I thought you were going to the funeral."

Burying her face against his shoulder, she clung to him. "I went, but I couldn't stay. I tried not to think about Mark, about the day he died, but I couldn't stop the memories."

He brushed several comforting kisses across her forehead. "You shouldn't have gone."

"I know, but I didn't want Seth to go without me."

"Is Seth all right?"

"Yes, he's the one who told me to leave. He's with his grandparents." She lifted her head and looked squarely into Jack's eyes. "My son has grown up a lot since Mark died. He's becoming quite a young man. I, uh, I want the two of you to get to know each other, to like each other."

"Honey, he's your son. I already like that about him."

She looked at Jack in an odd way, a way that sent a jolt of uneasiness through him. "What is it, Cathy? Just tell me."

"I need you, Jack."

He studied her expression for a full minute. "Are you saying what I think you're saying?"

"I'm saying I want us to make love."

When he didn't immediately respond, she asked, "Don't you want me?"

"Night and day," he told her. "With every breath I take. But honey, if there's going to be three in the bed, I'll decline."

"Three in the bed?" she asked, genuinely confused.

Suddenly she realized what he'd meant, and she laughed. Not the reaction he'd expected.

"You have no idea how really, really stupid that comment was," she told him. "The only time there has ever been three in my bed was when Mark was my husband."

He stared at her, uncertain if he'd understood her correctly.

"Don't you get it?" she asked him. "You were always the third one in my bed, the man in my heart and on my mind every time my husband touched me."

"God in heaven," Jack growled. Then right there in his yard, exposing them to any passersby, he kissed her with a brutal hunger that he couldn't suppress.

He swung her up into his arms, carried her across the yard and to the back door, not giving a damn who saw them. They barely made it into the kitchen before he set her on her feet, unzipped her dress and shoved it off her shoulders and down her hips. Seeing that she wore only a bra and panties— no slip and no pantyhose—he shrugged off his jeans and kicked them aside. Then he lifted her up and onto the kitchen table. While he unhooked her bra, she caressed his damp chest and belly before diving her fingers below the waistband of his briefs. When she curled her hand around his penis, he thought he'd die.

Where the hell had he put that extra box of condoms he'd bought at the drug store yesterday? He hadn't taken them upstairs, had he? No, he'd left them, along with the shaving cream and razors he'd purchased, in the plastic shopping bag that he'd put on the kitchen counter.

He leaned over her, kissed and then suckled each breast. Damn, he felt on the verge of exploding.

"Give me a second, honey."

"Jack." She held out her arms to him.

"I'm not quite ready," he told her as he backed away and hurried to the far end of the kitchen, where he'd left the Dunmore Drugstore bag lying on the counter. He raked through the contents, tore open the box of condoms and retrieved a gold foil wrapper. Within seconds, he had ripped it apart, taken out the condom and put it on.

When he returned to Cathy, he saw that she had taken off her panties and sat there in a partially reclined position, her legs spread wide, revealing the lush, dark bush covering her mound. After slipping between her thighs, he slid his hands under her hips and brought her to the edge of the table. She lifted her arms up and around his neck. He hoisted her hips and thrust inside her.

Moaning with pleasure, she hung on for dear life, undulating to the rhythm of his lunges. He eased his hands out from under her and moved them smoothly up her back. As if sensing that his embrace held her safely in place, she leaned back, tossing her long brown hair behind her as she went wild in his arms.

Within minutes they both came, first she and then he a second later. Panting and trembling, they clung to each other while their bodies enjoyed the aftershocks of their orgasms.

Cathy and Jack spent the afternoon alternating between making love and exploring the three stories and partial basement of Jack's house. Instead of going out to eat, they grilled steaks and prepared corn on the cob and veggie kabobs on the grill. Seth called on her cell phone around six, and she assured him that she was okay.

"You didn't go home, did you?" Seth had asked. "I called earlier and didn't get an answer."

"No, I didn't go home. I didn't want to be alone."

"Are you with Jack Perdue?"

"Yes."

"That's good, Mom. I'm glad you're not alone."

"Are you okay?" she'd asked him, wishing he didn't feel obligated to comfort his still-grieving grandparents.

"Yeah, I guess so. It's been a rough day for Nana and Granddad. Nana's been crying a lot. They need me, Mom. You understand, don't you?"

"I understand."

For now, she would not interfere. J.B. had shown he was willing to compromise when he agreed to allow Seth to spend weekends with her. But eventually, she would have to take Seth away from them, out of their home and away from the daily influence of J.B.'s narrow-minded beliefs. Just not yet.

During her hours with Jack, she had forgotten about the Fire and Brimstone Killer and had forgotten about Mark and how he'd died. Sweet relief, even if only temporary.

Her time with Jack seemed surreal, almost as if she were having an out-of-body experience. She was happy, truly happy, for the first time in a long, long time. And it wasn't just the great sex, which alone was enough to make her ecstatic. No, it was the sense of being accepted for herself, for who she was, flaws and all. And not just accepted, but appreciated. Jack had always had a way of making her feel special.

They had ended their day doing yard work, then showering together and making love again before falling into deep, manual-labor-tired sleep.

When the phone rang late that night, Jack uncurled his arm from around her naked body, reached across her and grabbed his cell phone lying on the bedside table.

"Yeah, Perdue here."

Because their bodies were so intimately aligned and he was lying halfway across her, she felt it when he instantly tensed.

"Son of a bitch!" He moved away from Cathy and swung his long legs off the opposite side of the bed. "I'm on my way." Pause. "No, no, I can find it."

Cathy sat up, reached out and grabbed Jack's arm. "What is it? What's happened?"

"Get up, honey, and put on some clothes," Jack told her as he flipped on the overhead light. "You can go with me, but you'll have to stay in the car. Understand? There's been another murder."

She slid to the edge of the bed and stood. "Who?" Her voice trembled.

He grabbed her by the shoulders. "Donnie Hovater."

"Merciful God!"

*   *   *

Fifteen minutes later, Jack parked in front of the house where Cathy had lived with Mark during the last years of their marriage. A row of emergency vehicles lined both sides of the quiet street located less than half a mile outside the city limits. One of the things she had always loved about this place was the two-acre lot that provided a huge front- and backyard. Residing here had combined the best of both town and country living.

When Jack opened the driver's side door, he turned back and told Cathy, "Stay here."

"If I promise not to get in the way . . . ?"

"As it is, Mike is going to chew my ass out for bringing you with me." When she looked at him pleadingly, tears in her eyes, he heaved a heavy sigh. "Just keep your distance and don't say or do anything. Understand?"

"Yes." She got out and followed him.

At the edge of the driveway, he paused when he saw Mike, who from the looks of him had also come straight out of his bed. It was only then that Cathy checked the time. She glanced down at her wristwatch and noted that it was 1:48.

Mike threw up his hand and motioned to Jack. Then, when he saw Cathy, he frowned. While Jack walked toward his boss, she stayed at the end of the driveway but scanned the yard and the front of the house. Suddenly her heart leapt into her throat. Missy Hovater sat on the porch steps, her eyes glazed over as if she were in shock. A slender redheaded paramedic stood over her, talking to her. Cathy eased back out into the street and went around several vehicles, doing her best not to get in the way as she circled around and entered the yard from the other side. Everything maternal within her wanted to reach out to Missy, but what could she possibly do that the medic couldn't?

She managed to get close enough to hear what the young man was saying to Missy and yet was still far enough away not to be intrusive.

"Miss Hovater, please let us help you. You're in shock, and unless—"

"Don't touch me," Missy cried. "I'm contaminated!"

"Please, miss, just let me put this blanket around your shoulders to keep you warm." He held the blanket out to show her.

"Get away from me!"

Another medic, a little older, approached and pulled the young man aside. "We'll have to sedate her and take her to the hospital. Trying to talk to her isn't working."

"Wait!" Cathy called out to them before she realized what she was doing.

Both men turned to her. "Who are you?" the older guy asked.

"I'm Cathy Cantrell. I'm a friend of the family. Missy knows me. Please let me talk to her."

The two men exchanged concerned glances. Then the older medic said, "Go ahead, ma'am. See what you can do."

Cathy took the blanket from the young medic, walked over to Missy and sat down beside her. "Missy, may I put this blanket around your shoulders?"

Missy looked at her, a blank expression in her eyes. She nodded. "All right, Mrs. Cantrell."

Cathy draped the lightweight blanket around the girl, then curved her arm over her shoulders and held her. "You're not alone, Missy. I'm here. I'll help you get through this."

Missy turned and looked directly at Cathy. "He's dead."

Cathy took a deep breath and glanced at the older medic, who nodded his head. "Yes, darling, he's dead." She gently stroked Missy's back, massaging her soothingly.

"I'm glad he's dead." Missy trembled uncontrollably. "I've thought about killing him so many times, but I just couldn't work up the courage to do it."

Cathy's breath tightened in her throat. My God! Had Missy just confessed to killing her father?

Chapter Twenty-seven

Cathy rode in the ambulance with Missy, holding her hand all the way to the hospital. Dunmore General was a county facility with an excellent emergency room and a small psychiatric unit. From her home to the hospital, Missy clung to Cathy's hand as if it were a lifeline. She kept talking, often incoherently, about her father. Some of her ramblings made sense, some didn't. But from what Cathy could make out, Donnie Hovater had not been the man everyone believed him to be. His daughter's accusations painted a very ugly picture of the minister.

"I begged him not to," Missy kept saying over and over again. "He wouldn't stop. I hated it. I hated him. I'm glad he's dead."

"Hush, sweetie, hush." Cathy had known that with every word she spoke, Missy cast suspicion on herself, not just as her father's murderer but as the Fire and Brimstone Killer. She didn't believe this battered little girl was capable of such brutality, but when pushed beyond the limits of endurance, everyone was capable of just about anything.

The doctor admitted Missy to the psychiatric unit of Dunmore General after an initial examination and a brief questioning by Mike and Jack. But when the nurse started to wheel Missy away, she screamed for Cathy not to leave her. With the attending physician's permission, Cathy was allowed to go with Missy.

Jack accompanied them, but once Missy was settled, he left the room after giving Cathy a quick good-bye kiss.

"How much trouble are you in for taking me to the murder scene with you tonight?" she asked as he started to close the door.

"Nothing I can't handle."

"I'm sorry. I know I promised to stay out of the way, but when I saw Missy and realized what bad shape she was in, I knew I had to do something."

"It's okay, honey. Mike didn't take more than a couple of inches off my hide. And you did what you had to do, what's your nature to do. You comforted a young girl in pain."

"Do you have to go?"

"Yeah, I need to get back to the scene of the crime," Jack explained. "Mike's called in the task force, so the ABI unit could arrive at any time."

"Missy did not kill her father."

"Let's hope not," Jack said. "I hate to leave you here, but I'll be back as soon as I can."

Jack had left several hours ago, and Cathy had been sitting at Missy's bedside ever since. She stood up and slipped out of the room while Missy slept. For nearly an hour after Missy fell asleep, she had continued to clasp Cathy's hand, and whenever Cathy moved, Missy's eyelids fluttered in a fretful manner.

Cathy went straight to the nurse's station and asked where she could go to use her cell phone.

"There's a small waiting room down the hall on your right. You can use your phone there or use the hospital phone that's provided for visitors."

The waiting area was a room approximately twelve by twelve with one vinyl sofa and half a dozen chairs. Cathy slumped down on the sofa, opened her shoulder bag and retrieved her phone. She dialed Jack's number. He answered on the fourth ring.

"Hey, honey, how's it going?" he asked.

"Missy is finally sleeping. They had to give her another injection about an hour ago," Cathy said. "Are you still at the crime scene?"

"No, we finished up there about half an hour ago and left it to the CSI team from the state. Morgan is calling a task-force meeting for eight o'clock, so we're going over the preliminary evidence on the Hovater case right now."

"Can you tell me if there is any evidence against Missy?"

"Honey, you know I can't—"

"I know. Sorry I asked. I'm just so worried about her. If half of what she's been saying is true, Donnie raped her repeatedly for years." Cathy drew in a shaky breath, doing her best not to cry.

"Cathy?"

"Hmm?"

"Call Elliott Floyd and either have him or someone he recommends handle the legal stuff for Missy," Jack said.

"You think she'll need a lawyer?"

"Do it as a precaution. After all, she practically confessed in front of witnesses. Even if it turns out that there is no physical evidence against her, she'll be questioned, and for that alone, a good lawyer at her side won't hurt."

"I'll call Elliott at six," Cathy said as she checked her watch. Ten till five. But first she had to make another phone call.

"As soon as the task-force meeting ends, I'll try to get away and come by the hospital to pick you up. If you're ready to leave before I get there, call Lorie."

"Yes, sir."

"Sorry, honey. I'm used to giving orders. I know you're perfectly capable of taking care of yourself."

"I am, but I kind of like your being concerned about me. Shows you care."

"Oh, I care. I care a whole hell of a lot."

"Jack?"

"Yeah, honey?"

"Donnie was the killer's fifth victim. Y'all have to find this person and stop him before he kills again."

"We're trying."

As soon as they said their good-byes, Cathy sat there and stared at her phone, wondering if she should make the call she wanted to make. After all, she didn't know for certain that Lorie's suspicions had any basis in fact. Just because Lorie had told Cathy that she suspected Ruth Ann had been sexually abused as a young girl didn't mean she actually had been.

"Do you remember when the Whitmore girl was raped by her uncle a few years back?" Lorie had asked Cathy. "Well, Ruth Ann took an unusual interest in the case. She even went to court every day during the trial. And from some of the offhand comments she made, I put two and two together and came up with the obvious—that she'd been a victim of abuse when she was a kid."

If Ruth Ann had been sexually abused as a young girl, who better to help Missy than another survivor? But what if she made the phone call and Lorie was wrong about her cousin's wife?

Nothing ventured, nothing gained.

She would wait until 5:45 to call Ruth Ann, and then at six she'd phone Elliott. In the meantime, she decided to go downstairs to the twenty-four–hour snack bar and get a cup of coffee and maybe a candy bar out of the machines.

Derek Lawrence had arrived before the others. And after being told about the things Missy Hovater had said at the scene and later in the ER, both times with witnesses present, and her reaction to her father's murder, he'd immediately put together a scenario with Missy as the killer.

"She wouldn't be the first girl to kill her abuser," Derek said. "Let's say this guy has been raping her for years, possibly since she was a little girl. She's been powerless to stop him. She's had to endure the pain, the shame and degradation and the feelings of helplessness for years. Finally she snaps and decides to fight back. She sees all ministers as evil because of her father's actions, so she takes it upon herself to punish them."

"Why not start with killing her father?" Wayne Morgan asked. "Why kill four other ministers first?"

Derek shrugged. "Any number of reasons. Possibly to throw suspicion off herself when she did kill her father. Or it could be that she wanted to test her method—death by fire."

"Or it could be that Missy Hovater is just an innocent victim," Jack said.

"Yes, that, too, is possible," Derek agreed. "But from what you've told me, she was at home when her father was killed, and she didn't call 911 when she saw him burning to death. Neighbors heard his screams and made the call. And they found Missy sitting on the porch steps. Apparently, she had sat there and watched him burn."

"That's total conjecture," Mike said. "No one knows what she did or didn't do, only that when the neighbors first saw her, she was sitting on the steps mumbling to herself and when anyone tried to approach her, she started screaming."

"She was traumatized," Derek suggested.

"Traumatized by having witnessed her father's murder or traumatized by having committed the murder?" Mike asked.

"Take your pick," Derek replied.

"No one saw Donnie Hovater being doused with gasoline and set on fire, unless his daughter didn't do it and she witnessed the event," Morgan said. "I take it that she was in no condition to be questioned?" He looked straight at Jack.

"No, sir. After her initial examination in the ER, she was

given a sedative and sent straight to the psych unit on the fourth floor. We were given strict instructions not to question her without her doctor's consent."

"Do you have a guard posted at her door?" Morgan directed that question to Mike.

"No. It didn't seem necessary. The psych unit is locked down twenty-four-seven and has its own guards on duty around the clock."

"I'd get somebody over there ASAP," Morgan said. "We'll want to question her as soon as the doctor gives us the green light. And keep somebody there until we figure out if we've got any evidence that we can use to charge Missy Hovater."

"All right. I'll handle that now."

"Wait," Morgan called to Mike. "Did y'all find a lighter at the scene? Did y'all search Missy Hovater?"

"Nope," Mike replied. "We didn't find anything. No lighter. No matches. And we didn't search Missy because the child was wearing nothing but a gown, a gown with no pockets."

Morgan nodded. Then, when Mike quietly left his office, Jack offered Morgan a cup of coffee, which he accepted. "Want any more?" he asked Derek, who shook his head, declining a second cup.

"How old is Missy Hovater?" Morgan asked as he brought the mug of coffee to his lips.

"Seventeen," Jack replied. "Why do you ask?"

"The Fire and Brimstone Killer's victims have been spread out over the middle of North Alabama," Derek said. "This means he or she had to have a means of transportation to get to the victims. An educated guess would be that he or she drove their own vehicle, and driving a vehicle would require a driver's license."

Jack rubbed his chin. "My guess—educated or not—is that Missy Hovater did not possess a driver's license nearly twenty months ago when Mark Cantrell was killed. The Hovaters didn't live here in Dunmore when Cantrell was murdered, and as far as we're aware, Missy Hovater didn't know Mark Cantrell."

"Good points," Derek said. "Let's say that Missy isn't the Fire and Brimstone Killer. It's still possible that she killed her father."

"You mean a copycat killing." Jack hated to admit that the same thought had crossed his mind. What better way to get rid of an abusive father than to murder him and blame his death on an unknown serial killer?

Cathy checked on Missy periodically over the next couple of hours and was glad that the medication had helped her rest.

"She'll probably sleep another hour or so," the nurse had told Cathy. "You might want to take this opportunity to go down to the cafeteria for breakfast."

"Thanks, I'll grab a bite later."

When she left Missy's room, she paused when she saw the uniformed deputy sitting in a folding chair outside the door.

He stood up the moment he saw her. "Good morning, ma'am."

"Good morning." She glanced at his name tag. "Deputy Glenn. May I ask why you've been posted outside Missy's door?"

"Sheriff Birkett's orders, ma'am."

"Oh, I see." She offered him a halfhearted smile before heading down the hall toward the waiting room.

She pulled from her pants pocket the piece of paper on which she had jotted down a name and telephone number earlier this morning. Elliott Floyd had recommended a Chattanooga law firm to represent Missy.

"I'll call him myself," Elliott had offered, "and fill him in on the situation. Give me until around eight-thirty, then call his private number and work out the details with him yourself."

The waiting area was no longer empty. An elderly couple sat in the corner, haggard expressions on their lined faces. When she entered the room, they glanced her way. Then the man returned to reading the newspaper and the woman to her knitting.

Cathy made her way to the private nook near the windows overlooking the roof of the one-story ER, a 1980s addition to the hospital. She removed her phone from her purse, checked her wristwatch—8:35—and carefully dialed the number Elliott had given her.

He answered on the third ring. "Camden Hendrix here."

"Mr. Hendrix, this is Catherine Cantrell. Elliott Floyd called you earlier this morning and—"

"Yes, Ms. Cantrell, Elliott filled me in on the case. Have the authorities tried to question Ms. Hovater?"

"No, not really, but they have posted a deputy outside her hospital room."

"I see. Okay, give me the name and phone number for the hospital, then her doctor's name, the one in charge of her there in the psych ward. I don't want anyone questioning her until after I've spoken to her."

"Then you'll represent Missy?"

"If Elliott Floyd asks me for a favor, I usually comply."

"Thank you. I don't know what your usual fee is, but—"

"I'm not holding you responsible for the bill, Ms. Cantrell. Elliott explained your involvement. I'll represent Ms. Hovater pro bono. As I said, as a favor to Elliott. That, and I hate the thought of a young girl being victimized by her own father."

"Again, thank you, Mr. Hendrix."

"I'll try to rearrange my schedule so that I can be in Dunmore by sometime this afternoon. It's only a two-and-a-half-hour drive from Chattanooga."

Dial tone. End of conversation. She didn't know Camden Hendrix, but Elliott Floyd had sung the man's praises.

"He's the best of the best. The man never loses a case."

Cathy slipped her phone back into her purse and left the waiting room. Just as she approached the nurse's station, she saw Ruth Ann Harper coming up the hall, directly from the elevator. She threw up her hand and waved. Ruth Ann walked straight to Cathy.

"Thank you for coming."

"How is Missy?" Ruth Ann asked.

"She was still sleeping when I left to make a phone call."

"You said that they're keeping her sedated."

"That's right."

"Will they allow me to go in and see her?"

"Yes. I've already spoken to the nurses, and they've gotten in touch with Dr. Morrison. I also explained that you're a close family friend. And I told a small white lie. I told them that Missy had asked for you."

"I don't know if I can help her. I'm afraid I might say the wrong thing."

"She needs someone who understands what she's been through." Cathy's gaze locked with Ruth Ann's. She saw the realization in the other woman's eyes.

"How did you know about me?" Ruth Ann asked.

"Know about . . . ?"

"Don't pretend with me, please. When you called me, I suspected you knew something, and just now, when you said what you did about Missy needing someone who understands what she's been through, I knew for sure."

"I don't know anything about your past," Cathy said. "It was Lorie. She picked up on some things you said a few years ago, and . . . well, she told me that you'd taken a special interest in the Whitmore girl's rape case."

"And here I thought I hid my feelings so well that no one would ever suspect anything."

"Look, Ruth Ann, whatever did or didn't happen to you is none of my business. I neither want nor need to know. The only reason I called you is because I hoped you could help Missy."

"A long time ago, someone helped me," Ruth Ann said. "I guess it's past time for me to do the same. I'll talk to Missy and do whatever I can to help her."

Cathy grasped Ruth Ann's hand. "Thank you."

"Would you take me to her?"

"Come on. Her room is just down the hall."

When they entered Missy's room, they found her awake and restless, her slender young body curled into a trembling fetal ball.

"I thought you'd left and weren't coming back." Missy held out her hand to Cathy, who rushed forward and took the girl's unsteady hand.

"There's someone here to see you," Cathy said.

"I don't want to see anyone." Missy looked at her visitor and turned away. "No, please, no."

"What happened to you was not your fault," Ruth Ann said in a soft voice as she approached Missy's bed. "You're not to blame. Do you hear me?"

"I am. He told me I wanted him to do what he did. He told me that I tempted him."

Ruth Ann and Cathy exchanged glances, both of them consumed with sympathy for the abused child. And that's what Missy was, just a girl of seventeen, close to the same age as their own children.

Missy cried quietly, her entire body shaking with the force of her almost-silent sobs.

Ruth Ann paused beside the bed. "What your father did to you was not your fault. He was sick, and what he did to you was wrong. Believe me, I understand how you feel."

"How could you possibly understand?" Missy asked, her voice quavering with emotion.

Ruth Ann laid her hand gently on Missy's back. "Because when I was a young girl, my father raped me repeatedly, from the time I was ten years old until the night he died."

Chapter Twenty-eight

Both Cathy and Ruth Ann accompanied Missy Hovater when she was taken to the sheriff's office for questioning on Monday following Donnie Hovater's death late Saturday night. The authorities had been unable to find a close relative. It seemed that Donnie Hovater had been an only child and his parents were deceased. Missy's mother had been raised in a series of foster homes and had never known either of her parents. For all intents and purposes, Missy Hovater was alone in the world. ABI agent and head of the Fire and Brimstone Killer task force Wayne Morgan looked as if he'd rather eat glass than have to interrogate a young girl who had been brutalized by her father's sick cruelty.

Camden Hendrix had shown up at the hospital yesterday afternoon, but Missy had been completely uncooperative. The only people she would talk to were Cathy and Ruth Ann, so they had acted as go-betweens for Missy's lawyer. Cathy didn't know what she had expected Cam Hendrix to look like, but certainly not the big, ruggedly handsome guy whose winning personality instantly put her at ease. Elliott Floyd had sung the man's praises, filling her in on his reputation as one of the South's premiere attorneys.

"He came from nothing. Literally. And now he's filthy rich and famous, or at the very least notorious." Elliott had chuckled. "He's one of the most sought-after trial lawyers in the country, and his firm has even branched out into international law. He's an advisor to Griffin Powell. I assume you've heard of him."

Yes, she'd heard of *the* Griffin Powell, the mysterious former University of Tennessee quarterback who had disappeared off the face of the earth shortly after college graduation. The man had shown up ten years later, a billionaire philanthropist who established the Powell Private Security and Investigation Agency, some said, as a front for his illegal businesses. But that was only one of many rumors about the wealthy mystery man.

Cathy also knew that Jack's sister, Maleah, worked for the Powell Agency and that she had used her contacts in the agency to persuade former FBI profiler Derek Lawrence to help the Fire and Brimstone Killer task force. Free of charge.

They entered Mike Birkett's office, she and Ruth Ann flanking Missy. The girl's face went chalk white as soon as she saw Agent Morgan.

"Come on in, Missy." Cam Hendrix stepped forward and pulled out a chair for his client. "Have a seat right here." He glanced at Cathy and Ruth Ann. "Y'all sit on either side of her. I'll stand."

Jack, Mike, Derek Lawrence and two people Cathy had never seen before crowded into the small office, but all of them stood along the back wall, doing their best not to bring attention to themselves. Thankfully, Missy seemed oblivious to their presence.

"Miss Hovater, I intend to do this as quickly as possible," Agent Morgan said. "I'm afraid I'm going to have to ask you about Saturday night and what you know about your father's death."

"About his murder," Missy said.

"Yes, about his murder," Morgan agreed. "Can you tell

me exactly what happened that night? And please take your time."

"Where do I start?" Missy placed her hands on the table, one hand folded over the other.

"Start wherever you'd like."

She swallowed hard. "He came to my room, the way he always did. And he—we had sex."

"Are you saying that your father raped you, that he forced you to have sex with him?" Cam Hendrix injected the question into the cross-examination process.

"Yes," Missy replied.

"And this wasn't the first time, was it?" Cam asked.

"No, my father had been raping me since I was twelve."

"Miss Hovater, after your father left your room, what happened then?" Agent Morgan asked.

"Nothing. I just lay there for a long time."

"Did you know when your father went outside?"

"I heard the doorbell ring."

"What time was that?"

"I don't know. I didn't look at the clock."

"When you heard the doorbell ring, what did you do?" Agent Morgan pulled out a chair and sat across from Missy. "Did you leave your room? Did you . . . ?"

"No, not at first." Missy eased her hands up and off the table. "But then I heard someone screaming." She brought her clasped hands close to her body and held them over her midsection, just below her breasts. "I got out of bed and listened. I called for my father, but he didn't answer."

"What did you do then?"

"I put on my gown."

"You changed out of your . . . ?"

"I was still naked."

Looking downright uncomfortable, Agent Morgan continued, "After you put on your gown, what did you do then?"

"I followed the sound of the screams and realized they

were coming from outside. I went out onto the porch, and that's when I saw him."

"Saw who?"

"My father. He was on fire," Missy said, her voice eerily calm. "I stood there and watched while he burned."

"You didn't cry out for help? You didn't rush back into the house to call 911?"

"Isn't it obvious that Missy was in shock?" Cam Hendrix said. "She could hardly have been expected to act in a rational manner."

"Yes, certainly. It's a reasonable assumption," Agent Morgan agreed. He focused directly on Missy. "Did you see anyone else?"

"Someone else? Where?"

"Did you see who doused your father with gasoline and set him on fire?"

"No, I—I didn't see anyone else. I don't remember seeing anybody except Daddy. He kept screaming and screaming, and then he didn't move anymore and he stopped screaming. I wasn't sure he was dead, but I hoped he was."

Silence. The tense atmosphere in the room pulsed with life. No one said a word.

"Is that all for today?" Cam Hendrix asked, breaking the unnatural quiet. "Missy was just released from the hospital this morning, and as you can tell, she's already exhausted."

What everyone could plainly see was that Missy Hovater was sitting there staring off into space, an unnerving smile curving the corners of her mouth and a peaceful expression on her pretty face.

A ripple of uncertainty crept up Cathy's spine.

"Yes, that's all for now," Agent Morgan said. "We can postpone further questioning until Miss Hovater is feeling better. Of course, you know the routine, Counselor. She's not to leave town, et cetera, et cetera."

"Missy will be staying with my family," Ruth Ann said.

"My husband and I are hoping to work out something with social services so that we can become her foster parents."

Mike Birkett opened the door for Ruth Ann, who, with her arm around the girl's shoulders, led Missy out of the office. Cathy followed them. As she passed Jack, he reached out and gently grasped Cathy's arm. She looked at him, questioning his actions.

"We need to talk," he told her. "Can you wait for me outside, or do you need to leave with Mrs. Harper and Missy?"

"I came in my car," she told him. "I planned to go from here to Treasures. I'll wait for you."

Cathy helped Ruth Ann get Missy situated in the front seat of her Volvo before turning to Cam Hendrix. "Do you think they believed her?"

"Yes, I think they believe she didn't set her father on fire, but they also believe that she intentionally did nothing to help him and that she's glad he's dead."

"Can they charge her with a crime?" Ruth Ann asked.

He patted Ruth Ann on the back. "They could, but I don't think they will. It's my job to make sure they don't, so stop worrying. You just take good care of Missy and leave the rest to me."

Heaving a sigh, Ruth Ann shook his hand and then got in the car and drove away.

Cam Hendrix turned to Cathy. "The Harpers are taking on quite a responsibility by bringing Missy into their home. She's going to need a great deal of therapy as well as TLC. I've known cases like hers before, and sometimes these young girls never recover."

"If anyone can help Missy, John Earl and Ruth Ann Harper can."

"May I give you a lift somewhere, Ms. Cantrell?"

"No, thank you. I have my car."

Jack came out of the building and stood there watching her with Missy's lawyer. He called out to her, "Ready to go get that cup of coffee, honey?" He stressed the one-word endearment.

Cathy smiled. She knew what he was doing. He was warning off Cam Hendrix, letting him know that she wasn't available. "Be there in a minute," she told Jack.

"Boyfriend?" Cam asked.

"Yes."

"Lucky man."

"He thinks so."

Cam laughed. "Smart man."

As soon as Cam walked off, heading toward his Mercedes in the adjacent parking lot, Cathy turned toward Jack and smiled. He came up to her, looked past her into the parking lot and grunted.

"I don't trust lawyers," he said. "And smooth-talking, rich, handsome guys like that are bad news for lonely widows."

Cathy laughed. "Then I'm safe from him. I'm not a lonely widow."

Jack slid his arm around her waist and pulled her to his side. "You certainly aren't, and I intend to make sure you stay that way."

She looked up at him. "What did you need to see me about?"

He frowned. "Seth."

"Seth?"

"He came to see me yesterday afternoon."

"About you and me or about Missy?"

"About Missy. He's got a crush on her, but I figure you already know that, don't you?"

She nodded.

"He's very worried about her, and he wanted to ask me to do whatever I could to help her. He knows I'm on the task force and thought I could use my influence with Mike and the others to get them to handle her with kid gloves."

"Oh, Jack. I had no idea he'd come to you and ask you to intervene. I'm sure he wasn't intentionally asking for any special favors for Missy."

"Don't worry about it, honey. Seth didn't do anything wrong. I just wanted you to know how concerned he is about her. I realize you don't need any advice about how to handle your son, but you might want to talk to him, help him work out the anger and frustration he's feeling. He doesn't understand how a father could abuse his own child the way Donnie Hovater did Missy. And I don't think he'll get any help on that front from his grandparents. I figure they're the type of people who aren't going to want to talk about it."

"You're right, they aren't. But he and I talked yesterday, probably before he came to see you. I have to admit that I'm as dumbfounded as Seth is as to how a man who appeared to be a fine, upstanding preacher could be such a monster. Seth told me that he wanted to see Missy, and I told him that she wasn't ready to see him, that it might be a while before she'd want to see any of her friends."

"We had a man-to-man discussion," Jack admitted. "He stayed at the house a couple of hours, and we talked about a lot of things. I hope you don't mind. I don't know how much I helped him, but I tried."

"I don't mind at all. Thank you." She stood on tiptoe and kissed Jack's cheek. "I think you could be a very positive influence on Seth. He needs a man to talk to, and I can't think of anyone I'd rather have him go to for advice."

"I'm not so sure how good an influence I'll be, but I can give it my best shot. I think maybe Seth's a lot smarter than I was at his age and a hell of a lot more grounded. And I have a feeling that was your doing."

Cathy caressed Jack's cheek. "Sometimes . . ."

"Sometimes what?"

"Nothing, really. Just sometimes I wish things could be different. I wish I could change the past."

He grabbed her hand and held it. "It's bad to look back.

The past is over and done with. All we have is the here and now."

Cathy laid her hand in the center of his chest and smiled. "Will you come for dinner tonight?"

"Why don't I pick up some barbeque and bring supper with me?"

"Sounds like a plan."

"Think about me a few times today."

"I will," she told him. "You think about me, too."

"I'll think about tonight."

She kissed his cheek again before walking away, her emotions all over the place. Happy. Worried. Eager. Uncertain.

How long would it be before she'd have no choice but to tell Jack the truth about Seth?

John Earl had debated whether or not he should be at home when Ruth Ann arrived with Missy Hovater. He certainly didn't want to do anything to upset the girl or cause her any undue distress. But in the end, he had decided that if he and Ruth Ann were going to bring this young girl into their family as a foster daughter, the sooner she accepted him as a friend, the better. He realized that she would be wary of him at first, that because she had been abused by her father for so many years, she might see him as the enemy. She would need time to learn to trust him. He was, after all, a man, and the poor child had learned from her horrific experiences that men could not be trusted.

When Ruth Ann had spoken to him about Missy, about her desire to help the girl by making her a part of their family, he had been reluctant. But seeing how important this was to his wife, he had finally agreed. Perhaps in helping Missy, Ruth Ann could actually help herself. Until the recent series of clergymen murders, John Earl had thought perhaps, at long last, she had been able to put the past behind her. Of course, she could never forget the years of sexual abuse she endured or the way in which her father had died, but he had hoped those things no longer haunted her. But then the old nightmares had returned to plague her on a routine basis.

"They're here." Felicity jumped away from the window and let the curtain fall back into place. "What do we say? What do we do?"

"Don't do anything other than say hello," John Earl advised. "She'll probably want to go to her room, and she may not want to interact with any of us, other than your mother, for a while."

"I think bringing that girl into our home is a mistake," Faye Long said.

"Grandmother, how unchristian of you." Felicity glowered at Faye.

"I think it's awful what Missy's father did to her," Charity said. "I don't blame her if she did kill him."

"We'll have no more talk like that," John Earl told his elder daughter.

"Did she ever tell you what was going on?" Felicity skewered her sister with her sharp glare. "You two are friends, and friends tell each other secrets. If Missy really is the Fire and Brimstone Killer, maybe she'll confess to you."

"Oh, shut up!" Charity shook her head in disgust. "Don't you dare say stuff like that to Missy." She looked to her father. "Daddy, warn Felicity that she'd better behave herself."

Before John Earl could caution his younger daughter, she answered her sister. "I'll behave. I like Missy. But I have to admit that I don't know why Mother was willing to give up her craft room to make Missy a room of her own when I've been having to share a room with you all my life."

Charity glared at Felicity, who promptly stuck her tongue out at her sister.

The back door opened, and Ruth Ann called, "We're home."

John Earl took a deep breath, gave both of his daughters a quick be-on-your-best-behavior glance and prepared himself for the first day of their new life.

Ruth Ann led Missy into the family room, her arm around the girl's slender shoulders. Everyone waited, barely breathing, all of them wanting to put Missy at ease.

"Welcome to our home," John Earl said. Then quickly added, "Welcome to your new home."

With a wide, deer-in-the-headlights look in her eyes, Missy glanced quickly from John Earl to Faye, who forced a smile and nodded, to Felicity and finally to Charity.

"Hi, Missy." Felicity lifted her hand and waved.

"We're glad you're going to be staying with us," Charity said.

"Missy's had a rather tiring morning," Ruth Ann told them. "I think she'd like to go to her room and rest for a while before lunch."

"Certainly, certainly." John Earl recognized that desperately lost and frightened expression on Missy's face. He remembered only too well that same look on Ruth Ann's face shortly after her father died in the fire that had destroyed her home.

As soon as Ruth Ann escorted Missy through the family room and into the hall that led to her former craft room at the back of the house, everyone else released the anxious breaths they'd been holding.

"Boy, she looks like a zombie," Felicity said.

"If you'd gone through what she has, you'd look pretty rough yourself," Charity told her.

"Girls, keep your voices down," John Earl told them. "Sound carries down the hall, and you do not want Missy to hear you talking about her."

Felicity shrugged. "If show time is over, I'm going outside to sit in the gazebo and listen to my iPod."

"Lunch will be ready in about an hour," Faye reminded

them. "Sitting down to our first meal with that pitiful child will be an ordeal for all of us. I still say it was a mistake for Ruth Ann to—"

"Mother!" Ruth Ann stood in the doorway, a hostile scowl on her face. "I'm ashamed of you." Her gaze scanned the others in the room, going from one to another and then settling back on her mother. "Missy prefers to have lunch in her room. I'll fix her a tray after we've eaten." She fanned her hands in a shooing manner. "Go on about your normal routines. Keeping things as normal as possible will be good for Missy, and it will certainly make the transition easier on all of us."

John Earl went over and kissed his wife on the cheek. "Erin has been handling things at the office, but I should head on down there soon. I think I'll skip lunch. I had a big breakfast this morning."

"You go ahead, dear," she told him. "And take Erin some of those oatmeal raisin cookies I made last night. I know she likes them."

"I'll bag up a few on my way out the door."

John Earl was using a busy schedule as an excuse to leave, but he knew that Ruth Ann was better equipped than he was to help their daughters and her mother adjust to the new situation. After all, they were all women, and women understood one another in ways men never could.

Punishing Donnie Hovater for his many sins had given her great satisfaction. Of all those whom God had chosen for her to destroy, none was as worthy of the Lord's fiery wrath than the man who had repeatedly raped his own daughter. She knew now that, without any doubt, he had been evil personified.

She knew evil. She was a product of evil, and yet, through God's gracious and forgiving love, she was blameless. God's Son had atoned for her sins when He died on the Cross, and even those such as she, born from sin, born in sin, were washed clean and would be allowed into the eternal sanctuary of heaven. She would sit at the right hand of God. She would be blessed among the saved, for she had done the Lord's bidding while here on earth.

"What, Lord? Yes, I hear You. I know my work is not done. There are others who must be punished. I believe I know the name of the man You have chosen for Your angel of death to visit next."

She closed her Bible and placed her hand atop it where it rested in her lap. Breathing in the fresh, sweet outdoor air surrounding her, she recalled the genuine pleasure she had known as she had watched Donnie Hovater writhe in agony and scream for mercy. He had burned quickly, his cries for help going unheeded. Had he, in those final moments of his life, repented of his sins, or had he gone to the hereafter an unrepentant soul?

Did it truly matter? She believed that there was no atonement for men such as he. His evil had been too great, the damage he had inflicted unforgivable.

"Yes, Lord," she whispered, a feeling of power encompassing her as she allowed her Savior to send the Holy Ghost into her heart and mind and body, to fill her with the strength of His righteousness.

Quietly, reverently, she recited the words from the first book of Revelations, the words God had placed on her lips. "'And I looked, and behold a pale horse: and his name that sat on him was Death, and Hell followed with him.'"

She closed her eyes, smiled, and continued talking to God, plotting the demise of another blasphemous false prophet.

Chapter Twenty-nine

During the weeks since Donnie Hovater's murder, life had returned to normal for almost everyone in Dunmore, even for Cathy to some extent. But the normalcy was shadowed by doubts and fears and the ever-present certainty that it was only a matter of time before the Fire and Brimstone Killer struck again. Personally, Cathy felt a little guilty for being so happy. Jack spent every weeknight with her, and Seth spent weekends. And last Saturday, the three of them had shared the entire day together. Jack had borrowed Mike's boat, and they'd gone to the river. She had been amazed at how well her two guys had gotten along. But why shouldn't they, when they were so much alike?

But there was a problem with the way her son seemed to be bonding with Jack—how long before Jack figured out that Seth was his son? Lorie kept telling her that she needed to tell them both the truth sooner rather than later.

"I need more time," she'd told her best friend. "I need to be sure about Jack, about our relationship."

"Don't put it off until it's too late," Lorie had said. "You don't want either of them finding out some other way."

This morning—this glorious Fourth of July Saturday—
Cathy had decided that she would tell Jack the truth tomorrow evening, after Seth had returned to his grandparents'
home. But for now, she didn't want anything to interfere
with their day-long celebrations. Jack would be here soon to
pick them up and drive them to Spring Creek Park for the
holiday festivities that included barbeque and chicken-stew
dinners for sale, cold beer and soft drinks, family picnics,
country bands playing late into the night, baseball games,
fireworks displays and blankets spread out under the stars.

"Mom?"

"Hmm?" Cathy placed a package of napkins on top of the
overstuffed picnic basket and barely managed to close the
lid.

"I've been thinking about when school starts in August,"
Seth said. "I'd like to come and live with you full-time then.
Do you think Granddad and Nana will be okay without me?"

Cathy drew in a deep breath and released it slowly as she
allowed the joy of the moment to encompass her. "Yes, I believe they'll be okay. After all, it's not as if you'll be cutting
them out of your life. You can see them whenever you'd like,
and they'll always be your grandparents."

Will they? an inner voice asked. *How will J.B. and Mona
react after I tell Jack and Seth the truth? Will they still be
able to think of themselves as Seth's grandparents?*

"What's the matter, Mom?"

"Huh?"

"You've got this really peculiar look on your face."

She brushed aside her concerns. Time enough to deal
with the aftereffects later. Today was going to be a good day,
one more building block in the foundation of the life she hoped
to construct with Jack and Seth . . . if she was lucky—very,
very lucky.

"It's nothing really," she lied. "I was just wondering how
you'd feel about Jack staying here occasionally."

"Oh."

"I know it might be awkward for you and Jack, at least at first, but—"

"Are you going to marry him?"

"Uh, I don't know," she replied, not the least bit surprised by her son's question. After all, he'd been raised to believe in the sanctity of marriage and that living together out of holy wedlock was a sin. "Jack and I haven't discussed marriage."

"Why not? You love him, don't you?"

"I care deeply for Jack." *You love him. Admit the truth to yourself even if you can't admit it to your son.* Yes, she loved Jackson Perdue, with all her heart. And if he asked her to marry him tonight, she would say yes, a thousand times yes.

"Hey, I'm not saying get married right away or anything, but anybody can see that the guy's nuts about you. And I think he's okay. You know, as far as stepdads go, Jack wouldn't be all that bad."

"Oh, he wouldn't, would he?"

"We get along okay," Seth said. "We actually like a lot of the same things, sports and stuff like that. And he really listens to me when I talk to him. He doesn't treat me like I'm some dumb kid."

Cathy smiled. "That's because you're not a dumb kid. You're a smart kid."

They heard a car pull into the driveway. Seth went to the back door and looked outside.

"It's Jack." Seth lifted the heavy picnic basket loaded down with food and supplies and carried it with him as he met Jack at the back door.

"Ready to go?" Jack asked when Seth opened the door for him.

"Sure are," Seth replied. "I'll take this on out to our car." He hoisted the basket up to show Jack, then headed outside.

Jack came over to Cathy, leaned down and kissed her. She returned the kiss, and when he raised his head, they both grinned. He scanned her from head to toe.

"Honey, you look good enough to eat."

She laughed. "Save your appetite for food today."

"I'll try to be on my best behavior, but, woman, you look way too good in those blue jeans."

The car horn honking reminded them that Seth was waiting in the Jeep Cherokee. Jack slipped his arm around her waist.

If only every day could be like this.

Erin had come to the park with Clay. As far as anyone knew, they were merely acquaintances and this was just a friendly date. Her on-again/off-again sexual relationship with Clay was their private business, something neither of them advertised. Love had absolutely nothing to do with how they felt about each other. All her love, every ounce her heart held, belonged to John Earl. He was everything to her. If only he would realize how much better she would be for him than that insipid Ruth Ann. The woman was practically a saint, or at least John Earl thought so. It wasn't enough that she was raising two children of her own, but now she had taken in Melissa Hovater and the entire town marveled at her kindness. Even Clay had made some stupid comment about what a great person John Earl's wife was.

"The woman has a heart of gold, doesn't she?" he'd said. "Can you imagine her becoming a foster mother to a girl who's suspected of killing her own father?"

Erin knew that John Earl wasn't 100 percent in favor of Missy living with them. He hadn't actually come right out and said it, but Erin was good at reading between the lines. Sometimes she could almost read John Earl's mind. He was concerned about the Hovater girl's influence on his own two daughters, and Erin couldn't say that she blamed him. Felicity was already a handful, a bit of a wild child who seemed to enjoy embarrassing her devout, highly respected parents.

And Charity, although quiet and rather moody, seemed to be a paragon of virtue, like her mother.

"Here's your peach ice cream." Clay held out the two scoops in a cookie-dough waffle cone, one of Erin's favorite desserts. "Better start licking." He chuckled. "It's already melting."

She took the cone from him, smiled and ran her tongue around the edges. "Thanks."

"It's hot as blue blazes. Why don't we find us a nice shade tree somewhere?"

She caught a glimpse of John Earl as he and his family settled themselves around one of the concrete picnic tables near the outdoor grandstand set up for the bands and singers. When the love of her life put his arm around his wife's shoulder, Erin cringed. Damn that woman!

"What's the matter, sugar?" Clay asked.

"Huh?"

His gaze followed hers, and he grunted. "Give it up, baby doll. Old John Earl won't ever be yours."

She snapped her head around and glared at Clay. "Never say never."

"You're living in a dream world. That man's not going to cheat on his wife, and even if he did, he wouldn't leave her."

"Maybe. Maybe not. You never know what might happen."

Ruth Ann might get run over by a bus. Or one day, John Earl could wise up and figure out what he was missing. The one thing Erin knew for certain was that sooner or later, one way or the other, he would be hers.

Ruth Ann had been reluctant about encouraging Missy to join the family today for the Fourth of July celebrations at the park, but John Earl had insisted. After all, if Missy had stayed at home, Ruth Ann would have felt obligated to stay with her. For the past few weeks, since that poor child had been living with them, he had noticed subtle changes in his entire household. His mother-in-law, seldom cheerful or easygoing, had become sullen and irritable. It was apparent that she disapproved of John Earl and Ruth Ann becoming Missy's foster parents.

"Don't you think you have enough to deal with as it is?" Faye had asked him. "I feel sorry for the girl, for what her father put her through, but God help us, it's unfair for anyone to expect Ruth Ann to be a mother to Missy. Don't you understand that she's reliving all her own horrible memories?"

"She may be reliving her past with her father," John Earl had said. "But at least she's dealing with it while she's awake. Her nightmares have stopped—or haven't you noticed? Ruth Ann hasn't had more than a couple of bad dreams since Missy came to live with us."

Where Missy becoming a member of their family seemed to have had a positive effect on Ruth Ann, it had had a negative effect on Faye and on Felicity, who seemed to resent all the attention her mother lavished on Missy. Charity was the only one who appeared to be unchanged. She was as she'd always been, his sweet, steady, tenderhearted daughter, who did her best to please everyone.

"Do I have to stay here with the rest of you?" Felicity whined. "If I promise not to get in trouble—"

"I'd rather you didn't wander off," Ruth Ann said as she and Faye spread the checkered tablecloth over the concrete table. "We're going to eat soon, and I don't want your father to have to search the park for you."

Felicity glowered at her mother and then turned to her father. "Daddy, please." She glanced at her wristwatch. "It's eleven now. Just tell me what time to be back, and I promise I won't be late. I want to hang around some of my friends and not get stuck with . . ." She rolled her eyes skyward. "With my family."

He knew she had stopped herself short of saying "with Charity and Missy." His daughters possessed different personalities, and although they'd been close as children, they had grown apart during their teen years. And in the past couple of years, Felicity occasionally acted as if she hated her sister.

"Be back here at twelve-thirty." His gaze connected with Ruth Ann's, and he immediately recognized that look of disapproval in her eyes.

"Thank you so much." Felicity gave him a quick hug and then all but ran off into the crowd. He turned to Charity and Missy. "Why don't you two take a walk, look around and enjoy the day? Just be back here at twelve-thirty."

"That's a good idea." Charity turned toward a somber Missy.

"I'm not sure," Ruth Ann said. She laid her hand on Missy's shoulder.

"Teenagers do not want to be stuck with their parents all day," John Earl told her.

"Come on, Missy," Charity said. "I saw Seth with his mom over at the waterfall. We could go say hi."

"All right," Missy replied and followed Charity, who glanced over her shoulder and gave her parents a reassuring look, as if saying *I'll take care of her.*

As soon as the girls were out of earshot, Faye grumbled as she removed a gallon of sweet tea from one of the picnic baskets they had brought from home. "Mark my word, that girl is going to be trouble."

"Mother!" Ruth Ann glared at Faye.

"For heaven's sake, it's not that I don't feel sorry for her." Faye laid a package of white paper napkins on the table and reached into the basket for the plastic forks and spoons. "But she is not your responsibility, and you can't work miracles, you know. You cannot change what happened to her."

"Of course I can't. No more than I can change what happened to me. But I can help her to stop feeling guilty, to stop blaming herself for what her father did to her, just as John Earl helped me."

"I tried to help you," Faye said. "I did my best." Faye slammed the boxes of forks and spoons down on the table, and then turned abruptly and walked away.

Ruth Ann heaved a deep sigh.

John Earl placed his arm around her shoulders. "Everything will be all right. It'll just take time for Faye and Felicity to adjust to having Missy as a part of the family."

She looked into his eyes. "I hope you're right. Felicity's behavior and her attitude in general seem to have gotten worse lately."

"Give her a little more of your undivided attention and she'll come around." He kissed Ruth Ann's forehead. "Why don't you take this opportunity to walk around and absorb some of the Fourth of July spirit in the park? I'll finish up here and put the food out a little before twelve-thirty."

"I think I will take a walk."

"Just don't follow the girls. They'll be fine on their own."

She smiled at him. "You know me too well."

Standing near the spring-fed pond, she scanned the park, now overrun with holiday celebrators. She knew so many of these people. Sheriff Birkett, his mother and his children were sharing lunch with Seth Cantrell and his mother and her boyfriend. Wonder what Seth thought of his mother having an affair? He had been raised to know that sex outside of marriage was a sin.

She smiled to herself. Some of these people were such hypocrites, even those who professed to be ministers of the gospel.

Her gaze settled on Patsy and Elliott Floyd, who were working their son's food booth, both of them dutiful parents. Even Patsy, with all her good qualities, was not above sin. But her sins could never compare to the evil inflicted on others by her male counterparts.

You, Patsy Floyd, are safe from God's wrath here on earth.

Boisterous laughter coming from the covered pavilion across the pond caught her attention. Reverend Dewan Phillips, his wife Tasha and a dozen members of their congregation were sharing an early lunch.

They all revere that man almost as if he were a demigod. They've put him up on a pedestal, believing him to be a saintly person. Poor fools. Their little tin god has feet of clay. The Lord knows what is in his heart.

Pure evil.

Yes, Lord, I hear You.

The time is right. I must act soon.

When Lord?

Yes, of course.

I will make preparations for tomorrow night. Guide me, Heavenly Father. Show me the way.

In humble silence, her words heard only by God, she recited John 16:13. "Howbeit when he, the Spirit of truth, is come, he will guide you into all truth; for he shall not speak of himself; but whatsoever he shall hear, that shall he speak: and he will shew you things to come."

Chapter Thirty

Jack lay beside Cathy, his arm draped across her naked belly, his nose nuzzling her shoulder. She had never been happier in her life. She was in love again, gloriously, passionately in love. And although they had not exchanged the words, she knew in her heart that Jack loved her, too.

How many people actually got the second chance that fate had given them?

Yesterday had been wonderful, a true celebration of not only the country's independence but Cathy's freedom. She was living her life by her rules and making her own decisions, as she should have been doing all her adult life.

Even today had been good. Church with Seth this morning had been followed by lunch out with Jack and a walk-through of his house. She had been eager to show Seth the renovations in progress and brag just a little about the plans she had drawn for Jack's contractor. And despite the continued tension between her and her mother, her in-laws seemed to be making a genuine effort to accept Seth's decision to live full-time with her when school started next month.

Things couldn't be better with Seth. He liked Jack, and the two were getting along great. Seth wanted to come home, to live with her, and he'd even accepted the possibility that she might one day marry Jack.

All she had to do to keep her hard-won happiness was continue lying to the two most important people in her life. But if she told Jack the truth tonight, as she had promised herself she would, what would happen? How would he react? Would he ever forgive her for keeping his son from him all these years?

And what about Seth?

Would he hate her?

She eased Jack's arm up and off her, and then she slid out of bed.

"Where are you going?" Jack asked in a relaxed, sexy voice.

She grabbed her robe off the foot of the bed and put it on before facing him. "We need to talk."

He sat up in bed, allowing the sheet to slip down and around his hips. "Sounds serious." He studied her closely. "What's wrong, honey?"

"Get up and put on some clothes," she told him. "I'll fix us something to drink. Which do you prefer iced tea or iced coffee?"

He tossed back the covers and stood, boldly naked. "I'd prefer your staying in bed with me." He reached down and picked up his discarded jeans from the floor. "I thought everything was fine, that life was good for us. For you and me and even for Seth." He put on his jeans and then snatched his shirt off the nearby chair, where it had landed when he'd flung it aside in his haste to strip off hurriedly an hour earlier.

"We have to talk," Cathy said. "I've put this off too long as it is."

Leaving his shirt unbuttoned, he closed the gap between them, grabbed her gently by the upper arms and looked down into her face. "Tell me you aren't having second thoughts about us."

"No second thoughts," she assured him. "As a matter of fact, I want you to know that I love you now more than I did seventeen years ago."

He sucked in a deep breath and tightened his grip on her arms. "Is that what this is all about—you need to hear me say the words?"

"No, Jack, really, that's not—"

"I love you, Cathy."

Oh God. Oh God. Why now? This simply made telling him the truth about Seth even more difficult.

"Damn, woman, you're scaring me," Jack told her. "Take that frightened look off your face."

"Finish getting dressed and meet me in the kitchen."

She pulled away from him, and he let her go without protest.

"Cathy," he called to her as she reached the door.

Without turning around, she replied, "Yes?"

"If this is going to be bad news, maybe you'd better fix me something stronger than coffee or tea."

"Okay." She hurried out of the bedroom, practically running away from him.

She'd barely had time to uncork the bottle of wine—the strongest liquor she had in her house—before Jack entered the kitchen. Fully dressed, but with his hair slightly mussed, he paused on the other side of the room and rubbed the back of his neck.

He eyed the two half-full wine glasses sitting on the table. He blew out a damn-it's-bad-news breath.

When he came toward her, she held up both hands, signaling him to halt. He stopped and stared at her.

"Is it that bad?" he asked.

"Oh, Jack, I don't know how to tell you. I—"

"Good God, whatever it is, just say it."

She squared her shoulders and looked him in the eyes. "You haven't pressed me to explain why I married Mark so soon after you left."

"Is that what's wrong, why you're so worried? Whatever the reason, it's all water under the bridge. We have to let go of the past and be grateful for what we have now."

"This is part of our past that affects our present and our future."

He nodded. "Okay. Go ahead. I'm listening."

She wrung her hands together and then threaded her fingers in a prayerlike gesture. "A couple of months after you left, Mark came to Dunmore to conduct a gospel meeting. He was staying with his parents. I remembered him from church, of course, but he was years older, and our paths hadn't really crossed outside of church. I knew he'd been a widower for a couple of years.

"I needed guidance, so I went to him because I thought, as a young minister who had lost the love of his life, he might understand the situation I was in better than our regular preacher, Brother Fulmer, who was stern and judgmental." She swallowed. "Not only did Mark understand, but he was sympathetic, and during the next two weeks, while he visited his parents after the gospel meeting ended, we talked often and he came up with a solution to my problem."

"You've lost me," Jack said. "What was your situation? What problem did Mark Cantrell solve for you?"

"He offered to marry me and take me with him when he left town so that no one would ever know the truth."

Jack stared at her, clearly puzzled.

"I was seventeen, had just graduated from high school, and suddenly I was pregnant and unmarried and I'd just been told that my baby's father was missing in action in the Middle East and presumed dead."

She waited for the information to sink in and for Jack to realize that he was her child's father.

"You were pregnant?" His voice lowered to a deep huskiness. "With my baby?"

She nodded. *Please, God, let him understand. Let him forgive me.*

"You married Mark Cantrell because you were pregnant with my child and thought I was dead."

"Yes. After you left, I received only one letter from you, and then I didn't hear from you again. When I found out I was pregnant, I went to see your mother. She told me what had happened to you."

"Did you tell her that you were pregnant?"

"No. No, I didn't tell her."

"So Mark Cantrell offered to marry you and take on the responsibility of another man's child. He must have loved you a great deal to—"

"Mark was still in love with his wife, and I was in love with you. In his profession, he needed a wife, a helpmate, and . . . He knew he could never father a child of his own. When he and his wife had tried to have a baby and she didn't get pregnant, they underwent numerous tests and discovered that Mark was sterile."

"If Mark was sterile, then what about Seth?"

Hadn't he understood what she'd said? Hadn't she told him that he was Seth's biological father, not Mark? Oh God, no. She hadn't mentioned Seth. Did he think she had lost that baby—his baby—and gotten pregnant again by Mark?

Apparently the shocked expression on her face revealed the truth as surely as a verbal confession. "You didn't lose my child, did you? Seth was that baby. Seth is my son."

"Yes, Seth is yours."

Jack stood there and stared at her, but didn't say another word, not for several minutes. Cathy wanted to beg him to say something, but she waited patiently, allowing him time to absorb the information.

"I understand," he said. "Under the circumstances, it

makes sense that you'd agree to marry Mark. What I don't understand is why, after you found out that I was alive, you never contacted me to tell me I had a son."

"I didn't know for quite some time. My mother chose not to inform me when she learned, through local Dunmore gossip, that you were alive. Mark and I lived out of state, and it wasn't until Seth was nearly two years old and we were visiting that I ran into Mike and he mentioned you."

"That was fourteen years ago. For the love of God, Cathy, why didn't you tell me then?"

"I didn't know what to do," she admitted. "I wanted to tell you, but . . . My mother and Mark convinced me that it wouldn't be fair to any of us if I did. Mark and I had just begun to have a real marriage, and he'd been so good to me. He thought of Seth as his, and Seth, even at two, adored his father." When she saw the hurt look in Jack's eyes, she corrected herself. "He adored Mark."

"If you ever loved me, how could you have kept the truth from me? I had a right to know that I had a son." He paused for a gasping breath. "I have a son." He closed his eyes and clenched his teeth.

She moved toward him, but when she reached out to touch him, he flinched.

"Please, Jack, try to understand how it was. Try to see my side of things. I was young and stupid and let Mark and my mother make all my decisions. I was wrong, so very wrong for keeping Seth from you. If I had it to do all over again, I'd—"

"You'd do what?" He opened his eyes and glared at her. "You wouldn't do a damn thing differently, because you wouldn't have the backbone to stand up to your mother or anyone else for that matter. Weak, spineless, helpless Cathy. Damn you!"

"I am not that same easily manipulated girl I was. I've changed. I've grown a backbone. If not, do you think I'd be standing here telling you the truth?"

"Lady, you're a day late and a dollar short!"

He marched past her, ignoring her outstretched hands, flung open the back door and stomped outside. Cathy ran after him, catching up with him in the driveway. She grabbed for him. He shoved her aside and got in his car.

"Jack, don't leave like this. Stay, please. Let's talk this out. Don't go." Tears sprung to her eyes.

Jack started the car and backed out of the drive. Cathy followed him for half a block until his car disappeared as he turned at the end of the street several blocks away. Then, barefoot and wearing only her robe, she stood on the sidewalk and cried.

Tasha and Dewan hosted an informal get-together the first Sunday night of each month, with the deacons and their wives and children coming to their house for coffee and dessert. During their years in Dunmore, they had made many friends, but none as dear to them as Dionne and Perry Fuqua, a couple only a few years older than they were. Dionne was an elementary school teacher and Perry the high school football coach. They had married young, had children in their early twenties and were now parents to a twelve-year-old and a fourteen-year-old, both boys.

While the boys watched TV in the den, the adults sat in the living room talking, discussing everything from local politics to global warming.

"It's getting late," Dionne said, interrupting her husband midsentence in his tirade against irresponsible fathers missing from their children's lives, a pet-peeve with the devoted father of two. "It's nearly ten-thirty."

"Stay for a while longer. I want to discuss plans for adding on a Sunday school wing to the church and expanding the sanctuary," Dewan said. "Tasha just put on a fresh pot of decaf coffee."

"Yes, do stay. The boys will want to see the end of their

program before y'all leave." Tasha stood and gathered up the empty dessert plates. "Honey, would you get the cups for me?"

Perry glanced at his wife. "Mind if we stay until eleven?"

She smiled. "Okay, but only until eleven. Remember, I'm teaching summer school, and I can't sleep late tomorrow."

Dewan gathered up the cups and saucers from the coffee and end tables and placed them on the tray where Tasha had set the plates. As he lifted the tray, he asked, "Anybody want more pie?"

"Not me," Dionne answered.

"Maybe just a small slice," Perry said. "Tasha makes the best blueberry pie I've ever tasted."

Dionne shook her finger at him. "What happened to that diet you were planning to go on?"

"I'll do that tomorrow," he told her.

Both couples laughed.

"I'll check on the boys and let them know we're leaving in thirty minutes," Dionne said as Dewan carried the tray into the kitchen.

"I'll cut you a small piece of pie and bring it with the fresh coffee," Tasha said. "When we come back, you and Dewan can discuss building plans while I show Dionne what I've done to the nursery."

Even though the baby wasn't due until early September, she had been unable to wait to redecorate their third bedroom. Dewan had painted the walls a pale yellow, and they had bought white furniture, including one of those new round baby beds. They had waited such a long time for this child, a child conceived in love and wanted so desperately.

"We should discuss baby-shower plans," Dionne said. "Several of the ladies have already mentioned it to me. Your child is going to be surrounded by a congregation of honorary aunts and uncles."

* * *

She had been watching the house for nearly an hour, waiting for the lights to go out so that when she rang the doorbell the odds were that Reverend Phillips would be the one to open the door. There was a chance he would recognize her, but what did that matter? If something went wrong, and she was unable to follow through with the Lord's plans to punish the reverend, then she could come up with some excuse for being in his neighborhood and ringing his doorbell. But if things went well, Dewan Phillips wouldn't be able to identify her, because he would be dead.

The lighted face of her digital watch allowed her to check the time in the dark. The watch had been a birthday gift, one she treasured.

Ten-forty. She should have waited until later, but she was so eager to do God's bidding that she had sneaked away early.

Wait. Be patient.

But she didn't want to wait. She was pumped with adrenaline and filled with the Spirit. The Holy Ghost had entered her and guided her every move. The Almighty's desire to punish Dewan Phillips raged inside her, begging for release.

Nothing could go wrong.

No one could hurt her.

She couldn't be stopped. Not when she was guided and protected by a higher power.

Slowly, carefully, she slipped out of the car, opened the trunk and removed the gas can. After checking her pocket for the lighter, she crossed the street. Glancing around, she saw no one, just a couple of stray dogs half a block away. She noted an SUV in the driveway and wondered why either the reverend or his wife had parked outside of their double garage. People often used their garages for storage, making it impossible to park their vehicles inside. That was probably the reason.

She made her way quietly across the yard, her gaze fixed on the front door. A smile warmed her from within. Courage roared inside her like a mighty lion. While doing the Lord's work, she was invincible.

Be careful. Don't do anything foolish.

She didn't need to worry. God would take care of her. The Holy Ghost possessed a power unknown to mortals, a power that now surged through her veins.

Cloaked in the Spirit, held in the very palm of the Lord Almighty's hand, she knew no fear. She walked up to the front door and rang the bell.

The door opened. A tall black man's outline was silhouetted in the doorway, his muscular body backlit from the light inside the house.

"Yes, may I help you?" he asked.

His voice sounded odd, but he was probably surprised to see a stranger on his doorstep at this time of night.

She smiled. *God has sent me to you.*

"Are you sure you're at the right house? This is Reverend Phillips's home."

Without a moment's hesitation, she uncapped the gas can she held behind her back, then hoisted it high and threw the contents straight at her target. Before he had a chance to react, she dropped the can, flipped open the lighter and using both hands locked the flame. She tossed the open lighter toward his chest. The lighter hit the edge of his gasoline-soaked silk tie.

Burn in hell for your sins.

The Holy Ghost surged through her, the feeling stronger than ever before.

She backed away from the man on fire and watched him burn. Then she quickly bent down, picked up the metal torch lighter and put it in her pocket.

A woman's voice screeching for help warned her that she must leave quickly. She had accomplished her goal and done God's bidding. It was time for her to return home, to rest, to recoup, to prepare herself for the next time.

She yanked the gold chain from her neck and tossed it down on the sidewalk. Then, without a backward glance, she walked away, crossed the street and got in her car.

Jack sat on the back porch, his gaze unfocused as he went over in his mind, again and again, what Cathy had told him. He wasn't sure how he felt, other than being pissed as hell. But what lay beneath the anger?

He had a son.

He was Seth Cantrell's biological father.

The logical part of his mind understood why Cathy had married Mark Cantrell and even understood her reasoning about why she'd never told him the truth. But his gut told him he had every right to be angry and hurt, to never forgive Cathy for what she'd done.

I was young and stupid and let Mark and my mother make all my decisions.

Damn Elaine Nelson!

And damn Mark Cantrell. *He couldn't have a son of his own, so he stole my son from me.*

Why had he thought, even for one minute, that this time around, he'd get it right? He should have known better than to believe he could finally live a somewhat normal life. He had actually thought he and Cathy had a chance. God, what an idiot he was.

A real home and a happy family weren't in the cards for him. Never had been. Never would be.

Stop feeling so damn sorry for yourself. You're not the first man who's been in this situation, and you won't be the last.

He had no idea what to do. Would Cathy tell Seth? And if she didn't, did he have the guts to do it? He sure as hell had the right.

Jack wished he could cry. But the last time he'd shed a

tear, he'd been a bruised and battered boy, scared to death of his stepfather. He held the tears inside, a pain without any form of release.

When his cell phone rang, he hesitated checking the caller ID, halfway certain it would be Cathy. But when he saw that it was Mike, he answered.

"Yeah, what's up?"

"The Fire and Brimstone Killer has struck again," Mike told him.

"Who?" Jack asked.

"We're pretty sure the intended victim was Reverend Dewan Phillips."

"What do you mean the intended victim?"

"The reverend and his wife had company, Perry and Dionne Fuqua. Perry and Dewan are about the same size, close to the same age . . ."

"Fuqua got turned into a human torch instead of the reverend?"

"He's still alive. It doesn't look good," Mike said. "But we caught a break. Seems Fuqua's wife saw a glimpse of the killer as she ran off."

"She?"

"Yes, she. Our Fire and Brimstone Killer is definitely female."

Chapter Thirty-one

Jack felt like shit. Not only had he gone all night without any sleep, but he'd been working with the ABI team since midnight on the new Fire and Brimstone Killer case. The urgency of the situation at work had left him with no choice but to push aside his own personal dilemma. Mike had left the office thirty minutes ago, leaving Wayne Morgan, Jeremy Vaughn and Karla Ross here at the office with Jack. They had gone over the information from the crime scene and Dionne Fuqua's description of the person she had seen leaving the Phillipses' yard moments after she heard her husband's first agonized screams. There hadn't been any point in bringing in a sketch artist, because the deacon's wife had not seen the woman's face.

Medium height, medium build, which covered 80 percent of the women in Dunmore.

"All I saw was a woman hurrying away. I never saw her face, and it was too dark to see her hair color. She was wearing pants, and she was carrying something square, about the size of an overnight bag, in her hand."

The first officers on the scene had taken Mrs. Fuqua's statement, and Mike had chosen not to requestion the lady whose husband had died less than an hour ago. Perry Fuqua was the sixth victim, a man who had simply been in the wrong place at the wrong time. No one had any doubts that Dewan Phillips had been the intended victim, and only the fact that Deacon Fuqua answered the door at the Phillipses' home had saved the reverend's life.

"I don't think Missy Hovater is our killer," Karla Ross said, breaking the silence that had lingered in Mike's office after he left.

Her boss, Special Agent Wayne Morgan, who was busy preparing a fresh pot of coffee, paused for a half second and asked, "What makes you say that? You must have a specific reason."

"Yeah," Jeremy Vaughn from the Huntsville PD added. "We're pretty sure the locket found on the Phillipses' side-walk belongs to her. It has her name engraved on it, and the picture inside the locket could be her mother. You've got to admit that there's a strong physical resemblance."

"Sure, the locket probably belongs to her, but I think it was planted at the scene to make us suspect her," Karla said. "The killer has been very careful not to leave behind any evidence the first five times. Why would she be so careless this time?"

"Good point," Derek Lawrence said as he entered the room without knocking or alerting the others beforehand.

All eyes focused on the former FBI profiler.

"Glad you decided to join us," Jack said, the tone of his voice gruffer than he'd intended.

"I'll let your surly attitude pass this time, considering you've been up all night," Derek told Jack. "Our killer wouldn't be careless enough to leave behind evidence, not at this stage of the game. If she left something, she did it on purpose."

"Let me get this straight," Special Agent Morgan said. "You believe the killer left the locket to cast suspicion on Melissa Hovater."

Derek nodded.

"How did she get hold of Missy's necklace?" Detective Vaughn asked.

"And why single out Missy?" Morgan asked and then shook his head before anyone could respond. "Yeah, sure. I get it. Missy was a suspect in her father's murder, so why not point the finger at her and lead us in the wrong direction."

"It's going to be rough on the girl having to be questioned for a murder we're all pretty sure she didn't commit," Karla said.

"That's why Mike has gone to see the Harpers," Jack reminded them. "He wanted to talk to them and explain the situation. The last thing any of us want is to traumatize Missy Hovater more than she's already been traumatized."

"I'll be as gentle as possible when I question her," Morgan assured them. "But I have to question her. If she can ID the necklace, she should be able to tell us where she kept it and who had access to it."

"If she took the locket with her to the Harpers', then I'd say that narrows down the possible suspects," Derek said.

"To the people living in the Harper house." Detective Vaughn lifted the coffee pot off the warmer and brought it over to the desk where Karla sat. "More?" he asked. When she nodded, he filled her mug to the brim.

"That's right," Jack said. "The people living in the Harper house or anyone who has visited them recently and had free access to the house."

"At least we now know that our killer is definitely female," Derek said. "That rules out about half the population. And just in the Harper household alone, we have four females—Mrs. Harper, her mother and her two daughters."

"Any other new, brilliant insight into the case?" Jack asked.

Derek eyed him with curiosity and hitched his thumb toward the door. "Got a minute for a private chat?"

Jack huffed. When he glanced around the room, each person avoided making direct eye contact with him. Okay, so he needed an attitude adjustment this morning. Who wouldn't, considering the news Cathy had laid on him last night?

"Sure thing." Jack opened the door and held it for Derek.

They walked through the outer office, where Mike's secretary nodded at them and a couple of the deputies acknowledged them with a smile or a wave. Once they entered the entrance hall, Jack turned to Derek.

"Let me have it with both barrels," Jack said.

"What's wrong?"

"Personal problems."

"How bad?"

"Bad enough."

"Take some time off to deal with them."

Jack shook his head. "That won't work. There's no easy solution. For now, I'm better off working."

"Then bring it down a notch," Derek suggested. "For your own sake as well as for the people you're working with."

"Yeah, I'll do that." He looked right at Derek. "Are we good?"

Derek grinned. "We're good."

When the two men returned to Mike's office, they came in on a conversation about—what else?—the identity of the killer and what motivated her to kill clergymen and in such a gruesome way.

"She's pissed," Karla said. "Some preacher screwed with her in some way and messed up her mind. Right? We figure out the motive, we're one step closer to figuring out her identity."

"Sounds reasonable to me," Detective Vaughn agreed.

"Our killer won't stand out," Derek told them. "Not the way you'd think. I still believe that she appears to be relatively normal. She's got a hard-on for clergymen, all right. She's handing out punishment as if she's on a mission from God. Somewhere in her past is a clergyman who, like Karla said, screwed with her and messed up her mind."

"This leads us back to Missy Hovater," Morgan said.

"Her father sexually abused her for years. She hated him, wanted him dead."

"And yet none of us believes she killed him," Karla said.

"Our killer is screaming. We just can't hear her. All the rage is inside her, but it's not evident to anyone looking at her. Missy Hovater might have hidden her rage in the past, but now it's out there for the world to see. Our killer's rage isn't. The Fire and Brimstone Killer has internalized her anger, kept it bottled up inside her. Oh, she's screaming all right—screaming in silence. And we all know that silence is often the deadliest kind of scream there is."

Cathy had been awake all night. Right after Jack stormed out of her house, she had called Lorie, who had come over and stayed until half an hour ago, when she'd gone home to shower and get ready for work. They had talked until Cathy was hoarse. They had cried until Cathy's eyes were red and swollen. They had damned all men in general, but Jack and Mike in particular. And now, in the cold, hard light of day, Cathy had to face the truth—she might have lost Jack forever. And then there was Seth. She needed to talk to Jack again as soon as possible to find out if he intended to tell Seth that he was his biological father. But regardless of what Jack did or didn't do, she realized that she owed it to her son to be totally honest with him.

After turning on the shower to let the water get steamy warm, Cathy stripped out of her gown and robe, kicked off her house shoes and laid out two clean towels and a washcloth. She took her time, lathering her hair, scrubbing her body, shaving her legs and underarms. In a way, she felt that she was preparing for battle. The normal routine that usually took her less than half an hour took nearly fifty minutes, but by eight-thirty she was dressed, her hair done and her makeup applied.

She was battle ready.

And she had made some decisions while the deliciously warm water had peppered her body. To hell with Jack. If he couldn't forgive her, then losing out on their second chance would be his fault, not hers. She had to talk to Seth. It was her place to explain things to him, to help him understand why she had kept the truth from him and from Jack all these years.

With her stomach tied in knots, she decided to skip her regular breakfast and prepare coffee and whole-wheat toast. But just as she slid two slices of bread into the toaster, she heard a knock at the kitchen door. When she looked through the half-glass door, she saw Seth standing there, a frantic expression on his face.

Oh God, had Jack already spoken to him? Was he here to confront her?

Bracing herself for the worst, she wiped her hands off on the towel hanging over the sink and hurried to the back door. The moment she unlocked the door, Seth stormed in, a wild look in his eyes.

"We've got to go to the sheriff's office right now." Seth's words ran together as they rushed out of his mouth so quickly that Cathy barely understood what he'd said.

He held up what Cathy assumed was her morning newspaper. "Slow down and tell me what's going on."

"Here, take a look for yourself." Seth opened the newspaper and held it out for her to see. "It's happened again. Just last night."

Cathy read the headline: *Fire & Brimstone Killer Strikes Again*.

"Who?" she grabbed the newspaper out of his hands and scanned the article. "Deacon Perry Fuqua?"

Seth grabbed her by her shoulders, startling her so that she dropped the paper to the floor.

"Mom, you have to go with me to talk to Sheriff Birkett. Please, let's go now. I have to tell them I was with Missy last night."

"What are you talking about? Why do you have to tell—?"

"Felicity called me to tell me that Mike Birkett came to their house just a little while ago and talked to her parents. The sheriff took Missy in so that the task force can question her. They think she killed Mr. Fuqua, just like they think she killed her dad. She didn't. I know she didn't."

"Calm down, Seth." Cathy pulled his hands off her shoulders and held them securely between them. "How do you know she didn't?"

"Weren't you listening to me? Because I was with her last night when Mr. Fuqua was killed, and I have to tell them that I was."

"Seth, look at me."

Reluctantly, he lifted his eyes, and his gaze connected with hers.

"Were you really with Missy last night?"

"Yes. I . . . uh . . . I slipped out of the house, and she did, too, and we met. It's not the first time."

Cathy suspected that Seth was lying to her. When he was a little boy, she could always tell when he wasn't telling her the truth, and even now her maternal instincts still acted as a lie detector.

"Mom, please, please . . ."

"All right. Let me get my car keys and purse." She picked up her purse off the kitchen counter and then lifted the keys off the rack by the door. "By the way, how did you get here? I didn't hear a car drive up."

"I walked. I left a note for Nana and Granddad."

Cathy moaned. She'd deal with J.B. and Mona later.

"Hurry up, Mom."

Fifteen minutes later, they arrived at the sheriff's office in downtown Dunmore. She barely got the car parked before Seth opened the door and jumped out. Rushing to keep up with him, she got out, locked the car and ran to the front entrance. Seth paused long enough to hold the door for her.

"We need to see the sheriff right now," Seth told Mike's secretary.

"Sheriff Birkett is in a meeting," she replied.

"You don't understand. I'm a witness," Seth said. "Well, sort of. He's questioning Missy Hovater right now, isn't he? I've got important information about Missy."

The woman looked from Seth to Cathy, apparently uncertain if Seth was dangerous or just overzealous.

Before Cathy could reassure Mike's secretary, Seth blurted out, "Get Jack Perdue. He'll vouch for me. He and my mom are dating and—"

"What the hell is going on out here?" Jack opened the door marked with Mike's name and stopped abruptly when he saw Cathy and Seth.

Oh God, please don't let him assume that we're here because I told Seth the truth about his paternity.

Seth ran toward Jack. "I've got to talk to the sheriff. Missy didn't kill Mr. Fuqua. She was with me last night. I swear she was. I'm her alibi."

Cathy held her breath as Jack reached out and laid his hand on Seth's shoulder. Tears burned her throat, and it was all she could do not to cry out loud.

"Missy isn't here," Jack said in a calm, authoritative voice. "Reverend and Mrs. Harper are bringing her in later for questioning, along with her lawyer. I don't think Missy will need an alibi, but if she does, I'll call you and you can come back in and give a statement."

Seth's shoulders sagged as he released a pent-up breath. "She didn't kill anybody, not even her father, that son of a bitch."

Jack glanced past Seth, his gaze settling on Cathy. Her heartbeat accelerated alarmingly. "Take him home."

"Come on, Seth, let's go," Cathy said.

"Thanks, Jack," Seth said. "When Felicity called me, she thought for sure y'all believed Missy was the Fire and Brimstone Killer."

"Go home with your mom," Jack said. "The three of us will talk later. Okay?"

"Okay."

Jack squeezed Seth's shoulder as he looked at his son. Cathy knew that he wanted to grab Seth and hug him. But he didn't. He released his hold on Seth and then turned and walked back into Mike's office.

He had all but ignored her.

As soon as his mother took him to his grandparents' home and his grandfather met them at the door with a reprimand, Seth knew what he had to do. He'd been thinking about it for a while now and had already pretty much made up his mind. After the way his mom had responded to his hysteria about Missy this morning, he felt certain he was making the right decision. His grandparents loved him and needed him, but his mother understood him. She didn't expect him to be perfect. She just wanted him to do the very best he could.

He'd been putting this off, not wanting to upset his grandparents, but after his mom left, he told Nana and Granddad that they needed to have a serious talk.

"It's not as if y'all won't see a lot of me," Seth tried to explain. "I'll be over here all the time. It's just I think it's time for me to move back in with Mom now. I should be with her."

"I won't hear of it," Granddad said. "You're just a boy and certainly not old enough to make this type of decision for yourself. Wait another month or two. Please. Your mother isn't the best influence on you and—"

"I'll soon be sixteen. I'm old enough to know what's right for me."

"Seth, sweetheart, are you sure?" his nana asked.

"Yes, ma'am, I'm sure."

"I do not want you living with your mother and being exposed to her fornicating with that man." Granddad's face turned red as he balled his hands into tight fists. "She is setting a bad example for you."

Seth knew it would be futile to argue with his grand-father, a man who could see only one side of any issue—his own side. "I think Mom and Jack will probably get married."

His granddad huffed.

"You could wait awhile, at least until school starts, and give us time to adjust to the idea that you're leaving us," Nana suggested.

"He's not leaving now and that's final!" Granddad stormed out of the room.

Nana patted his arm. "Give him a little time, please."

"I will. He didn't give me a chance to say that I'll think about waiting until school starts to move in with Mom."

"That's good, that's good. Thank you, dear."

He could see the sadness in Nana's eyes and hated that he had put it there. "I love you, and that won't change just be-cause I'm living with Mom. I hope you can persuade Grand-dad not to take Mom to court over this. He's got to know that, at sixteen, the judge will allow me to choose who I want to live with."

After he and Nana talked for a while, he felt better about the entire situation. Nana had a way of counteracting Grand-dad's negativism with her positive attitude.

"I think I should spend some time with Mom today," Seth said. "I want to explain things, to tell her that we've talked and—"

The doorbell rang, but before Nana could respond, some-one pounded on the door. "Mona? Mona, let me in. It's Elaine."

"That was certainly fast," Nana said.

"What's she doing here?" Seth asked.

Nana rolled her eyes and sighed. "I have a feeling that your grandfather called in reinforcements." She walked to the door, opened it and barely had time to move out of the way before his other grandmother stormed into the living room.

Grandmother pinned him with her sharp, narrowed gaze.

"What is this I hear about your wanting to move in with your mother?"

"J.B. certainly didn't waste any time," Nana said.

"J.B. is worried, as well he should be," Grandmother replied, never taking her eyes off Seth.

"I'll leave you two alone to talk," Nana told them. "I imagine I'll find J.B. piddling in the garage."

As soon as Nana left, Grandmother glowered at him. "You will not move in with your mother. Do you hear me? She isn't a suitable role model for any young person. She is living in sin with that Perdue man!"

"I like Jack," Seth said. "I think my mom loves him, and he loves her. I hope they get married. Mom deserves to be happy."

"She'll never be happy with Jackson Perdue. He was a good-for-nothing boy, and he hasn't changed. He was all wrong for my Cathy seventeen years ago, and he's still all wrong for her."

"Don't you think that's Mom's decision to make, not yours?"

Grandmother gasped. "You're being impertinent. It's her influence, isn't it? She's become someone I hardly know." Grandmother ranted, seeming to lose control of her anger. "The only time in her life when she defied me, she wound up in trouble, and if she doesn't watch out, she'll wind up pregnant and unmarried again. How she can give that man a second chance is beyond me. He doesn't deserve a second chance."

Seth suddenly felt sick. His stomach knotted painfully. "What do you mean she'll wind up pregnant and unmarried again?"

Grandmother stared at him, her cheeks flushed, her eyes wide as she realized she had inadvertently blurted out some horrible family secret.

"Was my mother pregnant with another baby before she had me?" he asked, and all the while his mind was calculating the years.

"Seth, please, I—I didn't know what I was saying. I didn't mean to—"

"Was I that baby? Was Mom pregnant with me when she married my dad . . . when she married Mark Cantrell?"

"Mark Cantrell was your father," Grandmother declared. "In every way that mattered. He loved you. He was a good father."

Seth swallowed hard.

"Seth?" Grandmother reached out for him.

He sidestepped her and ran toward the front door.

"Seth!" she screamed. "Please come back. Let me explain."

He rushed out onto the porch, down the steps and into the yard. He could hear his grandmother calling his name over and over again. Ignoring her, the rush of blood pumping through his body filled his ears with its roar as he ran up the street.

Mark Cantrell wasn't his father. Not his real father. His mother had been pregnant with him when she'd gotten married.

He didn't want to believe it. Had his mother lied to him his entire life? Had the man he had called Dad, the man he had loved and respected and tried to emulate, not been his biological father?

Winded from his fierce run, Seth paused on the corner of Mulberry and Fourth to catch his breath.

Grandmother had no reason to lie to him. In fact, she had been horrified when she'd realized she had blurted out the truth.

And what was that truth?

If Mark Cantrell wasn't his father, then who was?

You know, an inner voice said. *You know there's only one man it could be.*

Yes, he knew. There was no doubt in his mind that Jackson Perdue was the man who'd gotten his teenage mother pregnant.

Chapter Thirty-two

She sat alone in the gazebo. Alone with her thoughts. Alone with God.

Had she made a terrible mistake last night? Surely God would not have allowed the wrong man to die. No, she had to believe that the man she had mistakenly thought to be Dewan Phillips had been God's chosen sacrifice. She might make a mistake, but the Lord Almighty did not. Reverend Phillips was not innocent. It had simply not been his time. But his time would come.

God will show me the day of his punishment.

For now she would wait and pray and be thankful that no one suspected her of being the angel of death.

Perry Fuqua's wife had seen a woman running away from the Phillipses' home last night. Too bad for Missy. If the Lord hadn't instructed her to leave Missy's locket where the police could find it, she never would have done such a thing. But her work was far too important to God to risk being stopped before she completed her holy mission.

I'm sorry, Missy. I know you have endured so much misery, but I'm sure you will be all right. The Lord has told me that no real harm will come to you. By casting doubt on you,

the police will have someone to focus on—leaving me free to
continue doing God's work.

She needed time to reflect on last night's events. It was
the first time that she had misunderstood God's instructions.
She had been so sure that He had wanted her to punish
Dewan Phillips. But instead His wrath had destroyed Perry
Fuqua.

Forgive me, Lord, for not listening more carefully.

You must know that as the Apostle Paul believed, so I be-
lieve.

"I have fought the good fight, I have finished my course, I
have kept the faith: henceforth there is laid up for me a
crown of righteousness, which the Lord, the righteous judge,
shall give me at that day." II Timothy 14:7-8.

But you have not finished your course, she heard God
whisper in her ear.

Your work is not done. There are others to be punished.

She dropped to her knees, her hands folded in prayer, her
eyes filled with tears. "I am Yours to command. Lead me to
the unholy blasphemers, and I will do Thy will, wise and just
Jehovah."

Cathy had tried to telephone Jack several times, but apparently whenever he noted that she was the caller, he
wouldn't answer. She understood that he was working, that
the new Fire and Brimstone Killer case took precedence
over everything else, but the least he could do was give her
one minute of his time. They needed to talk as soon as possible. All she wanted was to set up a time and place for them to
meet to discuss Seth.

How would she ever be able to explain to her son why she

had lied to him his entire life? And that's what she had done. She could make every excuse under the sun, but in the end, the truth was the truth. She had allowed him to believe that Mark Cantrell was his father, and even though Mark had been a good father to Seth, he had not been his biological father.

If she couldn't get in touch with Jack, then she had two options—either go ahead and tell Seth the truth or wait and hope Jack didn't talk to him first. She hated both options.

As she paced the floor in her living room, trying to decide on a course of action, two things happened simultaneously. Her phone rang, and Seth, using the key she had given him, opened the front door and walked in. She smiled at Seth as she picked up the portable phone from the charger. When she noted the strange expression on his face, she gripped the phone tightly. He stood there, only a few feet from her, his whole body tense and his eyes riveted to hers. She glanced away momentarily to check caller ID, hoping it was Jack, but when she saw it was her mother, she silently groaned.

"It's probably Grandmother," Seth told her.

"Yes, it is. How did you—?"

"She's calling to warn you that she told me Mark Cantrell wasn't really my father."

Cathy dropped the phone. It hit the floor with a loud thump.

"What did you say?"

You heard him. You know what he said.

What had possessed her mother to take it upon herself to reveal Cathy's deepest, darkest secret?

"Granddad got upset when I told him that I definitely planned to come and live with you. He called Grandmother to come over and try to talk me out of it. She became really frustrated when I told her that I liked Jack Perdue and hoped you married him. That's when she spit it out—the truth that you were pregnant when you got married."

"Seth, please, let me explain."

"Explain what? That you and Jack Perdue had sex and you got pregnant and you suckered my dad—scratch that—you suckered poor old Mark Cantrell into marrying you when you couldn't get Jack?"

"You've got it all wrong."

"What part have I got wrong?"

"Mark knew I was pregnant, and he knew who my baby's father was," Cathy said. "We were not in love, but eventually we grew to love each other. And your father . . . Mark loved you as if you were his own."

"But I wasn't his, was I? I was—I am Jackson Perdue's bastard!"

Dear God, her worst nightmare was coming true right before her very eyes and there wasn't anything she could do to stop it from happening. The best she could hope for was that Seth would give her a chance to explain everything. But even then, was he mature enough to understand and to forgive her?

"I loved Jack. And he loved me." Cathy tried to keep her voice calm, despite the fact that her emotions were screaming. "You were conceived in that love."

"Why the hell didn't you just get an abortion instead of—?"

"Never suggest such a thing. Not once did the thought ever cross my mind. I loved and wanted you from the moment I knew I was pregnant. You were my baby. A part of Jack and me."

"Does he know?"

Cathy took a moment to steady her nerves before replying. "Yes, Jack knows."

"How long has he known? Did he know back then, before you married someone else?"

"No, he didn't know back then. I didn't tell him." *How could I have told him when he was missing in action half a world away and presumed dead?* "I—I told him last night. I realized that it was way past time for me to be honest with him . . . and with you. I intended to tell you, too, as soon as—"

"How'd he take the news that he has an almost-sixteen-year-old kid?"

Cathy froze. What was the best way to respond to his question?

Seth laughed, the sound a harsh, sarcastic chuckle. "Don't bother answering. The look on your face says it all."

"No, Seth, you don't understand."

"I hate you. You don't know how much I hate you. I hate you, and I hate Jack. Damn you both!"

He turned and stomped toward the door. When she followed him and grabbed his arm, he shook her off, opened the door and rushed out onto the porch. She tried to catch up with him, but he ran off down the street, his long legs flying at a speed she couldn't equal. She called his name several times, then stood there in the middle of the road and watched him disappear.

Cathy wrapped her arms around her waist. She couldn't move, could barely breathe. She had to find Seth and talk to him. She had to make him understand.

But would he listen to her? Probably not.

First she needed to tell Jack what happened, even if it meant barging in on him at work. She had no choice.

Of all the public-service assignments she was forced to do to repay her debt to society, Felicity found only one of any real interest to her. Her position at the animal shelter would last two weeks, and today had been the first day of her second week. She had become fond of several dogs, one in particular, a mutt she had nicknamed Freckles because the pup had small black spots all over his white face and neck. Because her grandmother disliked animals in general and dogs in particular, she and Charity had never been allowed to own a pet. But now that she was older and could care for a dog all by herself, surely she could talk her dad into letting her adopt Freckles.

She had called her mom and told her not to pick her up at noon when her morning shift at the shelter ended.

"I want to have lunch with Dad," Felicity had said. "It's only five blocks from here to the church. I can walk there in no time."

Preoccupied with Missy, her mother had easily agreed to her request. Mom had her hands full with Missy's problems, the latest of which was her being questioned in yet another murder case. To say that her mom had been neglecting the rest of them ever since Missy had become a member of their family was an understatement. Missy had been a nuisance for quite some time, ever since Felicity realized that Seth Cantrell had a thing for her. Seth was blinded by Missy's blond beauty and her damsel-in-distress persona. Now the whole world felt sorry for Missy. Yeah, okay, even she did, at least to a certain extent. Imagine being repeatedly raped by your own father. Yuck!

Felicity arrived at the church at twelve-fifteen, quickly made her way downstairs and hurried toward her father's office in the basement. Her footsteps were muffled by the cushioned layer of industrial-strength carpet that covered the basement floor. The outer door to the minister's office stood wide open, so Felicity walked in, expecting to see Erin McKinley at her desk. But the outer office was empty.

As she opened the door to her father's private office, she started to knock but stopped dead still when she saw Erin and her father kissing. Erin had her arms around Felicity's father's neck, and he was gripping her on either side of her waist.

Shocked beyond belief, Felicity backed up slowly, quietly turned around and ran into the hallway. She was halfway up the stairs when she heard her father calling her name.

He had nothing to say that she wanted to hear.

Her father was an adulterous blasphemer.

Just how long had he been having an affair with his secretary?

Oh, mercy! Her poor, sweet mother!

"Let her go, John Earl." Erin came up and grasped his arm. "Maybe it was for the best. Better that she know now, that everyone knows."

John Earl glared at his secretary, a woman he had thought of as a loyal employee and a good friend. He'd never thought of her as anything more and had had no idea she harbored any romantic feelings for him. Not until today. Not until a few minutes ago, when she had kissed him.

They had been talking, just talking. He'd been using her as a sounding board for his concerns about the situation with Missy. Erin had been consoling him, agreeing with him that perhaps Ruth Ann's kind heart had led her to take on Missy as a charity case while neglecting her own two daughters, at least temporarily.

"Ruth Ann is a good woman, but she isn't perfect. And she doesn't love you the way I do. I'd never put anyone else's needs before yours," Erin had told him. "You would always come first with me."

That's when she had thrown her arms around his neck, told him again that she loved him madly and then kissed him. Thrown off guard by her actions, it had taken him a few seconds to respond by grabbing her waist and pushing her away. Unfortunately, Felicity had walked in and seen Erin kissing him and had jumped to the wrong conclusion.

John Earl grasped Erin's shoulders and looked directly at her. "Erin, I'm sorry if I've ever done anything to lead you on, to make you believe that I reciprocated your feelings."

She stared at him, her eyes wide and filled with disbelief. "But I love you. I've loved you forever. I know that if you'll only admit it to yourself, you love me, too."

He gave her shoulders a sound squeeze, then released her. "I believe it best if you go home for the rest of the day. Tomorrow, we'll discuss how best to handle your resignation."

"You're firing me?"

"No, no," John Earl assured her. "But under the circumstances . . . I'll give you an excellent reference and help you find other employment. Now, please, Erin, go home. I need to call Ruth Ann and tell her what happened, and then I need to find my daughter and explain to her that what she thought she saw—"

Erin slapped him, then spun around and marched back into the office. He had to admit that he hadn't seen that slap coming any more than he had the kiss.

Half a minute later, with her leather bag hung over her shoulder, Erin swept past him without a glance. He returned to his office, picked up the phone and called his wife. He had to put a lid on this before it exploded in his face and his entire family got hurt.

"Jack?" Officer Grimes stuck his head in the door of Mike's office, where the task force was sharing a working lunch, barbeque from Big Ed's Barbeque & Ribs. "That Cantrell kid is back. He wants to talk to you."

"Seth Cantrell?"

"Yep. And from the way he's acting, I'd say if you don't come out and talk to him, I'll have to handcuff him to stop him from coming in here."

Jack glanced around the room. "Will you folks excuse me?" He looked at Mike and nodded toward the door. When he headed out, Mike followed him. They paused just beyond the open door.

"I need to take half an hour," Jack said. "It's personal."

"Problems with Cathy's son?"

"Yeah, something like that."

"Can't it wait?"

"I don't think so," Jack told him. "Otherwise, I wouldn't ask for the time."

"Okay. Go do whatever you need to do."

Jack thanked his old buddy and then scanned the outer office for Seth. He saw him across the room, about ten feet away. The boy looked like hammered hell.

When he approached, Seth squared his shoulders and looked Jack right in the eye. In that instant, Jack realized that Seth knew the truth.

"Let's get out of here," Jack said. "I've got a thirty-minute lunch break. We can take a walk and talk."

Seth nodded.

They walked in silence as they exited the sheriff's department and crossed the street. When they reached the small park in the center of town, a block away, Jack pointed to a wooden park bench. "Let's sit."

They sat, one on each end of the bench.

"Let's hear it," Jack said.

"I know."

"Know what?"

"That you're my father, my biological father."

Jack sucked in a deep breath. "Yeah, it seems that I am."

"She lied to me," Seth said. "She lied to both of us. I hate her. I hate her so much. And I hate you."

Seth hung his head and stared down at the ground.

Jack felt his son's pain. So this was what it was like to have a child hurting and not be able to help him. More than anything, he wanted to erase the agony he saw on Seth's face and heard in his voice.

"Exactly what did your mother say to you?"

"Nothing much. I didn't give her the chance. I didn't want to hear any of her lies."

"My guess is that she told you the truth. It might have been sixteen years too late, but give her credit for finally telling both of us."

"That's just it—she didn't tell me. Grandmother told me.

She didn't mean to, but she got so angry when I told her I liked you and I hoped my mom married you that she just blurted it out."

"Elaine Nelson always was a real piece of work."

Ignoring Jack's assessment of his grandmother, Seth asked, "Was Mom telling me the truth when she said that she just told you last night?"

"Yes, she was telling you the truth."

"How'd you feel when she told you? I bet you hate her, too, don't you?"

Did he hate Cathy? She had kept the truth about his son from him for sixteen years, and if he hadn't come back to Dunmore, he might never have found out he was a father. It had been less than twenty-four hours since he had learned the truth about his relationship with Seth, not nearly enough time to figure out how he felt or what he should do. But time enough to realize that when Cathy had married Mark Cantrell, she had done it because she believed she was doing the right thing, the best thing for her child.

For his child.

"No, I don't hate her," Jack said, in an honest gut response.

"How can you not?" Seth asked, all his youthful agony quivering in his voice.

"Because I've had some time to think about it, and I realize that, under the circumstances, your mother did what she thought she had to do to protect you."

"Protect me how? I don't understand."

"Cathy and I were a couple of kids. She was seventeen, fresh out of high school, and I was twenty, home on leave from the army. We had two weeks together and fell head over heels for each other the way only kids that age can. I was careless. I got her pregnant.

"I had no idea she was pregnant, and she didn't have any way of letting me know. I was sent to the Middle East during the Gulf War and wound up a POW. The army told my family that I was MIA and presumed dead. By the time I could let Cathy know I was alive, she had already married Mark Cantrell."

"Mom thought you were dead?" Seth's eyes, a duplicate of his own, stared at him, and Jack knew his son had desperately needed complete honesty.

"Yes, so you see, she did what she did because she felt she had no choice if she wanted to protect you. She married Mark Cantrell to give you a father. And from what I've learned, he was a good dad to you, wasn't he?"

"Yeah, he was a good dad, but . . ."

"But what?"

"But when Mom found out you were alive, she should have told you. She should have told me."

"You're right. She should have, but she didn't. And we're both going to have to find a way to forgive her, because we both love her and we know she did what she believed was best for you."

Seth stared at him in disbelief. "You still love her?"

Jack clamped his hand down gently on his son's shoulder. "Yeah, I still love her. I'm mad as hell at her right now, and a part of me would like to wring her pretty little neck, but somehow, someway, she and I are going to work our way through this." He squeezed Seth's shoulder. "What about you and me? Do you think you could give me a chance to be a father to you?"

"Do you want that, to be my father?"

"I do. More than you'll ever know."

"Maybe. Yeah. Okay. I guess."

"We won't rush it," Jack told him. "We'll take it slow and easy. It'll be a new experience for me, having a son."

"I don't really hate you," Seth said.

Jack grinned. "I know, Son, I know. What about your mom?"

"I'm not sure."

"You love your mother."

"Yeah, I love her," Seth said. "But she lied to me, and it was a big lie."

"She made a mistake. She's only human. We all make mistakes."

"Dad would want me to . . . I mean, Mark would want me to forgive her. He taught forgiveness."

"Look, Seth. Mark Cantrell was your father in every way that mattered, and I'd be a fool not to appreciate the fact that he was there for you when I wasn't. Don't ever feel guilty about loving him or thinking of him as your dad."

"You mean that?"

"Yes, Son, I do."

"I guess I feel the way you do." Seth tried to smile, but the effort failed. "I love Mom, but I'm mad as hell at her."

"I'm sure she'll give you all the time you need to work through your feelings, but you should tell her that you don't hate her and you're working on forgiving her."

"I can't talk to her. Not yet." Seth looked at Jack pleadingly. "Would you talk to her. Tell her how we feel. I mean, how I feel?"

Damn! He needed more time himself, so he understood how Seth felt. But at least he could call Cathy and let her know that he and Seth both still loved her. "Sure thing. I'll call her. In the meantime, if you want to talk to me again, I'm here for you."

When Seth stood, Jack did, too. Father and son faced each other.

"I wish Granddad and Nana didn't have to find out," Seth said. "This will break their hearts."

"It's not your place to have to tell them. Your mother should be the one to explain things to them."

"When you talk to her, will you tell her that?"

"Yes, I will."

"Thanks, uh, Jack. It's okay if I call you Jack, isn't it? I know you're my father, but—"

"Jack's fine."

* * *

Seth wasn't sure exactly how he'd wound up stopping by the Harper house, but after leaving Jack in the park, he had walked around for a while, feeling as if he had no place to go. He wasn't ready to talk to his mother, and he couldn't face his grandparents. He didn't think Grandmother would tell them what she'd done. No, that wasn't her style. She'd wait and let someone else give them the bad news. She wouldn't take the blame for anything.

As he walked by the Harper's, he wondered how Missy was doing and if she'd been able to hold it together during her second interrogation by the task force. He supposed he could have asked Jack about it, but he'd had other things on his mind at the time. Besides, it wasn't likely that Jack would have told him anything.

Should he just go up to the front door, ring the doorbell and ask to speak to Missy? Would Mrs. Harper tell him to go away? Or would Missy refuse to see him? While he stood on the sidewalk thinking about what his next move should be, Felicity came dragging up the street, barely keeping out of the slow flow of midday traffic. What was wrong with her? She looked like she was sick or something. Maybe he should go help her.

He called out to her. "Hey, Felicity. What's wrong?"

She looked up from where she'd been staring sightlessly down at the pavement. When she saw him, she broke into a run and came barreling into him.

"Oh, Seth, I'm so glad to see you." She wrapped her arms around his waist and laid her head on his shoulder. "I need somebody to talk to."

"What's going on?" He tried to prize her away from him, but she held on tight and started crying. "Hey, what's going on?"

"You won't believe me when I tell you," she sobbed.

Before he could reply, a car slowed as it passed them, and

Seth recognized the driver as Charity Harper. She pulled into the driveway, killed the engine and got out.

"Maybe you should talk to your sister about whatever's bothering you," Seth suggested.

She lifted her head from his shoulder, nodded and then grabbed his hand. "Charity needs to know. But I want you to come with me when I tell her. Please."

"Yeah, okay. I guess." He had enough problems of his own without getting involved in whatever was going on with Felicity, but he could hardly tell her that, could he?

Charity waited on the sidewalk as he and Felicity walked toward her. "Hello, Seth." When he responded with a nod, she turned her attention to her sister. "What on earth is the matter with you?"

"Let's go to the backyard," Felicity said. "I don't want Mom to see us talking. She'll ask me all sorts of questions, because I'm supposed to be with Daddy right now."

"Don't be so melodramatic," Charity said. "The way you're acting, you'd think somebody died."

"Right now, I could kill Daddy," Felicity admitted.

"Felicity Ann Harper! What a thing to say about Daddy."

"When I tell you what he did . . ." Keeping a tight hold on Seth's hand, she motioned for her sister to follow her the long way around to the backyard.

Grumbling under her breath, Charity went with Felicity as she all but dragged Seth around the house and straight toward the gazebo. When they neared the small enclosure, Seth noticed that someone was sitting inside. Missy! The girl he'd come to see. When they approached, she laid aside the book she'd been reading and rose to her feet.

"What's she doing here?" Felicity complained loud enough for Missy to hear her.

"I'm sorry," Missy said. "If you don't want me here, I'll go back inside."

"You don't have to leave," Charity said. "This is your home and your yard, and you have as much right to use the gazebo as Felicity and I do. Isn't that right, Felicity?" Charity nudged her sister in the ribs.

"Yes, that's right," Felicity said begrudgingly.

"There's plenty of room in the gazebo for all of us," Charity said. "Come on, let's sit down and you can tell us why you want to kill Daddy."

"What!" Missy's eyes widened as she glared at Felicity.

"Oh, I don't suppose I really want to kill him," Felicity said, "but Mom will when she finds out what he's been doing."

"What are you talking about?" Charity frowned at her sister.

"I caught Daddy red-handed with his secretary. They were kissing!"

"I don't believe you." Charity's face went chalk white.

"Don't believe me then, but I'm telling you that I saw it with my own two eyes. I walked in on them in a lip-lock."

"I thought your parents were different," Missy said, her voice little more than a whisper. "I believed they loved each other and had a perfect marriage and were perfect parents. Oh, Felicity, I'm so sorry."

"Uh, yeah, thanks." Felicity hung her head and then sighed heavily. "Gee, Missy, I'm the one who's sorry. Having a father who's cheating on his wife isn't anywhere near as bad as having a father who . . . well, who did what your father did to you."

"Raped me, you mean."

"Yeah." Felicity looked to Seth as if begging him to help pull her out of the hole she had dug herself into. "I've about decided that there are no good parents. Except maybe your mom, Seth."

"My mom's a liar." The words came out of his mouth before he knew what was happening. Damn, why had he said that?

"Huh?" Felicity said.

"What?" Charity asked.

"What did she lie about?" Missy reached out and caressed Seth's arm.

"I found out just this morning that Mark Cantrell wasn't my biological father. My mother was pregnant when she married him. My dad wasn't my dad. My mom has lied to me all these years."

"Well, looks like we've all got something in common," Felicity said. "We've all got at least one rotten parent." She glanced from person to person as she said, "Missy's father raped her. Our father is cheating on our mother. And Seth's mother lied to him about who his real father is. I say parents can't be trusted. Maybe my dad and your mom deserve something bad happening to them just like something bad happened to Missy's father."

"Felicity!" Charity scolded her.

"I don't want anything bad to happen to my mom," Seth said. "She made a mistake. People make mistakes. You shouldn't wish for something bad to happen to your father."

"Well, I do," Felicity said. "I want him punished for what he did. Him and that awful Erin McKinney, too."

Chapter Thirty-three

"You didn't have to come in today, you know," Lorie said. "Besides, I'm thinking we should start closing Treasures again either every Monday or Tuesday, at least during the summer."

"I'm better off here than I would be at home," Cathy said. "I'd be climbing the walls without something to keep me busy."

"You're not doing much better here. You're as nervous as a cat in a room full of rocking chairs."

Cathy forced a fragile smile. "At least here I'm not alone waiting for the phone to ring, hoping Jack will call or Seth—"

"I could strangle Jackson Perdue," Lorie said. "How dare he lay all the blame on you. It's not like you got pregnant all by yourself. What the hell would he have done if your positions had been reversed? You could have had an abortion or given your baby up for adoption, but you didn't."

"I have to believe that once he's had a chance to think things through, he'll understand. I just wish he'd call. When I stopped by the sheriff's department, Mike said that Jack was out for lunch and he'd give him the message to call me ASAP." She checked her watch for the dozenth time in the past half hour. "That was nearly an hour ago. It's obvious that he's avoiding me and Mike is helping him."

"Mike's another man I'd like to strangle."

The over-the-door bell chimed to alert them that a customer had entered the store. Lorie groaned.

"Speaking of strangling someone . . . that's Bitsy Cavanaugh," Lorie said quietly. "She's a regular. Always buys several things and then returns half of what she buys."

"I'll take care of her, if you'd like for me to."

"That would be—"

Cathy's phone rang, instantly immobilizing her and Lorie.

"Well, answer it," Lorie told her.

With an unsteady hand, Cathy clasped the phone and glanced at the caller ID. "It's Jack."

"So talk to him. Go in the back. I'll take care of Bitsy."

Heading for the back storeroom, Cathy answered on the third ring. "Hello."

"Cathy, it's Jack."

"Yes, I know."

"I . . . uh . . . I'm sorry I haven't returned any of your earlier calls. I needed a little time to think."

"I understand."

"Look, we need to talk, face-to-face. May I come by tonight?"

"Yes, of course."

"I think you should know that Seth came to see me."

Cathy's stomach knotted painfully. "What did he say to you? What did you say to him?"

"He's hurt and angry with you and me, but we had a good talk. He's a smart kid. He's got a good heart. You did a fine job with him."

For half a second, Cathy couldn't breathe. Jack's compliment had taken her totally by surprise.

When she didn't respond, Jack said, "Seth doesn't hate you." Pause. "And neither do I."

She sucked in and released a quivering breath.

"Cathy?"

"I'm here." And hanging on by a thread. She was on the verge of bursting into tears.

"We'll find a way to work through this," he told her. "I love you, honey, and Seth loves you. But we've got a mess on our hands, and I don't know what it'll take to clean it up."

"I'm willing to do whatever it takes. If only I could make you and Seth understand how it was for me, why I did what I did, why I kept everything a secret."

"One thing at a time," Jack said. "Right now, give Seth some time and a lot of space. He needs you to talk to his grandparents, to Mark's parents. It's your job to tell them the truth. Seth was afraid that he'd have to do it, but I told him that it wasn't his place to do it."

"I'll go over there this afternoon and talk to them, but only to tell them that both you and Seth know the truth. J.B. and Mona have always known that Seth wasn't Mark's biological child. They knew Mark couldn't father a child."

Jack grunted. "I don't know if that's going to help Seth or make things worse for him. He loves them, and he's worried about how they'll take the news."

"You care about Seth, don't you?"

"My God, Cathy, did you think I wouldn't care? He's my son. Besides that, I'd already begun to care about him simply because he was yours."

"Oh, Jack." Tears pooled in her eyes. She swallowed hard.

"Talk to your former in-laws and explain things. I'll stop by tonight, and we'll talk. We'll figure out where we go from here."

Several minutes after the conversation ended, Cathy stood alone in the storeroom and cried. Grateful tears. Jack still loved her. Seth still loved her. And where there was love, there was hope.

* * *

After Seth left the Harpers, he called Nana to tell her that he was okay and for her not to worry about him.

"What's wrong?" she had asked. "Whatever it is, come home, dear, and let's talk."

"You need to talk to my mom first. I—I'll come home after you talk to her."

He'd been walking around Dunmore for the past hour, his mind a mixed jumble of thoughts and feelings. And even though his own life was one big mess, the thing that kept bothering him had nothing to do with his personal problems. He couldn't get Felicity Harper off his mind. The crazy way she'd been acting and the horrible things she'd said about her father worried him. He wished he could shake this bad feeling—a feeling that Felicity intended to do something to her dad.

I hate him. I wish he was dead.

I could kill Daddy.

He had known Felicity for years, and the older she got the weirder she got, but until today he'd never believed she was capable of actually killing somebody. Maybe he should have figured it out sooner. If he had, he might have saved a few lives. But even now, he could hardly believe what he was thinking.

Strange as it seemed, it all made some goofy kind of sense. Felicity was a rebel. She hated her parents' Christian lifestyle, hated being a preacher's kid, hated anything that was even vaguely normal. She disliked her grandmother, thought her mother was a doormat, grumbled all the time about how her sister was the favorite child and had made no secret of how much she resented Missy's presence in her home. The only person she admired was her dad. And now he had let her down in the worst way possible.

Felicity was one gigantic mass of hate and anger and resentment.

She had called her father an adulterous blasphemer who should be punished for his sins.

Maybe he was wrong. God, he hoped so. He'd always liked Felicity, despite her being a royal pain in the butt. But he could not shake the gut feeling that she might be the Fire and Brimstone Killer.

He had to tell somebody. Jack, maybe. But what if he was wrong? The last person he needed to confide in was a sheriff's deputy. He could always confront Felicity, but if she was a killer, what would stop her from trying to kill him?

He wondered if anyone else had drawn the same conclusion he had and, like him, didn't know what to do. Missy might have picked up on something since she'd been living with the Harpers. She and Felicity mixed like oil and water.

Seth looked around and noted that he had walked all the way back to Main Street. It was nearly two o'clock, so downtown wasn't overrun with the lunchtime crowd. Finding a private spot underneath the storefront canopy of a closed business, he called Missy. She answered quickly, on the first ring.

"Hello, Seth."

"Hey, I'm not bothering you, am I?"

"No, I . . . uh . . . I was hoping you'd call. I've been thinking about calling you."

"Yeah, what about?"

"About Felicity," Missy said. "I'm worried about her. She's acting really strange."

"Yeah, I know. Felicity is the reason I called. I think maybe she's going to do something really stupid. We need to stop her."

"I know. I think maybe she's going to hurt her father. I've never seen her so angry. I wanted to talk to Charity about it, but she ate a quick lunch and went back to Bright Side."

"Where's Felicity?"

"I don't know. She left a little while after you did."

"Where are her parents?"

"Ruth Ann and Mrs. Long are both out looking for her," Missy said. "Her dad called and explained what had happened with his secretary. It seems she kissed him, and he was totally shocked. They're not having an affair. He sent her straight home after it happened, and he's going to have to fire her."

"Does Felicity know?"

"No. She disappeared before her mom could tell her, so Ruth Ann and her mother are trying to find her. And Reverend Harper is still at the church, waiting there in case Felicity shows up again. They're all worried sick about her. And so am I."

Just say it, Seth told himself. *Tell Missy what you're thinking and see how she reacts.* "I know this sounds crazy, but I've been thinking . . . What if Felicity is the Fire and Brimstone Killer?"

Missy gasped. "Oh, Seth, surely not. You know what that would mean?"

"Yeah, it would mean she killed my father and yours."

"My father deserved what he got, but yours didn't."

"We have to talk to somebody, tell them what we suspect."

"Who can we trust?"

There was one person he'd been able to talk to all his life. He could talk to her about anything. He might still be angry with her, and he certainly hadn't forgiven her, but she was the only person he could talk to who would take him seriously and at the same time would help him see where he might be completely wrong.

"My mother," Seth said. "Can you pick me up on Main Street near the drugstore and we'll go to Treasures together? We'll tell my mom everything. She'll know what to do."

Erin wanted to die. Her life was meaningless without John Earl. She had loved him for years, had devoted herself to him and he had tossed her aside like yesterday's garbage. He was like all the others, taking what he wanted without any thought of her feelings. He was a vile, egotistical bastard, and she hated him. She wished he could know the pain she felt. He deserved to suffer. It would serve him right if he ended up like the other preachers had. Burned at the stake. Turned into a human torch. Punished for disappointing those who loved him.

He had sent her home, and home is where she'd stayed. She couldn't go back to the church office today and face him, not after what had happened.

How could he expect her to come to his office tomorrow and talk to him in a calm, rational manner? He intended to fire her. He might ask her to resign, but it amounted to the same thing. He was sending her packing. Oh, he'd give her a decent reference and think he'd done a good deed.

Son of a bitch! Sanctimonious asshole!

Maybe she should go see him and show him just what she thought of him. She'd tell him what he could do with his letter of reference. She'd tell him to stick it where the sun don't shine.

Better yet, she'd set the damn thing on fire and watch his reaction before she exacted her revenge.

"I think I'll work in the stockroom for a while since you don't seem to need me out here," Cathy told Lorie. "I could use a little quiet time to think about things."

"You have a big night tonight." Lorie said. "First a meeting with J.B. and Mona to tell them that Seth knows Mark wasn't his father and then later, Jack's stopping by to talk." Lorie gave her a sympathetic look. "What did Mona say when you called her?"

"Nothing really, just that she's concerned about Seth because he hasn't come home. She wanted me to tell her right then and there what was going on. I told her I'd explain everything when I stop by after work."

"Maybe you should leave now and go on over there."

"J.B.'s not there. He's gone to Huntsville and won't be home until around five," Cathy said. "I suppose Mona will call Mother and I'll have to deal with her, too."

"Your mother should fess up and admit she's the one who spilled the beans to Seth."

"Mother takes credit for anything she considers good, but she never takes the blame for anything that goes wrong."

"Everything's going to work out, you know. Jack and Seth will both come around. Jack's already told you that he still loves you and—"

Cathy's cell phone rang. She picked it up off the counter where she'd placed it by the cash register. "That's odd. It's John Earl's office." She answered on the second ring. "Hello."

A hoarse, unrecognizable voice said, "Ms. Cantrell, this is Erin McKinley, Reverend Harper's secretary. I apologize for my voice." She coughed a couple of times. "Allergies. I have a mild case of laryngitis."

"Oh, I'm so sorry," Cathy said.

"I'm calling for John Earl. He would appreciate it if you'd come over to his office as soon as possible. It seems he wants to talk to you about his daughter Felicity and your son, Seth."

"What about Seth and Felicity?"

"I really don't know, Ms. Cantrell. I'm simply relaying a message. I believe there's some sort of problem with his daughter that involves your son."

"And you say that John Earl wants me to come over there now?"

"Yes, ma'am. Can I tell him you'll be here soon?"

"Yes, of course."

"Thank you."

When she hung up, Cathy turned to Lorie. "That was strange. John Earl's secretary said that he wants to see me ASAP to talk to me about Felicity and Seth."

"That is strange. What could be so urgent that he needs to see you right away?"

"I don't know. She just said that there's a problem involving Seth and Felicity. I can't imagine what it could be. I just hope Seth hasn't done something stupid because he's angry with me."

"Why don't you go on over there and talk to John Earl now. I'm sure whatever it is, he's already dealing with it. Felicity's a handful, but she's basically a good kid." Lorie laughed. "Actually, she reminds me of myself at that age. I was always doing something I shouldn't, always screwing up. But my folks weren't as understanding and supportive as John Earl and Ruth Ann. If they had been . . ."

"I'll try not to be long," Cathy said. "But if for any reason I can't make it back here to Treasures this afternoon, I'll call you."

"Don't worry about it. I can hold down the fort. Just go find out what's going on with Seth and Felicity."

"Give me my purse, will you." Cathy held out her hand. "It's under the counter beside yours."

Lorie pulled out the small leather clutch and handed it to Cathy. "And remember to cut Seth some slack. He's going through a pretty rough patch right now. If he's done something he shouldn't have, point out to him that everyone makes mistakes and forgiveness works both ways."

Cathy groaned. "All things considered, I guess I can overlook almost anything he's done."

Seth glanced at Missy, who clutched the steering wheel with both hands and glued her gaze to the rearview mirror as she backed her car out of the parking lot on Main Street.

"I haven't driven anywhere since my father died," Missy said. "I'm sort of nervous."

"We could have walked to Treasures," Seth told her. "Or if you want me to, I can drive. I've got my permit. I'll be sixteen next month."

"It's okay. We'll get there a lot quicker if we drive instead of walk, and it's important that we talk to your mother as soon as possible. If we're right about Felicity . . ."

"Maybe we're wrong. Maybe I've jumped to conclusions. Just because she's weird and was talking trash about killing her dad doesn't mean she's the Fire and Brimstone Killer."

"You're right, it doesn't. But what if she is and we don't tell anybody and she actually kills her father?"

"I keep going over the facts," Seth said. "Whoever killed my dad and yours and the other clergymen had it in for men of God, right? And this person has to be all screwed up in the head. Also, the killer has to have access to a car and has to know how to drive. And don't forget that whoever planted your locket at the last crime scene had to be someone who had access to it, which means somebody in the Harper household. Whoever did that doesn't like you, otherwise she wouldn't have tried to frame you. All the evidence adds up to Felicity."

Missy shivered. Her whole body rippled with tremors. "Maybe not. What if it's someone else in the Harper house?"

"Like who?"

"Mrs. Long, maybe. She's a strange old woman, and it's obvious she doesn't like me."

"But does she hate preachers for any reason?" Seth asked. "I'd think she might have a fondness for them since her son-in-law is a minister, and so was her husband."

Missy slammed on the brakes so quickly that if he hadn't been wearing a seat belt, Seth would have gone sailing through the windshield.

"What the heck?"

"Oh, Seth, it could be Mrs. Long or . . . No, no, I won't believe it's her."

"Who? Mrs. Long?" Seth asked, but Missy shook her head. "Why did you stop in the middle of the street? If another car comes along, we could get hit from behind."

Missy nodded, took her foot off the brake, gave the car enough gas to propel it forward and then she glanced at Seth.

"If I tell you a secret, will you swear to me that you won't tell another living soul?"

"Yeah, sure. What is it?" Seth watched the play of odd emotions crossing Missy's face. Whatever she was going to tell him must be pretty horrific.

"Swear to me. Say the words."

"I swear I'll never tell."

"Ruth Ann's father did to her what my father did to me. He raped her from the time she was a little girl until the day he died. That's why she took me in, why she's been trying to help me."

"Shit! That means Mrs. Harper must have hated her father and could hate all ministers."

"It gives her a motive," Missy agreed. "But it also gives Mrs. Long a motive. She must hate what her husband did and probably hates herself for not being able to stop him."

"So you think she's stopping other ministers from doing bad things?" Seth asked. "But my dad was one of the good guys. Why would anyone kill him?"

"I don't know. All I know is that someone in the Harper house could be the Fire and Brimstone Killer. I just don't know who. It could be Felicity or Ruth Ann or—"

"Turn off here and hit the alley behind the street," Seth told her. "Treasures has a parking area in back."

Missy turned off North Main and quickly made a right into the alley. She pulled her car into an empty slot at the back of the Treasures building, and she and Seth got out and hurried to the back door. Finding the door locked, Seth banged on it with his fist. Finally, Lorie opened the door and stared at them, obviously startled by their unexpected appearance.

"What's going on?" Lorie asked.

"I need to speak to my mother right away," Seth said.

"She's not here," Lorie told him.

"Where is she?"

"She got a call from John Earl's secretary. Something

about a problem with you and Felicity, some trouble y'all had gotten into," Lorie said. "She left a few minutes ago to go over to the Baptist church and talk to him."

Seth's gaze met Missy's and he knew she was thinking what he was—that something was wrong, bad wrong.

"Somebody lied to Mom," Seth said. "Felicity and I haven't gotten into any trouble. There's no reason Reverend Harper would need to talk to my mother about me. And his secretary isn't at the church. She went home for the afternoon."

"You two come on in." Lorie held open the back door. "Tell me what's going on. I can see that you're both scared spitless."

Seth allowed Missy to enter first, and then he followed her and waited for Lorie to close and lock the back door. Standing in the narrow hallway that separated the bathroom and the storeroom, Seth gave Lorie a condensed version of his and Missy's theory.

"Do you think we're wrong to be worried?" Missy asked.

"No, you're not wrong," Lorie said.

"What should we do?" Missy looked at her pleadingly.

"Call Jack," Lorie said. "I have no idea what's going on, who called Cathy and why, but I don't like it. If you two are right about—"

"I'm going to the church now," Seth told her. "Mom could be in trouble. You call Jack and tell him to meet me there, and I'll call Mom's cell phone and warn her. He looked at Missy. "Can I borrow your car?"

"I'm going with you," Missy said.

"No, Seth, wait," Lorie called to them as they pushed her out of the way and headed for the door.

When she parked her car in the church lot, she didn't pay any attention to the other vehicles. People used the lot for various reasons, not all of them associated with the church. It had been years since she'd been inside the Dunmore Baptist Church, and she didn't know her way around inside, so she entered through the unlocked front doors. Just inside the vestibule, she found a directory listing and discovered that the minister's office was in the basement. The carpeted staircase leading down to it was well lit. Once she reached the lower level, she found a bright, cheerful hallway with pale cream walls and numerous rooms, most of them Sunday school rooms with gaily decorated doors.

When her cell phone rang, she opened her purse, reached in and removed the phone. Seeing that the caller was Seth, she answered immediately, but the phone suddenly went dead. She tried returning the call, but discovered that the reception here in the church basement was terrible. That was probably the reason her phone wouldn't work properly. As soon as she talked to John Earl, she'd call Seth.

The door to the office marked REVEREND JOHN EARL HARPER stood wide open, enough so that Cathy was able to see inside to his secretary's desk. But she saw no sign of Erin McKinley or anyone else for that matter.

Odd.

Maybe John Earl had sent her on an errand, or perhaps she was in the nearby restroom.

"Hello," Cathy called as she walked into the outer office.

Silence.

"John Earl, it's Catherine Cantrell."

A strange noise came from inside his private office. She walked over to the partially open door and peered inside. No one sat behind the desk.

"John Earl?"

Then she heard that funny noise again. It sounded like shuffling and . . . and what? Moaning?

Her heartbeat accelerated.

What's the matter with you? You're acting as if you have

something to be afraid of, and you know good and well you don't. You're in a church, in the minister's private office. Where else could you be as safe as you are here?

Cathy entered the room and followed the peculiar sounds until she reached the side of the large oak desk. She saw what appeared to be a man's feet clad in leather loafers.

Was John Earl lying on the floor? Doing push-ups? Or had he passed out?

She took several quick yet tentative steps and stopped dead still when she got a full view of the man on the floor. John Earl had been bound and gagged. Blood trickled down the side of his head, from his hairline to his chin. He stared up at her, his eyes wild with fear. He kept moaning and shaking his head.

"My God, who did this to you?" Cathy rushed over to him, knelt down beside him and yanked the gag from his mouth.

"Watch out!" John Earl yelled.

Too late. His dire warning was the last thing Cathy heard before someone conked her on the head and knocked her out cold.

Chapter Thirty-four

Missy zipped into the parking lot, came to a screeching halt and stopped her car in front of the church.

"Mom's here," Seth said. "There's her car."

Missy jerked the keys out of the ignition. Then she and Seth jumped out of the car and ran up the porch steps. They went inside, leaving the front doors wide open. He followed Missy straight to the stairs that led down to the basement. She stopped abruptly on the first step and glanced over her shoulder at Seth.

"Why'd you stop?" he asked softly.

"What if whoever called your mom has a weapon of some sort, a gun or a knife or . . . we don't have anything to defend ourselves with or to defend your mom."

Seth absorbed the reality of what Missy had just said. "We need to be quiet and not let anyone know we're here. Understand? Our best chance of getting the upper hand is if we can take them by surprise."

Missy shivered. "Oh, Seth, maybe we should wait for Deputy Perdue."

"Look, why don't you wait for Jack," Seth suggested,

keeping his voice quiet. "I'm going downstairs. I have to find out if my mom's all right."

"I know. It's just that I'm scared."

"Go back into the vestibule and wait for Jack."

"But you might need my help." She looked down the staircase. "I'm going with you."

"Are you sure?"

"I'm sure."

"Then let's go. And be as quiet as you can. We don't want to give whoever's down there any advance warning, do we?"

Cathy's head hurt something awful. She tried to lift her hand to rub the back of her head but found that she couldn't move her arm. Her eyes flew open. Where was she? And what had happened to her? *Think, Cathy, think!*

When she tried to move again, she realized that her hands were tied behind her back, and when she tried to scream, all that came out was a muffled groan. She had been gagged!

Don't panic.

She inhaled and exhaled several times in an effort to calm her rioting nerves. Then she tried to focus but found her vision slightly blurred, probably a result of having been hit on the head. But who had hit her? And why?

After repeatedly blinking her eyes, her vision cleared enough so that she could survey the area around where she lay. There on the floor, only a few feet away from her, was John Earl, his hands and feet bound. And someone had replaced the gag in his mouth. She tried to get his attention but realized that he was staring straight up at something or someone standing behind her.

Cathy's heart raced as fear pumped a surge of adrenaline through her body. What was going on? Had she inadvertently walked in on a robbery?

Twisting around enough to move her head to one side, she followed John Earl's gaze up and behind her.

Terror gripped her. Her muscles went taut.

Standing there looking down at them, a frighteningly sweet smile on her face and a small red gasoline can in her left hand, the Fire and Brimstone Killer pronounced a death sentence on both her and John Earl.

"The Lord has sent me here to punish you for your sins," she said. "You, John Earl Harper, are an adulterer and a blasphemer. Pray for God's mercy. And you, Catherine Cantrell, are a fornicator and a liar who sinned against your husband and your son. God has told me that you must die, too. He wants me to make an example of you as a warning to other women. Ask your Heavenly Father to forgive you."

Jack pulled in at the Baptist church parking lot but didn't see any sign of Seth and Missy. He figured they had beaten him here by a few minutes at the very least, which meant they were already inside the church. He didn't know if the kids had simply concocted some elaborate story in the hopes of throwing suspicion off Missy for the recent string of murders or if there was some credence to their theory. But he knew one thing for sure—something about Cathy being lured to the church smelled to high heaven.

"I don't know what's going on," Lorie had told him when she'd called. "But my gut is telling me that Cathy's in trouble. I've tried calling John Earl several times, and there's no answer. The kids are on their way there now, and Seth's ready to take somebody apart. You know how protective he is of his mother. Even if Cathy's not in harm's way, if he thinks she is, he could do something he'll regret."

Before getting out of his car, Jack removed his Smith & Wesson from his hip holster, checked it and returned it to the holster. When he got out, he surveyed the area. On a Monday afternoon, this section of town was quiet, with only an occasional passing car. The parking lot was 90 percent empty, and he suspected the few cars there weren't related to any church business.

Finding the front doors standing wide open, Jack walked inside the vestibule and looked around, but didn't see a soul. Lorie had told him that her cousin's office was in the basement, so he quickly located the stairs and headed down, all the while hoping he would discover that he had no reason to be concerned about Cathy.

Cathy stared up at the girl who stepped around her in order to reach John Earl. She stood over him, smiling down at him. Acting as subtly as possible, so as not to bring attention to herself, Cathy managed to bend her knees, bringing her bound-together ankles up enough to propel her body into a creeping motion. She slithered slowly, quietly, carefully. Her purse lay within reach, there on the floor, to the side of the desk. Her cell phone was in her purse, resting securely in its own little open pocket. But even if she could get to her purse, how could she, with her hands bound behind her, open the purse and remove her cell phone? And would there be any service since there had been none earlier?

"Oh, let the wickedness of the wicked come to an end. God judgeth the righteous, and God is angry with the wicked every day," she recited the Scriptures to John Earl, a passage from the seventh chapter of Psalms. "God has judged you, John Earl Harper, and as His angel of death, I have come here to punish you for your sins."

John Earl tried to speak, but his words came out a mumbled plea to his daughter as his eyes filled with tears.

With her attention focused on her father, she paid no attention to Cathy, leaving her free to back up against her purse and grab it with her fingertips. She pushed the purse between her bound hands and struggled with the magnetic catch.

"I believed in you," his daughter said. "I trusted you

above all others. I thought you would never disappoint me, never hurt me."

Cathy prized her purse open and then slid her fingers inside to search for her phone.

"Oh, Daddy, Daddy . . . I loved you." A fierce, animal-like growl came from deep in her throat. "Damn you to hell!"

Cathy glanced toward John Earl. His daughter stood over him with the open gasoline can in one hand. *Dear God, no! No!* Cathy's mind screamed as she watched Charity Harper pour gasoline all over John Earl.

"No, Charity, don't do it!" Seth screamed.

Charity lifted her head and turned around, shifting her gaze from the unopened lighter she held in her hand to Seth and Missy standing in the doorway to the minister's private office.

"Go away," Charity said. "Do not interfere with the work of the Lord."

"This isn't the Lord's work," Seth told her. "This is the Devil's work. How can you even think about killing your own father?"

Charity laughed, the sound frighteningly maniacal. "That's just it, you see. John Earl Harper isn't my father, just as Mark Cantrell wasn't your father."

"I don't know what you're talking about, but whatever you're thinking, you have to know that your dad—that John Earl—hasn't done anything wrong. He wasn't having an affair with—"

Charity screamed. "Don't say that woman's name!"

Seth's heart stopped for a millisecond. He glanced down at where his mother lay on the floor, her eyes pleading with him to be cautious, to do nothing to send Charity completely over the edge. He nodded to his mom so she'd know that he understood.

"You don't want to do this," Missy said. "Whatever you think your father has done, it can't be as bad as what my father did."

Charity glared at Missy. "That's just it. What my father—my real father—did was every bit as bad and then some. At least your father didn't get you pregnant, did he?"

"What are you saying?" Seth asked. "Are you pregnant?"

Charity screeched with laughter, the sound utterly hysterical. "Not me, stupid. My mother. My grandfather raped her over and over again from the time she was a little girl, and dear, devout, good Christian woman that she is, my Grandmother Long didn't do anything to stop him."

"Yes, I know," Missy said, drawing Charity's attention directly to her while Seth cautiously moved toward his mother. "Ruth Ann shared the horrors of her childhood with me in order to help me."

"My poor, pitiful mother. She was only sixteen when she found out that she was pregnant with her father's baby," Charity said, her eyes glazed with madness. "I was that baby. I heard Mama and Grandma talking one day a couple of years ago. They thought they were alone in the house. They were discussing the night that Mama's father died in a house fire."

She looked from her two intended victims on the floor to Seth and Missy. "My grandmother poured gasoline on him while he slept that night, and she set him on fire. Finally, she did something to stop him. But it was too late then, too late for my mother and for me."

Lifting the red can in one hand and the lighter in the other, Charity whirled around and shouted at Seth, "Don't go near her. Once I have finished with John Earl Harper, I will bring down God's wrath on Catherine Cantrell. I believed all women would be spared, but I now know that wicked women must be punished as well and your mother will be the first."

"No—don't even think about doing it," Seth said.

"You don't understand," Charity told him. "I am following God's instructions. He chooses the wicked ones to be punished and sends me to do His bidding."

"Did you kill my father?" Missy asked.

"God's angel of death killed Donnie Hovater." She looked directly at Seth. "And Mark Cantrell and the others, too. Like my grandfather, who was also my father, all blasphemous men of God and wicked women must be punished. They cannot be allowed to continue their evil ways."

Seth watched helplessly as Charity upended the red can, poured the remainder of the gasoline over Cathy and dropped the empty can on the floor.

Jack stood several feet behind Seth and Missy, keeping his presence unknown for the time being. He had already called for backup and instructed headquarters that emergency vehicles should silence their sirens when approaching the church. An ambulance had been dispatched, along with units from the Dunmore Fire Department.

As he moved in closer, he drew his Smith & Wesson. When he reached the doorway, he slipped to one side, his presence shielded by the wall. Seth glanced over his shoulder, and his gaze met Jack's. Jack pressed his left index finger over his lips, issuing Seth a warning not to give him away. He knew how scared his son must be. Hell, he was scared out of his mind. He had to stop this pitiful young girl from harming anyone else. The thought of how close Cathy was to being set on fire frightened him more than anything ever had. He had faced down his stepfather's wrath and taken his punishment. Often he had faced death on a daily basis as an Army Ranger. But if anything happened to Cathy, if she were badly hurt, if she died . . .

"Charity, please don't do this," Seth said, his voice quivering slightly.

That's it, Son, keep talking to her. Keep her distracted.

Jack hated the thought of shooting a young girl, but he had to stop thinking of her as anything other than a threat to the woman he loved. He had been listening to the girl's ravings and had come to the conclusion that Charity Harper was mentally unbalanced. Anyone capable of such brutal murders had to be either crazy or pure evil or a combination of both.

"Don't try to stop me," Charity told Seth. "I don't want to hurt you. God doesn't want any innocent souls harmed, but I must do His bidding."

"God doesn't want you to kill my mother," Seth said. "She's a good person, a good mother."

"She's a liar and a fornicator!"

Using both hands Charity flicked open the lighter. The flame burned high and bright, a red-orange golden glow. She quickly activated the flame lock mechanism.

Jack stared at the tiny oval flame shimmering at the tip of the lighter Charity held tightly as she waved it back and forth, first over John Earl and then over Cathy.

"Please, Charity, please . . ." Seth took a tentative step toward her.

"Don't come any closer!" she screamed as she lowered the lighter toward her father.

Jack had hoped that it wouldn't come to this, but he had no choice.

He lifted his weapon and zeroed in on Charity. When Missy saw him, she gasped silently, then eased up beside Seth, tugged on his arm and pulled him aside. When Jack shot Charity, she might drop the lighter, and there was a damn good chance it would set Reverend Harper on fire. There was only one chance to prevent that from happening.

Jack aimed and fired. "Seth, grab the lighter!"

The bullet hit its target—the center of Charity's chest. She fell backward from the impact. Her eyes widened in shock as her body rebelled against the assault. She dropped to her knees, still clutching the lighter. She stared sightlessly at her father, then tossed the lighter toward Cathy as she crumpled to the floor, face down.

The lighter sailed straight toward Cathy.

Seth dove forward, his arm outstretched, his palm open.

Jack held his breath.

Realizing the lighter was a hairsbreadth from igniting the gasoline soaking her hair, skin and clothes, Cathy rolled backward against the desk.

Seth caught the lighter in his palm, then quickly snapped it shut and closed his fist around it.

Jack rushed into the room and clamped his hand down on Seth's shoulder. When his son turned to him, he hugged the boy. Seth hugged him, and then they both knelt beside Cathy. Jack jerked the gag out of her mouth and untied her wrists as Seth untied her ankles.

"Charity?" Cathy asked.

"Dead," Jack replied. He knew he had hit her in the heart. There was no way she could have survived.

"Help John Earl," Cathy said to Seth as Jack lifted her to her feet.

Jack slid his arm around Cathy's waist and held her against him as Seth and Missy untied John Earl. As soon as he was free, he rushed to his daughter, knelt down and pulled her lifeless body into his arms.

When the emergency crews arrived a few minutes later, they found John Earl still holding Charity, his face ashen with grief and his eyes filled with tears. Missy was clutching Seth's hand tightly, and Jack held a gasoline-soaked Cathy in his arms.

Chapter Thirty-five

Almost everyone in Dunmore had shown up during the visitation hours at the Baptist church on the day of Charity Harper's funeral. The funeral itself had been a private event attended only by Charity's family and a handful of close friends. Cathy had stayed at Seth's side during the service and afterward had taken him home, where Jack had been waiting for them. No one, not even John Earl and Ruth Ann, had blamed Jack, but Cathy knew better than anyone how he agonized over having had to kill Charity in order to save two other lives. What had transpired that afternoon in the church basement had brought Seth and Jack together in a way only a shared tragedy could have. They had bonded as comrades, as Cathy's protectors, and the trauma they had shared had helped speed up the healing process for all three of them

Two months later, the Harpers, along with their foster daughter, Missy Hovater, moved away from Dunmore. John Earl had been assigned to a church in Louisiana. No one ever mentioned that Charity had accused her grandmother of having set her husband on fire all those years ago. Somehow, in the grand scheme of things, it really didn't seem all that important. Ruth Ann had told Lorie that the family's only hope of ever having any chance at a somewhat normal life was to move as far away from Dunmore as possible.

For several weeks, Seth had nursed a broken heart over Missy's departure, but by Thanksgiving he was dating Bracey Carter, the girl he'd taken to the Homecoming Dance in October. Cathy was thankful that her son's feelings for Missy had been little more than a teenage crush.

Although she had longed for Seth to live with her his junior year in high school, he had opted to live with J.B. and Mona until next summer.

"Granddad and Nana need me more than you do right now," he had told her. "Besides, you and Jack need time to work things out before you have me underfoot all the time."

The holidays—Thanksgiving, Christmas and New Year's—came and went. Jack moved in with Cathy permanently on New Year's Eve. On Valentine's Day, he proposed. They set their wedding date for mid-March during Seth's spring break and moved into Jack's big, newly renovated Victorian home.

Maleah hadn't meant to eavesdrop, and God knew she wished she could walk away and pretend she'd never seen Griff and Yvette Meng talking quietly on the patio. Their conversation was none of her business.

But why had they waited until Nic had driven into Knoxville for the day to meet? For the past several months, Nic's marriage had taken a turn for the better, ever since Griff had confided to her about his frequent trips to Europe.

"I can't really explain everything," Nic had told Maleah. "But it seems that someone from Griff's past—the past he shares with Sanders and Yvette—has resurfaced and is posing a threat to them and to me and Barbara Jean. To anyone close to Griff."

She had wanted to question Nic further, but hadn't. If Nic

was satisfied with Griff's explanation, who was she to doubt him?

Maleah paused near the open patio doors and pressed herself against the wall to hide herself from view.

"It is not possible," Yvette said, her dark, almond-shaped eyes wide with concern. "Malcolm York is dead. We killed him. Whoever this man is, he is not York."

"I agree," Griff replied as he put his arm around Yvette's slender shoulders. "But he's been seen more than once by those who knew York, and they swear the man is his twin."

Yvette grasped the lapels of Griff's sport coat. "You have to find him, whoever he is. Use whatever means necessary. Take Meredith with you. Go back to France. I cannot relive that nightmare. Do you hear me, Griffin? I will not!"

Griff shook her gently, then wrapped her in his arms and held her. "I have to be totally honest with Nic."

Yvette jerked her head up and stared at Griff. "You cannot. She will not understand. If she knows . . . She will never forgive you. You will lose her."

"If I continue lying to her, I'll lose her anyway."

"Then tell her, but not yet. Wait as long as possible. Buy yourself some time." Yvette caressed Griff's cheek. "Without Nicole, you cannot be happy, and you deserve to be happy always."

Maleah heard the hum of Barbara Jean's wheelchair. She eased away from the wall and walked across the room, all the while wondering if she should tell Nic about what she'd heard.

How could she tell her best friend, who was just now getting her marriage back on track, that her husband was still keeping secrets from her?

Cathy stood in front of the cheval mirror and studied her reflection. She had chosen a simple, white silk and satin dress with a rounded neckline, a fitted waist and a billowing skirt that skimmed the floor. Today was the happiest day of her life. The early springtime weather had cooperated by giving her a warm, sunny day with the trees budding, flowers blooming and birds singing.

Lorie knocked on the door and stuck her head in. "Ready?"

"Ready." Cathy held up her bouquet of white roses.

Lorie disappeared, and the door opened wide. Seth stood there in his black tuxedo, looking every inch the handsome young man he was. She walked over to him and took his arm. They smiled at each other.

"Nervous?" he asked.

"A little," she admitted. "I've waited a lifetime for this day." She reached out and caressed Seth's cheek. "I love Jack with all my heart."

"He feels the same way about you." Seth grinned. "I know because he told me he did. And I told him he'd better take good care of you or he'd have to answer to me."

Cathy laughed. "What did he say to that?"

"He made me a promise. He said that he'd spend the rest of his life doing everything possible to make you happy."

The organ music began, signaling them that it was time for the wedding to start. Seth led her down the hall and to the doors opening into the Methodist church sanctuary. She watched as Lorie, wearing a spring green silk dress and carrying a yellow rose bouquet, walked down the aisle right behind Jack's sister, Maleah, who wore a spring pink dress and carried pink roses.

When the wedding march sounded, everyone in the church rose to their feet as Seth led her down the aisle. Jack waited at the altar, Mike Birkett at his side. Jack stepped forward and took Cathy's hand.

Seth gave Jack a pat on the back and then kissed Cathy's cheek. "I'm really glad my parents are finally getting married," he whispered so softly that only the three of them could hear. "I love you guys, you know."

"We love you," Cathy told him.

Seth took his place on the first-row pew, and during the ceremony, when Patsy Floyd asked, "Who gives this woman to be married?" Seth replied, "I do."

Read on for an exclusive extract of
Beverly Barton's new novel

Beg to Die

coming in 2010

Prologue

He pounded on her door and shouted her name. *Go away,* she wanted to scream. *Leave me the hell alone.* But she knew he wouldn't go. Not unless someone came and dragged him away.

Maybe she should call Jacob and tell him that Jamie was harassing her again. As the county sheriff, he could hold Jamie in jail overnight. Or she could phone Caleb and ask for his help in getting rid of an unwanted midnight visitor. Caleb had gotten plenty of practice lately as the bouncer at Jazzy's Joint. He'd thrown Jamie out of the place several times recently.

But for some reason, she just couldn't bring herself to pick up the telephone. It wasn't that she wanted to see Jamie. Not tonight of all nights. But she'd been expecting him, had known somewhere deep down inside her that he would pay her a visit after his engagement party ended.

"Jazzy . . . lover, please, let me in."

His voice was slightly slurred, no doubt the result of numerous glasses of champagne, and not the twenty-dollars-a-bottle stuff either. Probably Moet's Dom Perignon or Taittinger Comtes de Champagne. Or possibly Roederer Cristal or

Pommery Cuvée Louise. Something like that cost no less than eighty bucks a bottle. In hosting the big bash celebrating their only grandchild's upcoming nuptials, Big Jim and Reba Upton had spared no expense. Everybody in Cherokee Pointe had been talking of nothing else. The Uptons had hired a catering service out of Knoxville for the engagement party and the rehearsal dinner, the same service the bride's parents had chosen to cater the wedding reception next month.

While Jamie continued banging on the door and pleading with her to talk to him, Jazzy curled up tightly on the sofa and placed her hands over her ears. Jamie had been engaged twice before and hadn't followed through with wedding plans either time. But it looked as if his engagement to Laura Willis might actually end in marriage. If for one minute she believed Jamie's marrying another woman would put an end to his obsession with her, she'd be the first in line to offer them congratulations.

Sure, there had been a time when she'd dreamed of becoming Jamie's wife, but that had been years ago, when she'd been young and foolish. That stupid dream had died a slow, painful death as maturity had given her a firm grip on reality. No way would Jamie's rich and socially prominent family ever accept her; they still saw her as nothing but a white trash tramp who'd gotten pregnant at sixteen.

Did she still care about Jamie? Yeah, somewhere in her heart remnants of that passionate first love still existed. Only a few years ago, she had still been as obsessed with Jamie as he was with her. For the past ten years he had floated in and out of her life, just as he had floated in and out of town. But this time, when he'd returned a few months ago·with a new fiancée in tow, Jazzy had turned him away when he'd come to her. And one night, when he hadn't taken no for an answer, she had threatened his life. Or, to be more precise, she'd threatened his manhood. And what truly frightened her was the realization that she would have shot him—shot his balls off—if he'd come after her again.

"Jazzy . . . don't be mean. Please, doll baby, let me come in. Just one last time. Don't you know how much I love you?"

No, damn you, no! You don't love me! You never did. You're not capable of loving anyone except yourself.

While she sat on the sofa, hugging herself, wishing she could block out the sound of Jamie's pleading, memories washed over her, flooding her senses. The first time Jamie had kissed her. The junior/senior prom, when she'd given him her virginity and had known she would love Jamie forever. The day he'd cried when he told her he couldn't marry her even though she was carrying his child. The night he had returned to Cherokee Pointe after his first year of college. They'd made love repeatedly for forty-eight hours, leaving bed only when necessary. The first return visit, years ago, when he'd brought home his first fiancée—and Jazzy had welcomed him into her arms, into her bed, not caring about his bride to be.

How many times had she forgiven Jamie? How many times had she given him just one more chance? Time had run out for them. She knew it, even if he didn't. She'd turn thirty soon; she had wasted enough of her life waiting for Jamie Upton to give her what she wanted, what she'd always wanted from him. Marriage.

"Jazzy . . . Jazzy . . . baby, please, talk to me. Even if I marry Laura, it doesn't mean we can't still be together."

A cold, deadly calm settled over her heart. She stood, squared her shoulders and walked to the door. Her hand hovered over the knob. *You're the only one who can end this thing once and for all,* she told herself. *Do what you have to do to free yourself from Jamie.*

Simultaneously Jazzy unlocked the deadbolt and turned the knob. When she eased open the door, Jamie took full advantage and shoved his way into her apartment. Before she could say a word, he grabbed her and kissed her. Impatiently. Brutally. His tongue thrust inside her mouth.

For a split second, she savored his savage possession. Then common sense took charge. She broke away from him, her breathing ragged. He reached out for her, but she side-stepped his grasp.

"I need you, Jazzy. I'm aching, I want you so bad."

"What we once had is over," she told him. "It's been over for a long time. I've accepted that fact. It's time you did."

"I don't love her. I'm marrying her because Big Mama is giving me no other choice. She expects me to marry Laura."

Jazzy laughed, mirthless chuckles. "And God forbid you ever go against what Big Mama wants."

"I'm sorry." His shoulders slumped. "I know I'm a spine-less bastard. But if I don't keep Big Mama happy, I could lose everything. Big Daddy's told me this is my last chance. If I screw things up with Laura, he'll write me out of his will."

Jazzy almost felt sorry for him. Almost. "You know I'll never be your mistress. I draw the line at fooling around with a married man."

Lifting his gaze from where he'd been staring at the floor, he looked directly at her. "Would you let me stay tonight? Just for a little while. A couple of hours." He held up his arms in an "I surrender" gesture. "Just let me hold you. I swear, I won't do anything you don't want me to do. I need you, Jazzy. One last time. Please, lover. Please."

Against her better judgment, she nodded. "You can stay an hour. That's all." When he opened his arms to her, she shook her head. "Sit down on the sofa. I'll fix us some cof-fee. I think you could use some. You should sober up before you head home and try to explain to your fiancée where you've been."

"Hey, honey, if you're planning on getting your gun while the coffee is brewing, there's no need. Believe it or not, I want us to be friends. I'd prefer lovers, but I'll settle for friends. I just can't imagine my life without you in it."

Oh, hell. Why had he said that? *Don't go soft. Not now. You've heard Jamie's line of bull before. You know the guy can sweet talk his way out of any jam—or into any woman's bed.* But not her bed. Not ever again.

"You aren't going to get to me," she told him. "Remember, I've heard it all before. I'm the girl you honed your persuasion skills on."

"You may not believe me, Jazzy, but . . ." He came up behind her, but didn't touch her, just stood very close, his breath warm on her neck. "In my own selfish way, I do love you. I always have. And I always will."

Odd how a part of her wanted to believe him, maybe even needed to believe him. When she turned to him, he reached out and caressed her cheek. She sucked in her breath.

"Please, Jazzy." He looked at her with those sexy hazel eyes, his expression one of intense longing. "Baby . . . please."

She didn't protest when he pulled her close. Gently. And kissed her. Tenderly. All the old feelings resurfaced and for a moment—just a moment—she wanted him in the same old way. He allowed her to end the kiss. Then he stood there staring at her, waiting for her judgment call.

"I can offer you coffee and conversation for an hour," she told him. "That's it. Take it or leave it."

"I'll take it." A sly, seductive grin curved the corners of his lips as he turned and walked over to the sofa, then sat and crossed one leg over the other knee.

You're a fool, Jazzy told herself as she rushed into the kitchen and prepared the coffeemaker. Being nice to Jamie wasn't the answer. But God in heaven, old habits died hard.

Tonight she would say goodbye to Jamie. This time would be the last time. And if he ever came to her again, she knew what she'd have to do. She'd have no choice, not if she wanted to save herself.

* * *

The man had to die! It wasn't that she wanted to kill him or anyone else, but he had left her no other choice. Not only would he have to die, but she feared others would have to forfeit their lives, also, if they interfered. Of course, it wasn't entirely his fault; after all, he was only human, a mere man, with all the weaknesses inherent to his sex. But he was the worst of his kind, spineless and weak. He gave in to his baser instincts without regard to how his actions might harm others. He reveled in the depravity that plagued most men and many women.

Her hand settled over her belly. In order to protect herself—and her baby—she needed to plan a strategy that would put suspicion on someone else. But not just anyone. She wanted that woman to pay with her life, and what better justice than to have her executed for murdering her lover? After all, the whole town knew she'd threatened to kill him.

She stood in the shadows, waiting and watching, knowing where he was and what he was doing. He was with that woman, making love to her. How could he do this? He had sworn his love was true. Lies. All lies! They were fornicators. Sinners. Evil to the core. Both of them deserved to die. To be punished.

She shouldn't act hastily, in the heat of the moment. That was the way mistakes were made. She had made mistakes in the past, but not this time. She had trusted when she shouldn't have, but never again. She needed to be calm and in control when she ended the son of a bitch's life. There was no need for her to kill him tonight. As long as she eliminated him before his wedding day, everything would be all right.

She would not kill him quickly. A quick death was too good for him. He needed to die slowly, painfully, tortured and tormented. The thought of listening to his agonizing screams excited her. Her mind filled with vividly gruesome impressions of his last hours on earth.

"Everything I do, I do for you, my sweet baby. I won't let anyone hurt you. They think we aren't good enough for them.

They think they can sweep us out the door and pretend we don't exist. But I won't let that happen. You don't have anything to worry about. Not now. Not ever. Mother's here . . . Mother's here."